DEMON CHASER II

David Berardelli

DEMON CHASER II

"One Foot in Hell, But Still with Great Shoes"

GRAVESTONE PRESS

DAY ONE - REACHING FLORIDA

Chapter 1

Flea Marketing

An endless sea of cars, pickups and RVs--most carrying out-of-state tags--filled the dusty parking lot.

The flea market, a long chain of covered wooden booths, offered everything from oranges to costume jewelry, tools, electronic equipment, clothing, DVDs, guns, ammunition, and lawn furniture. Folks in baggy shorts, tank tops, flip-flops, and baseball caps flocked the booths and the fast-food plaza.

Wearing a black form-fitting tee shirt, red shorts, and custom-designed black sneakers with a red T covering each toe, Tiffany LeBouf inched down the aisle. Her thick honey-blond hair slid across her back like a shimmering curtain of gold.

This was her first time in Florida. It was just as crowded as California, but hotter, brighter, and more humid. As she edged down the congested aisle, the excitement on the faces of the people swarming the booths uplifted her spirits.

Chip, the weird little guy who pulled her out of Hell, checked out a booth selling potted plants twenty feet ahead. His shock of wild red hair stood out like a roving fireball among the crowd. She knew to keep an eye on him. He would get into serious trouble if he picked up something and ate it.

Being an inferior demon with the spirit form of a flower, Chip's idea of a happy meal was a plate of crushed eggshells, burnt coffee grounds, and a pitcher of fresh spring water. He also had no qualms about grabbing a plug of dirt from a potted plant to suck on, even with people watching.

Earlier this morning, a middle-aged couple had picked up Tiffany and Chip outside Louisville and dropped them off here, just a few miles north of St. Augustine.

Chip's tiny green eyes lit up when they climbed into the back of the light-blue Lincoln Town Car and saw the woman, Alice, chattering away on a cell phone.

Chip had a strange contempt for cell phones. Thought they were silly. He even hinted that they were first thought of in Hell by the demons Balboa Whip and Breath Mint--or whatever those nasties called themselves.

Tiffany couldn't help thinking that maybe Chip had a point. He hadn't been up here in fifty years. The last time he was sent up, no one had ever heard of a cell phone.

The driver's name was Bertram. He and Alice smoked cigarettes and chattered away about their divorced daughter Belinda, who had two small boys, spent a fortune for Day Care and lived a few miles from the high school, where she taught Social Studies, drove a second-hand Toyota Supra, liked Bruce Willis movies, and dabbled in gardening.

Bertram let his wife do the talking while he drove. He reminded Tiffany a little of her father, who also never said too much.

"Give you a good deal on a necklace, young lady."

Tanned and bony in his frayed brown tee shirt, suspenders, and patched black corduroys, the gray-haired man winked devilishly. The burning cigarette stuck between his cracked lips framed his seamed face with billowing gray tendrils.

"No thanks."

"It's marked thirty. I'll take twenty." He lifted it carefully from the glass case and handed it to her.

Ignoring the strong mix of cigarette smoke and sweat emanating from him, she took it.

She had seen tons of jewelry in her short lifetime. In Hollywood, where she spent the last four years of her life, you quickly learned what was real. This went for five bucks, tops, in any costume jewelry store. But she didn't want to hurt the man's feelings. She handed it back. "I really don't wear jewelry."

"Fine-lookin' young lady like you?"

Marilyn Monroe seldom wore jewelry in her private life. She said it took the attention away from her looks. When she was alive, Tiffany had always wanted to be known as the New Millennium Marilyn. She never liked things moving around on her wrists or around her neck and was pleasantly surprised when she learned that she and her idol shared this uniqueness.

"I just don't like how it feels." She hoped he'd understand.

"On you? It'll spark like fireworks."

She knew he was feeding her a line. She felt sorry for him. One brief probe, using the powers

7

she had developed since she and Chip escaped from Hell, had told her all about this man. He sold junk because he was afraid he wouldn't have enough money to live on from his retirement as a plumber. His wife no longer paid attention to him, even made him sleep on the couch when he came home drunk. Aside from a grown daughter who never saw him and a few drinking buddies who didn't even know his name, he had no one.

"Tell you what. I paid five for it. You can have it for eight. I'm only making, what? Three?"

"But I really don't--"

"Go ahead, cupcake." Chip, munching on wet dirt from the plug of grass in his hand, had snuck up to her. "That trinket'll look just dandy hanging around that gorgeous swanlike neck."

"Gorgeous? Swanlike?"

He shrugged. "Best I can do. It's too noisy around here for me to concentrate on something nicer."

Tiffany gazed into his eyes, searching for the familiar impish glint. Chip was a demon. A trickster and a jokester. Nicer just wasn't his style.

"Are you feeling okay?"

"Hey, you told me to behave."

"Sure did. When Bertram and Alice picked us up. That was hours ago."

He shrugged. "I thought I'd try working on my issues."

"Speaking of issues. . ." She pointed to the plug.

He shrugged. "I have the munchies."

8

"Obviously." She lowered her voice. "But I don't want the necklace."

Chip winked at the vendor. "She's hoping I'll buy it for her. Aren't they just precious? They honestly don't think we know what they're doing."

The vendor moved closer to Chip and whispered, "This lady...she's...with you?"

Chip grinned. "Abso-damn-lutely."

The vendor squinted, looking Chip up and down.

"Problemo? Looks like you've got some sort of weird eye-thing going on."

The vendor shrugged. "Guess I've seen just about everything now."

Chip lowered his voice. "This lady's kind of special--if you know what I mean. She doesn't go in for flash. Or money. Or tall, good-looking rich dudes in custom suits driving expensive cars. She can see through all that."

"Ya don't say?"

"I guess you could say we've been through Hell together. Besides, she goes for other stuff."

Tiffany wanted to slap Chip. Or shove her tennis shoe into the seat of his pants. If only he hadn't mentioned the Hell thing...

"Other stuff?" the vendor asked.

"Quality."

The vendor blinked. "Quality?"

"There ya go."

"You're...quality?"

Chip chuckled. "I guess you might say I hide it pretty well, huh?"

9

The vendor scratched the back of his neck. "I guess she must know what she's doin'."

"Most of the time, but sometimes she forgets herself and gets lost in one of her blond moments. When she does that, it's almost impossible to figure out where she misplaced all those leftover brain cells she usually--"

"Chip?" Tiffany decided it was time for him to shut up.

"Yes, muffin?"

"Stick a sock in it."

"Yes, ma'am..."

"I was you?" He glanced at Tiffany, then gave Chip a solemn look. "I'd buy this lovely lady whatever she wants."

"You've just convinced me, sport. Besides, she's giving me that look. When she does that, you know she's ready to kick some serious ass." Chip tossed the plug of grass into the crowd, reached into his pocket, and produced an imaginary twenty.

"Get your change." The vendor pulled a battered shoe box from under the cracked wooden counter and opened it.

"I knew it." Her neck grew warm. "That remark about your issues. It was just...baloney."

He winked. "What'd you expect, lamb chop? Have you forgotten my roots already?"

"You're being cruel," she whispered. "He has to pay rent for this booth."

"I'll bet he got that necklace for next to nothing."

"He paid five dollars for it."

"And you believe him?"

She sighed. I'm probably being naïve again. But she couldn't help it. You just can't change who you are. Not even when you're dead.

"Here's your change."

"Keep it," she said.

His gray brows bumped together. "But it's twelve bucks."

"He doesn't care," she told him. "He just inherited money."

Chip blinked. "I did?"

"Shut up," she whispered.

"Congrats. And thanks." The old man winked at Chip. Then he wrapped up the necklace in a white Walmart bag and handed it over.

Chip stared at the bag.

The vendor shrugged. "They were free."

"Gotcha."

Chip followed Tiffany outside, where the blinding afternoon sun turned the long uneven row of windshields into a jagged line of blinding starbursts.

"How long do I have to keep fixing your practical jokes?" she asked. "That poor man has to put up with rude, nasty people all day. He doesn't deserve to be swindled by someone who doesn't even have to worry about money anymore. And that line you fed him about my going for quality..." She shivered, thinking about it again.

"Babykins, when will you start developing an evil side? You promised me in Ohio that you would do interesting things while we're here. I assumed you meant interesting bad things, but I'm beginning to think it was just a line."

11

She dropped the bag on a chipped wooden tabletop as they passed.

"You're gonna leave that there? After I paid for it?"

"Yes. And you didn't pay for it."

"What was I supposed to do? Tell him we're demons and that we only whip out money after we conjure it up?"

"One, I'm not a demon. And two, telling anyone about our imaginary money trick would be really stupid--even for you."

"Why don't you just put that on and make me feel better?"

"I don't wear jewelry and it won't make you feel better if I put it on."

"Ouch. You can be cold, girl."

"When the occasion calls for it."

"What's wrong with being bad as well?"

"You know I'm not comfortable with bad."

"Need I remind you what you did in Ohio just a few days ago?"

She hated when he brought that up. Sending the demon Gutril back to Hell was not the sort of thing you could easily forget. However, it had been totally necessary.

"I wish you'd just stop bringing that up," she said. "If he hadn't been so obnoxious, I probably wouldn't have done what I did."

"But at least we're still up here. And need I remind you why we're still up here?"

She didn't need reminded and didn't even want to think of it just yet. It made her feel dirty, used. Evil. If it weren't for the fact that it kept her from going back down, she would have told them all to shove it.

"I haven't forgotten."

"I suggest we get our minds back on track and find a ride to Orlando. We've only been given a few days to get this done. We don't have time to ass around."

"Sometimes you make me feel like a little kid."

"Really? I've never seen a little kid hauling around a pair of such perfectly perky, playful puppies--"

"Will you please stop?" He could be such a jerk.

"If you insist."

"When we finally meet Breath Mint, I intend to--"

"The super's name, my beautiful, bountiful, but oftentimes brainless butt-kicking babe, is Braithwaite."

"It sounds like Breath Mint. And don't call me brainless."

"Might I remind you that this dude is a super demon? With a nasty temper? We don't want to antagonize him by screwing up his name, do we?"

She didn't care. From what she learned, demons didn't deserve any consideration.

"I'll try to remember."

"We've got to play by his rules. Otherwise, he'll send someone after us and we'll find ourselves down in Olivier's rock garden, being peed on for the next five hundred years."

"I'm aware of all that."

13

"Then why the attitude? I thought you liked being up here."

"I guess I'm just nervous. Belching Waiter sounds really disgusting."

Steam trickled out of Chip's small, pointed ears. He groaned, ran a hand through his thick red mop, and farted loudly. "Tifferoo, for such a breathtaking babe, you can be such a blonde."

14

Chapter 2

Cal & Digger

Cal Krebs was not exactly the world's best scammer.

For the last five years he had been scraping by, hitting the tourists so he wouldn't have to rely on wages to live. Wages were for chumps. Wages made you do stupid things for money. Made you kiss some dork's ass. And get up early in the morning. And get on I-4 and fight with ten thousand other chumps just so you could end up in some dork's office, kissing his ass.

Cal hit the streets every day around lunchtime, bumming quarters, lifting purses, and picking up spare change from restaurant tables. It was small stuff, but what else could you do after you flunked out of high school, didn't want to learn a trade, and lived in your car?

Stealing from tourists wasn't too difficult. Most didn't even know what you were doing. Some were so happy being in sunny Florida that they would give you a few bucks without even thinking. Others weren't so obliging, but if you were good at reading faces, you could always tell when it was time to split. It also helped if you were a good runner.

Cal was a great runner. At six-one and one-forty-five, he could fly like the wind. Especially when someone was chasing him.

But everything changed just a few days ago.

15

Whenever someone else shows up on your turf, it's usually a bad deal. It can turn into a fight or sometimes just a heated argument. If the confrontation's bad enough, the cops show up. Then you find your ass in jail, rather than out there where you belong, conning pocket change.

But once in a lifetime your luck shifts, even turns around. Things even turn out great for a change.

For Cal Krebs, the last few days had been awesome.

Digger was his name. Couldn't be his real name, of course. Probably some stupid nickname from school. He might have dug ditches during the summers. Or maybe he was one of those dudes, liked mining for valuables on the beach. Scavenger sounded scary, even disgusting, so he probably settled on Digger. Chicks probably considered it cute. Cuddly, even.

Only a few days ago, the dude just showed up from nowhere.

Weird. One day Cal was going to ask him how he did that.

International Drive had been Cal's turf for months. Fairly easy pickings, so quite naturally he didn't want to share. But when he saw how Digger operated, it changed everything.

Digger had the Touch.

Cal had only seen dudes like him a few times before. The really great ones were on TV, on the religious channel. Standing before thousands of folks, telling them all about the Lord as if they'd actually seen him and chatted with him...

16

And you'd believe them. They could make you reach into your pocket and give them every dime you had. They'd tell you anything and you'd be totally convinced they knew what they were doing.

You'd never see Digger standing on a stage, talking to thousands of people. And he sure didn't look like those guys. He wasn't neat, didn't dress well and could care less how his hair looked. Kind of like Tommy Culky, the kid everyone made fun of in school because he didn't care about the same stuff everyone else cared about.

Digger dressed okay but you could tell he really wasn't comfortable. Like Gary Cooper in that old Mr. Deeds movie, where he inherited twenty million bucks. Deeds looked all right when those fruity butler dudes dressed him up, but you could tell he didn't like it one bit and wouldn't be happy until he ripped off those fancy threads and hightailed it back to Mandrake Falls, where life was much simpler.

Dig was like that, although he didn't look anything like Gary Cooper. More like Steve McQueen, only shaggier and with a slight paunch.

But Dig's looks didn't matter. Or his clothes. When you had the Touch, you could do exactly as you pleased.

Cal had no idea where Dig came from. That didn't matter, either. All Cal cared about was that Dig promised to teach him a few tricks. Cal knew he couldn't learn the Touch. Hell, everyone knew you had to be born with something super cool. But Cal could learn whatever he would need in this scamming business. They were partners. And partners shared. Digger was weird, but Cal could tell Digger liked him.

Take that cell phone Dig carried around. Dig just wasn't a cell phone type of guy. Always went hyper whenever he had to use it. Cal asked him about it, but all Dig said was that it was someone he had to report to, once in a while.

"You got a boss?" Cal couldn't understand how a dude like Dig would need an actual boss.

Digger shrugged. "Sort of."

"Whaddya mean, sort of? Is he or isn't he?"

"He…likes to know where I am and what I'm doing."

"Then he's your boss."

Dig didn't say anything. Dig obviously didn't even want a boss. Cal didn't think he needed one. Why would you anyone when you were so good at what you did?

"Dig, you got a boss, you'd better tell me about it."

Dig got this really bummed out look on his face and suddenly smelled funky. Like sweat, only worse. Cal wondered if the dude had some sort of chemical imbalance. Cal didn't want it to jinx him or fuck up his Touch. Cal figured the best thing was not to ask about it.

Two days later, the phone was gone.

"Where'd it go?" Cal asked.

Dig shrugged. "Lost it."

"What about that guy, wants to know where you're at?"

Dig went pale and let loose with that funky smell again.

18

Time to let it go—this time for good. It messed with Dig's head, and when his head was wrong, his Touch suffered. And nothing mattered but the Touch.

Cal figured Dig must have told Mr. Boss Man where to shove it, then chucked the cell phone. This was good because Dig wouldn't have to worry about giving this Boss any of his earnings. He could share them with Cal instead.

They worked International Drive a few days, driving around in Cal's beat-up silver Pontiac T-1000 and fixing it whenever something went wrong. That was another good thing about Dig—he was totally freaky with engines. All he had to do was pop open the hood and listen for a few seconds. He would then reach in there and make some minor adjustment. The Pontiac would purr like a contented female.

Dig was unbelievable. Cal needed to stick with this guy. A dude like him could do anything.

After spending most of the day on International Drive, they drove back to Orlando. Because of its stores, bars, and restaurants, Colonial Drive did some seriously good business. Tourists spent their money there whenever they drove around in their rental cars, looking for interesting places.

Since it was rapidly approaching the end of the dinner hour, the eateries were gradually losing their customers. A surf'n turf place less than a block west of Semoran showed about a dozen customers in its front window. Cal pulled in, eased around the brick building, and stopped just short of the rear exit. "Think you can get us some money?"

Dig opened the door. "No problem."

A well-dressed middle-aged couple came out of the building, arm in arm. Cal figured them for maybe five bucks—especially if they enjoyed their meal. When tourists were happy, they gave you more money.

Dig walked right up to them and said something. Grinning, the guy dug right into his pocket and handed Dig some bills.

How the hell does he do that?

Dig got back in the car.

"How much?"

Dig counted the bills. "Sixty." He stuffed them down his pants pocket.

Sixty bucks. Un-fucking-believable. "Man, I wish I could do that!"

"I'll teach you."

"When?"

"Soon."

Cal knew better than press the issue. He had never seen Dig irritated and didn't want to. Cal didn't want to ruin a good thing. And if he was an expert at anything, it was irritating folks. "Where to now?"

Dig shrugged. "You want to find a motel room?"

"Like to find some girls, too."

"Girls?"

"Yeah. You know. Long hair? Curves? Legs up to here? Smell good?"

Dig sighed. "I know what girls are."

Cal pulled back out onto Colonial and stopped at the intersection. The Pontiac coughed a couple of

20

times. "Dammit. I wish I could get rid of this piece of shit. I've been hauling this thing around since high school."

"I keep it running."

"A new ride would be better."

"How?"

Dig knew some neat shit but acted like he had never actually done anything before. "It's new, dammit. With all the bells and whistles. Smells better. Flies."

"Like that one across the street?"

A gorgeous shiny red Mustang sat in the front lot of the Ford place next to the building. It had that look that said, I'm here, big boy, take me.

"Yeah. Like that one."

"Want it?"

Cal discovered he was almost salivating. "I'd kill for her!"

"Her?"

"Can't you tell she's a lady?"

"How?"

Cal shrugged. "She's sleek, gorgeous, covered with paint, and really hot."

Digger stared, squinting as usual. You had to explain things to him the same way you'd talk to an alien in a sci-fi movie. Dig acted like he grew up in a monastery on some remote mountaintop. He probably had a mother who never let him do any good shit when he was little.

Mothers can really fuck up a guy.

"Just messing with you, Dig."

"I knew that." He turned dead-serious, but anyone could tell he was just play-acting—probably so Cal wouldn't think he was a dweeb. "You really want her?"

How could anyone ask such a dumb question?

"Does a bear shit in the woods?"

"I think so." Digger turned serious again. Cal couldn't tell if he was wondering about the car or about bears. "A bear can shit basically anywhere it wants."

"Dig, you're weird."

"We need to ditch this."

"Are you serious?"

"If you want that other car..."

The light changed. Cal went straight and pulled into the vacant lot of a closed tune-up garage. If anyone else had been talking like that, Cal would have figured them nutso and told them to kiss his ass. But Dig didn't joke around like other dudes.

"Might as well give 'er a shot," Cal said, shrugging.

They got out, trotted back to the Ford place, and crouched in some bushes outside the chain link fence.

It was close to nine o'clock; the dealership was locked up tight. No one walking around in there, but Cal didn't exactly get a warm fuzzy about all this. Security cameras scanned the lot. A giant lock holding a heavy chain looped around the double gate kept anyone from opening it. A seven-foot-tall chain-link fence sealed the works.

"Any suggestions?"

"We just go on in and take her." Dig made it sound simple.

"What do we do? Turn into Superman? Or just become invisible?"

Dig blinked. "Super-man? Who's he?"

"You've never heard of Superman?"

"No..."

"Dig, sometimes you worry me."

Digger walked right over and covered the lock with both hands. He stood there quietly, hunkering down a little.

Cal wondered what the hell he was doing. Dig didn't even seem to care about the heavy passing traffic. Some asshole would notice him standing there. He was standing directly in the security light beam.

After about half a minute, Digger dropped his hands to his sides.

The lock clicked open. The weight of the chain made the whole works thump to the ground.

Cal stood back in amazement. Awesome. "How'd you do that?"

Digger shrugged. "It's just a trick."

Was he serious? "Know any more like that?"

"Sure."

"How about starting up that baby? I don't think I can pop the ignition on a computerized ride."

"Pop the ignition? Computerized?"

Dig must be feeding him more bullshit. How could a dude who knew so much cool stuff not know about computerized rides?

Or popping the ignition? Or Superman?

Maybe he did spend time in that monastery. Cal had heard some seriously weird things about monks. He just hoped Dig wouldn't go weird on

23

him one night and cop a feel or something. "How long have you been out of touch with the real world?"

Dig scratched the back of his neck. "What year is this?"

"Hey, it ain't important. We'd better get out of here, and fast. That surveillance camera's giving me a bad feeling."

"What is that?"

This dude jokes about the strangest things. "It's a camera. No doubt hooked up to the Police Station. Cops are probably on their way here, as we speak."

"Let's say hi." Dig pulled Cal by the arm.

"What the hell--"

"Smile and wave."

This dude's as crazy as a bedbug. "Why would I wanna do that?"

Digger shrugged. "To confuse them."

"How's this gonna confuse them?"

"They'll probably think we're crazy."

Dude's got a point. Cal waved—reluctantly at first, then more enthusiastic when Dig began jumping up and down, grinning stupidly and waving both arms.

"I think we made our point." Cal risked a nervous glance at the main highway. Dig might have the Touch and all but doing that was probably one of the dumbest things Cal had ever done in his life.

And that said quite a bit.

Digger went over to the Stang. "Is this thing electrical?"

24

"You have been out of touch."

"I'll get it started."

"Do it fast, okay?" Cal could have sworn he just heard a distant siren.

"We'll be long gone even before you have a chance to get nervous."

"Too late for that." Cal wanted to slap Digger silly. Too late for that, as well. "Any longer and they'll be tossing our asses into cells."

Dig blinked. "Don't cells have locks?"

"Well, yeah..." Cal regarded the heavy-duty padlock and chain lying on the ground. Then it registered. "I get it. I may be slow, but I get it."

DAY TWO - Meeting Braithwaite

Chapter 3

Conducting Business

Dark and air-conditioned, the Oasis Lounge echoed with the clinking of glasses and the chattering of the tourists and locals filling its chairs and barstools.

Seated by himself, Daniel Grove enjoyed his vodka martini while the International Drive traffic roared past the tinted windows. Alyssa and Tonya, his two regular clients, were due in. The transactions would be brief and casual. The girls, both successful attorneys, were smart enough to know how to handle their business without arousing suspicion.

But as smart and as savvy as they were, they just could not stay away from the coke. For Daniel, this was a good deal. Their habit gave him just enough kicking-around money to keep him happy.

Getting away from the office was just as important as the extra money. Specializing in web design and graphics packed entirely too much stress into Daniel's carefree lifestyle. If he could generate enough business with the coke, he would no longer have to worry about stressing himself trying to resolve other people's web problems.

But right now, he didn't have much choice. As the only son and heir of billionaire Richard Grove, Daniel discovered early on that his future came with a long list of irritating requirements. Discarding a successful software service in favor of providing daily coke to a couple of lady lawyers just wasn't an option.

Alyssa, in her tan business suit and open-toed black spikes, sashayed into the room and slid her perfect round ass onto the seat next to his. Her sweet lilac scent brushed his cheeks, settling warmly into his nostrils. Her large, heavily lashed dark-brown eyes remained dead-steady on him.

Daniel instantly felt the familiar stirrings when her left hand rested on his right thigh beneath the table. He had to remind himself that this was just business. But there was no reason why he couldn't try having a little fun in the meantime...

"Hi," he whispered. "Come here often?"

Alyssa said nothing. She tapped his thigh.

Hot lady lawyer being a bitch. As usual.

But a little persistence might just be all he needed to melt the ice.

"My name's Daniel. Wanna find a motel room, order a couple of thong outfits, and spend a fun evening, putting them on one another?"

Her hand swatted his thigh.

So much for trying to melt the ice... Alyssa had obviously been a lawyer too long. She needed to get on the Yellow Brick Road and take a quick jaunt to Emerald City to ask the Wizard for a sense of humor.

He pulled the small roll of bills trapped within her tight fist and pocketed them in exchange for the small white envelope he carried in the same pocket.

"Call you tomorrow, same time," she whispered. He didn't even see her slip the envelope into her large tan leather handbag as she left the room.

Ten minutes later, auburn-haired Tonya, in her simple plaid skirt and loose-fitting cream blouse, took a seat beside him.

"Hey there," he said pleasantly. His technique and charm might work better on Tonya. She wasn't as serious as Alyssa. "Wanna mess up the sheets a little before we get down to business?"

Tonya gave a brief smile and rested her hand on his thigh.

"Tell ya what. I'll even straighten them out before we leave."

"You're funny." But her brief smile had already disappeared.

So much for wasting some good-natured foreplay on the wrong babe...

He slipped her the tiny white envelope. She gave him his money, got back up and disappeared quickly in the crowd out in the motel lobby.

Daniel drank some of his martini. Lady lawyers definitely needed work in the personality department. But at least they made good money. Half a dozen more like those two and he could toss his laptop into Lake Eola. It had taken him nearly a year to develop a solid connection for a steady supply of top-grade stuff. When your supply was reliable, you could count on a steady thriving business.

But he still wouldn't mind luring one of them— or both—between the sheets.

28

"You've got possibilities," said a deep voice close behind him.

A huge dude with dark, deep-set eyes, short black hair and a broad face sat alone at a corner table, drinking red wine. He was dressed in a dark suit that fit his massive frame perfectly. You needed money for a custom fit when you were hauling around that much girth. Lots and lots of money.

Dude obviously suspected something. Daniel didn't think the man was a narc. From what he knew about narcs, they didn't dress very well and always looked nervous and clueless. And they didn't drink wine while they were working. Usually coffee. Or Bromo-seltzer.

But if he wasn't a Government boy, who was he? And why would he want to draw attention to himself?

Daniel decided not to talk to this dude. Assuming the defensive would probably be best. Too many weird people wandering around these days. He sipped more of his drink and tried not to appear nervous.

"That was nice stuff you just handled," the man said. "You do that often?"

Daniel checked the entrance. Some scattered crowds flocked the lobby, waiting to check in. Others studied the dinner menu on the easel outside the glass doors of the restaurant. It wouldn't be difficult to get up and fade away. If someone looking like Tonya could do it, he should be able to.

Daniel just shrugged. A shrug was okay if you didn't want to talk. It didn't make you look guilty and made you look less suspicious.

"That bit of business you just did." Big dude lowered his voice. "I'll bet you make just enough money to want to do it all the time."

Weird. How the hell could this dude hear all that from over there?

Daniel instantly felt the underside of the table for a bug. He had seen something like that on NCIS. Government men were always bugging things. They bugged their ears, their undershorts, their glasses, their hats. If they wanted to nail someone, they would surely bug the furniture.

Maybe this dude really was a narc.

But wouldn't he have made his presence known right after one of Daniel's transactions?

Maybe he was on the take. That happened a lot. Narcs didn't make all that much money; they probably wouldn't turn down a little pocket money if they were offered some under the table.

"What are you talking about?" Stupid might be the best way to go here. When you acted stupid, people generally left you alone. "Business? I'm here, having a drink. Trying to, anyway."

The man barked laughter. "You trying to tell me that you're just sitting here, having a drink, and every five minutes, a well-dressed bimbo comes in, plants her ass down, whispers some shit at you, slips a tiny white envelope in her bag, then gets up and leaves? And you don't know what that's all about?"

This big boy saw entirely too much.

30

More people came in. The bigger the crowd, the easier the getaway.

Daniel wouldn't have any trouble outrunning him. The man looked close to fifty. His massive size would also prevent him from moving quickly. Barely thirty, Daniel still retained his long-distance runner's body from high school. He could fly if he had to.

"Join me," the man said. "Let's talk."

Daniel remained frozen. He didn't trust strangers. All you had to do was check out one of the theme parks—even Walmart—and you'd see enough weirdos wandering around to make you want to lock yourself in your apartment for the rest of your life.

"C'mon. I don't bite. Not usually, anyway. That is, when I'm in a good mood."

"Are you in a good mood?"

The big boy laughed. He shrugged and held out his hands. "Is this place still standing?"

Daniel glanced around the room. This boy sure said some weird things. "Seems to be..."

"Then I'm in a good mood."

"What did you want to talk about?"

"You sure are suspicious."

"This is Florida, you know."

"You can say that again. Idiots running around, looking for directions when they should be trying to find out where they left their brains."

He had that right. But it was really a no-brainer for the locals. "How do I know you're not one of them?"

31

The big man eased forward. His dark, deep-set eyes didn't blink. "Kid, the only important thing you need to know is that you don't want to piss me off."

***

Braithwaite sat back and drank more wine.

It had only been a week since he and his three inferiors had come up through one of the thousands of landfill tunnels connecting this world with the Darkworld. Although Balberith, his predecessor, had already given him a detailed assessment of Modern Mankind down in the Castle of Demons, Braithwaite's evaluation upon his arrival told him Balberith had been uncharacteristically generous.

Mortals obviously thoroughly enjoyed the latest toys Braithwaite, Balberith and the other supers had provided them. Everyone had computers, cell phones, and high-definition TVs. Plastic, one of the inventions Balberith had developed nearly a century ago, had taken over. Not only was the substance destroying the planet, but mortals also couldn't live without it. They used it to manufacture just about everything. They also used it to nuke their food and bottle their tap water, which large companies sold all over the world.

Other signs of emotional and social decay abounded, clearly demonstrating Mankind's frantic rush toward its ultimate annihilation. Kids having kids. Kids driving drunk, texting, killing one another. Trashing homes. Shooting at one another in moving cars. Home invasions. Road rage. Cyberbullying. Identity theft.

32

Hell's campaign had reached its final stages. The Dark Prince would soon leave the basement of Hell to reclaim his Kingdom.

Braithwaite was confident he would be one of the twelve reigning super demons when the Reclamation came to pass. The next few decades would be crucial.

Braithwaite liked challenges but he also liked things simple. Nudging mortals over the edge would be child's play.

Take this Grove kid, for instance. Born to the right family and given every possible advantage, yet he chose to act like a colossal idiot.

Braithwaite was forced to demonstrate a character trait he hated most of all. This trait was useless in Hell but vital up here. Finesse. He had to exercise his diplomacy skills for the benefit of the Legion of Demons.

It shouldn't be difficult. The Grove kid had a lot going for him. The boy was good-looking, bright, well-dressed, educated, and ambitious.

But only a dunderhead would conduct such risky business in a crowded place like this. Plainclothes cops sat three tables down, trying to pass as tourists. One of them had even used a cell phone twice in the last half-hour.

To make sure the cop hadn't voiced his suspicions to his contacts about the Grove kid, Braithwaite caused the phone to slip from the cop's grip and fall to the floor. It was promptly stepped on by the middle-aged couple wandering by.

Manipulating this boy was essential. Grove's old man was high up in the Central Florida Chapter

33

of the Diocese. His kid should be demonstrating considerably more brain activity. Supplying two well-dressed sluts with white powder in a crowded bar was not a smart way to acquire success and power. Nor was it the proper way to protect the Diocese.

The kid got up from his chair. He looked like he wanted to bolt from the room. Before the boy could decide, Braithwaite sent over the suggestion

(join me)

and Grove quickly turned right back around. He approached Braithwaite's table and sat down facing him. As soon as his scrawny young butt touched the seat, he glanced around stupidly.

"Kid, you really need to learn how to handle sluts better."

"What are you talking about? Those two ladies—"

"Kid, let's not waste any more of my time. Sound cool to you? Sounds like a nifty plan to me."

The kid was still trying to figure out why he hadn't left when he wanted to. His thoughts rang cloud and clear: Why the hell am I here when I just got up to leave?

He really needed to focus better. At this rate, he should either try his hand at politics or just go ambulance-chasing with the rest of the well-dressed walking dung heaps.

"How long have you been supplying them?"

The boy eyed the door again. I've got to get the hell out of here!

Time to set his frightened little mind to rest. "How would you like to pull in twenty or thirty grand a week?"

The boy immediately stopped eyeing the door.

Braithwaite sighed. About damned time he found the right button. This boy was truly his father's son.

The boy's eyes grew. "Twenty or thirty...grand?"

"Sometimes more. You don't mind working Sundays, do you?"

"That much money a week?"

"An occasional holiday here and there?"

"Twenty thousand bucks?"

Braithwaite scratch his jaw. This kid definitely had gotten focused in a hurry.

"Who would I have to kill?"

"Let's just take this one step at a time, all right?" Braithwaite held out his hand. "The name is Waite. Brett Waite."

"Mr. Waite. I'm—"

"You're Daniel Grove."

The boy stiffened. "H-How do you—"

"I know all about you, kid. Your old man is Richard Grove, the senior partner of Glaser Enterprises. How's that for breaking the ice?"

The boy's eyes had grown enormous. "Wow! You're really good!"

Braithwaite had more wine. "Kid, keep the adoration on low simmer, okay? I'm not exactly in the right frame of mind to give out autographs or attend a ceremony for knighthood. Or even best director."

35

Chapter 4

Picked Up by A Trio of Mellow Fellows

Four lanes of heavy South Orange Blossom Trail traffic roared past.

Chip sniffed the air. With the toe of his tennis shoe, he touched the blades of bleached grass poking through the jagged cracks of the sidewalk. He did this same thing in Ohio, when they first came up from Hell.

Tiffany knew why he wasn't munching on dirt as well. She didn't see any. Just sand and long, jagged lines of fire ants. Cigarette butts, candy wrappers, and more sand littered the walk. A crushed Wendy's cup and a couple of mashed Coors cans sat at the corner. Spray-painted graffiti smeared the walk straight ahead. Down the street, a building painted pink and yellow huddled behind a neon sign that said, The Babe Palace. Next to it, a purple building advertised Chicks A-Plenty.

This was definitely not the best section of town she'd ever seen. It reminded her of East L.A.

"Happy now?" Chip asked.

"Huh?"

"We're no longer in that tacky little Ohio town."

She knew what he meant. When the deputy had dropped them off in downtown Raven just days earlier, she couldn't believe her bad luck. She had escaped Hell only to end up in a place where the locals wore overalls, chewed tobacco and drove

36

beat-up pickup trucks and old cars with their taillights held on with duct tape.

But she also met Lou Gates, her one true love, in that tacky little town. She and Chip were only in Raven a few days, but because of Lou, it was an experience she would never forget. She would treasure the memories forever.

She didn't want Chip to know how much she missed Lou. Chip wasn't the romance-minded type. Being stuck in a rock garden behind the Castle of Demons for more than two thousand years would take the desire out of anyone.

"It wasn't a bad little place," she said softly.

She expected him to say something cynical, but he just went back to sniffing the air.

"Methinks we've got a bit of old-fashioned walking ahead of us, milady," he said a little later in a horrible cockney accent.

"Tell me something."

"Let loose with your innocuous but most likely irritatingly intrusive inquiry."

"How do we find Bath Water in a busy place like this?"

He groaned. "You mean Braithwaite?"

"Whatever."

"That, me lassie, poses a genuinely terrificoso question."

"How about giving me a terrificoso answer?"

"I would, save for one terrificoso reason."

"What's that?"

"I've got none."

"Really? You could've fooled me."

37

"That's why I be the bestest of the best," he said with a grin. "The ultimate Trickster." He spun around and farted so loudly, a passing pickup truck honked its horn in response.

"I think you just found yourself a friend," she said flatly.

"Good grief. I hope he doesn't circle around and want to get chummy. I'm not exactly a social-minded kind of guy."

"Don't worry. I was just being sarcastic."

"Cool. But getting back to your irritating habit of screwing up a certain super demon's name—"

"I know, I know. You also said we need to find him quickly. I just don't see how we'll be able to in all this chaos."

"We've got no choice. It's the only reason we're still up here." He blinked. "You were being sarcastic?"

"That took a few seconds..."

"My timing's off. It's the humidity. The noise. No dirt to munch on for my daily mineral high. I'll probably be back to normal when we go back down."

"Normal?"

He shrugged. "A figure of speech."

She didn't want to think about returning to that horrible place. She wasn't even supposed to be down there. If Gutril hadn't been wandering the Valley of Decay, looking for someone to annoy, she'd still be in that beautiful, quiet gray pasture.

But the fact that she was yanked into Hell didn't make her a demon. And she didn't care why

38

they'd sent her and Chip up here—she could never commit an act of evil. It just wasn't in her makeup.

"I don't intend to go back," she said firmly.

"Really?"

"You know?"

"Baby cakes, you've been sending out enough signals since I brought you back up. Any moron could figure out your motives."

"But I didn't think you could."

"What kind of moron do you think I am?"

"The smart kind?"

"A smart moron." His ears twitched. "I like that."

"Well, since you now know how I feel—"

"It doesn't matter. You don't have much choice. Neither do I. We're both sort of doomed."

"I refuse to think that way."

"Don't expect me to pump sunshine up that fine ass. I'm not the perfect choice. Especially since I wasn't supposed to be sent down there, either."

His somber expression told her he was dead-serious.

"You never did say what you did to be sent there, did you?"

Noperino."

What did you do?"

When?"

She sighed. "To be sent down there."

"Would you believe I stuck firecrackers in the Pope's undergarments while he was wearing them?"

"Which one?"

"The pink silk pair with the red racing stripe down the front flap."

"I meant which pope, silly."

"I'll bet you didn't know popes wore silkies, did you?"

"How would I know that?"

"That's right. You wouldn't."

"So…which was it?"

"Huh?"

He was so aggravating. "Which pope?"

"Does it matter?"

A beat-up white van squealed to an abrupt stop at the curb beside them. The side door squealed open. A churning gray cloud of marijuana-scented smoke billowed outside, brushing her face.

"Tifferoo?" Chip coughed. "You still here? I can't see anything!"

"Still here." She fanned the smoke away. "But I think I'm getting high."

The cloud cleared. Three young men in dirty sweatshirts and jeans sat inside, grinning stupidly behind their smoldering cigarettes.

The one who pushed open the door gestured. "Get in, baby. Let's party!"

The driver said, "Get in, Blondie. And dump the runt."

"Runt?" Chip tilted his head.

"No thank you," she told them.

"Yeah. Runt." The guy beside the driver sat up in his seat. "Got a problem with that, asshole?"

"With what asshole? I see three of you."

"Get in, baby," the guy in back coaxed.

Tiffany hated it when people were nasty. "This is my friend," she said. "I don't appreciate you calling her runt."

40

Chip looked at her. "Her?" he whispered.

The driver said, "Her?"

"Do your stuff, Ms. Trickster."

Grinning impishly, he pushed out his skinny chest and forced both hands through his thick red tresses.

"Shit!" The guy in the back practically popped a vertebra in his neck.

The one who had called Chip a runt studied the smoldering stub stuck to the paper clip pressed between his thumb and index finger. "Where the fuck did you get this stuff, Myron? I coulda swore—"

"From Buff Boy. Top-notch Colombian."

"Top-notch Colombian, my ass! You just called a chick a runt, Norbert."

"Man, thought she was a guy!"

"She ain't, though, is she? Even has titties. Small, but they're there..."

"I can make them a little bigger," Chip said in his high-pitched female voice. "I just don't see the point. It's not like we're gonna have sex or anything..."

"Man, I'm so fucked up..." Norbert shook his head.

A motorist behind the van yelled. Someone else honked.

Myron said, "You ladies wanna party?"

"Not really," Tiffany said. "We need to find a business associate—"

"We'll take you," Myron said.

"But you don't know where we have to—"

"We'll take you anywhere," the driver said.

41

"Anywhere?" Chip asked.

More honking.

"Get in!"

"Guess it's better than walking," Tiffany said.

Chapter 5

Daniel's New Boss

The middle-aged waitress brought them fresh drinks.

His martini was strong. Daniel Grove made a conscious effort not to turn stupid and guzzle it down. He didn't want to be hauled in on his way home. That happened twice before, in his wild college days, with Dad bailing him out both times. Dad drove him home, planted Daniel's butt in a kitchen chair, and threatened to toss him out on his ear and pull all their financial help. This way, Daniel would see how hard it was to function on his own. While Dad ranted, Mom went on and on about her younger brother Bill, who had spent half his life in Rehab.

Truly a giant bummer of an afternoon.

But right now, Daniel needed something to calm his nerves. This was weird, to say the least. Bad enough a casual observer could figure out what you were doing with two hot, spaced-out babes in a crowded bar. It was even worse when you got up to leave and found yourself sitting at the casual observer's table.

Am I that messed up?

Not on one martini.

He stared at his glass. Drugged, maybe?

First bugged. Now drugged.

How else could he explain his head suddenly going apeshit while he wasn't looking?

43

But none of that mattered. Not now, anyway. All Daniel cared about was what this big dude had just said.

Twenty or thirty grand a week.

It had to be a con. No one saw that kind of jack. No one, that is, except for the big drug guys and those gun runners. And, of course, the Hollywood crowd, and Big Tech.

But if it was a con, Daniel wanted to know right off.

"What's your proposition?" he asked, trying to sound as businesslike as Dad would under the circumstances.

"You don't waste any time, do you, kid? I like that."

"Life's too short."

Grinning, the man calling himself Waite swatted Daniel between the shoulder blades. Damn! It felt like someone had tapped him with a twenty-pound sledgehammer. This dude was not only huge, he was also incredibly strong.

Although sitting, Waite appeared extremely tall and probably weighed three hundred pounds. His powerful low-pitched voice sounded like Orson Wells and the method in which he sat, sipping wine, was reminiscent of Wells portraying Macbeth or perhaps Henry VIII. Daniel could easily visualize Waite wearing a black cape and strutting around with a silver-handled ebony cane.

Despite his initial skepticism, Daniel didn't think Waite was a con artist. The man's attitude defied pretense. The method in which his small,

44

steady black eyes focused on Daniel defined total confidence. The cut of his suit—

Armani, perhaps, or Versace—suggested aristocratic taste.

Anyone who could afford one of those boys—custom-tailored, no less—had to be swimming in money.

Waite also knew Dad. That was a good sign, wasn't it? It should be. Dad never wasted his valuable time with the wrong people. Choose your sphere, he always said. You can't pick your relatives, so select your contacts wisely. These are the people who can make you rich or drag you down.

Dad would probably be around a long time. He was in great physical shape. Played golf, tennis and racquetball. Went to the sauna. Drank booze socially and never to excess. Watched what he ate. Didn't do anything stupid. Dad was only fifty-seven; he'd probably live another thirty years.

Daniel loved Dad, but thirty years was an incredibly long time to wait for your inheritance. Daniel would be sixty in thirty years. A giant bummer. He might as well be dead.

Waite put down his wine glass. "You need a manager, kid."

A manager? For what?

"I'm doing all right."

"Those sluts will never make you rich. They're strictly small potatoes. Pocket change."

Pocket change? Those babes had successful practices. They had both been interviewed on Good

45

Morning, Orlando, and were featured in Florida Businesswoman Magazine.

"They each make two hundred K a year," he said. "They're local celebs and they're only twenty-eight years old."

"Two hundred K? That's chicken feed."

Two hundred K? Chicken Feed? What was this dude smoking?

"I spend that much on cigars." Waite winked devilishly.

Something's definitely off about this dude.

"To put it in a nutshell, don't deliver what they want when they want it. Get what I'm saying?"

"Not really."

"I know the type, kid. Let me put it another way. Don't piss them off."

Daniel knew what he meant. The girls were babes, but everyone who knew them said they turned nasty when someone crossed their path.

"You want to make money, kid? Big money? A boatload of cash?"

"Who doesn't?"

"You've got the head for it—just like your dad. But you're disorganized. Your lack of experience will bite you in the ass if you don't fix things right now."

Waite appeared sincere. But it still sounded like a con.

"Kid, I know how to make money. So does your dad, but you don't want to learn from him."

"I don't?"

"He's put up boundaries."

"How?"

"He's cut a few corners; I'll give him that. But he's always made sure his ass is clean and that the end result will be above board and respectable."

"Glazer's worth eleven figures."

"On paper."

"He's got a stock portfolio that'll choke a horse."

"What happens if he needs a few hundred million in one lump?"

Daniel knew what Waite was getting at. But he wasn't sure he wanted to deal with anything on such a grand scale. Selling coke to a couple of babes a few times a week was one thing. Since mostly everyone did coke nowadays, no one really cared who did it or dealt it anymore.

But running an illegal business for big money?

This was something that could put you away for quite a while.

"I don't think Dad would ever want such a huge chunk of money in one lump."

"Good thing. He couldn't get it. It would collapse his corporation."

Like it or not, the man was absolutely right.

"Kid, you can make a fortune in this town if you work it right."

Bummer. This was definitely a con. "I've heard that one before."

"It's true."

"Where do I start?"

"Tourists. Where else?"

Yep, a con. Time to finish my drink and leave.

"Kid, they come here for the weather, the theme parks, and the beaches. They bring money—

lots of it. And they don't want to take it back home. They want to take stories back home. Things they can tell their friends after work over beer."

"I've never heard it put quite that way."

"Tourists are idiots, believe me. If they see a sign that says, "surrender all your money at the door," they'll do it in a heartbeat."

"I know all that. I've lived here long enough."

"Fortunately, there are several classes. The most popular are the poor slobs saving up their money all year long so they can take the family to the theme parks. The rich come here to buy property and whatever else strikes their fancy. They're more cautious and much harder to approach. When you target them, you have to do it discreetly. They can't realize what you're doing."

"So then, you want to stay clear of the poor tourists altogether?"

"There ya go."

"You don't like fleecing the poor?"

Waite boomed laughter. His huge hand swatted Daniel on the shoulder. A knot of heat rushed across his shoulder blades. "Good one, kid. I like that."

Daniel rubbed his stinging shoulder. He couldn't help wondering what was really going on. Who Waite was. If he had other clients.

"Kid, you'll do fine with a little direction."

"And Dad won't be involved in this at all?"

"If he suspected you were involved in something illegal, what do you think he'd do?"

"He'd tell me to stop doing it."

"Your father isn't exactly a saint."

48

Daniel knew all about his father. Dad had been working deals and making private calls from his den ever since Daniel could remember. Dad also had a slew of associates he met almost daily at the country club. Dad had mentioned several by name, but didn't talk about much else. "I know," he said.

"How?"

"For one thing, he's a member of a secret club."

"It could be made up of priests."

"They can't possibly be priests. They're all rich and powerful."

"Has he asked you to join this club?"

"He wants me to continue building up my business and invest small amounts of money in mutuals and new companies to gain business savvy. He doesn't want me taking any risks. He doesn't even trust me enough to tell me the name of his club."

"Do you know its name?"

"I overheard him talking about it in his office."

Waite lowered his voice. "You heard him mention the Diocese?"

Daniel couldn't speak. This was truly weird. Almost like in Raiders of the Lost Ark, with everyone whispering about the location of the Ark.

"Want to know how I know about it?"

This was a no-brainer. Waite was wealthy, powerful, and well-connected. He was probably a member himself. How else could he know?

"Let's just say I know and leave it at that, shall we?"

Daniel had more of his drink.

"Kid, your father has done some things in his past that he's not proud of. Everyone has. You've got to shatter a bunch of legs to make an omelet."

"You mean eggs?"

"Whatever. But when it comes to his only son and heir, he's as protective as momma bear. He doesn't want you falling into the wrong hands and he doesn't want you doing anything to mess with the family name. He won't want you involved in something that might get the Orlando cops sniffing after you."

"That would be a giant bummer."

"Then I guess we'll have to be careful, won't we?"

Daniel didn't like doing anything his father wouldn't approve of. He also didn't like doing anything behind his father's back. But Waite's statements rang true. And if that much money could be made, why would Dad disapprove?

This could be much worse than being hauled in for drunk driving. Wearing an orange suit and sharing a bunk for the next ten years with someone named Bubba or Chocolate Charlie would be all it took to get Dad to revamp his will.

"If I'm caught, Dad'll kill me. Mom, too."

Waite shrugged. "You can only die once, kid. Believe me, I've tried changing that, but so far, I'm unable to alter the process."

"Process?"

"Dying just once. Pay attention. I get pissed off when people ignore me."

"I'm not ignoring you. I just don't want to get caught."

50

"You won't."

"You sure?"

"Guaranteed."

How could anyone guarantee that?

"I just can," Waite said.

"Can what?" Daniel asked warily.

"Guarantee that."

How the hell?

Waite chuckled. "Anyone can read your expression."

"It's that obvious?"

"A tad. So what do you say?"

Daniel couldn't argue with this sort of logic. Nor could he dispute the man's ideas. Or his wardrobe. "I like the money aspect, but I just don't know."

"Trust me, kid. I know exactly what I'm doing."

"Last time someone said that, I ended up in the drunk tank with him, watching him trying to swim with his head stuck in the toilet bowl."

Chapter 6

At the O-Town Café

Dressed in his single-breasted dark-blue Versace and cream-colored silk tie, Richard Grove pushed open the glass door of the O-Town Café and found a vacant window seat in the half-filled air-conditioned room.

He knew he shouldn't be worried by his son's phone call. Daniel didn't sound distressed in any way. He'd only wanted to get together to discuss something important.

Daniel normally never phoned these days. The days of calling for money, thankfully, had long passed. The boy had been on his own for the last several years. Using his computer programming skills, he had built a solid, respectable business. Aside from holiday and birthday visits, Richard and Mildred rarely saw their son these days.

Due to the nature of the call, Richard abruptly canceled his two-thirty appointment with Central Florida Builders & Developers. He had made a promise to himself when the boy was just a toddler that he'd always support him. Too many parents neglected their children these days. When kids weren't exposed to the solid family unit, they never learned camaraderie or a sense of belonging.

Which explained what was happening in most households nowadays.

It was important to give his son his space. When Daniel finished college and expressed the desire to venture out on his own, Richard and

Mildred did what they could to see that the boy was given whatever resources were required. Mildred wasn't wild about their son's decision to move into a garden apartment in Winter Park, but she didn't protest. Not too much, anyway. The apartment was only a few miles from their comfortable Casselberry ranch home. Twenty minutes, tops, even with traffic. "Spitting distance," as Daniel had quipped.

But they both knew this was the beginning of a new phase in their lives. For Daniel, it was the beginning of his new life as his own man. For Richard and Mildred, it was the beginning of their new life without their son.

Daniel, accompanied by a huge, broad-faced man in a dark, custom-fitting double-breasted suit, came in at just a few minutes past three. Daniel's companion moved in a straight line, like that of a charging elephant. Waiters, waitresses, and customers automatically ducked out of his way.

"Hello, Daniel." Richard was happy to see that his son looked well. Daniel, as always, was nicely tanned. And the fuller cheeks conveyed the message that he was eating well. "Haven't seen you in quite a while."

"Work keeps me pretty busy. I'll drop by one of these days."

"Your mother would love that. So would I."

Daniel seemed uneasy. Richard hoped he hadn't gotten involved in something questionable. His companion looked like trouble.

The Mob?

Unlikely. Daniel dealt with computer people. He liked the bar scene but chose his clubs wisely

53

and stayed away from the Trail and the seedier areas entirely.

But this man definitely carried the smell of danger about him. His eyes were small and very dark, like smoldering coals. Similar to Mr. Balbor, a former associate, who Richard hadn't seen in several years. Balbor's eyes gave you that same uneasy feeling.

"Dad, this is Mr. Waite."

Richard extended a hand. Waite took it and smothered it with his own. The grip was hot and excruciating. If the handshake hadn't been so brief, Richard suspected his hand might have been crushed.

What on earth was his son doing with such a beast?

Daniel had obviously brought him for a reason. Richard hoped it wasn't to ask him to invest in some get-rich-quick scheme. Richard was always open to promising ideas but had a bad feeling about this man.

"Mr. Waite," he said. His hand throbbed. "Please have a seat."

Waite slid his chair back and sat. His chair groaned in protest. He looked around. "How's the chow here?"

"Very good. I take it you're not from Orlando?"

"What gave me away? My debonair way? Sophistication? Cultured method of speech?"

Richard went silent. The man's humor took him aback. He found his voice. "Might I inquire where you are from?"

Waite's broad face spread into a fleshy grin. The smoldering coals settled directly on Richard. "I hail from the same neck of the woods as one of your former colleagues."

Richard tried reading the other man's expression. The grin told him nothing. "Really. That is very interesting."

"My friend Balbor sends his regards."

Richard froze. My God. Balbor's successor had finally arrived.

But why Central Florida? And why so soon? The Diocese had been doing quite well the last few years with the tourists keeping the economy flowing nicely. And despite the dips in the Dow and the latest recession, Glazer still held its own.

"A pleasure meeting you, Mr. Waite. But I'm surprised you've decided to come here first. Might I ask how you met my son?"

"We hooked up at a motel bar."

That made sense. Waite would want to take in the local color right off. However, Richard didn't want his son exposed to Diocese matters quite yet. He was much too naïve and inexperienced.

But now was not the time nor the place to voice his doubts.

"My son has agreed to show you around?" Richard hoped he didn't sound too obvious.

"Your son demonstrates intelligence and business sense," Waite said. "I've decided to give him a few pointers. Business-wise, of course."

"That's very generous," Richard said tactfully. "Just how do you—"

"I haven't decided yet." Waite glanced around the room. "They have waitresses here, don't they?" he asked. "Or are those skinny bimbos wandering around carrying trays of food just for decoration?"

A slender brunette about eighteen years old appeared, her notepad ready, her pretty face arranged in a polite smile. She was understandably intimidated by Waite's enormous presence. The name Ashley was stamped in white block letters on the shiny black tag pinned to her white blouse. "May I help you?" she asked softly.

"What were you doing back there?" Waite said. "Not your hair, obviously."

She looked down at her notepad and trembled. Richard could tell Daniel wanted to say something. Not wise. Richard pushed his foot forward beneath the table, preparing to tap his son's shin if necessary.

"I want a large, juicy steak," Waite said. "The bigger, the better. Blood-rare. I want the plate soaked."

She scribbled his order.

"That plate had better look like it got a smidge too close to the latest summer slashfest."

She kept scribbling.

"Also, a baked potato smothered with butter and sour cream. And a bottle of your best port wine."

After Daniel and Richard gave their orders, Waite said, "And try bringing it here before one of my friends here dies of starvation or old age."

She hurried away.

"You scared her," Daniel said.

56

Waite grinned. "I kinda put a little extra fire in my delivery." He tilted his head. "Think I went a tad overboard?"

"We don't want her scared..."

Waite put his elbows on the table and leaned forward. He lowered his voice. "We don't?"

"She might mess up our orders."

Waite nodded, then straightened. "Then I'll just have to make sure she dies a long, horrible death."

Richard and Daniel froze.

Waite grinned devilishly. "But I'll see that she has time to fix her hair first."

Richard and Daniel continued to stare.

"Isn't that kind of...harsh?" Daniel managed.

Waite shrugged. "What? The hair thing? Or the death suggestion?"

"She's probably only making eighty bucks a week and tips. She doesn't need—"

"Need what, kid?"

Daniel shrugged. "She's seems like a nice girl. And she's cute."

Richard hoped the boy would shut up. Infuriating a protector was always a bad move. "Daniel, I think you'd better—"

"Grove, let the boy get it off his chest. He's having a genuine attack of testosterone." Waite nodded. "I like it."

"Mr. Waite—"

"He doesn't know yet," Waite said.

"You...didn't tell him?"

"Tell me what?" Daniel watched them closely.

"I thought it would be a treat to give him the good news with you present."

"Dad? What's going on?"

Richard wasn't prepared for this. He had always wanted his son to learn the facts in a much different setting. Not in a crowded restaurant. And certainly not from a super demon.

"Think I should educate him before or after our meal?" Waite stared at Richard. The smoldering coals actually glowed. "I suggest right now. It might be quite a while before we get our food."

Richard knew better than stir the pot. "I agree," he managed.

"Dandy. Dinner theater antics always stimulates the old appetite." Waite faced the window, where traffic sat at the light.

Directly across the street, a shiny silver BMW inched to a stop.

"Kid, see that silver job out there?"

Daniel nodded.

"Want to see it smoke?"

"Smoke?"

"You know. Burn. Ignite. Flames, sparks, fumes—all sorts of charcoal and smoldering stuff moving around. The whole shebang. Emphasis on the bang."

Daniel glanced nervously at Richard. Richard avoided his son's gaze. His boy was about to become a man. For Daniel, life would never be the same.

Waite's broad cheeks stretched into an easy grin. "Having a good window seat at a spectacle

58

intensifies the wonder and the true meaning of a genuine miracle." He turned back to the window.

And winked.

Outside, long tongues of flickering flames jumped out from beneath the hood of the BMW.

Chapter 7

Wild Ride

The beat-up van weaved recklessly through the heavy afternoon traffic.

The boys were acting way beyond silly. The driver made screechy bird noises, the boy beside him giggling after each loud belch. Myron, sitting close beside Tiffany, pounded his chest like a gorilla each time he looked at her.

Tiffany had been to several Hollywood parties where everyone was much too stoned to act rationally. These three were just as stoned and even sillier. She was surprised Frankie hadn't wrecked the van.

"So where are you taking us?" she asked.

"How about we just drive around and boogie?" Myron said, coughing out smoke.

The gleam in his glazed eyes made her uneasy. "What exactly do you mean by boogie?"

Myron and his friends brayed laughter. "Boogie, baby. You know. We find a room somewhere, then you and Red take off your clothes—"

"And boogie!" his friends chirped in unison.

"I see." This wasn't so different from Hollywood after all. "An orgy."

The threesome howled.

"You're turning them on, Tifferoo," Chip whispered. "Cool it."

"I think they're doing it themselves."

60

"Gonna boogie," Myron sang, his voice cracking. "Gonna boogie, boogie, boogie, all night long..."

"We really need to make our appointment," Tiffany said, growing angry.

"You don't wanna boogie?" Myron pushed his greasy ponytail over his shoulder and sent over a thick cloud of B.O.

"Our appointment's really important."

Myron's blinking chestnut eyes went out of focus. He sucked in another huge lungful of grass, let it back out, and suffered a wet coughing fit.

Tiffany wiped some cold spittle off her cheek. "Thanks so much for sharing."

Norbert snatched a half-finished bottle of Jim Beam from underneath the front seat, unscrewed the cap, and sucked down a giant swallow. He handed the bottle to Frankie, who upended it and offered it to Myron. Myron gulped down some and offered it to Tiffany.

She had no intention of drinking from that bottle. It smelled of grease and oil. Just because she was dead didn't mean she had to lower her standards. "No, thank you."

"You're not one of those chicks, are ya, baby?" Myron asked. "Always says no?"

"I've been known to say yes on occasion."

He chuckled. "Bet you said yes a shitload of times."

She glared. "What's that supposed to mean?"

"Means I seen ya before. Look like the main dom lezzy bitch in a bondage flick I just saw."

"Sorry, but it wasn't me."

61

"Sure looked like ya. Flick was even made here in Orlando."

She sighed. "You must have me confused with some other dom lezzy bitch."

"You weren't in Bountiful Bound Biker Babes of Babylon?"

"As terrific as that sounds, I don't think so."

"Ya sure? Or just pulling a number on me?"

"I think I'd remember being involved in something like that."

"Some really hot bitches in that flick. Wow." Myron shook his head. "I mean wow..."

Chip said, "You never told me you did those."

She groaned. "Listen carefully, now. I never told you because I never did any."

"You sure?"

"Have a belt." Myron handed her the bottle again.

"I'm just not in the mood."

"C'mon. Loosen ya up." He elbowed her in the side.

"Don't do that again, okay?"

"You mean this?" He elbowed her again.

"That's what I meant."

He sucked down more and belched loudly.

"It sure is hot in here." Chip frowned. "Something wrong with the air-conditioning?"

Myron's rough, unshaven face moved closer, his foul miasma brushing heavily against Tiffany's mouth and nose. "How come you don't want any, baby?"

"It's a little early for me."

"You don't want to get shitfaced?"

"I'd rather make our appointment sober."

"What kind of appointment?" Frankie asked.

She turned to Chip.

He shrugged. "Go ahead, buttercup. What harm can it do?"

"We're supposed to meet a super demon somewhere in downtown Orlando. His name is Belching Waiter. Or is it Breath Mint? Whatever his name is, we have to meet him."

"Braithwaite." Chip sighed.

"A super demon?" Myron squinted.

"No shit?" Norbert said.

"Where'd you meet up with this super demon?" Frankie asked, grinning.

"We haven't yet. We're here. With you."

"Then how d'ya know you're supposed to meet him?"

"They told us down in Hell what we're supposed to do. Actually, they didn't tell me. They told him—her."

The trio stared at her for a full ten seconds, then howled laughter.

"Super demon," Frankie said, nodding.

"Sounds heavy," Myron said. "We oughta stick with these babes."

"What for?" Norbert asked.

"This Belching Waiter dude might know where to get hold of some better stuff."

"I dunno," Norbert said. "I'd rather just boogie and get shitfaced."

"You wanna come up here, Red?" Frankie patted the console. "Plant your tight little ass on this."

63

"Yeah!" Norbert chugged down more Jim Beam. "Let's rock. Red first. Then Blondie."

Frankie patted the console again.

Chip scratched his chin. "How come you want little ol' me and not my bodacious buddy?"

"Ol' Myron's got dibs on Blondie."

Tiffany sighed. It was becoming clear that these three weren't going to take them where they wanted to go. "This isn't exactly what we had in mind."

Frankie shrugged. "Want out? Just climb on my lap and push the door open." He winked. "You might get lucky."

"I might block your view. You wouldn't want to have an accident, would you?"

The threesome squealed laughter.

Myron slapped her on the back. "Know something, Blondie? You're a riot."

"Thank you, but I really wish you wouldn't do that."

"This?" He elbowed her in the side. "Or this?" He swatted her back again.

A clot of heat flared up at the base of her neck. You're not evil, she reminded herself. You don't like hurting people.

"Ya one of those babes? Don't like being touched?"

"I'm afraid so."

"I thought all chicks liked getting down and dirty."

"I'm sort of a neat freak. I used to watch Odd Couple reruns when I was little."

"You're right, Myron," Norbert said, giggling. "She's a riot, all right."

"C'mon, babe," Myron coaxed. "Get down and dirty or jump out. How fast we going, Frankie?"

"Um, lemme see..." Frankie scrunched down to eye the dash. He rubbed his nose. The van swerved, nearly sideswiping the tour bus beside them. "Forty-eight. No. Forty-three. No. Sixty-four . . ."

"Can't you see?"

"Would help if I opened my eyes."

Norbert cackled loudly.

Tiffany knew she had to do something about this. These idiots were too far gone. "I'm not getting a warm feeling about you guys," she said.

"You want a warm feeling, baby?" Myron's foul breath made her gag. "I'll give you one." He elbowed her a third time.

Frankie and Norbert laughed hysterically. Norbert said, "I think Blondie's got the hots for ya, Myron."

"That right, baby? Like what ya see?"

"Not really."

"If I were you, Myron," Chip said, "I'd lay off. My friend can be a serious ass-kicker when she's riled."

"What about you, Red?" Norbert asked.

"I'm not much of an ass-kicker."

"How about an ass-wiper?"

"How's that?"

"Crawl up here so I can wipe my ass with that red mop."

"Wow," Chip said. "I haven't felt this desirable since Olivier tried selling me to Mastiphal for the shrunken heads of two Muslim terrorists and the pickled testicles of a former U.S. President."

"Your friend sounds like she wants an ass-whipping." Myron elbowed Tiffany one last time.

"I told you not to do that." Not a demon. Not a demon.

Norbert twisted around in his seat. His eyes were glossy and out of focus. He gripped a large automatic pistol, pointing it at her face. "Like my gun?"

"Wow. It looks brand-new."

"I stole it."

"That makes it hot, doesn't it?"

Frankie rapped the wheel with his fist. "Blondie, you've got a serious pair of 'nads for a babe. C'mon up here. Give me a lap-dance and I'll see if I can keep this van between the lines."

"Before I do anything, I'd like to know why your friend has a hot pistol."

"I like hot pistols, Blondie," Norbert said, giggling.

"Really?" Tiffany focused on the gun.

"Love 'em." Hot. "They turn me on." Hotter. Hotter... "In fact—"

Scorching!

A high-pitched wail of agony exploded from Norbert's lungs. Steam rose from the gun, turning his flesh bright red.

"Motherfuck! Ahhhh! Christ! Owwww! What the fuck?"

66

He waved the gun hysterically, struggling to release it. It stuck to his flesh. The slab barrel thumped Frankie on the back of the head. He slammed his side against his door, losing his grip on the wheel. They whacked into the bumper of the Dodge pickup in front of them.

The smell of burnt flesh and released sphincter overpowered the reek of marijuana.

"Jeez Louise." Chip sniffed and coughed. "Someone cut a serious slice of nasty Limburger in here!"

Frankie and Myron scrambled in their seats, trying to dodge the flailing pistol. Frankie mashed down on the brake pedal and slammed it into park. Myron tried to snatch the gun from his friend's grasp. His fingertips touched the searing barrel, sizzling his flesh. His ear-shattering shriek bounced off the walls of the van.

A bulky man with long hair, a full beard and tattoos covering his huge hairy arms jumped out of the Dodge truck, rushed over, and pounded on Frankie's door.

Tiffany pushed the side door open. Chip crawled behind Myron's twisted, jerking form and joined her out on the curb.

The two large, bearded passengers of the Dodge pickup hurried over to the open doorway and pulled Myron out onto the macadam. The driver had Frankie in a headlock. Norbert screamed while struggling with the gun.

Distant sirens drowned out the traffic noise.

Chapter 8

Protégée

Fire trucks, ambulances, and squad cars arrived in minutes.

Police rerouted the heavy rush hour traffic. Cops stayed busy with crowd control while paramedics tended to burn victims. A white news van pulled up to the curb, its cameras rolling. A tow truck sat at the intersection, waiting for the firefighters to finish dousing the mysterious blaze that had turned a sparkling silver BMW into a charred, smoking husk of metal.

Daniel stared numbly at the chaos. Wow. Was this real or what?

Shaking himself out of it, he stared at Waite. The big dude was grinning.

"Not bad," Waite was nodding in approval. "I'm a little rusty, of course, but when you haven't done something in five hundred years, you sort of lose your sense of timing. With practice, I'll get it back."

Dad sat hunched over, staring at his water glass. No shock whatsoever had registered on his face.

Reality suddenly slapped Daniel squarely in the face. The last hour could now be explained. Waite's eerie perception of Daniel's business dealings in the Oasis Lounge. Waite's knowledge of Dad, of Glaser. Of the Diocese. Why people ducked out of his way, cringing at the sound of his voice.

And his recent mention of five hundred years.

He was either totally nuts, or not real.

Other things also made sense. Dad's frequent business trips. The fact that they had never known difficult financial times, even when recessions plagued the country. Those secret phone calls coming in for Dad during supper or in the middle of the night.

The short brown hairs stood up on the back of Daniel's neck.

Everything was now crystal-clear. Dad's success had nothing to do with proven business tactics, savvy, or good luck. The Diocese was obviously much more than a group of shrewd, lucky business guys. And the big man calling himself Brett Waite wasn't just a man who knew how to make big money.

Daniel's voice struggled out of his throat. "Where are you from, Mr. Waite?"

"Daniel..." Dad sat bolt upright.

"Stuff a cork in it, Grove." Waite's grin hadn't relaxed at all. He was one smug dude enjoying himself. "Where do you think, kid?"

Daniel couldn't say the word aloud. Sometimes it sounded like you were clearing your throat when you uttered it. Other times, a cough. It was just a short, harmless four-letter word people uttered when they were bummed-out or when they forgot something. The softest, most innocuous cussword you could think of.

Such a small word, yet it stayed in his throat.

It was also a place. A place that, only minutes before, Daniel did not even believe existed.

But the times had shaken his former skepticism. During the last few years, news stories even more intense than any slasher flick plagued the airwaves and the Net. Acts of extreme violence and hatred, convincing him the world wasn't the same safe, quiet place he'd known as a child.

And when this mystery dude popped out of the blue, mentioned fireworks, then, with a wink, turned the street into something right out of Beirut, you suddenly realized what religious people and doomsayers alike meant when they said evil wasn't confined to Hell.

Waite's gaze hadn't left Daniel. "Methinks the kid's figuring it all out. Got it all worked out yet, kid?"

Daniel couldn't look him in the eye. He didn't know if it was fear or repulsion. The cold heavy lump in his throat and the throbbing emptiness in his gut made him tremble.

Another siren screamed down the street. Two cops directed the crowd away from the curb.

Waite continued staring at Daniel. The big man didn't even care about the burn victim the paramedics struggled to squeeze out of the BMW.

The nervous waitress appeared, watching the chaos. "That poor man," she said softly, sighing.

"Isn't that just all sorts of awful?" Waite's eager eyes focused on the large round tray she placed onto the collapsible stand she pulled open. "Some people just don't care where they stage their theatrics. In front of a crowded restaurant, where people are trying to enjoy their meal, no less!"

She carefully picked up Waite's huge plate.

"Enough of that nonsense. I'm famished." Waite rubbed his palms briskly together and slid a napkin over his ample lap. "A weenie roast always stimulates the old appetite."

She gingerly placed the bloody dish on the setting in front of him. Waite meticulously sank the sharp edge of his knife into the huge slab of meat. He carved out a small triangle, popped the dripping piece into his mouth and swallowed it whole. "Perfect." He dabbed at his mouth with his napkin. "I'll let you keep your job. Tell the manager to give you a big, fat raise. Just don't take so long the next time."

Without a word, she placed the other two orders in front of Daniel and Dad.

Dad said, "I'd like a double bourbon on-the-rocks."

Daniel could tell Dad was upset. Dad rarely drank before supper.

"Yes, sir." Then, in a soft voice, "Will there be anything else?"

Waite said, "If there is, I'll give you a friendly yell."

She scurried back to the kitchen.

Turning away from the activity in the street, Daniel found that he had lost his appetite.

"Aren't you eating, kid?" Waite seemed concerned. "That grilled chicken looks good. For grilled chicken, that is. Personally, I never saw the sense in it. Not enough blood for my taste."

Daniel stared at his plate but quickly found that he could not focus on anything right now. Especially food. Enjoying a meal while someone

71

less than fifty feet away was just pulled from his burning vehicle seemed…well, he just couldn't do it.

"Kid, you're pissing me off. Face reality. Grow some balls. Pull your head out of your ass. In that order." Waite drank some wine. "And oh yeah, eat your goddamned chicken."

Dad silently picked at his chef salad.

Waite put down his fork and licked some blood from his lips, then blotted his mouth with his napkin. "Kid—"

"Mr. Waite, my boy's understandably upset."

"What the hell for?" Waite sucked in a big forkful of baked potato. "The fact that I don't like grilled chicken? Where I'm from? Or is he also pissed that our waitress took too long and doesn't have a clue what to do about her hair?"

"I think the car fire was what actually upset him. Both of us, in fact."

"Ah." Waite nodded. "I see. A little too much flash, ya think?"

"It was kind of, well, violent. A man was driving and there were people passing."

"I get you."

"You really must understand that we—"

"I must admit that I might've overdone things a tad. All cooped up down below for too long. Too anxious to show off."

"I'm glad you understand."

Waite nodded. "I should be a little more subtle next time, I guess. Less flame, perhaps?" Waite squinted. "And keep the smoke more in the

72

background for effect." He shrugged his massive shoulders. "I told you, I'm a tad rusty..."

"Mr. Waite..." Dad finally met Waite's gaze. "I think my boy's a little young for all this. . ."

Waite stared at Dad the longest time. Then he sat back in his seat and crossed his huge arms over his big chest. His voice lowered. "Grove, how old were you when we took you in?"

Dad lowered his head and silently pushed his fork through his salad. He said nothing.

Waite uncrossed his arms. "Enough said, then? No more whining? Playing with your food?" He picked up his wine glass. "Now that we've gotten all the bullshit out of the way, a toast is in order. To my new protégé."

Chapter 9

Looking for Breath Mint

Tiffany and Chip squeezed through staggered tangles of pedestrians clogging up the walk.

Chip's expression was even sillier than normal. She knew him well enough to tell when something was bothering him.

"Something on your mind?" she asked.

"I guess you told me the truth after all, honey bunny."

"When?"

"When you promised me you'd do some interesting things." He chuckled. "That was pretty cool. Hot, actually—if you want the technical term."

"They didn't give me much choice." Doing that made her feel as if she had actually acted like a demon in spite of her good intentions. "Norbert shouldn't have been waving around a loaded gun."

"It wouldn't have hurt either of us, muffin."

"It would've hurt or killed someone else. There's a lot of traffic out there."

"So?"

"You don't care if some innocent person was accidentally shot?"

He shrugged. "Honeykins, I haven't spent the last few centuries down there for doing good deeds."

She sighed. Getting angry with him would accomplish nothing. He couldn't help being the way he was. "Anyway, Frankie was too stoned to drive.

74

Especially in such heavy traffic. He could've killed someone."

"What was wrong with Myron? He really fancied you."

"He slobbered. And I don't like being manhandled."

"He manhandled you?"

"You saw him elbowing me. He was no better than the wolf guy."

At the intersection, the blackened husk of what looked like a BMW was hauled away on the flat bed of a tow truck.

The crowds brought traffic to a standstill. A large square-shouldered cop stood in the center of the intersection, his whistle chirping like a hysterical bird. His arms flopped in erratic directions.

"What's he doing?" Chip asked.

"Directing traffic. What's it look like?"

"It reminds me of a dance the slave girls did for the pharaohs in ancient Egypt. Good thing he's wearing that blue suit. His paunch totally grosses me out."

"C'mon." She pulled his elbow. "We'd better cross."

Chip stopped as they were about to pass. "What happened here? Somebody decide to use their car to roast weenies?"

The whistle screeched in their direction. Out of the corner of his mouth the cop barked, "Keep moving!"

"No offense, Mr. Officer Person, but that doesn't exactly answer my—"

75

"Move or I'll have you arrested!"

"For what?"

The cop spat out the whistle. It hopped down his chest, stopping by its chain over his belt buckle. He placed his fists on his ammo belt. "Raising my blood pressure, for starters."

"If you really want your blood pressure raised, my delicious friend here can make her luscious melons do all sorts of crazy things you'd never in your life expect to—"

Tiffany elbowed him in the side. "Shut up. And please don't include me in your perversions."

"It's the only fun I get these days."

A young guy in baggy shorts and a stained white tee shirt sat on a stool near the double glass doors marked Orange Avenue Bistro. A sign tied around his bearded neck said KEEP DEVELOPERS OUT OF THE EVERGLADES. He watched them behind his smoldering cigarette.

"Did you see what happened?" Chip asked. "Chuckles over there has a hugantic hornet crawling around in his undershorts and won't tell me."

"Car caught fire."

"How?"

He shrugged. "You see a crystal ball in my lap?"

"Just the beginnings of a pot belly."

A frown. "Smart guy, eh?"

"He has his moments," Tiffany said.

He puffed out tendrils of gray smoke. His blinking blue eyes focused on Tiffany. "Just started cooking. And me without my marshmallows."

She ignored his lecherous stare. "Is the driver all right?"

"I knew that, I'd be working in an air-conditioned hospital, not baking myself to a crisp out here with this stupid sign."

"Thanks for your time."

He held out his hand. "Got a couple bucks? Standing out here in this heat makes a guy thirsty."

"You're sitting," Tiffany said.

"Chick's bright," he told Chip.

"She has her moments, too."

"Bright and gorgeous? She for real?"

"Not really. Just appeared in a bright cloud one day during one of my hallucinations."

"Musta been a real doozy." His hand remained open.

"When she touched down, I actually felt like a real man for the first time in two thousand years," Chip said with a wink.

"I'm hip, believe me." The guy's hand hadn't budged.

"Still want that handout?" Chip asked.

"Is the Pope Catholic?"

"I think he has to be," Tiffany said.

Chip slipped him an imaginary twenty. The guy jumped up, yanked off his sign, tossed it against the brick wall, and disappeared around the corner.

Chip stared at her.

She said nothing.

"No words of wisdom this time? Nothing about whatever he's got in his hot little hand has probably already disappeared?"

77

She hoped Chip's twenty wouldn't vanish until the bartender brought that jerk his drink. "Nope." Then she turned and walked away.

"So tell me about that," he said, joining her.

"About what?" she asked.

He sighed. "The smoking vehicle."

"What about it?"

"Do modern cars do stuff like that?"

"They're all computerized. They'll turn themselves off whenever their system goes out of whack."

"Ever see one that just lit up?"

"Not a BMW."

"What's that?"

"Expensive."

Chip suddenly stopped walking and began sniffing. "We're getting close."

"To what?"

"The super demon—what else?"

"Is it that rotten egg odor I remember from down there?"

"Most likely. I caught a whiff while Chuckles was motioning us on."

"How come I don't smell it?"

"You haven't spent hundreds of years down there. After that much time, your sniffer becomes sensitive."

"You think Barf Wafer caused that fire?"

"Possibly. He's always been a blow 'em-up kind of guy. And it's Braithwaite."

"That would mean he's close."

"If he caused that fire, he is."

"Why would he do something like that?"

78

"To make a point. To vent. Or he might just be feeling good."

"He blows things up when he feels good?"

"He's a demon, angel. When a demon feels good, he causes explosions. Or accidents. Sometimes he makes people disappear. Or do really stupid things."

"He does that on good days?"

"Correctamundo."

"What about bad ones?"

"When a super's on the rag, you find the nearest rock, slide underneath, and wait."

"For what?"

"The next Millennium."

79

Chapter 10

Ashley Parker

Momma's dirty red Toyota Supra sat in the driveway as Ashley Parker pulled her ten-year-old black Honda Accord over to the curb.

Momma usually left for work around six. She'd been waitressing at the Fly Trappe on Michigan Avenue the last five years and got home just before three in the morning, usually half-drunk.

It hadn't always been that way. Momma never drank much at all while Daddy was living with them, just a little wine when they went out for dinner. Momma was much different in those days—carefree, friendly, laughing a lot. But when Daddy left with the airline stewardess he'd met on a business trip six years ago, Momma had never been the same. She had been slipping away ever since, a day at a time. Ashley feared that one day she would come home and find Momma sitting in a chair, comatose, her spirit gone forever.

Ashley found Momma in the kitchen, her flowered housecoat open, her plaid pajamas exposed. Her hair was a mess. "Back already?" Momma cracked an egg over the skillet, dropped it in and tossed the shell into the sink.

"It's after five, Momma."

Momma yawned and pushed a hand through her tangled brown tresses. Her slippers scraping the scuffed tile, she shuffled over to the fridge and pulled a loaf of sourdough bread. Then took out two pieces and stuck them in the toaster. "Meet anybody rich?" She left the loaf on the counter and, without bothering to close the refrigerator door, went back to the stove.

"Probably." Ashley closed the door and kept a close watch on the skillet. Momma had already started three skillet fires. Ashley didn't want to die that way.

Momma picked up the spatula and tried flipping the egg. "Shit, forgot to put in the butter." She went over to the coffeepot and poured a cup. "Grab yourself a rich one while you're young."

"Yes, Momma." Ashley reached around her and turned off the flame. "I'm going to my room now."

Momma was silent as she scraped the egg out of the skillet.

Ashley closed her bedroom door, stripped out of her uniform, and went to get her shower ready. Her cell phone rang.

She opened her purse and got it out. "Yes?"

"Ashley?" a man's voice said softly.

"Speaking."

"This is Daniel Grove."

"Yes?"

"I saw you today."

"Really? Where?"

"The O-Town."

"How'd you see me?"

"I was one of your customers."

That didn't tell her anything. She'd waited on at least a hundred people and hardly remembered any of them. Waitressing was not the sort of profession where you brought your work home with you.

She wondered why he was calling. And how he'd gotten her number. "Okay..."

"I was there with my father and another man."

"Okay..." She began wondering what he wanted.

"You'd remember him."

This guy was beginning to sound like a certified weirdo. That was all she needed— especially after dealing with so many others in one day, then coming home and having to deal with Momma. "Care to describe him for me? Just so I don't have him confused with anyone else?"

"That would be difficult."

"What? Describing him? Or confusing him with someone else?"

"I'll let you decide. He's about six-six and probably weighs in in at around three-fifty. Short black hair. He's huge, loud, and arrogant. Aside from that, he's plain mean."

The image registered instantly. Mean was an understatement. Loud and arrogant didn't even cut it. The man seemed almost evil.

A bully. The kind who gives off negative vibes.

Some of those vibes might have even drifted into the street, influencing that horrible car fire.

"I vaguely remember him."

"I thought you might. He leaves a distinct impression."

"He certainly left one on his chair. It had to be reupholstered and fitted with stronger screws as soon as he left."

"Whoa. . . That's terrible." He laughed.

"Oops. I kinda let that one slip, huh?"

"I won't tell anyone if you won't."

"Sorry, but he kind of bugged me. Hurt my feelings, too."

"Really? I hadn't noticed."

"He practically told me my hair is...icky."

"Your hair looks fine. Just great. Very fetching."

"That's the kiss of death for a guy, you know. Mentioning a girl's hair without the usual bow or curtsy? And thank you for your bow and curtsy."

"It's the least I can do."

She could only guess what this guy was doing with him. He seemed so nice and polite. And fun to talk to. Good-looking, too, with soft blue eyes and a warm smile. It was probably a business meeting.

But that still wasn't the main issue.

"How'd you get my number?"

"I kinda told your boss I forgot to leave a tip, and would it be okay if he gave me your number so I could give it to you personally?"

"Really?" She only remembered the customers who didn't leave her one. "Was the service that bad?"

"No. Of course not."

"I'm surprised. I get kind of distracted when someone—especially a man—mentions my hair in a bad way. It's never happened before, but it's

83

something a girl doesn't respond to very well, ya know?"

"I can imagine. And I did leave a tip."

"Then you lied to my boss?"

"Yeah. I did."

"That wasn't very nice."

"I know. I need to quit doing that. If I keep up the lies, word'll get out and someone'll think I'm a politician."

"Can't have that. But why'd you lie?"

"I had an ulterior motive."

"Sounds sinister and a little kinky."

"That's highly possible. Truth is, I wanted to see you again."

The guy she remembered appeared too prosperous to waste his time on someone waiting tables. "So that's why you called? To see me again? And apologize for your friend?"

He laughed. "That last item wasn't exactly high on my list. But you're right, I really should apologize."

"Because he'd never do it himself?"

"You must know him."

"Actually, I never had the misfortune to come across him before."

"Well, you're right. He doesn't apologize."

"I would've probably fainted if he had."

"Would you like to go out for dinner? Around six-thirty?"

"Dinner? You and me? Tonight?"

"Unless you'd rather postpone it until Christmas. Or maybe Arbor Day. Is there a problem?"

84

She stared at the clock on her nightstand. "It's already five-thirty." She didn't know why she'd said it. She never needed much time to get ready. Just a quick shower, then find something to wear and fix the face.

"It doesn't give you much time. I'm sorry. I should've thought of that."

Her last date was nearly a year ago. A customer. A nice-looking guy around forty. The dinner was great, but she hadn't heard from him since.

"Actually, I'd love to. As long as you don't bring along your friend."

"No need to worry," he said. "He's got other plans."

"I'm so sorry to hear that. . ."

"Want me to ask if he can reschedule so he can join us?"

"I really wouldn't want to be responsible for having him juggle his schedule. Unless you really do want to wait for Arbor Day..."

"I don't think my stomach can hold out. That's ten months from now!"

"Let's tempt fate and try and have fun without him, then."

"Sounds like a plan."

"I just hope he won't feel slighted."

"Doesn't matter. I'm not bringing him, no matter how much you insist."

Chapter 11

In Enemy Territory

With Tifferoo just a few yards ahead in the crowd, Chip stopped about twenty feet from the revolving doors of the glittering glass and metal skyscraper.

Hordes of well-dressed males and females whizzed through the revolving glass doors, many jabbering away on cell phones, others glancing at their watches. Things to do, appointments to make.

The smell ended here. Braithwaite was somewhere within this steel fortress. Chip could feel the cold aura brushing against him, its sourness making his essence throb like an open wound. The same sourness that drifted down the castle walls to the rock garden, where Chip and a dozen others spent the last several centuries, staring at the darkness.

Going inside seemed lame. Worse, it was stupid—even lame-brained.

Braithwaite was the worst of the bunch. He was evil, powerful, nasty, vicious, and arrogant, and those were his "good" qualities. His favorite hobbies were destroying people's brains...and turning them into inanimate objects...and forcing them to do evil things.

Disappearing in the sunset with Tifferoo sounded much better than stepping inside and dealing with the super demon. Much more pleasant, much less traumatic.

It wouldn't work. Braithwaite had helluva reach. As the super demon grew more organized, he would summon more inferiors to help him handle the workload. At the peak of Balberith's reign, he had brought up more than two thousand inferiors. Some were good, some weren't. But all had one thing in common: they were impossible to spot.

So even though fading away seemed the smart thing to do, he knew they could not get away with it.

At least, not now.

Like Tifferoo, he didn't want to go back down. Nothing to do but stand in that rock pile, getting pissed on while watching the eternal darkness. His only reprieve came when Olivier plucked him out of the slimy rocks once or twice each century to come up here for a quick errand.

Their few days in Raven had convinced him how much he missed being up here. How great it was to have powers—even limited ones—once again. He could do tricks up here. And use his brain. He was free to do as he pleased.

If it was the last thing he did, he'd find some way of—

Someone touched his shoulder, jolting him.

"You okay?" It was Tiffers.

He gazed into those big beautiful blue eyes and the dark, bleak images instantly went away. But he knew better than let her know how he felt. He had to maintain his mischievous persona. Otherwise, she would freak, and both of them would be doomed. "Why'd you sneak up on me?"

"What were you doing?"

87

"I was deep in thought."

"Really?"

She could be so nasty for such a sweet babe. "I've been deep in thought before."

"When?"

He shrugged. "About sixty years ago, then maybe a hundred and twenty before that."

"Really?"

"Correctomundo. And when I'm doing my deep-in-thought thingy, I tend to wander off and lose myself."

"Good thing it doesn't happen very often."

"Tifferoosky, you keep up with the smartass, you'll have me thinking you actually are a demon."

She flinched. He knew that would rile her. Good thing, too. It was the only thing he knew of to keep her in line. "Perish the thought. Anyway, your sudden pensiveness has me worried."

"Why?"

"I thought I'd lost you in this crowd."

"I know where I am."

"But I didn't."

It worried him when her clueless blonde mentality made a sudden appearance. "Lamb Chop, who do you think you're talking to?"

"I don't mean now, silly. I meant before."

"I was right here before. I'm right here now."

"I see that."

"I'm always right here."

She frowned.

"Something confusing you? Your forehead's all crinkly and messed up."

"You...don't seem to be moving."

"Why do I have to be moving if I'm just standing here?"

"Why are you doing that?"

"Doing what?"

"Just standing here."

"The scent stopped right here." The dark, bleak images instantly came back.

Tifferoo blinked. "Him?"

Chip nodded.

"Then don't you think we'd better go in?"

She had a very good point. An excellent point, in fact. And they didn't have much choice. But he just couldn't budge from his spot.

"Think you can follow me in?" she asked.

He tried thinking up a good zinger, but it wouldn't come. Braithwaite had him spooked. He could only nod at Tifferoo and let her take his hand.

The air-conditioning, potted plants, and furniture in the high-ceilinged foyer provided a pleasant respite from the harshness of the hot, busy street. A directory drilled into a square marble pillar showed visibly from the entrance.

His eyes immediately jumped to the bottom line.

Waite Business Diversities & Consultations
Brett Waite, Owner & Manager

"You think that's him?" Tifferoo asked.

Even disguised, the name made him tremble. "What would you call yourself if your name was Braithwaite?"

"Breath Mint? Belching Waiter? Bath Water? Brat Whipper?"

"Droll, honey bunny. Very, very—Brat Whipper?"

"You asked, didn't you?"

Her dry wit brought him back. Not all the way, but enough to remind him he wasn't alone. Not like the last two times he'd been up here.

He followed her over to the shiny elevators and stood there, staring at their distorted reflections in the metal. And feeling very small and insignificant.

"Why aren't we pressing the UP button?"

He didn't reply. He was thinking of grabbing her hand and rushing blindly out into the street. And finding some place to hide for the next hundred years.

"Are you scared?"

"I'm way past scared, muffin. I'd have to be ten times braver to be scared."

"So why don't we just turn around and leave town?"

If only it was that simple. "Supers usually bring along packs of inferiors when they come up. It wouldn't be difficult to send a few of them after us."

"You don't think we ought to at least try and take our chances?"

"We don't know how many others he's brought along. I don't think we should try anything stupid. Not yet, anyway."

"Does this mean you want me to push the UP button?"

He couldn't reply.

Numbly he watched her slender index finger moving toward the UP/DOWN panel.

An explosion of ice raced down his back when the button glowed red.

Chapter 12

Two Visitors

The blonde, followed by Olivier's miserable inferior, sashayed into the office.

Braithwaite watched her intently. Not bad. A knockout, in fact. She also exuded a strong sense of independence. Facing a superior obviously did not intimidate her.

Very good. He hated cowardice. The pathetic stinkweed cowering behind her, for instance. Braithwaite could not believe Olivier had picked that anorexic mess to hunt down Gutrillus. From what the Legion had heard, this blonde was directly responsible for that nasty bit of business.

"So you're the Limboite I've been hearing about."

"I'm the only Limboite I know of," she said.

He lit his cigar and watched her closely. Still no fear. The only dread Braithwaite could smell came from the idiot hiding behind her. The Limboite was apparently unaware of the powers of a super demon.

But that only stood to reason. She hadn't been down there long enough to learn what was what. And the only demon she knew was Gutrillus.

A piss-poor example, at best.

He wanted to give her a demonstration. Maybe turn her friend into a pile of upchuck for a few minutes. Add some peas, maybe a little tuna for texture and aroma, and voila! An interesting conversation piece for a few pleasant moments.

Later, perhaps.

"I've heard you were responsible for sending Gutrillus back down."

"I gave him the initial nudge," she said. "Chip zapped him and brought him down."

"Chip?"

She gestured to the stinkweed.

Braithwaite sighed. Some of those nicknames the inferiors chose—especially those conjuring up a cute image—put him in a foul mood. Didn't these morons have any self-respect?

"You think highly of this inferior?"

"We're partners."

"Cozy. Sorry I can't appreciate the moment. I don't do moments." He shrugged. "Bad for the complexion."

She just stood there, watching him.

Braithwaite pushed a thick plume of gray smoke in her direction. She made no effort to wave it away. One obstinate bitch. He could have fun with her.

"My name, as you've no doubt seen in the lobby, is Brett Waite. You may call me Mr. Waite. Or a simple sir will do. I really get off on Your Excellency, though. Your Highness also grabs my immediate attention. But I guess we'll have to improvise a tad. These idiots wandering around might get the wrong idea. Mortals are much too easily confused."

The blonde and the inferior nodded.

"I assume you've heard of my powers."

"We saw the fire," she said indifferently.

"Impressive, wasn't it?"

93

She just shrugged.

Damn. This was one seriously stuck-up bitch. He knew when he first heard about her coming from that flesh factory in California that she would be a problem. Good thing she was hot and sizzling on the eyes. Otherwise, he would have to give her a serious skin condition or do something interesting to those perky titties.

Right now, he'd have to be satisfied making things more difficult for them.

How about if he made them blind?

As interesting as that sounded, it wouldn't work. They wouldn't be able to find the shit bug if they couldn't see.

Something less physically intrusive, perhaps?

How about giving them less time than originally planned for their errand?

Sounded like a dynamite plan.

Braithwaite sat forward. "I'm going to trust Olivier's judgment and keep you up here for the time being. I've brought along a skeleton crew with me to start up my campaign. One inferior has taken over Orlando's illegal drug trade. Another has eliminated several major pimps. This will enable us to revitalize Central Florida's somewhat sluggish prostitution trade. A third was supposed to handle tourist crime and target the theme parks. He has disappeared."

"Is he still in Florida?" the blonde asked.

Braithwaite gave her one of his humorless grins. "If I knew where he was, I wouldn't need you two—capisc?"

No reply. He could tell the blonde knew she had just pressed the wrong button.

"The others have been ordered to report to me every day. I haven't heard from this one."

"What's his name, sir?" the stinkweed asked.

"Cletis. Know him?"

"Not by that name."

"I'm told he prefers to be called...Digger." That nickname was ridiculous. Just as bad than Chip.

"Now I know who he is."

"I'm real pleased. Impressed as well. But mostly pleased."

"Really?" the stinkweed asked.

"Of course I'm not pleased. Or impressed. Go find him. If you do, I might be slightly tolerant. Maybe a little less unpleasant. But if you want pleased and impressed, buy a puppy and toss it kibbles and bits."

"How long do we have?" the blonde asked.

"Three days."

"Three days?"

"Your hearing is superb. So is your memory. Now find him. You're wasting time." He opened the top drawer, pulled out a cell, and slid it across the desk blotter. "We'll need to keep in touch."

The blonde picked it up. "Did you give one of these to Digger?"

"I didn't realize at the time that he was such an imbecile. Who else but an imbecile could complicate such a simple job as dialing H-E-L-L-9-9-9 every morning? That walking shitpile either lost it or left it somewhere."

95

The blonde shrugged. "Accidents happen."

This bimbo was really pissing him off. He was going to find an interesting place for her when their time was up.

"I'm so happy to hear such worthless drivel. If you want to improve things, you might work on your conversational skills while you're trying to find that damned shit bug."

Chapter 13

Dinner Date

The Orlando Crab Shack hummed with activity. Fresh-faced waiters sporting buzz cuts scurried up and down the aisles, toting large metal trays. The air-conditioned room smelled strongly of sautéed seafood, crab boil, and garlic toast.

Dressed in a tan blazer, maroon shirt unbuttoned at the collar, and black slacks, Daniel Grove eagerly ate his shrimp. He blotted his mouth frequently with his napkin and ate directly over his plate.

Ashley could see why. That blazer looked expensive.

"How are the oysters?" he asked.

"Just great." She hadn't eaten since before lunch and had sucked down six oysters, half of her baked potato, and three scallops before realizing it. She hoped Daniel didn't think she always ate like a pig. "I haven't had any in such a long time."

He grinned behind his wine glass. "Glad I'm here at such a joyous occasion."

"So is my stomach." She had a small sip of wine and reminded herself to go easy. The last time she overdid it was two years ago, when she'd gone through her "crazy stage." To rebel against Daddy leaving and Momma taking refuge in her whiskey bottle, Ashley quit school, left home, and lived on the streets for more than a year. She settled in with the wrong crowd and soon found herself pregnant. But doing coke daily, drinking at night, and barely

97

eating had taken its toll, terminating the pregnancy. To help her through her miscarriage, she lifted some cheap vodka from the local liquor store. It had made her so sick that she nearly died.

She promised herself then that she would never be that stupid or reckless again.

"Tell me about the O-Town," Daniel said.

"Interested in working there?"

"I'm just curious."

She suspected he had something in mind. She hardly knew him but could tell he was very bright and savvy about most things. Most of the people she saw nowadays seemed to have something wrong with them. She just hoped he wasn't weird. "I'm having too much fun to talk shop, actually."

"How are the working conditions?"

"It's a restaurant."

"I noticed."

"That's right. You were there. You didn't eat much, though..."

He went silent for a few moments. "I wasn't very hungry."

"So you went to a restaurant anyway?"

"It was more of a business meeting than anything else."

"So that's why you went? Not just to see me?"

"I didn't know about you at the time."

"You learned quickly."

"I did, didn't I?"

"And that I was apparently having a bad hair day."

"Only according to one person. And that was definitely not me."

98

"Good thing. Otherwise, I wouldn't be here."

"I'm glad you are. I'd hate to be sitting here all alone, eating this great food and talking to myself."

"That would be so interesting to watch."

"I don't think it would make the Sentinel. Or even the news. Tell me why you like the O-Town."

"Well, for one thing, I love the frantic pace. And I've always been partial to a hot, sweaty kitchen. As well as dealing with hungry, obnoxious people. And, of course, everyone talking and shouting at me at the same time. It's really a delightful environment."

"Sounds like it. How would you like to be working somewhere else?"

"What is this? A fresh, new way of sweeping a girl off her feet?"

"I guess you could say that."

He couldn't be serious. But he wasn't smiling.

"We've only just met. You don't even know what side of the bed I like."

"We'll flip a coin. Whoever loses gets the side I don't want."

"And if I win?"

He shrugged. "Then you get the side I don't want."

"That sounds fair."

Something was definitely on his mind. He didn't seem the type to fall for someone waiting tables. He would most likely go for the daughter of someone rich. But she couldn't tell what he was thinking from his jokes. "What are you getting at?"

"What's keeping you there?"

"The chef has a crush on me."

"I'm serious, now."

"So was he until I told him I wanted a dozen kids."

He blinked. "You're kidding..."

"What do you think?"

"I can only hope you're kidding."

"Of course I'm kidding. Now...what's all this about?"

"I'm feeling you out."

"Really? Most guys like to do that manually."

"Out—not up."

"Sorry. Sometimes I lose my sense of direction when I drink wine."

"Don't drink so much wine."

"Good idea. I don't want to miss anything—especially if you're doing something fun and interesting."

"Seriously, what's keeping you there?"

She ate a little of her salad. "It's hard to find a really good job without a high school diploma."

"You didn't graduate?"

"It's a long story."

He shrugged. "I've got the time."

"I don't think I could tell it very well right now."

"Why not?"

"My mind is on something else."

"Such as?"

"I'm trying to decide why you're so interested."

He blotted his mouth. "How would you like to make three or four times what you're making now?"

"You must be insane. I sometimes make a hundred bucks in tips in one day."

100

"How often?"

She shrugged. Sometimes twice in the same month."

"How about the other days?"

She was lucky if she averaged fifty but didn't want him to know. "Not quite that much."

"I'm serious, now."

"So am I. One day I had this customer who wanted to take me—"

"I'm serious about you leaving that place."

"What would I have to do? Be a drug mule?"

"I'm starting up a business and need someone to handle the phones."

"A receptionist?"

"Sort of."

This sounded too good. "Receptionists don't make that much. Do they?"

"Mine would."

The way he suddenly turned so serious startled her. She sensed a red flag making its appearance. "Is this, well, legal?"

He lowered his voice. "I'm starting up an escort service."

She stiffened. "Isn't that a fancy term for prostitution?"

"Orlando's a major tourist town. Rich people from all over the world come here to enjoy themselves."

"Isn't that what Disney, EPCOT, and all those other fun places are for?"

"A rich man comes to town. He stays at one of our best hotels and is driven around by a top-notch limo service. He's only here for a day or so to conduct his business and expects—"

"Someone to dump a hooker in his lap while he's trying out the rides?"

***

Daniel had hoped this would go better.

Ashley was a bright babe. She deserved much better than waiting tables. Working as a waitress is difficult, back-breaking work. Ashley had to put up with obnoxious customers every day of her life. Some were probably almost as bad as Mr. Waite.

Daniel could already feel a chemistry developing between them. He had hoped he could make his pitch without causing her to dislike or distrust him. The way it played out, there would be very little personal risk. Mr. Waite had assured him of this.

"This service is available everywhere," he told Ashley. "Why shouldn't someone cash in on it?"

"It's not legal."

"The average visiting businessman is here for only a couple of days."

"So?"

"He'll spend even more money if he enjoys our accommodations. That would benefit all of us and—"

"I'd be afraid, Daniel."

"There's no way you'd be in any danger." Waite had told him that very same thing, just hours ago. Daniel had been just as skeptical. But that was before the car fire. Before Daniel discovered Waite's true identity.

"How can you guarantee that?" Ashley asked.

Daniel could not tell her about Waite or the Diocese. But he had to be honest. He owed her that. Being vague might not be such a bad idea. "Neither of us will get our hands dirty."

"Is your nasty friend involved?"

"Indirectly." At least that was the truth.

"I don't trust him."

"He's rich and powerful. He and his associates have helped my father in countless business ventures."

Her eyes grew. "Your father's involved in illegal stuff, too?"

He lowered his voice to a whisper. He hoped he wasn't about to make a huge mistake. "My father's company owns several large parcels of land bordering the theme parks. He's one of the five richest men in this state."

Her jaw dropped. "Wow..."

He had seen that same look before. It was the main reason why he seldom told anyone about his family. But Ashley was different. He couldn't see her turning into a starry-eyed, greedy slut just to get in with his family.

He just hoped he hadn't scared or intimidated her.

"Your friend...he's actually helped your father?"

"His associates have."

"And everything was legal?"

"Everything."

"But not in this case."

"Look at the casino industry and what it's done for many struggling states. Prostitutes work in just about all of them. The only reason the local cops don't crack down is because of the billions in revenue pouring in."

She swallowed another oyster. "That's too complicated for my tiny little mind to wrap around."

"Take my word for it. When local politicians are involved, the cops have an unwritten hands-off order."

"Then there's nothing for me to be afraid of?"

"You sit at a desk and answer the phone. Just write down the appointments and make the appropriate calls. Plain and simple."

She drank more wine. He could tell she was thinking it over. He was reasonably confident she would take the offer.

"What do you say?" he asked.

"I don't think so, Daniel. Thanks, but no thanks."

Chapter 14

The Search Begins

The supper crowds had thinned but traffic still clogged the streets. Out-of-state tags could be seen on nearly every vehicle inching down Orange Avenue.

Tiffany knew the meeting with Breath Mint had been stressful for Chip. The elevator ride back down was spent in silence. Except for an occasional twitch of his ears, he showed no signs of life. But at least he perked up once they had left the building. He began sniffing the air immediately.

At the corner, a crowd waited for the light to change. A tall, skinny black teen turned and glanced at them beneath his red do-rag. He wore baggy black pants pulled halfway down to his knees. His red and gold plaid undershorts showed clearly.

"I can see his drawers," Chip whispered.

"It's the style," she whispered back.

"Is it the style to show Mister Smiley from the front?"

"Mister Smiley?"

"Hey, I'm trying to be polite here."

"Polite? You?"

"Please answer the question."

"In my shock and confusion, I forgot what it was."

"Read   the   old   lipperoos. Is…it…the…style…to…see… Mister—"

"You can see that from here?"

"I'm just asking if it's the style."

"Showing Mister Smiley is a definite no-no."

"It's all right to show your butt crack, but a no-no for Mister Smiley. Is that the idea?"

"You don't want to see Mister Smiley, do you?"

"I'd rather have a lobotomy with a dull ice pick."

The teen glanced at them again.

"Your shorts are showing," Chip said.

Tiffany quickly turned away and waited anxiously for the light to change.

"Say what, man?" the teen said, squinting.

"Your undershorts. I can see them."

The teen frowned.

"You don't get it, do you?" Chip asked.

"Whazzat you say, man?"

"I don't want to see your undershorts. My bodacious buddy doesn't want to see your undershorts. And unless I'm totally off base, no one in this crowd wants to see your undershorts."

"You be dissing me, man?"

Chip blinked. "Huh?"

The teen showed a mouthful of glittering gold teeth. "Don't you be dissing me, man. Don't you be conversating no bad dialogue 'bout me or my threads, man—know what I be sayin'?" He gave Tiffany a quick once-over. "Fine bitch, man—know what I be sayin'? What she be doin', hangin' out wi'-choo? Yo' baby momma?"

Chip turned to Tiffany. "What language is that?"

"Jive."

106

"You be Class-A weird, man. You too, Momma, you be hangin' with this skinny white dude."

"He's the second son of a third cousin of one of my illegitimate children," she said.

"I didn't know we were related," Chip said.

"Only by marriage."

"I thought you said I was illegitimate."

"Not you. Your cousin."

He nodded, his ears wiggling.

Watching them warily, the teen backed up quickly, bumping into two middle-aged women shoppers. He veered around the crowd and rushed across the street moments before the light changed. As he ran, he kept his hands pressed to his groin so his pants wouldn't slide down.

The crowd began crossing.

"You know," Chip said as they followed, "judging by that pleasant little exchange, I really don't think mortals need help from any super to nudge them down the tubes."

"You don't think Boiled Wafer can make things worse?"

"I sure am glad you didn't call him that back there. He was in a really foul mood."

"He's a demon. When are they in a good mood?"

"That's beside the point. He's peeved over Digger's vanishing act. He's probably hoping the other supers haven't heard about it yet."

She didn't see what all the fuss was about. Breath Mint was loud and obnoxious. She'd seen dozens of jerks just like him in Hollywood. She

107

wouldn't be at all surprised if some of the supers had been Hollywood big shots as mortals. "He didn't seem very scary to me."

"Buttercup, do you realize what that boy is capable of?"

"He just didn't impress me at all."

"He would have if he had gotten pissed. I thought he was going to do something disgusting with me."

"He's not going to try anything as long as we're working for him."

"The point is, sweet pea, you don't want to mess with him."

"I'll try to remember that. Meanwhile, tell me what we need to be doing."

"Looking for Digger."

"I thought his name was Cletis."

"His nickname is Digger. Weren't you paying attention?"

"It was impossible not to. Broad Waist is awfully loud. He's like a bad TV actor who overacts so everyone notices him."

Chip looked around quickly. "Precious, you need to keep it down. He could be right behind us, you know."

She turned and scanned the crowd rushing by. Except for the males in the group, no one seemed to care about them. "I don't see him."

"He's a shape-shifter. Like Gutril, only much worse."

"He doesn't need to shape-shift." She patted her back pocket. "Not as long as we have his cell phone."

He stiffened, his gaping eyes fixed to her pocket. "I forgot about that."

She sniffed. "What's that funky smell?"

He grinned sheepishly. "I tend to lose my cool when I'm scared."

"I guess I should be used to that by now."

"I didn't lose my cool much in Raven. No need to."

They resumed walking.

"So what's this Digger guy look like?"

"Messy. Slow. Stupid."

"I can't wait to meet him. How do you know him?"

"I saw him wandering around the Castle a few times."

"What was he doing?"

Chip shrugged. "Sniffing around."

"For what?"

He shrugged.

She suspected he was being evasive. "You're keeping something from me, aren't you?"

"Just waiting for you to ask the right question."

"All right... What else do you know that'll help us find him?"

"He's a trickster, like me."

"What else?"

"His spirit form might help us a smidge."

"What is it? And why is he called Digger?"

"He's a dung beetle."

She stopped walking. "I guess that's why Breath Mint called him a shit bug, isn't it?"

"Yes, dearest. Our Man of the Hour is what you might call a salivating shitster."

109

Chapter 15

Home Awful Home

A light-colored Olds sat in the drive behind Momma's Toyota.

Ashley sank in her seat as Daniel pulled the Corvette over to the curb.

Terrific. Momma had brought home someone. It was bound to be an interesting evening.

Daniel killed the lights and switched off the ignition. He turned in his seat. He smiled but didn't say anything. He was probably waiting for her to do something important, such as opening her door or thanking him for a pleasant evening. Or maybe both. Maybe he wanted her to kiss him. Or at least shake his hand. Maybe just a smile would do.

She was content just sitting here. Maybe he'd let her take a short nap. They could even just sit here for a while and talk. That would be pleasant, wouldn't it?

Yes. It would be. Anything would be better than walking in on Momma and her date.

"What's wrong?"

She smiled, but her facial muscles, heavy and awkward, made it difficult. She never could hold things in. "What makes you think something's wrong?"

"You're not getting out."

"This seat's comfortable. That wine made me…sleepy."

"I don't think that's quite it."

"What makes you say that?"

"Your smile. It was, well, kinda sorry."

"Not enough sparkle?"

"Actually, it looked more like a frown."

"They say a smile is nothing but a frown turned upside down."

"Yours looked more like a frown turned right side up."

"Sure it's not just how I look in the dark?"

"Reasonably."

She let her head rest against the seat. Daniel's dash clock said it was nearly eleven. Momma probably faked another headache. A customer may have shown interest. Judging by the Olds, whoever she brought home had money. But nothing would come of it. Momma just couldn't hold herself together long enough to keep a man interested.

"Something going on that you don't want to deal with?" he asked.

"Momma brought home one of her customers from the bar."

"Bummer."

"To say the least."

"Want me to go in with you? Or would you like to stay out here for a little while and wait for them to pass out? We could talk—maybe even fool around. But only if you really and truly want to."

It brought another smile to her lips. This one was actually easy and felt more like a smile. "It's all right. But I appreciate the offer."

"Offer? I must be losing my touch. And my sex appeal."

She patted his arm. "Don't worry, you're just fine. Sweet, too."

"But not sexy enough to get you to forget about your mom and concentrate on jumping my bones instead?"

"It's just that, well, she does weird things to my head."

"No shit?"

"Does it show that much?"

"Since I parked the car, your bubbly turned to tragic in a single nanosecond."

"I told you, she screws me up."

"Fight it. Think funny, sexy, bizarre thoughts."

"Bizarre?"

He shrugged. "Best I can do when my mind ain't working."

"What's wrong with your mind?"

"It's all messed up. My date climbed in there and rearranged things."

"It wasn't intentional."

"Of course not."

"Trust me. If my mother wasn't messing with my head, I wouldn't be messing with yours."

"Amazing how orderly things can be when you approach them calmly and with a clear head."

"I wish my head was clear."

"Anything I can do to help?"

"Can you do any quick carpentry work?"

"I can't even manage any slow carpentry work. Why?"

"If I had a back door to my bedroom, I could sneak in without having to go through the living room. I'd even climb in through my window if I could do it without ripping my clothes."

"That would require steps."

"Can you do steps?"

"Not in the next five minutes."

She sighed. This was ridiculous. She should not be acting this way. She just had a great time and was letting Momma ruin the rest of the evening. "I'm being silly."

"You're female."

"Thanks a lump."

"Just trying to squeeze out one last smile."

She couldn't help it; she let loose with another one. And leaned over to kiss him on the cheek.

He grinned. "Wow. Didn't think that would even work. Not only a smile, but a kiss, too?"

"I had a great time, Daniel."

"Me, too. If you want me to come in—"

"No." She pushed open her door. No reason she should be afraid to enter her own house. And certainly no reason to drag Daniel into this. "I'll be fine."

"You promised to think about my proposition."

She stared dumbly at him. Her mind had gone blank.

"The receptionist thing."

At the restaurant she promised to reconsider it. "I will. And thanks again for a lovely evening."

One of Momma's old Genesis labels flowed softly from the CD player. Momma sprawled on the couch. Her blouse was unbuttoned. A well-dressed fat man about fifty sat beside her. He had

113

glossy eyes and a lopsided grin. When Ashley came in, his eyes bulged as he gawked at her.

Momma pushed herself back up and smoothed out her hair. "You're home early," she said, buttoning up.

"Sorry, Momma." Ashley hated apologizing for coming home but the situation had made her feel guilty. "Did the bar close early?"

"I left." Momma's eyes blazed. "Got this killer headache."

Bringing someone home for a few drinks and a little wrestling on the couch would work wonders for anyone's headache. Momma was apparently too drunk to realize how lame that sounded. "Well, I'm off to bed, so I'll—"

"Your baby daughter?" the man chimed in a high-pitched voice. "Cute."

"Adorable," Momma said with obvious contempt.

"Looks just like her mother," he said with a grin.

Momma ignored his comment. She blocked Ashley's path. The reek of whiskey swelling from her raked against Ashley's skin. "Stay and meet my friend."

"I'm sorry, I just thought you might like some—"

"Say hello to Mr. Collins."

"Hello."

He stood to his full height—which was about the same as Ashley's—and bowed, showing her a huge bald spot. "Call me Teddy."

114

"Well, I guess I'll be going to bed. Nice meeting you."

"Stay for a drink," he said.

Ashley hurried down the hall to her room.

Momma bullied her way in behind her, slamming the door and leaning against it. "Why'd you have to come home now?" Her venomous whisper sprayed hot whiskey scum onto Ashley's face.

"I live here, Momma…"

"You interrupted everything."

"I didn't know you'd be coming home early. Or that you'd have one of your headaches. Or that you'd be bringing home company."

"You saw the Olds in the drive, didn'tcha?"

"Of course."

"You couldn't just take your friend somewheres else for an hour or two? You coulda taken him to meet your old girlfriends."

Ashley forced herself to ignore the bitter inference. It had been over two years since she had gone to live with some friends who had also quit school and taken to the streets. Two years and Momma still brought it up whenever she thought she needed extra venom.

Momma's drunk, she reminded herself. She can't help how she's acting.

"I'm going to bed now. Just make believe I'm not even here."

"Yeah, right." She yanked open the door. "Now the fat fart's gonna be thinking of you." Momma slammed the door behind her.

Ashley sank on the edge of the bed and forced herself not to cry.

116

Chapter 16

Checking Out the Local Color

Traffic clogged the streets. Loud, happy folks cluttered the sidewalks. A knot of leather-clad teen girls covered with tattoos and silver studs shared a joint. At the end of the block, a huge two-story brick building thundered behind a neon sign that said, Orange Avenue Strut Hut.

At the end of the single line filing into the building, a tall, well-dressed woman around forty snarled into her cell phone. "I don't care, Steven," she barked. The glittering silver dreamcatchers hanging from her earlobes danced wildly. "I don't want you going over there!" She threw up a bare arm. Tiffany caught a whiff of Chanel. "That's another thing I don't care about. You can tell me it was innocent till you're blue in the face—"

"Sounds like ol' Steverino won't be getting any when he goes home tonight," Chip said to Tiffany.

"Shush." Tiffany swatted him on the arm.

The woman glared at Chip, then lowered her voice. "I don't care, Steven. That woman bothers me!"

"Maybe if ol' Steverino was getting enough at home," Chip told Tiffany, "he wouldn't have to sneak back to his ex."

The woman's large dark eyes bore into Chip. "This is a private conversation—if you don't mind!"

Chip scanned the line of people just ahead. "You're kidding."

"Do I look like I'm kidding?" she snapped.

"Actually, you look kind of mental."

"Listen, you…"

"And little constipated. Your face is splotchy and your makeup's all smeary and messed up. Maybe if you had more roughage in your diet…"

"Just shut up and mind your own business!"

"What should I do first?"

"Both!"

Chip shrugged. "I'd like to, but you and Steverino—"

"His name is Steven, dirtbag."

"Steven Dirtbag?" Chip gave a low whistle. "I'll bet he went through hell growing up."

The woman's cheeks blistered. "Smartass. Like I said, this is private!"

Chip gave the crowd another quick scan. "How can anyone have a private conversation in this crowd?"

"Steven, I gotta go. There's this really irritating weirdo bothering me."

Chip turned to Tiffany. "She's the one trying to have a private conversation in a crowd of drunks and I'm the weirdo?"

"You want a belt in the mouth?" the woman growled, moving closer.

"Thanks. I usually wear mine around my waist. It keeps my pants from falling down."

"You're an asshole," the woman snarled. "And not amusing at all. I oughta just put you out of my misery—"

"Careful," he said. "You're liable to have an accident."

118

"You stupid little…" The woman looked down at the dark stain gathering at her crotch. "Oh, shit. Shit, shit, shit!" She dashed down the street, babbling loudly.

Tiffany stared after her. The woman was loud and rude—even nasty—but didn't deserve to be humiliated. This reminded her of the time Chip messed with that woman's eyebrow in the Raven Police Station.

"I sincerely hope you didn't do what I think you did," she said.

"I have no control over someone else's bladder, precious. I'm destined for bigger and better things. Tricks and illusions for all—"

"What did you just do?"

"I tricked her into thinking warm down under. When she looked down, I made her think dark. When she finds a rest room and realizes her panties are dry, she'll really have a bird. Poor Steverino."

"That was mean, you know."

"Tell me. Why do crazy women like her always manage to trap a man?"

She shrugged. "She's pretty."

"That's it?"

"That's all men seem to care about."

"Obviously."

"How old were you when you died?"

"When I actually died? Or when I went down to the dark place for stealing donation money from the Catholic Church?"

"That's what you did?"

"Sure. Let's go with that."

"What about the Pope's underwear thing?"

119

"The Pope never showed me his underwear. Or his thing."

"You mean that was a fib?"

"Actually, it was an out-and-out lie."

"You should be ashamed."

"I am. And you should've known better."

"One of these days I'll learn." He was so impossible. "C'mon. Let's go inside. You're having entirely too much fun out here. Besides, we might find Digger in there."

"Tifferoo, what are the chances of us walking into the first bar we come across and bumping into a dung beetle from Hell?"

Tiffany didn't reply. She was too busy switching her footwear to something stylish, yet understated and comfortable.

Inside, deafening music blasted through ceiling speakers, vibrating the polished tile floor. Flashing neon poured through revolving spots fastened to the rafters. A mountain of tattooed, spiked flesh smothered the dance floor. Glossy-eyed folks in their twenties and thirties jerked their sweaty limbs in time with the erratic beat.

Chip found a small round table and two chairs in a remote corner.

A waitress in a black tank top, tight white shorts, and silver platforms appeared. Her skinny neck and the upper part of her bony chest glinted under a thin sheen of sweat. Her headset had mashed down her hair, pasting dirty blond bangs to her glistening forehead. Her gingery perfume, mixed with sweat, drifted toward Tiffany.

"What's your order?"

120

"Where do you have that plugged in?" Chip asked, studying her.

The waitress scowled. "He's not serious, is he?" she asked Tiffany.

"I'm afraid so. Just ignore him like I do and he'll stop."

The waitress sighed. "All right. Let's try this again. What's your order?"

Tiffany ordered a strawberry daiquiri, Chip a pitcher of ice water.

The waitress's forehead wrinkled. "Ice water?"

He gently patted his thick red mop. "Keeps the ol' petals shiny and perky."

The waitress called in the order, then vanished.

Chip watched her. "Is that headset thingy like a cell phone?"

"See there? You figured it out all by yourself."

"Munchkin, sometimes you can be really cruel."

"Sometimes you deserve it."

"That's beside the point."

"All right," Tiffany said. "Now that we've got the headset mystery solved, tell me more about this Digger guy."

"You really want to know?"

"I think I have to if we intend to look for him."

"Well, for one thing, I don't think he'd like this place. He's more the outdoorsy type."

"Athletic?"

"I wouldn't call him that..."

"What would you call him?"

"Just your average slob who likes messing around with dung."

That was an image she didn't need floating around up there. "So you're telling he's probably always dirty?"

"I'm sure he'll try to stay reasonably clean so he doesn't stand out. But that's difficult when you're always playing around in the patties. He's not what you could call a neat freak."

The waitress brought their drinks and disappeared in the crowd.

A trio of young men approached their table. The man in front—neat, dark-haired, slender, and handsome—stopped about two feet to Tiffany's right. His bronze skin was smooth and evenly tanned, his features sharp and strongly Latino. His shiny black hair was brushed straight back—not one hair out of place. His dark eyes, prominent beneath the cultured black brows, wandered up and down Tiffany like the probing antennae of an inquisitive insect. It took her back to Hollywood, where evaluations by lascivious celebs and casting directors proved a daily occurrence.

"Hey, Baby, want to dance?"

"No, thank you."

"I'm Roberto Jackson." His smile showed dazzling white teeth.

"Is that supposed to mean something?" she asked.

"It means a lot to the ladies of Orlando."

"How about that?" Chip said, shaking his head. "Roberto Jackson. In the flesh. As we live and breathe. So to speak."

122

The man's grin relaxed abruptly. "What's a lady as sweet and as fine as you are doing with this jerk?"

"He's not a jerk all the time," she said.

"Gee, buttercup, I didn't think you'd start with the insults so soon."

"It just slipped out."

"When ain't he a jerk?" Roberto Jackson asked.

"Yeah," Chip said. "When ain't I?"

"When you rescued me from the Valley of Decay before those nasties could grab me and take me into the woods."

"As I already told you, I was ordered to do that. It was either that or stay in that damned rock garden another thousand years."

"And as I told you, I don't care why you did it. I'm just glad you did it. I'm really happy to be alive again."

Roberto Jackson watched them both in confusion. "Well, he's sure a jerk right now."

"That's only because I don't have to rescue her," Chip said. "Or do I, lamb chop?"

"I'm okay. But thanks anyway." To Roberto Jackson, she said, "If you knew him, you'd think he's cool. A little weird, maybe."

"I don't want to, baby. I only want to get to know you."

"You wouldn't want to."

"Let Roberto be the judge of that. You're definitely high-class."

"How would you know?"

"Your clothes, they fit your fine form perfectly. And those shoes..." He nodded in approval. "They look real expensive."

"Like them?" She crossed her legs and did an impromptu pose. "Just something I slipped on before we came in. They're Cole Haan Amelia Air Sling Pumps. I just love 'em to death."

Roberto Jackson grinned devilishly. "I'll bet I can get them off before you even know what I'm doing."

She turned to Chip. "Any suggestions?"

He shrugged. "Show him your wart. The big one I told you about in Ohio."

"I might not need it here."

"Your call, then."

"Listen, Roberto. Why don't you try and pick up someone else? I guarantee you'll have much better luck."

"I'm Roberto Jackson. I'm never turned down."

"Never?"

"No, ma'am."

The man's buddies shook their heads solemnly.

"Join me on the dance floor," Roberto Jackson said. "I'll show you some really smooth moves. Then I'll take you outside and show you my ride. I got this special ride for special ladies. It's a convertible."

She tried a gamble. "You wouldn't know someone named Digger, would you?"

"Describe him."

124

"To the average mortal, he doesn't look a day over thirty," Chip said. "He's messy—probably because he likes his shit."

"Shit? You mean...?" Roberto Jackson imitated snorting something up his nose.

"Coke would be an improvement," Tiffany said.

"I don't remember no one like that," Roberto Jackson said. "But I got friends."

"That's nice," Chip said. "I'm getting a super warm feeling about that." He belched. "Oops. Sorry. I guess my warm feeling's gone."

"You are pissing off Roberto," Roberto Jackson said.

"Wouldn't want that to happen," Chip said. "Not while we're busy being such good friends."

Roberto Jackson glared. "How would you like it if my amigos took you outside for a little tune-up?"

Chip shook his head. "If I'm still out of tune after a couple of hundred years, a little quiet time with your amigos just ain't gonna swing it."

Roberto Jackson sighed, then turned back to Tiffany. "Like I said, I've got friends. I might be able to find this Digger guy for you."

"Could you? That would be so nice."

"It would come with a price, though..."

"What would that be?"

He grinned, flashing his teeth again. "You would have to come home with Roberto."

"Really? Sounds expensive."

"It would be worth it. All the ladies of Orlando know what a bargain Roberto is."

"Want me to split?" Chip said. "Since you're in good hands with the one and only Roberto Jackson..."

"You go on outside," she said. "I'll be out in just a minute."

Roberto Jackson gawked at her. He apparently wasn't accustomed to rejection. "You wouldn't be trying to pull something on Roberto, would you?"

"Why would I do that?"

"You might be afraid of leaving your friend alone."

"You want him to come with us? Maybe as a chaperone?"

Roberto turned to his friends and said something in Spanish. The threesome laughed.

"That wasn't very nice," Tiffany said. "Calling my friend a skinny Anglo faggot whose mother should have stayed away from her pet monkey when she wanted a child?"

"I'm offended and outraged," Chip said. "My mother didn't even like monkeys. Not even when she died. But she did have this pet chinchilla she was quite fond of."

Roberto stared at Tiffany. "You...speak Spanish?"

"This is America, isn't it?"

Roberto's dark eyes glistened. "Baby, you're really turning on Roberto."

Tiffany stood up. "Really?"

His grin grew. "I think you're one fine, hot momma."

"You're fine, too." She looked him over, then sighed. "Except for your hair."

126

His hands automatically shot up in unison, gently patting the sides. "What's wrong with Roberto's hair?"

"Roberto's hair is messy."

His jaw dropped. "Messy? What the fuck you mean, messy?"

A heavy black comma slipped down over his forehead, the tip of it poking his eye. Gasping, he magically produced a plastic comb and brushed it carefully back. When he lowered his arms, the comma broke free and fell again. Panicking, Roberto Jackson produced a small pocket mirror from his tight slacks and worked furiously.

The thick comma refused to stay put.

Chattering away in heated Spanish, Roberto Jackson frantically ran for the rest rooms, his buddies close behind him.

Tiffany and Chip went back outside.

"That was admirable, baby cakes. But I'd still like to see you do the wart thing."

DAY THREE - The Hunt for The Dung Beetle

Chapter 17

Goodies for Breakfast

This modern world sure was jam-packed with really neat stuff.

Digger couldn't understand how people could be so wasteful, especially since they seemed to have so much. In the old days, no one threw away much of anything. You used everything and recycled what you didn't need anymore. The only ones who threw away the best stuff were people like Caligula. But that was only because Caligula was one crazy, bad dude who had everything.

Nowadays, people didn't seem to care much about anything. They tossed stuff out of their moving vehicles all the time: candy, burgers, cigarette butts, beer cans, bottles. Digger had found some weird things in these big green metal containers everyone called dumpsters. Clothes, books, fancy plastic equipment called computers and keyboards, even dead dogs and cats.

Caligula was as cruel as a person could possibly be, but nowadays, many people acted just as nasty. They killed one another for no good reason, set fire to things, even tortured one another. Digger had even seen some mortals almost as bad, even, as Braithwaite.

The mere utterance of the name made him shiver.

But at least Digger had Cal as a friend. Cal knew this place and knew how to get them away fast. And these cars they kept taking could even keep Digger far enough away of the super demon. Hopefully, Digger might even be able convince Cal to leave Florida and get even farther away.

But right now, there were some cool things to do in this place everyone called Orlando. And since so many people were always coming in from other places, Digger could stay hidden much better.

Something lying on the pavement a couple of feet from the dumpster glinted in the morning sun.

Digger went over to have a closer look.

Wow. His broad face stretched into a big grin.

Looked like a big wad of dried-up fruit stuck to some brown leaves.

A dog might have found it in the dumpster, chewed on it, then discarded it.

Didn't matter. Finders, keepers.

Digger loved dried-up fruit and leaves. He was rarely able to find such a delicacy down in Hell. He usually had to settle for whatever Sibrius and the other two-headed pit bulls left in their wake.

Digger's mouth watered as he went over to the dumpster to look for something to carry his new treasure in.

Breakfast would be a feast this morning.

Cal might even appreciate having some. After spending the night with that skinny young harlot they'd found at that dark, smoky tavern the night before, Cal should be starving.

***

His head throbbing, Cal forced himself up on an elbow and tried to figure out where the hell he was.

Looked like a motel room.

His clothes lay in a wrinkled heap on the floor. A white bucket sat on top of the TV. A half-empty jug of Wild Turkey and three cans of Coke cluttered the dresser.

A chick lay beside him, snoring softly, her face buried in the pillow. Her medium-length bleach-blond hair covered her neck. The sheet was pulled down, showing her back, flat ass, and a portion of a skinny thigh. A heart tatt highlighted her right shoulder. A purple SHAZAM stretched across her lower back. A tiny golden star marked the center of each dimpled butt cheek.

Cal vaguely remembered driving here and buying the room from some fat dork with thick glasses. Digger mentioned checking out the places off the main drag. He then split, probably to hit on more tourists.

Wasn't natural, a dude not wanting to get laid.

Fighting the fireworks going off in his head, Cal tried remembering what happened before they got here. Some dive just off the Trail called Shangri-La. The drinks were strong but pricey, the hookers taking up nearly all the barstools. Place stunk of cigarettes and B.O. Cal was already a little smashed from three shots of the Wild Stuff by the time the hooker joined them. Hell, he could hardly see her face in the dark room. Didn't matter. The

130

rest of her seemed all right. Bitch smelled good, too.

Cal handed her some bills. Two hundred, he remembered. She stuffed them down her tiny gold clutch. Then she suggested getting a room.

That was about it until he passed out.

The door clicked open. A widening beam of blinding light invaded the room.

Groaning, Cal covered his eyes and waited for the darkness to return.

Digger came in carrying a small brown paper bag. Something seriously foul-smelling followed him in, rushing toward the bed when the door slammed shut. He plopped down in the chair near the door and grinned stupidly. You'd think he'd just hit the Lottery.

"Step in dogshit?" Cal wrinkled his nose.

Digger opened the bag, pulled out what looked like a clump of dead leaves with brown snot clinging to it, and shoved some into his mouth. "Have some?" He held it out.

"You're shitting me, right?"

"It's pretty tasty. Fresh, too."

"Rather eat my tennis shoe."

"Aren't you hungry?"

"Not for monkey food."

The hooker yawned and sat up. The sheet slid down, exposing her small chest. A tatt spelling out PEARL in red letters covered the top of her right tit. Her face wasn't bad but nothing to write home about. A long, slender white scar ran down the side of her neck. She also sported moles and a little facial hair. Her eyes were a nice shade of blue, although a tad small.

"Somebody mention food?" she said in a tiny voice.

Cal picked up his clothes and shrugged them on. "I'm about to grab some breakfast."

"What about me? I eat, too."

"This is end of the line for you, baby."

She found her short leather skirt and tank top and wriggled into them. Her hair was a mess, but she didn't seem to care. She slipped on her black spikes, picked up her clutch, opened it, pulled out some bills, and counted them.

"Think we stole some?"

A shrug. "Happens all the time."

"Dig and I don't steal from hookers."

"Just checking, baby."

Dig munched loudly on more leaves. He didn't even seem to notice the hooker at all. He was one weird dude.

"You guys are okay." The hooker snapped her clutch shut. "How 'bout I give you a quickie before I leave?"

"How much?"

"Forty."

"Kinda high for a quickie."

"I'm good. Said so yourself. Said so four times."

"Yeah, but a quickie's what? Five minutes, maybe?"

"That's why it's called a quickie, baby."

"That's almost five hundred bucks an hour."

"You can't figure it that way."

132

"That's what it comes out to, right?"

"A quickie's a quickie. Do it for an hour, it's not a quickie no more."

"You didn't do nothing for my friend."

"He left before I could get my clothes off." She frowned at Digger. "Woulda given him a good time, too." She wrinkled her nose. "Maybe if he had a bath or somethin'..."

"Bye," Cal said. "See you in my wet dreams."

She closed the door softly behind her.

"We need to check out these theme parks everyone's talking about," Digger said, still munching.

Cal couldn't understand Dig sometimes. Instead of whipping off a piece, he wanted to see a fucking theme park. Cal remembered an old Twilight Zone episode he'd seen, weird things happening to some guy right after he hit his head. Maybe Dig hit his head. It might explain why he wasn't interested in women.

"Why the theme parks?"

"They've got animals."

"So?"

"I like animals."

"After breakfast."

"Sounds good. Promise?"

"I just said so, didn't I?"

"Sure you don't want some?" Digger held out the bag. "There's plenty."

"I'm more in the mood for a sausage biscuit."

"Then a theme park?"

"Yeah, dammit. Then we'll go to your fucking theme park."

Cal had to get this boy on regular food. It might put his head on straight.

Eating dead leaves and gooey brown shit didn't seem normal.

134

Chapter 18

A Bright New Career

The soft light-blue walls of Daniel's new office encouraged a calm state of mind. The tinted windows overlooking downtown Orlando brought in only as much softened sunlight as the vertical blinds would allow. The awfully expensive, adjustable tan leather chair fit his frame perfectly. The table below the window, stocked with his favorite brands of coffee and an assortment of delicious doughnuts and éclairs, sweetened the atmosphere. A cushioned leather couch encompassed the opposite wall.

Just twenty feet down the hall, the spotless rest rooms smelled faintly of sandalwood. Thick carpeting covered the entire floor.

The perfect office.

Daniel hated it.

For the last three years, he had been content running his small company out of his Winter Park apartment. He could bum around in sweatshirt and baggies, take a sandwich break whenever he wanted, pop open a beer, even slip into his trunks for a quick dip in the complex pool. He could work eight hours. Or ten. Or just three, if he wished. Frequently he took a day off just for the hell of it. He was his own boss. And he didn't have to fight the horrendous I-4 rush hour traffic twice a day.

Mr. Waite wanted him here, on the premises. The new escort service needed to be run efficiently. Moving his consultation business proved no

135

problem; Daniel merely bundled up his laptop and fax/printer, brought everything to the new Magnolia Avenue address and set up in this office three floors down from Mr. Waite. Here, Daniel could supervise what was going on across the hall, where the answering service was being organized. He could also learn the nuts-and-bolts procedure of building a business from scratch. Under the guise of Waite Information Systems, the Help Desk could run perfectly.

However, Ashley remained foremost on his mind. He'd originally wanted her to work here, but later decided it wouldn't be in her best interests. The idea scared her, for one thing. She would not know what she was getting into. And since Waite was only three floors away, Ashley would be constantly on edge. And if she were on edge, it would be much more difficult to start a relationship with her.

She knew Waite only as a loud, arrogant man. She had no idea he was a super demon. Daniel never wanted her to find out.

Besides, countless other girls much more qualified than Ashley could better fill the position.

After a quick coffee break, Daniel would make some calls to a local employment center to see who was available for an immediate interview.

Daniel poured a cup of vanilla blend from the Mr. Coffee and stood in front of his huge, tinted window.

The Orlando skyline was clear, the traffic on I-4 just as chaotic as usual. Hard to believe the situation in this town could worsen. But it would, and very quickly. Mr. Waite would see to it. He thoroughly enjoyed making things worse.

Yet another important reason for not bringing Ashley into the picture.

His cell buzzed. Mr. Waite's name showed prominently on the display.

His pulse hastening, Daniel switched it on.

"When can we expect our new receptionist to start?" Waite asked in his usual abrupt manner.

Daniel's pulse thumped even worse. Dealing with Mr. Waite was always stressful. Best underplay it, make him think things were under control. "I've got a few calls to make before I select someone—"

"Didn't you tell me you wanted that skinny brunette from the Cafe?"

"Actually, I've been thinking it over and—"

"And didn't I tell you she'd make a lousy receptionist?"

Daniel sighed in relief. "You're absolutely right, sir."

"A receptionist has to be on the ball, and a waitress who doesn't jump for her new customers isn't on the ball."

This sounded like Waite was easing Ashley out of the picture. A good move overall.

Yet Daniel wanted to defend her. Ashley was on the ball. She was also funny and very perceptive. The Café was busy when they had gone there. It was lunchtime. Every waitress working there was up to her neck in hungry, demanding customers.

137

"She's smart enough to handle a job like this, sir," he said.

"Then what's the holdup? Did you tell her how much money's involved?"

"She's frightened."

"About what?"

"Getting caught."

"Kid, you're in the big leagues now. Know what that means?"

To Daniel, it meant dealing with someone who could inflict intense agony upon anyone with a mere glance. "I sure do," he said softly.

"When you want something, you go after it. Understand?"

Daniel didn't reply. He suddenly realized he had messed up.

"Kid? Did you hear me?"

"Yes, sir."

"Have her here this afternoon. Understand?"

That didn't give him much time. If he wanted to save Ashley from serious stress, he'd have to contact the first agency he could find and take anyone who was available. "I'll find someone with better qualifications and—"

"Get the brunette. This has to be in place quickly. Once the calls start coming in, you can hire two more females. You can even fire her once you find two others who are better qualified. Just get her here. We need to start this up."

Daniel pulse pounded. "But sir... You just said--"

"Several important colleagues are coming over from Europe and I want them to be thoroughly

138

entertained this weekend. I expect them to be at the airport within the next two hours. She'd better be handling those phones long before then."

Waite hung up.

Chapter 19

Breakfast Chatter

While Dig watched the passing traffic out in front, Cal went into Ye Olde Doughnut Shoppe on International Drive and bought one glazed, one sugar, and a large black coffee.

Cal had wanted a bigger breakfast. Maybe a sausage biscuit, or some bacon and eggs. A full stomach might get rid of the stupid fireworks still going on in his head.

But they just didn't have the time. The Stang stuck out like a turd on white carpeting. Even the world's dumbest cop would spot it.

They needed to make tracks.

Cal went outside and pulled a sugar doughnut from the bag.

"What's that?" Dig asked.

Was this boy for real? "A doughnut. What's it look like?"

"A doe-nut?" Dig stared stupidly at it.

"Don't tell me you don't know what a doughnut is..."

"I don't know what a doe-nut is."

Cal waited for Dig to break out in laughter, but he didn't. But that didn't mean anything. Dig's wit was pretty damn dry.

Hell, even a fucking Bedouin knew what a doughnut was.

"Dude, where have you been?" Cal decided to play along. "Doughnuts have been around for centuries."

140

"I haven't."

"Haven't what?"

"Been around for centuries."

Cal shook his head. This wasn't the time for stupid jokes. "Here." He handed it over.

Dig held it carefully between his thumb and index finger. You would have thought he was holding something disgusting. "What's the hole for?"

Now he knew this boy was kidding. "Um, you stick your thumb through it so you can eat it without getting any on your hands."

Dig kept gawking at it. Cal could tell it was an act. This dude certainly could lead you on. Maybe the dry wit came from having the Touch. Cal could handle that if it meant having the Touch.

"I wonder who thought of that," Dig said, shrugging.

"How should I know? I look like a stupid baker?"

"I don't know what stupid baker looks like."

"They wear white shirts, white pants, white aprons, and white hats."

"Why so much white?"

Cal sighed. "Who knows? Maybe they have an arrangement with the local hospitals and give them free doughnuts in exchange for their clothes. Stop fucking around and eat the damn thing."

Digger stuck his thumb carefully through the hole. He sniffed, frowned, then licked the side.

Cal groaned. "You're supposed eat it, not lick it."

141

Dig looked like he wanted to throw up. "It tastes weird."

Cal shook his head. "You scrape shit off the bottom of your shoe for a quick snack and have the balls to tell me a doughnut tastes weird?"

Digger took a small bite, then frowned.

"Now what's wrong?"

"Where are the nuts?"

"Doughnuts don't have nuts. Not unless you ask for them."

"Why's it called a doe-nut?"

"Just eat the damn thing, all right?"

"I like nuts. Especially when they're mixed with rotten fruit."

Cal finished his glazed and sipped the hot coffee. "Let's get back to the car. I need to buy some clothes. And a toothbrush." He tossed the empty bag in a trash can.

Lights flashing, a squad car sat behind the stolen Mustang outside the motel room. A tall, broad-shouldered cop stood between the two cars, talking on his radio.

Damn. Cal loved that Stang. Those were the breaks. "We need to get the fuck outa Dodge."

Dig gawked at him. "I thought this was Orlando..."

"You really need to save the good one-liners for when I'm in the mood."

Dig nodded. "I get it. You're not in the mood, right?"

"Your momma didn't raise any idiots, did she?"

"Actually—"

"Just shut up and find us another ride to lift."

"Lift?"

What was wrong with this dude? He was beginning to sound like someone who had just landed on the planet. "Steal, dammit. Heist. Grab. Nab. But do it fast. That cop's probably already got backup on its way."

Dig pointed. "How about that one?"

A late-model maroon Riviera sat near the side entrance of the restaurant in the lot next to the motel.

Todd nodded approvingly. "Looks helluva lot better than the back seat of that fucking squad car."

Chapter 20

A Major Decision

Groggy from a night of troubled sleep, Ashley sat up in bed.

Her restlessness, fueled by Momma and her drunken date, caused her to toss and turn much of the night.

When she finally drifted off, she found herself lost in the woods at night, searching for the clearing that would take her home. Teddy and Momma appeared, blocking her path. Both were laughing and drinking from large glasses. A large hole had been dug in the ground at their feet. A strong, foul smell oozed from it. Momma gestured for her to come closer.

Ashley tried backing up, but some invisible force pulled her closer.

Mr. Waite's head suddenly emerged from the inside of the hole. His eyes glowed red. His teeth were long and sharp.

He laughed: a loud, horrible moaning sound. A swollen knot of heat escaped from his mouth, rushing toward her face.

Her heart thumping, she sat up and surveyed her surroundings.

Darkness. Strange shapes.

She squinted, forcing her eyes to acclimate. The shapes gradually grew more vivid. Her nightstand. Dresser. Vanity. Chair.

Her bedroom, thank God.

Her armpits tingled with sweat. Shivering, she lay back down, thinking of the dark woods and that foul-smelling hole. Trying to interpret its meaning.

Her thoughts looping, she drifted back to sleep.

She awoke what seemed like only moments later. The small digital clock on her nightstand told her it was time to get up.

She tiptoed to the bathroom.

Hopefully, she could perform her morning ablutions and leave the house quickly. She suddenly had the strong urge to be somewhere else. These surroundings made her nauseous. She didn't know if it was because of the dream or the confrontation with Momma the night before; she only knew she wanted to be away.

Her cell buzzed.

Who would be calling so early?

The Café, telling her to work another double?

She toweled herself off, wrapped another towel around her dripping hair, and snatched up the phone.

"Hope I didn't wake you," Daniel said.

It was nice to hear his voice. To talk to someone who didn't make her feel guilty about anything. "I had to get up to answer the phone anyway," she quipped.

He laughed. "Guess I deserved that."

"No problem. I was already up."

"What happened after I dropped you off?"

"My mother was having a private little binge."

"How'd she take the interruption?"

"Not well."

"Was her binge partner irritated as well?"

145

"Teddy actually enjoyed my grand entrance."

"Nice guy?"

"If you like sloppy, leering drunks."

"You're all right, aren't you? I mean, they didn't—"

"I'm fine. I just went right to my room."

"So that was that."

"Sort of."

"Meaning?"

No need for anyone to know her problems. But she did want to confide in Daniel. Although they didn't know one another very well, she felt she could give him a heads-up.

"Last night convinced me more than ever that I need to find somewhere else to live. Unfortunately, I can't think about doing that right now."

He didn't reply.

She shouldn't have said anything. She might have put a damper on things by turning him down at the restaurant. But maybe she could fix it. "I've also been thinking more about your offer. I want you to know that."

A pause. "Well, whatever you decide, I'll respect your wishes."

"Has something come up?"

Another pause. "Not really..."

"How come I sense something in your voice, then?"

He sighed. "I just don't want to be responsible for getting you involved in something you're not comfortable with."

His tone sounded different. "Daniel, has something happened?"

146

"I've been considering the illegalities, possible problems. Stuff like that."

"Didn't you tell me this would be a high-class operation? That I wouldn't have to worry about anything going wrong?"

"Yep. I said all that."

"Was it the truth?"

"Still is."

"Why so hesitant, then?"

"I've thought a little more about it and decided that I'm not comfortable trying to convince you to do something you're dead-set against doing."

Was she dead-set against it? As great as this all sounded, it was an escort service. She wouldn't be an escort—that wasn't the issue. But she'd be arranging things. No matter how she thought about it, she'd be breaking the law.

But somehow it didn't sound as bad this morning.

"Maybe I'm not as dead-set against it as I thought I was."

"Now you sound like something's changed."

Maybe she had changed her mind. Was it because of Momma? The confrontations? Watching Momma deteriorate by the day certainly didn't help.

"Ashley? Still there?"

That was the problem. She was here and didn't want to be.

Should she accept the job? Was she considering it because of Momma? Because it might provide a means of escape?

Should she tell Daniel about her dream? He would probably laugh and tell her she was basing

147

her fears on Waite's brashness, his arrogance. Anyway, it was just a dream. Dreams meant nothing.

"I'm still here." Her heart had tugged when she said it.

"I have this feeling you're far away."

"I am and I'm not."

"You sound...strange."

Actually, she felt better than usual. Was it because of Daniel's call? Because someone had suddenly entered her life? Someone who actually wanted to help her?

Or was it because she suddenly felt her life was about to change?

"Daniel, what's the pay?"

"Six hundred a week."

Wow. And she wouldn't have to be on her feet all day, developing varicose veins. She would be able to save all sorts of money. Maybe even get her own place.

The door burst open. Momma, wearing the clothes from the night before, staggered in. A strong mix of B.O. and dragon breath floated over, brushing Ashley's nostrils and making her gag.

"We outa aspirin? Can't find any in the medicine cabinet. Got any in yours?"

"There's half a bottle above the sink, Momma."

She hurried past, shoving Ashley's bathroom door open. It slammed against the wall.

The familiar sounds of her mother coughing and hacking echoed off the walls.

"Baby...get in here and...damn! Missed the crapper!"

148

Ashley stared at the phone in her hand. The bars of morning sun coming in made it shine like a polished gem.

An omen?

"Daniel, tell me where you'd like me to be," she heard herself whisper.

"What was that? Ashley, what's going on? Are you all right?"

"I can come over this afternoon. Is that soon enough?"

Chapter 21

Mingling Amongst the Tourists

Crowds flocked the restaurants and flooded the souvenir shops.

The Church Street area roared with heavy late morning traffic. Foreigners shuffled along, taking pictures of street signs, buildings, and even bums begging for change.

Dressed in a sleeveless light-blue blouse, tan Capri's, and a pair of black BCBGirls Put Pumps, Tiffany stayed close to Chip in the slow-moving crowd. Upon closer inspection, she decided the black didn't quite go with the tan Capri's. She changed the pumps to red, adding a sparkling diamond stuck to the center of each heel strap.

She loved having total control over her wardrobe. This perk alone made her even more determined to stay up here. Breath Mint was too smart to do anything to jeopardize their hunt for Digger. That gave her and Chip a little time to plan an escape.

Like their assignment in Raven, they only had three days. Right now, accomplishing their task seemed downright impossible. Finding someone in Orlando would be much more difficult than looking for him in a town the size of Raven.

"Isn't there anything more about the Digger guy you can tell me?" she asked. "Aside from his disgusting hobby?"

Chip sucked on a clump of dirt he yanked from the window planter they'd just passed. "What could be simpler? A dung beetle stays close to dung."

"This is a big place. There's probably dung everywhere."

He looked down at her feet. "Why'd you change your shoes?"

"Didn't like the black. If Digger's seen playing around in dung, he's liable to be arrested, isn't he?"

"In that case, the local police station might be our best bet." He glanced at her feet again. "You're right. Red's better."

"Thank you. I thought so, too."

"Why the diamonds?"

"I thought the straps needed something extra."

"I thought you didn't like jewelry."

"Not on my skin, silly."

"My police station idea might work. I could do the zany lawyer impression I did in Ohio. The locals loved me. They wanted to get in touch with my agent and have him book me at their local saloon for a weekend spot. The feed store was looking for a dynamite act as well."

It infuriated her when he refused to stay focused. "We can't just hang around while we wait for him to be brought in. It could take weeks before he does something stupid."

"You're taking all the fun out of this, baby girl."

"You can't be serious."

"Serious is my middle name."

"I thought it was Tactful."

151

"My folks were playing Scrabble when I squirted out of my mom and rolled into the koi pond."

"Such a pleasant image."

"It had a happy ending. A frog let me share his lily pad until my old man found his fishing rod and reeled me in."

It was so hard, getting him to pay attention...

"Getting back to the subject... If Broad Wafer thinks we're taking too long, he'll send us right back down there."

"Good point. But just remember the ground rules. First of all, his name is Braithwaite. Secondly, if we don't find Digger, we get sent down. And thirdly, once we do find Digger, we get sent down."

"But at least we're safe as long as we're looking."

"And as long as Digger doesn't pop up too soon."

"What does he eat when he's not playing around in dung?"

"Dead leaves, dried fruits. Grass, if he can't find enough dung."

"I just don't understand why he'd vanish. He wouldn't want to get on Boring Waiter's bad side, would he?"

"I sure wouldn't. And it's Braithwaite."

"Even you froze up when you were in the same room with him."

"I've seen what he can do."

"Hasn't Digger?"

152

"He's been down there just as long as I have, so yeah."

"It doesn't make sense that he'd come up here to work for a super, then disappear."

"That's something you can ask him. If we ever find him."

A tall, gray-haired man jabbering away in German grabbed Chip by the arm and held out his camera. Chip took it. "Thanks. I've always wanted one of these babies. We can't use them where I come from. The light just isn't right." He resumed walking.

The tourist quickly grabbed Chip's elbow and pointed to his left, where a family of five waited in front of Church Street Station. "Nehmen Sie unser bild!" he shouted, nodding eagerly.

"Sorry, slick." Chip shrugged. "My German's a tad rusty. Last I used it was, I recall, in the Eighteenth Century, when a mean-looking dude with bad hair named Ludwig Van Something was trying to write his Second Symphony, and one of the supers controlling Europe at the time ordered me to play a nasty little game with the man's inner ear—"

"Peek-ture!" The German pointed to the camera. "Peek-ture!"

"He wants you to take his picture," Tiffany said.

"Ah. Here I was thinking I was just given a free camera."

When the man rejoined his family, Chip examined the camera. He clicked away while the family stood very still.

153

"Ein mehr, bitte!"

"How's that?"

"More!" they urged. "Ein more!"

Chip clicked again.

The man rushed over, took the camera, and shook Chip's hand vigorously. He ran back to his family to resume their tour.

Tiffany smiled. Chip might actually be changing for the better. "Not many demons would take a family's picture and give them back their camera."

"How do you know what I did, sweet cheeks?"

His impish grin told her she might have been premature in her latest observation. "What did you do?"

"I took several really dynamite shots of their tennies and hairy ankles." He wiggled his ears and chuckled.

"I should've known."

Across the street, more tourists took pictures while others leaned over parked cars, reading maps spread out over the hoods. Tour buses sat along the curb, waiting to be filled.

A large advertisement on the side of the first bus caught Tiffany's eye. "Wow."

"Something wrong, sweet pea?"

She kept silent as the idea quickly developed.

"Don't tell me you're still going through that weird female stuff. Like that peeing urge you had in Ohio. You should be over all that. Your bladder's only an illusion now."

"I'm getting an idea."

"Really? Wow!"

154

"Shut up. I'm serious."

"All righty rooty. Let loose with your latest litany, lady."

She pointed to a tour bus, where the sign

Kilimanjaro Safari Experience

covered a large collage of wild animals in a jungle setting.

Chip grinned. "Cool. Lions and tigers and bears—"

"Don't you get it?" He could be so dense. . .

"Get what, dearest? The lion thingy? The tiger thingy? Or maybe—"

"Where there are animals, there's dung."

Chip grinned. "You know something, honey bunny? You've developed a few more useful brain cells since you've been chumming around with me."

Chapter 22

Next on the Itinerary...

The Riviera could fly just as fast as the Mustang.

Cal was pleased and impressed. This ride handled some serious pickup and was a lot comfier. Nice, cushy adjustable seats and a back rest to die for.

Really cool, being able to pick up such a major ride so easily. No more shit about keeping the Pontiac running or worrying about it stranding him. Not even any crap about finding a dealer who wouldn't rip him off.

The only problem was picking which ride you wanted.

No doubt about it. Dig was definitely a keeper.

Cal got on the East-West Expressway and cut across town in no time. He wanted to get away from International Drive for a little while, maybe bum around Kissimmee while the cops hunted for the Riviera in the Orlando area.

He never had a problem getting around, although the damn toll roads always made him want to spit blood. In Orlando you could spend a fortune in tolls without ever leaving the County.

Cal pulled off the Expressway. He wanted to zoom through the toll lane, but the metal gate prevented that. Best stick to the rules. Otherwise, the cops would catch them long before he got used to this cool new ride. The cameras could pick up anything.

Cal tossed a fistful of change at the toll sack. The buzzer went off, the gate flipped up, and they got onto a four-lane road leading to Kissimmee.

Cal had never spent much time in Kissimmee. Too many Hispanics. Cal didn't hate Hispanics; he just didn't want to learn Spanish. In Kissimmee, the Hispanics running businesses spoke only Spanish and didn't want to learn English.

These roads were even more crowded here than in Orlando. As usual, most carried out-of-state tags. Billboards advertising the attractions, hotels, shopping malls, and vacation spots eclipsed the countryside and most of the skyline. Much of the area that remained pastureland spread out for miles and miles.

Maybe they'd get lucky and spot a cow or horse grazing off the main drag. Dig would get his rocks off playing with a cow or horse patty and they could get back to hitting the Orlando tourists. A steak dinner at a good restaurant sounded great. After dinner he'd pick up another hooker, buy a bottle, and shack up at a four-star motel.

But before they got busy doing all that, he decided to bring up something more important.

"Teach me something."

Dig continued staring out the window.

"How about teaching me to flip over these engines?"

"After we see some animals."

"I also want to learn how to mess with people's heads."

"That's no big deal."

157

Was he for real? How could he say something like that?

"You don't think that's a big deal?"

"Wow!" Digger jumped up and down, hitting his head on the roof of the cab.

Cal nearly swerved into the turning lane. "What the fuck?"

Jumping and squealing, Digger pointed to the huge billboard just off the main road.

A hugantic view of a jungle, with the words Kilimanjaro Safari Experience hanging over it in big brown letters, blazed at them.

Great. This weirdo spots an elephant and totally loses his mind...

Cal knew all about these places. This one, a glorified jungle tour with a fake African village, animal exhibits, and souvenir shops, really pulled in the suckers. Cal never went to these places—too many damn kids. Kids were assholes. They always got in your way. You couldn't even belt them without getting your ass in trouble.

"There! I wanna go there!" Dig looked like he might have a heart attack.

"Now?" Cal asked.

"Now! Right now!"

Chapter 23

The Meeting

Dressed in his dark-blue single-breasted Versace and gold cotton tie, Richard Grove nervously took a seat in the conference room.

Arranging this meeting had been tough. Getting everyone together on such short notice was frustrating. Richard's secretary had worked feverishly to locate everyone but met up with six dead ends. Two members presently conducted business in Belize while three vacationed in Europe and one investigated business interests in Quebec.

The demon calling himself Brett Waite had ordered the meeting. When a benefactor made such a demand, you did whatever it took to accommodate him.

"So then, our new benefactor has finally arrived." Impeccably dressed in his black Baroni, C. Dexter Larrabee sat on Richard's right. One of the four major investors of Glaser Properties, Inc., Larrabee, with his thick blond hair and clean-shaven face, presented a youthful appearance for his fifty-seven years. "It's about damned time."

"Better late than never." L. M. Shirley, the third senior partner of Glaser, rubbed a palm over his tanned bald pate. "It's been a long time since a superior has visited Central Florida. With the recent tanking of the economy, I consider this a stroke of luck. We can always use a helping hand as well as expert guidance."

159

"I agree." Douglas S. Baldwin, owner of two large chains of gas stations stretching from Jacksonville to Key West, sat up in his chair. The dark, pensive features on his handsome fifty-year-old face made one wonder if he actually knew how to smile. "I expected Balbor's successor to show up in Ohio. Talk about a squeaky wheel. Our Ohio Valley associates always seem to need extra attention."

"I'm surprised they haven't already found out about this new man's arrival," Shirley said.

"What makes you think they haven't?" Larrabee said.

"I wouldn't put anything past that group." Willis X. Jacobs, owner of several prime Kissimmee properties resting on six prestigious golf courses, displayed a scowl on his heavy, Karl Malden-like features

"We really shouldn't throw stones." Frank Reading, the fourth partner of Glaser, had graduated with Richard at the University of Miami nearly thirty-five years ago. Frank was a handsome version of Donald Trump, with darker, more natural-looking hair. "Phil Holeridge may be a whiner, but he is one of us. And we can't very well blame him for wanting consideration."

"Politicians," commented Larrabee sourly. "They may not have invented the wheel, but they certainly spent considerable time tweaking up the volume control on its squeak."

"Balbor spent nearly a decade up there," Jacobs said. "Other than strip-mining rights and the acquisition of crucial farmland, what do they need outside interference for?"

"More idiots up there," commented Shirley.

"And what do you call tourists?" Jacobs asked.

Oh boy, Richard thought dismally. Here we go again.

"At least tourists never stay," Frank said. "They come here, clutter up the roads, the stores, and the hotels, then fly back to Wisconsin. Or Michigan. Or New York—"

"And are immediately replaced by other tourists," Jacobs said testily.

"Well, yes, but—"

"No buts," Shirley said.

"Nothing but butts." Jacobs had a slug of coffee. "You know how many times I've almost been killed by an idiot in a rental car too stupid to realize that you stop at red lights here as well as everywhere else?"

"Tourists think different rules apply here in Fantasy Land."

"Tourists don't think."

"Where tourists come from, there are no red lights."

"Tourists should never have children," Jacobs said.

"Isn't that inbreeding?" asked Larrabee.

"Should be illegal. It produces cluttered roads."

"And more tourists."

"At least they pay our state taxes for us." Richard hoped they'd settle down until Waite's call.

161

"They support our theme parks nicely as well," Jacobs said.

"Our new benefactor." Douglas Baldwin sipped some coffee. "Tell us about him."

"His name is Brett Waite," Richard said. "He's an extremely arrogant individual."

"Tell us something." Larrabee had another bite of his bagel. "Am I imagining things? Or was he responsible for that mysterious car explosion yesterday afternoon on Orange Avenue?"

"You're not imagining anything."

"What was the reasoning?" Frank asked.

Richard sighed. He had hoped he wouldn't have to talk about this. Discussing it made him worry about Daniel working so close to a benefactor.

"It was a demonstration," he told them.

"What for?" Shirley asked.

"To show my son who we're dealing with. This man is, well, mentoring him."

"In what capacity?"

"I don't know."

Daniel's a grown man," Frank said assuredly. "He'll be able to handle this."

"I certainly hope so." Richard stared at the speaker phone on the desk. He had an uneasy feeling about this meeting. He hoped he was worrying about nothing. This could be nothing more than Waite introducing himself to the members. Or a discussion on a tentative itinerary for local business.

"When is he supposed to call?" Frank asked.

Richard glanced at his watch. "Any time now."

"We need to get on with this," Larrabee said. "I have a meeting with a potential client in an hour."

"I wouldn't suggest leaving right now," Jacobs said.

The phone buzzed.

The men jumped in their seats.

With an unsteady hand, Richard flipped it on speaker.

Waite's loud, abrupt voice exploded from the black box, vibrating the walls.

"This is Brett Waite. You there, Grove?"

"Yes, Mr. Waite."

"Who else is there?"

"My friends and colleagues, C. Dexter Larrabee, Lawrence Shirley, Douglas Baldwin, Frank Reading, and Willis Jacobs."

"C. Dexter Larrabee?" Waite asked.

Larrabee sat up. "Yes, sir..."

"What's the C stand for?"

Larrabee glanced around the table. Mostly everyone shrugged.

"Er, Charles, sir."

"You use the Dexter but not the Charles?"

Larrabee shifted uneasily in his chair. "It's a family tradition, sir."

"What? Not using the Charles?"

"Well, sir—"

"Is this family saga going to take long to unravel?"

"I was just going to say that my grandfather came over from Ireland—"

"I was afraid of that." Waite sighed. "Just forget I brought it up. Let's get on with this. How many belong to the Central Florida Chapter, total?"

Richard forced down a clammy lump gathering in his throat. "There are twelve of us, Mr. Waite."

A pause. "Twelve?"

"Y-Yes, sir..."

"I counted six."

No one said anything.

"Anyone want to add a little something to that?"

Richard felt his pulse quickening.

"I'm waiting—just in case anyone's interested."

The men exchanged fearful glances. Everyone turned to Richard.

Apparently I'm the spokesman, he thought. Lucky me.

"It was, um, very difficult getting everyone together on such short notice," Richard said awkwardly. "The others are out of state, tending to business—"

"Guess I didn't give you enough time, eh, Grove?"

"Well, sir—"

"I'll give you a break with this one. How's that sound?"

Richard didn't know how to respond.

"Where I come from," Waite said, "everyone's more interested in sniffing around for fresh stuff rather than doing anything else. So...what have you told your colleagues about me, Grove?"

"I told them you caused the car explosion yesterday afternoon."

"Pretty cool, eh?"

Silence.

"I said—"

"Yes, sir," Richard said.

"Very nice," Frank Reading said.

"An extremely impressive display, sir," Willis Jacobs added.

"Very impressive," agreed Shirley.

"Glad you appreciated my little demonstration. I was merely stretching, of course. Loosening up. I haven't been up here since the Black Plague. The flexing needs work. I'm looking forward to lots of practice."

Silence. Everyone sat stiffly, staring numbly at the speaker phone.

"I've called this meeting to tell you about my immediate strategies. I have contacts in Saudi." A pause. "Anyone else have contacts there?"

"I do," Baldwin said softly. "In fact, we all have contacts all over—"

Waite cleared his throat.

Baldwin shut up.

"I guess I didn't make myself quite clear," Waite said. "My last question required a yes or no answer. It goes like this. Yes. Or this. No. Understand?"

Silence.

"Good. I like it when people understand where I'm coming from. As for your contacts, save your chest-thumping for someone who actually gives a good shit. I care only about Saudi. Everyone understand?"

Everyone muttered an affirmative grunt.

"I'm pleased you're all paying attention. In a nutshell, I plan to bring several of them over here in the next few days."

"Where in Saudi?" Frank asked.

"And you are...?"

"Frank Reading, sir. A senior partner of Glaser."

"If you're the R in the company name, sounds like you're the least senior," Braithwaite said. "Or possibly the most junior."

Frank didn't reply.

"My contacts are from Egypt. Also, Pakistan and Iraq. My friends have expressed an interest in acquiring Central Florida land. They enjoy the climate here. They'd also like to learn golf, for whatever reason. I intend to satisfy their needs. Which is where you gentlemen come in."

The men gawked at one another.

Baldwin opened his mouth.

Richard quickly depressed the mute button before anyone could utter a word.

"He's not serious!" Baldwin gasped.

"Sounds serious to me," Larrabee said.

"How could anyone even consider bringing over terrorists to buy up our land?" Frank asked.

"This is insane!" Baldwin slammed his palm onto the table.

"You know what this could mean, don't you?" Jacobs said.

166

"Um, what could it mean?" Waite asked from the speaker phone.

Everyone gawked at Richard, then the desk phone. Then Richard again.

Richard's head throbbed. The mute button. It didn't work...

"The mute button works, Grove." Waite chuckled. "But you've obviously forgotten who you're dealing with. Gadgets are expensive toys—nothing else. They really don't stand up to demons, although I am quite fond of that new toaster oven you mortals have come up with during the last few years. And these nifty microwave things come in handy for fresh buttered popcorn. Anyway, don't put too much of your trust in gadgets like this hundred-dollar doorstop I'm using right now. Incidentally, where do you think this modern technology was first developed?"

Dead silence.

"Back to the subject." Waite's tone softened minimally. "Which one of you rocket scientists said something about my plan being insane?"

Everyone turned to Baldwin.

"No one wants to volunteer? All right, then. For that individual—and for those of you who might feel the same way—I'll say this. You're all bought and sold. Our property. But don't take it personally. You all know we're partners. We've been that way for centuries. You're the ones we make rich and we're the ones who tell you what to do to get even richer. Simple and direct—wouldn't you say?"

No one replied.

"Are there any questions?"

The men stared at one another, the panic clear on their faces.

"I'll let you know the particulars about my colleagues coming over. I'll also give you a little more warning when I decide to conduct another meeting. Hopefully, I'll be able to chat with more of you the next time."

Click.

Richard stared at the speaker phone. Had he heard correctly? Or was this Waite's idea of a sick joke?

Not a joke, he told himself. Yet he wished it was.

"He was serious, wasn't he?" Baldwin's voice had become a whisper.

"This is totally—" Larrabee stopped abruptly and gawked at the speaker phone. The others also stared as if a deadly snake sat coiled on the table, ready to strike.

"Think it's safe?" Frank whispered.

"I don't know," Richard whispered back. "I'm pretty sure it turned off when he hung up."

"Pretty sure doesn't cut it," Jacobs said.

"The red light's off," Baldwin noticed.

"Doesn't mean anything." Jacobs continued to stare.

"That's right," Frank said. "We're dealing with a super demon. Rules of logic don't apply."

"Richard, take a closer look," Frank urged.

"That's very dangerous," Richard said. "You look first."

"Don't tell me you're afraid," Frank said.

168

"I'm not afraid," Richard said. "I'm terrified."

Baldwin got up slowly. He moved toward the back of the phone and reached out with a trembling hand. Holding his breath, he pulled the jack out of its slot and let it drop.

Silence, followed by several deep sighs.

Richard swallowed another lump. Then, in a whisper: "M-Mr. Waite?"

Silence.

"A-Are you there?"

More silence.

Several sighs of relief.

"Gentlemen." Shirley's face was pale. "We can't sell to Arabs."

"I don't think we have much choice."

"What happened to free enterprise?" Jacobs poured a fresh cup of coffee. "There's nothing that says we're obliged to sell off our—"

"We're billionaires," Shirley said. "Together, we can buy this state, as well as two or three others."

"Except West Virginia," Jacobs said. "I hate West Virginia. The roads...well, the roads suck."

"What I'm trying to say is, we're too damned rich to be pushed around."

"So are they," Richard said anxiously. "They live in castles. Their toilets are made of gold. They own fleets of cars and limousines. They're accustomed to getting what they want."

"I wonder if he'd agree to a hands-off policy," Jacobs said.

"Does he sound like the sort who'd agree to something that's not his own idea?" Shirley asked.

169

"No," Baldwin said quickly. "He sounds like someone who'd convince Hitler to keep the ovens running twenty-four hours a day to save a few bucks on the power bill."

"I'm sure this new venture could triple our assets." Richard thought it was time to try and shed a little optimism.

"But at what price?" Larrabee said. "Selling off America to terrorists?"

"Japan owns American soil," Jacobs said. "So does Germany, Great Britain, China, and dozens of other countries. India owns just about every damned motel in Georgia and dozens of other states. And look at Iran. Bastards own practically every 7-Eleven in—"

"But we're talking terrorists," Shirley said.

"These aren't terrorists," Richard said. "They're sheiks and—"

"They're from a different century," Baldwin said. "They dress in custom-tailored thousand-dollar suits and are driven around in stretch limos. They drink thousand-dollar wines just like us, but they still behead people and keep harems."

"There's got to be some way of reasoning with this new man," Larrabee said. "There's a thing called morality here."

Frank chuckled. "Are you serious? We've all profited from the misfortunes of others."

"They don't even use deodorant," Baldwin muttered.

"It offends Allah," Larrabee said.

"I think we're looking at this all wrong," Richard said.

"How?" Shirley said. "Terrorists, Richard. Remember Nine-Eleven? Suicide bombers? Chemicals? America must die? That sort of thing?"

"I know what you're saying..."

"Then please tell us how we're looking at this all wrong."

"I'm seeing this in the perspective of the economy. For instance, how many recessions have we seen in the last thirty years?"

"Too many."

"How many times have we seen corporations go belly-up due to poor investments and stock manipulations?"

"But how does this—"

"Lastly, how many of us sitting in this room have seen financial trouble when the rest of the country has been crawling around on its belly, trying to scrape by?"

Silence.

Richard shrugged. "Anyone want to add to that?"

"But we're talking terrorists."

"We're also talking land," Richard said. "That's all they want. Raw land. And we have more than enough to sell. As I said before, they're just as rich as we are, if not richer. They'll pay whatever we demand. Any idea how much we stand to gain here?"

"Even if they bring over a battalion of terrorist trainees?"

"I honestly don't think they'll be doing that."

"You're being naïve, Richard."

"I'm trying to be optimistic. As I said, we've never had problems before. Not since we made the Pledge."

"Terrorists." Shirley shivered in disgust.

"Even so," Jacobs said, "we need some ground rules."

"Ground rules?" Larrabee sat up in his seat. "When a super demon's calling the shots?"

"We're not savages, you know."

"True," Baldwin said. "This is a civilized country."

Jacobs sighed. "These people scare the hell out of me. I've dealt with them at least three times during the last twenty years and they always make me feel...uneasy."

"Is it the suicide bombings?" Shirley asked. "The terror camps? The beheadings? The Allah thing?"

Jacobs nodded. "That and their stupid superstitions. Hell, they're liable to send over a group of suicide bombers if you happen to upchuck the sautéed camel testicle at their banquet table."

"What can we do about this?" Baldwin asked.

"I wish I knew." Richard hoped this situation wasn't as bleak as everyone thought. "I really wish I knew."

172

Chapter 24

Ashley's Big Chance

As Daniel carefully explained company policy, Ashley struggled to pay attention.

But it was difficult. She hadn't expected her new surroundings to overwhelm her so quickly. Her office, much larger than the manager's office at the O-Town Café, made her feel small and lost.

And everything was so bright. So expensive looking.

Massive potted plants decorated the lobby outside the glass doors. A huge print of the ocean covered the cream-colored wall facing her desk. The soft tan carpeting, so thick and luxurious, would feel like heaven if she was able to walk around in her bare feet.

The quiet, relaxed atmosphere, so different from the frantic tension of the O-Town, clearly demonstrated how quickly one's life could change.

She wished she could see the O-Town from her window. Looking down at it would be strange. She would feel as if she had triumphed, had climbed to a higher level. As if she had escaped.

Was she fooling herself? Maybe, maybe not. Even if she was, so what? She hadn't felt so good about herself and life in general in a long time.

But now was not the time to celebrate—not while Daniel explained the switchboard system. Pay attention, she told herself once again. Focus.

He demonstrated how to transfer calls and retrieve voice mail. Luckily, the switchboard had

173

only three lines. She had seen them much larger and more complicated in banks and other businesses. Thank God this wouldn't be that difficult.

A large black ledger sat opened on the desk blotter, its green lined pages staring up at her.

"Make sure you write down the exact times of the calls."

"No names?"

"No names and no notes. Just the times."

That sure didn't give her a warm fuzzy. But she guessed it would be wiser in the long run. The less she knew about any of this, the better she liked it.

"What's the pad for?" A thick notepad sat in front of the desk calendar.

"For show. Listen carefully to the message, make your call, relay every detail, and hang up. It's that simple."

"It sounds so easy, an idiot could do it."

"It is."

"Then why ask me?"

"Why do you think?"

His smile told her his reply. She couldn't remember the last time a man had made her feel so special. She wasn't surprised to discover just how much she truly missed it.

"Where's your office?" she asked.

"Just across the hall. By the way, the coffee serving tray is yours. Feel free to make a ton of coffee. We've got a catering service that delivers lunch daily, so don't bother with the junk food machines. There's also a water cooler, and the rest

174

rooms are halfway down the hall, toward the elevators."

"I spotted them on my way over."

"Anything else you need to know?"

"I think I can get by."

"You should only be on your own for a few days. We plan on hiring two more operators within the week. Then you'll have seniority."

"And company, since you won't be here to baby-sit me."

"You'll be fine."

"I hope so."

"By the way, that's a hot outfit you're wearing."

She hoped he would like it. She had picked out the pink sleeveless blouse and black pleated skirt specifically for him. She always thought it made her dark brown eyes larger and sexy. It was the first outfit she thought of when she told him she would come in for the new job. It immediately cheered her up, even eclipsed the unpleasant image of Momma staggering out of her bathroom, her hair matted, a foot-long clump of damp toilet paper stuck to her heel.

"I didn't think you'd noticed," she said softly.

"Oh, I noticed. I really did. I mean, I really and truly noticed."

His silly expression made her smile. "Then why didn't you say anything? It wouldn't be anything like that nasty friend of yours, commenting on my hair..."

He sighed. "I'm supposed to act...well, professional."

175

"I understand."

"Then you realize, of course, how uncomfortable I am right now. I'd much rather be home in my tee shirt and cutoffs, sitting out by the pool, using my laptop as a tray for my beer."

"I know what you mean. I'm used to my green skirt with O-Town stitched on the side and that stupid frilly blouse I had to wear with my nametag stuck out so prominently."

"I liked that stupid frilly blouse. I also liked where your nametag stuck out."

She felt herself blushing. "You would."

He shrugged. "Can't help what we are, right?"

"I guess."

"Tell me you don't like the setup."

"Setup?"

"You know. Boy meets girl, boy gets all hot and bothered and stupid. Boy acts like an idiot. Girl knows why boy acts like an idiot. Girl makes boy feel like an idiot…"

"I get it." She laughed.

"Maybe we can go out later on and celebrate with dinner."

"Celebrate what?"

"I'll think of something."

She laughed as he went over to the glass doors.

Before he left he said, "You're sure about all this?"

"I wouldn't be here, otherwise."

He didn't reply.

"Still feel funny?" She hoped she hadn't put him in a tight spot.

"I just don't want you to feel pressured."

"I'm fine, Daniel."

He smiled, then waved on his way to the glass doors.

She sat down and sighed. It was so nice, not having to spend all day on her feet. She hated the thought of getting varicose veins at her tender age. "Count on it," Momma had assured her, time and time again. "I'll bet you already have a healthy batch coming in."

Momma, she thought with great satisfaction, I just stopped them cold. Soon you'll be saying bye-bye to your favorite baby daughter. I'm sorry Daddy left, but that's not my fault. We both need to move on.

She went over to the coffeemaker, dumped four scoops into the filter, poured water from the jug, and got it chugging along. By the time she returned to her desk, one of the three phone lines blinked frantically.

Oh no. It's already starting...

Her hand shook as she picked up the receiver. It suddenly seemed just as heavy as one of those barbell plates Daddy kept in the garage. Her voice quivered but she somehow managed to force the words out. They came painfully at first, a scratchy knot of flame deep in her throat bursting loose. But when the thought

(you're only answering a phone)

emerged, the rest of it flowed like wine.

"Waite Answering Services, may I help you?"

A low-pitched masculine voice said, "I need someone tomorrow afternoon, one o'clock, Vistana Resort, Lee Vista Center, Room One-Seventeen. I want her no more than twenty-two, five feet tall, Asian, and multilingual."

The line went dead.

She reached for the notepad and stopped. Remembering Daniel's instructions, she hurriedly dialed the appropriate number, carefully repeated the message to some sort of recording, then jotted down the time in her log.

The heavy aroma of fresh coffee snapped her out of it. She got up rather shakily and managed to pour a cup without spilling any on her skirt. By the time she went back to the desk, her nerves had settled down.

I can do this, she told herself.

But a tiny voice inside her expressed doubt.

Chapter 25

Tramping Through the Savanna

The safari truck bounced down the bumpy jungle trail.

Tiffany and Chip sat in back behind a dozen others. A sign up front said, WILD ANIMALS AHEAD. Passengers with cameras and electronic equipment clicked away as the truck stumbled down the jagged dirt path.

In the seat in front of them, a small pigtailed girl around four years old peered over her mother's shoulder. Chip winked at her and wiggled his ears. The little girl giggled and ducked down in her seat.

Tiffany wondered how she and Chip could get away from this crowd without causing suspicion. She also wondered how they could possibly find Digger out here. The area spanned hundreds of acres, most of it heavily wooded. Their best bet was to try some way to cover the spots the truck couldn't access. Maybe they'd get lucky.

Chip stared at the little girl. A ribbon of white smoke trickled out of his left ear, dissipating when it drifted out the open window. The little girl's jaw dropped. She ducked down behind her mother again.

"Please stop teasing her," Tiffany said. "You'll make her mother freak."

"Me? Make someone freak?"

"How many people do you think can wiggle their ears and make smoke come out of them at the same time?"

179

He blinked. "You mean most of them can only do one or the other?"

"I've never seen the smoke thing before I met you."

"You see a lot of weird things down in Hell."

"News flash. We're in Florida."

"I keep forgetting that."

"How could you possibly forget that we're in Florida and not Hell?"

"The weather's similar. People are just as nasty up here."

"I don't remember seeing any theme parks down there."

"You weren't there very long, lamb chop."

"Are you trying to tell me there are theme parks down there?"

"They've got some really strange entertainment going on in the Castle at times."

"This place is much nicer than...down there."

"I saw some swamps on the way over that looked kind of funky."

She was beginning to think she should have left him back at the village. "Sometimes you're such a pill."

"And other times?"

"You're just plain obnoxious."

"Why all the compliments, angel? Having another one of your blond moments?"

"Try and behave. Please?"

The little girl peeked at him again. He crossed his eyes.

"Stop doing that. People will think you're crazy." His silly expression made her realize what she just said. "What was I thinking?"

"I really don't know about your mind, princess. I'm always much too busy admiring those goodies slightly lower."

"Oh, shut up and tell me something."

"How can I tell you anything if I have to shut up?"

She sighed. "How do we get off this truck?"

"Simple. We manipulate the driver."

"From here?"

"Oh ye of little faith..." He stared straight ahead.

Moments later, the truck slowed down and stopped.

A hundred yards off to their right, Nile crocodiles basked in the man-made river.

"What did you do?" she whispered.

"I tricked him into thinking he just heard a rattle in the engine."

"Good work. Now all we have to do is disappear when nobody's looking."

"No problemo."

"You have another idea?"

He winked. "Watch and learn, grasshopper."

She glanced at the tall weeds and the uneven terrain. "Before you do anything...will we be walking around in those weeds?"

"You want to look for Digger in an empty truck?"

"I was just thinking of my feet."

181

He looked down at them and grinned. "They are a couple of tasty-looking masterpieces, aren't they?"

He was so exasperating. "Will you please be serious? Just for a second or two?"

"All righty rooty. Just don't expect me to put on my serious face again."

"I'm just curious about what I should be wearing. These pumps just won't do it out there in the stickers."

"So change them. But do it fast. My shtick's about to start."

She closed her eyes. The pumps instantly turned into a pair of comfortable designer sneakers. "I'm all set."

He stood up. "Why'd we stop?"

"Yeah. Why the delay?" An irate female around thirty jumped up. She wore a black tank top and orange shorts. Angry red welts of sunburn stood out boldly on the damp skin just above her shoulder blades. She pulled off her sunglasses. "I didn't pay good money to bake in a hot truck."

"I think the driver's calling for help," Chip told her. "We're gonna be stranded here with those crocs over there, and they look hungry."

"Crocs are always hungry," commented an old man.

"What do they eat?" asked a middle-aged woman wearing a Gators cap and sunglasses.

"Whoever they want," the old man replied.

"Oh my God!" yelled another female.

The driver twisted around. "Folks, everyone's gonna be just fine. The animals cannot possibly

182

reach this road. We're experiencing slight engine trouble, but someone's coming over and—"

"Mommy?" cried the little girl in front of them. "Are we gonna get ate?"

"Those aren't even real crocs," someone said.

"They sure look real."

"Smell real, too."

"They can't get to us. There's a fence hidden in the woods. It's electrified. Saw it on some show."

"Don't care." A heavyset woman squeezed out into the aisle. "I'll take my chances walking back to the village. At least they got air-conditioning."

The others jumped up and bullied their way toward the front.

"Wanna see the giraffes!" cried the little girl, clinging to her mother.

The heavyset female pushed past the driver, knocking him back down into his seat.

Tiffany and Chip followed the eager column out into the thick brush.

***

The elephants grazed, pulling down tree branches with their trunks.

Digger's eyes grew. "This is so cool. I mean wow!"

Cal cursed himself for coming out here. This was really lame. And stupid. Sneaking into the bushes to watch elephants eat trees and dump huge piles of shit everywhere? I must be totally insane. That African village back there had air-conditioning, cold drinks, rest rooms, and seats with comfortable cushions. Nice-looking chicks wandering around, too. Most of them were probably eighteen or nineteen, dressed in tank tops and shorts. You could see some dynamite sunburn-marks in just the right places if you looked close enough.

But damn if this wasn't stupid...

Cal was a city boy. Running around in weeds and brush just wasn't his thing. Leave that shit for weirdoes like Jeff Corwin and that dinosaur guy, Nigel, or whatever the hell his name was.

"This sucks," he said, mostly to himself. "I could be getting laid or drunk. But no, I'm following around elephants—not chicks."

"Look at that." Digger's eyes bulged. "Isn't that awesome? All that dung?"

Cal snorted. "And me without my camera. We could do a show for the Animal Planet. How about this? The Most Extreme Shit-Squirters?"

"I'm going in there."

"Wait a minute." Cal didn't like the crazy glazed look in his friend's eyes. "Traipsing around out here will get our asses arrested. This is, like, private property. Didn't you see all those signs?"

"Nobody'll mind." Dig scaled the fence like a damned monkey and disappeared into the brush.

"Yeah. Right. Nobody'll mind. Shit." Cal slapped the back of his neck where a mosquito had just bitten him. Should have bought some repellent when they had the chance. Where the hell was the nearest truck? He wanted to flag it down and stay on it until he saw something with a roof. And a floor. And air-conditioning.

"Hey, Cal!" Dig crouched in some bushes about fifty yards from the elephants. He held something dark and round, about the size of a soccer ball. "C'mon in and look at this! It's awesome!"

Cal shivered. "What's that?"

"Elephant dung." He brought it closer to his face. "Fresh, too. And warm."

"Too much fucking information."

Digger gazed at it as though it was some sort of crystal ball.

This was incredible. How could someone cool enough to have the Touch be so totally fucked up? This was no different from the dried-up leaves and snot Dig had eaten at the motel room. Or that episode with the doughnut.

This boy needed serious help.

"Drop that turd, dammit."

"Why?"

"Because you can't make off with elephant shit."

"Why not?"

Cal didn't believe this conversation. "Listen carefully. A normal human being just doesn't do stuff like that."

"I don't care. I really like—"

"We need to get out of here. They catch us, they'll stick us both in a padded room."

"Why would anyone care what we do out here? We're not hurting—"

The roar of approaching bus engines made Cal jump.

"Now you've done it, brainiac. We're toast!"

185

Chapter 26

The Hunt Continues

Two trucks marked SAFARI SECURITY sat in the middle of the dirt path, their motors running. Half a dozen khaki-clad guards trudged through the bushes, barking into their radios.

Tiffany and Chip stayed hidden in a grove of scrub oaks just beyond the tall overgrowth.

"They sound really pissed," Chip whispered.

"They're probably worried about lawsuits," she said.

"This is private property. Besides, they've got some really huge animals wandering around, and they look hungry. Anyone who's not an idiot knows how stupid it would be to walk around out here."

"But they can still sue this place if they wander off and get hurt."

"Makes no sense, buttercup."

"Welcome to the modern world."

"Fifty years ago, things were much simpler."

"That was before computers."

"Exactly."

About thirty yards away, on the other side of the path, two figures emerged from the bushes. One was dressed in a baggy brown short-sleeve shirt and dirty jeans and carrying what looked like a basketball. His brown hair was as messy as Chip's. The young man behind him was taller and skinny, in a red shirt and black pants. His light-brown hair was cut very short. When the guards passed, the two figures bolted into the trees.

Although they were pretty far away, Tiffany could see smudges of dirt covering the first man's arms. "I wonder if that's the Digger guy."

"Who else would be hauling around an elephant turd?"

"My God. Is that what that is?"

"What else would you find among a herd of elephants, Babykins?"

Waves of nausea flooded through her. "I haven't been this grossed-out since…since I went to the State Fair as a child."

"Go on, muffin. Take us for a stroll down Memory Lane."

"I was having a lot of fun until my father took me to see the milking cows."

"What happened? One of them let loose with a brown spray when you were walking past?"

She blinked. "How'd you know?"

He shrugged. "You said you were grossed out. I just took a wild guess."

"Good guess."

"I'll bet that was a sight," he said, grinning impishly. "Little Tifferoosky covered in cow splatter."

"I was crying, and everyone laughed at me. I was even wearing my brand-new red dress."

"Good thing it wasn't a white one."

As soon as the security guys had moved on, the young men emerged from the trees and plodded down the weed-choked path. Their backs were showing, making it impossible to see their faces.

Chip turned, watching them. "Why are there two of them?"

"We can't exactly find out from here, can we?"

"Braithwaite did say Digger was by himself, didn't he?"

"That's what I got, too."

"But I see two of them."

"So do I."

"We need to find out what's going on."

"I need a better look at the other guy," she said.

"And just how do you plan on doing that?"

Tiffany smiled. "Now you watch and learn, grasshopper." She suddenly jumped up. "Hey, cutie! What's your hurry?"

The boy carrying the elephant patty glanced at her but kept on moving. His friend stopped abruptly and spun around.

The sounds of frenzied footsteps.

"The guards are coming back," Chip whispered. "We need to get away from here."

They hunkered down and scrambled back into the brush.

***

Twenty minutes later, Cal and Digger reached the short fence leading back to the wooden walkway, where trucks waited in the shaded pickup area down the road from the village.

Digger wanted to go back and pick up his trophy. It wasn't fair, Cal making him dump it in the bushes. That elephant turd was really fresh and sweet-smelling. It was a crime, leaving it there. Bugs and everything else would turn it all sour and funky.

"You still pissed about tossing that giant dingle berry?"

"I really wanted it." Digger couldn't believe how cruel Cal could be. He stood there, giving Digger that disgusted look of his. If Cal was a true friend, he would have seen how badly Digger had wanted that turd. But Cal was a modern guy. He'd grown up spoiled, just like all the other mortals. Everyone thought boxed food cooked in chemicals and frozen junk was good for you. Mortals could no longer recognize good, nutritious stuff anymore.

"You can't carry around an elephant turd in public. Hell, even I know that."

"It didn't smell that bad, did it?"

"It was a turd, dammit. The size of a fucking basketball."

"It was full of nutrients and all sorts of—"

"Don't wanna hear it."

"I'll be real careful about how I hold it."

"Then go back and get it. But don't say I didn't warn you."

"You really think everyone'll freak over something as fresh and as sweet-smelling as fresh elephant?"

Cal still looked disgusted. "Where have you been, man? People don't like gross, smelly things. Any idiot could figure that out."

Cal was so mean. He'd even made Digger wash his hands in that stream a ways back. Not only did Digger have to leave the turd in the bushes, he also had to wash off its rich smell.

Digger had seen some cool things in this modern world, but sure didn't like how weird people acted. They were nasty, ate foods swimming in chemicals, and didn't like smelling fresh things.

Ancient times were much better. At least no one pestered you about washing yourself so much.

They were soon trailing the latest group. Oldsters snapping pictures shuffled along, their orthopedic shoes squeaking quietly on the stone walk.

Cal had been quiet the last few minutes. Digger thought he was probably thinking of that blond lady they saw in the bushes. She sure was beautiful, even from a distance.

"I wonder who that lady was," Digger said.

"Doesn't matter," Cal said, sounding mad again.

"She sure was—"

"I said it doesn't matter. I'll probably never get to see her."

"She has to get back on a bus, doesn't she?"

Cal thought that one over. Then he frowned and gestured to the crowds gathering in front of the tour buses. "I don't know. There are too many damned buses lined up."

"We might see her again."

"How can you say that?"

Dig shrugged. "The buses all go back to the main parking lot, don't they? We could see her when she gets off."

Cal nodded. He suddenly wasn't wearing his mad face. "You could be right, Dig."

***

Dodging street vendors and screaming kids, Tifferoosky and Chip rejoined the crowd milling

190

around on the cobblestone walk outside the village of Harambe.

"Uh-oh." Tifferoo stopped walking and looked down at herself.

"What's wrong?"

"It's Broad Water."

"Huh?" Chip dropped his gaze to the sidewalk at her feet. He spun around, instantly scanning the crowds. Nothing but mortals wandering around, looking lost. "W-Where?"

"Here, silly." She squeezed the cell phone out of her back pocket.

Chip stepped back, nearly stumbling. He knew from the first moment he saw them in Ohio that he and cell phones would never get along. He'd even forgotten about the one Braithwaite had given her. Now that Tiffers had it in her hand, he couldn't take his eyes off it. It seemed to grow, the sunlight reflecting off it hurting his eyes. Something cold and slimy had encircled his neck. It was almost like Braithwaite, in serpent form, had slithered out of the little plastic box and wrapped himself around Chip's neck.

But something was odd. "I didn't hear it ring," he said.

"I had it set on vibrate."

"What's that?"

"It vibrates instead of rings. I didn't want to waste time picking a tune from the option menu." She pressed the piece against her left ear. "Yes?"

Chip chewed his lower lip. He couldn't imagine how she could stand there so calmly with a super demon on the line.

191

"No. Yes. Not yet. Kilimanjaro Safari. About an hour. All right." She pocketed the phone.

"What did he say?"

"Not much." She turned and followed the crowd.

Damn. How could she just have a conversation with Braithwaite and act like nothing happened?

He caught up to her. "You're not trying to drive me crazy, are you?"

She smiled. The tiniest glint of nastiness peeked at him from those big baby blues. "Is that possible?"

Funny. Real funny.

Tifferoo was beautiful and as sweet they came, but she also had a nasty streak. He didn't know if it was a natural babe thingy or something she'd learned in Hokeywood. Normally, that would be okay—especially when they went back down and had to fight demons again. But right now, they were up here. And they were dealing with a super demon.

"Tell me what he said, and please stop acting like a butthole."

"Okay. But only because you said please."

"Goody. Now...what did he say?"

"He wants us back in his office."

"When?"

"As soon as possible."

"Why?"

"He wants a status report."

"What do we tell him?"

"The truth."

"That we found Digger and lost him again?"

"Something like that."

"What about the guy with him?"

"We don't know who the other guy is."

They joined a swell of people lining up to board a bus with the sign DOWNTOWN ORLANDO painted on its side.

"What do we say when he asks why we lost Digger?" he asked.

"I'll tell him we were in the process of following Digger when the phone call interrupted us. And while I was busy answering the call, crowds of people got between us and Digger vanished."

The glint of nastiness had reappeared. He was always amazed how such a sweet female could possess an equally cold streak. "That'll really piss him off."

"He needs to leave us alone if he wants us to find Digger."

"I'm getting worried, Tifferoo. This place is really big and spread out. We have no idea where they went."

"We found him once. I'm sure we can find him again. Now that we know there are two of them, they might be easier to find."

"You don't think they'll stay here?" Lots of dung lying around."

"Lots of security guys, too."

"That raises a valid point."

"I think they'll try and get away. Most of the tour buses are heading back to Orlando. That might make it a little easier for us."

"I'm still trying to figure out where that other guy came from. Digger's not exactly what you'd call a social butterfly, Dearest. I've been around mortals before. I might be slightly of touch, but I've never known any to be particularly fond of elephant shit."

A warm breeze pushed some golden hair in her face. She brushed it away. "Maybe Digger bumped into him when he came up here, then decided to chum around with him."

"Why?"

"Digger might have wanted someone local to show him around."

"Doesn't matter. When Braithwaite gets hold of them, both their asses are toast."

Chapter 27

Mortal Life's Daily Challenges

After talking to the Limboite, Braithwaite's intercom buzzed.

"You have a visitor, Mr. Waite," Adele said from the outer office.

Braithwaite checked his Rolex. Three-thirty. He had more calls to make. Dortmunder, called "Slick" for his oil spill activities several mortal decades ago, headed Braithwaite's short list of calls. Dortmunder had gotten rid of three of Orlando's top drug traffickers and was also overseeing the Grove kid's escort service. He called yesterday afternoon to ask for more inferiors to help with the increased workload. They had to decide on a specific number and where to send the new workers.

Braithwaite also needed to touch base with the inferior Blunden, known as "Chopper," for his former practice of leveling forests. Blunden's present assignment of taking over local racketeering had begun three days earlier. He had already disposed of two of the city's top racketeers.

The next move was to appropriate the theme parks. Since Cletis had come up missing, a backup plan was needed. Braithwaite had to contact the Legion and order a dozen other inferiors brought up to make up for lost time.

"Who is it?" he asked Adele.

"Richard Grove. He says it's important."

"Send him in, then."

Braithwaite checked his Rolex again. He would make sure this only took a few minutes.

His face pale and drawn, Grove shuffled in.

"Sit down," Braithwaite said. "Make this brief. I'm busy."

Grove collapsed in the chair facing the desk.

Judging from his visitor's defeated demeanor, Braithwaite suspected something sour was going on. Braithwaite knew he wasn't going to like whatever it was. "You've got the floor," he said.

"Well, sir, I've come on behalf of the Diocese to ask a very large favor."

"Like I said, make it brief. I have businesses to run."

A deep sigh. "We're not pleased what...what you have in mind."

"Regarding?"

"This land deal. We're...worried."

"About what?"

"We're afraid your associates are affiliated with...with terrorist organizations."

Braithwaite groaned. Hypocrisy was all right under normal conditions, but not when it affected something he was working on. America was the epitome of hypocrisy. It murdered, corrupted, and abused people all over the world. But when dealing with a different culture, these idiots screamed religion and fair play.

Braithwaite found the situation amusing.

"Worried, eh?"

"Yes, sir..."

"Think I'm playing in the wrong ballpark?"

"Well, sir—"

196

"Profits are profits, right?"

"That's really not the issue…"

"You people are in on this for profits. Admit it. It's how you've all become so filthy rich, right?"

"Well…"

"Am I right?"

"Well, yes, but—"

"My associates are willing to pay three times what that land is worth."

"The profit margin isn't what is bothering us."

"Let me guess. Camel jockeys aren't exactly in your social circle."

Grove sighed.

"You prefer dealing with people who feed the poor and shelter the homeless? Their money is more to your liking, right?"

"Mr. Waite, you really don't seem to understand—"

"Grove, I know how to make men wealthy and powerful. The Legion's been doing it for centuries. You and your associates know this."

"We just think—"

"I know what you think." Braithwaite couldn't believe how stupid these mortals were. If they weren't Diocese members, he would've summoned them all here and turned them into mulch for the potted plants in the lobby. "You obsess over wealth but turn into girly-girls when something doesn't go your way. Isn't that about it in a nutshell?"

"We're just concerned…"

"This country is jam-packed with every conceivable profiteer, opportunist, crook, and schemer, which is why it is so popular with the

197

Legion. I'm not about to nullify a multi-billion-dollar land deal because a few wussies are soiling their undies. Get it?"

"We just don't want to sell our land to foreigners we're not familiar with."

"You only want to deal with foreigners you know?"

"We have a good system here. We don't want it jeopardized."

"You know who I am, Grove?"

Grove swallowed audibly. "Yes, sir..."

"Know who and what I represent?"

"Um..."

"Um is not an answer."

"Well yes, but—"

"But is not an answer, either. You know why I don't like but? I'll tell you why. It puts a damper on all the words in front of it. In other words, Grove, you just said yes, then but, which, to me, means no. Am I right?"

"Yes, but—I mean yes..."

"Good. Back to our original thread. Your good system. You know why you have one in the first place?"

"Yes..."

"Dandy. I'm real glad your long-term memory is working. Otherwise, I'd have to give it a little tweak. You don't want that, do you?"

"No, sir."

"Of course you don't. Know why? You see, if I go in there and do some tweaking, you're gonna have some problems you never had before. It's like

198

when someone who doesn't normally work on your car suddenly works on your car. Get it, Grove?"

Grove lowered his head.

"Let me give you a teensy-weensy example. I'll do just a miniscule amount of tweaking for now, just to show you how this could turn out slightly unpleasant for you. Are you ready, Grove?"

The idiot stiffened in his seat.

"For now, I want you to go right back and tell your bosom buddies what I just said about my land deal. If they don't like it, they can come here and tell me themselves. And in the meantime—and this is where the tweaking part comes into play—you might also remind every single mortal you encounter during the next twenty-four hours that you are one genuinely stupid asshole. I mean everyone. From Wifey Poo to every half-wit, nitwit, and witless twit you may come across in your everyday travels. Understand?"

***

A few minutes after Grove left, Braithwaite received a call from Dortmunder.

"Problem, sir. Just came up."

"Oh, fine." After the business with Richard Grove, Braithwaite was beginning to miss dealing with demons. At least they weren't wussies. Most of them, anyway.

"One of our girls is missing."

"One of the whores?"

"Sorry, but we're not that lucky."

Braithwaite groaned. "An escort?"

"I'm afraid so."

"The Grove kid know yet?"

199

"I wanted to tell you first. I'm not exactly sure how involved you want him."

"Like I told you, I don't want him doing any hands-on work yet. I want him to observe for a while. When did this happen?"

"I've just been told about it."

"Hold on." Braithwaite dialed the kid's number.

Grove answered on the second ring. "Sir?"

"Get your ass up here. Right now." He clicked off and got right back with Dortmunder. "Anyone looking for this bitch?"

"I've got a man on it right now, but it might take a while."

Ah, lovely. Braithwaite suddenly felt a strong need to vent. A traffic fatality or two, perhaps. "How long is a while?"

"There's no way of telling."

"I get it. Incompetence is all I've seen since we came up. You were here before. You should be used to this shit."

"Yes, sir. Because of cluelessness and stupidity, I was able to make nearly twenty million on contracts for oil spills and other jobs before the Government even suspected something sleazy was going on."

"How long did it take before they put out that contract on you?"

Dortmunder chuckled. "It was six months before they decided to use their hit squad. During that time, I made three million more in profits. But this was after the first two hits failed."

The intercom buzzed.

It was Adele. "Daniel Grove, Mr. Waite."

"Have him come right in."

The door opened. Grove, looking pale and confused, rushed right in. Braithwaite gestured for him to sit. "Tell me what happened with this girl," he told Dortmunder.

"One of our boys in Valet Parking told me he had the limo take them to Disney Village for a candlelight dinner at one of the hotels. According to their chauffeur, the girl went to the ladies' room and never came back."

"No one's seen her since?"

"Not a sign."

"You don't think one of her former pimps snatched her?"

"Two of them are out of the picture. I scared the third one so bad, he's probably in another country by now."

"Who was her date?"

"Some Hollywood big shot hosting a game show at Universal who wanted some high-class arm candy. He's really pissed."

"Find another female. The best one available. Give him a freebee, but make sure she gets her usual fee. He'll be happy once she pops him off a few times."

"Sounds good."

"You don't think he staged that fiasco, do you?"

"These high-priced celebs have to keep a low profile. He does something stupid, the paparazzi will show up and nibble at his short curlies."

201

"Some of these hotshots actually like the paparazzi," Braithwaite said. "But I'd guess none of them wants a shit peddler snapping shots of them slapping flesh with a hooker. You know where this leaves us, right?"

"Yes, sir. Traffic's increased quite a bit since I took over. There's a world of difference between the high-priced girls and the whores working the Trail. I can't possibly substitute a Trail tramp when the clients are expecting high-class for big bills."

Braithwaite hung up and lit a cigar. Mortals could fuck up anything. And they were every bit as irritating and stupid as they were during the Middle Ages. Give them the best education and the latest technology and they were still nothing more than walking shit-processors.

The Grove kid sat watching him nervously. Good. The more nervous you were, the more alert you were. The more you learned.

"Talk to your old man lately?"

"No, sir..."

"He and his friends have really pissed me off."

The kid said nothing. He didn't have a clue. The kid was young, impressionable. He needed to learn a few things. It would help him develop a hard competitive edge.

He also needed to be taught a lesson so he didn't do the same stupid things as his old man.

Braithwaite pushed some smoke across the desk. "Kid, your daddy and his chums don't want me doing business with Arabs."

The kid fidgeted. "We're all still a little gun-shy over Nine-Eleven, sir."

202

Braithwaite grinned. "Yeah, Agaliarept had a field day with that gig."

"Who, sir?"

"A colleague. One with a really dark sense of humor. He enjoys explosions and fires even more than I do."

"I thought...we all thought they were acting...on behalf of—"

"Yeah, yeah, yeah. That Allah thing. Praise Allah this, praise Allah that. Agaliarept thought up that snappy slogan on his own." Braithwaite chuckled. "Like I just said, he's been having a field day the last eight or nine decades with his dancing puppets."

"You mean he's the one responsible?"

"He loves sheep, kid. We all do. It's fun having your very own brain-dead remote-control toy. We also like it when someone else takes the blame for what we've been doing. But that's another subject. Getting back to you daddy..."

"What exactly did my father say, sir?"

"His friends are worried that my business associates will bring over suicide bombers and turn their precious land into a training ground for terrorists."

"Yes, sir..."

Now was the time to give the kid an example of harsh reality. "How's that new girl working out? The brunette."

The boy sat up. "She's doing fine..."

"Good. We both want her to do even better, don't we?"

The boy stiffened. "B-Better?"

"She's pretty and sufficiently bright. And judging by the colorful red blotches breaking out all over your face, she's already done a number on you."

The boy trembled.

"This tells me she's got the skills we need elsewhere. We both know what she should really be doing, don't we?"

Grove paled instantly. "I don't know what you mean, sir…"

"That call was from one of my men. One of our girls has disappeared. This leaves us one short."

The kid's eyes grew. "One…short?"

"Yeah. Know what that means, don'tcha?"

"But sir…Ashley was hired on as a—"

"The missing girl is young, skinny, brunette, and pretty. Just like your girlfriend."

"But I promised her—"

"Promises are all right if you're an idiot, but they don't have much cash value. Go give her the good news. Make sure she knows she can make a grand, possibly two, in one night. That should sweeten the pot."

Chapter 28

Status Report

Shortly after five, Adele buzzed Braithwaite, announcing his latest visitors.

The door opened. The blond Limboite and the stinkweed came in. She wore a sleeveless blouse, form-fitting Capri slacks, and a pair of expensive-looking tan leather pumps.

This bitch seemed to grow a tad easier on the eyes each time he saw her. Maybe when this was all over, he'd engage her in a little old-fashioned mortal sex. He didn't do it too often, mostly because he considered it silly and a waste of his valuable time. Explosions and fires were much more stimulating to the palate.

He might make an exception in this case, though.

Besides, servicing a superior would rid her of some of her irritating arrogance. For her own good, of course. She should be cowering in his presence. He didn't like it that she wasn't. Everyone should cower in his presence.

There must be something wrong with her.

"What kept you?" he said. "And where the hell is the shit-eater?"

"We spotted him at the Safari," she said. "He was with someone."

What the hell was she talking about? Cletis was a loner. A dung beetle. He had the social skills of a maggot, only he smelled worse. Not many creatures enjoyed being with a shit-eater. Just other shit-eaters. "Male or female?"

"Male."

"If you'd said female, I'd know you were lying. I've seen some genuinely stupid females up here, but we're talking about an idiot who'd rather watch a rhinoceros taking a dump than seek out a woman. Even the most patient female would pass at that."

"We have no idea who this other guy is."

"I didn't give him permission to team up with a mortal. Some idiot must have approached him to ask directions. This town is overflowing with idiots."

"We were too far away to see what was going on," she said.

"Um, couldn't you get a tad closer?"

"Security was all over the place. We had to hide."

This babe sure was irritating. He sighed. "And when you were finished hiding?"

"We lost sight of him when you called."

"When I called?"

She nodded.

"Are you saying I kind of distracted you? Took your eye off the big picture? Made things a tad hairier?"

"I didn't say that."

His blood began to boil. "What are you saying?"

"He slipped away pretty easily. He obviously knows someone's after him."

"Of course he knows. He's not a complete idiot. He knew he was in deep shit when he lost his cell phone."

"That makes it harder to keep an eye on him."

"It's your job. Yours and his." Braithwaite tilted so he could see the inferior hiding behind her. "That miserable idiot hiding behind you."

"Then you want us to resume our search?" she said.

Damn, she was irritating. "No, you may stay right here and do your fucking nails. Or let me watch you brush that luscious golden hair. Of course I want you to resume your search!"

They turned to leave.

He suddenly stood. The urge was too great. He had to show her who she was dealing with. It would make him feel better. "Come here. I want to show you something."

She walked over to where he stood at the window.

"Step closer. Pick someone from the crowd."

"Pardon?"

Stupid bitch. "I said, pick someone. Anyone."

"But why—"

"Pick someone, dammit."

She stared at the heavy swarm moving down the walk, then pointed to a man in a dark suit crossing the street with the flow.

"Good choice." Braithwaite closed his eyes. Fire. Smoke. Chaos.

He opened his eyes.

Dodging the crowds, the man bolted across the street like a gazelle.

Relief washed through Braithwaite like a splash of cool water.

"What's he doing?" Blondie asked.

"He's headed for the nearest drugstore."

She gave him a blank look.

He shrugged. "You can't set fire to a church without chemicals."

Her face paled. "But why?"

Braithwaite grinned in satisfaction. "Why not? I love explosions. They help me relax. They're a perfect outlet for having to deal with so many idiots with brain malfunctions."

She remained staring at the window. The arrogance had finally left the big blue eyes.

Braithwaite thoroughly enjoyed the moment. "Now go find that shit-eater. You've only got two days left."

***

A slender, dark-haired young woman in a pink sleeveless blouse and black pleated skirt sat hunched over on the sofa in the reception area. Her elbows rested on her thighs, her hands clasped so tightly together, her knuckles had turned white. Her dark, muddled thoughts drifted over to Tiffany.

The girl's world had crumbled. Darkness and cold terror made her tremble.

Broad Waist's image filled the girl's tormented mind.

"Mr. Waite will see you now," the middle-aged receptionist told the girl.

No response.

"Miss?"

208

The girl shook herself. She got up slowly and approached the door as if walking to her own death. She stared numbly at the door. Finally, she reached out with a shaky hand, pushed it open, slipped reluctantly through the gap and eased the door shut behind her.

"Tifferoo?" Chip nudged her.

"Yes?"

He jerked a shaky thumb toward the glass doors. "We need to get out of here. Like, now?"

After one last glance at the closed office door, Tiffany joined him.

Chapter 29

Ashley's Horror

"I-I wasn't h-hired for...for that, Mr. Waite..."

Ashley's pulse hammered as the wash of warm relief flooded down her back. She was surprised her voice even worked. It took three tries to get it out.

Mr. Waite appeared even bigger than she remembered. That wasn't hard to figure since he was sitting when she'd dealt with him at the O-Town. But now that he was standing, he dwarfed her. At nearly five-ten in her heels, Ashley found herself staring at his massive chest. The top of her head barely reached his slab-like chin. His mass blocked out the window behind him and most of his desk.

She forced her mind on the important issue. "I was hired to be a receptionist," she added, forcing the words out.

"I'm aware of that."

Couldn't he tell how distressed she was? He couldn't be as mean as he appeared, could he? Surely he possessed some understanding. According to Daniel, this man was a successful businessman. He should be able to read people. He would know when someone wasn't cut out for a certain job.

"I just started a few hours ago and—"

"And you're already well on your way to advancement."

"I don't consider that...advancement."

He shrugged. "From a desk job to a field agent in just a few hours? I consider that a super advancement."

Was he kidding? How could anyone consider being a prostitute an advancement?

"Mr. Waite, when Daniel hired me—"

"He obviously didn't appreciate your true potential."

Now he was being insulting. "I would never have hired on if I knew—"

"In a word, there's been a change of plans," he replied flatly. "I know, I know. That's six words, but it gets the job done, doesn't it?"

How could he be so glib about this?

She gathered up what courage she could find to maintain her position. She wouldn't agree to this, of course. The sooner he realized it, the better.

"Even if I wanted to, which I don't, I couldn't possibly do something like that. I'm just…not that way."

"Are you telling me you don't want to do it?" Waite raised his chin, dwarfing her even more.

"I really don't." Of course she didn't want to do it.

She hated Daniel for putting her through this in the first place. He said it wasn't his idea. But somehow that didn't matter.

He had trembled standing there in the doorway of the help desk area not fifteen minutes earlier, looking both frightened and angry. "I had no idea Mr. Waite was going to do this."

"But why, Daniel? Why?"

"One of the other girls, well, she came up missing. Mr. Waite needs a replacement in a hurry."

"Why me?"

"I don't know what to say, Ashley. I'm sorry. Really and truly."

She couldn't believe he'd betrayed her. Couldn't believe he hadn't stood up to Waite on her behalf.

"You're sorry. You've come here to tell me my life is ruined and you're sorry."

He said nothing. He stared at the floor. She could tell he wanted to escape, to avoid her gaze.

He'd become a total stranger. His eyes were cold, detached. They no longer resembled the beautiful blue eyes that had smiled at her over dinner the night before. Or even earlier today, when she'd first come in.

"Sorry isn't enough, Daniel."

Without another word, he turned and left.

The nasty Mr. Waite had done it. She didn't know how, but he had.

Waite remained gazing down at her, his small black eyes glistening with arrogance. "You're joining my stable of whores. You'll do it because you'll have to."

The word "whores" made the heat come back.

"But I don't have to," she said. Despite her efforts, she sensed her reserve slipping away. She gritted her teeth and forced herself to stay strong. "I didn't sign up to be an escort."

"But I've already told you, I'm changing the game plan."

"I don't care, I—"

"You'll do as I say."

His impassive expression told her he would not listen to reason. This was a mean, stubborn man.

She suddenly missed the O-Town. Strange, how you missed something you never liked when you faced something far worse.

They would take her back. She was certain of it. They always needed waitresses.

She would rather wait tables for the rest of her life than become a prostitute.

She took a deep breath. "I'm going to turn around right now and leave."

Waite grinned and waved. "Bye-bye."

That was easy. Maybe her defiance had somehow registered to him that she was stronger than she seemed.

She turned.

"Not so fast."

Some invisible force stopped her before she could take her first step.

"You'll need money for your new outfits. When you go out on your calls."

She opened her mouth to protest.

Mr. Waite's small, simmering black eyes suddenly grew brighter. A knot of searing heat plunged inside her, turning her thoughts into mush. Gasping, she grabbed her temples. The heat grew, becoming a blazing fireball growing rapidly in her head. She saw only a solid wall of blinding white before her. Her body trembled. Her muscles stood out in knots. She opened her mouth to scream, but dizziness took over. The floor shifted, swaying beneath her feet.

My God! What...what was that?

The fireball vanished. Instantly.

She slowly straightened. Her heart still thrashed. The pounding in her head had ebbed into a warm, heavy stillness. The floor swayed one last time.

"What...happened?" She barely heard her own voice.

"Changed your mind, didn't you?"

She stared at him, noting the smugness, the air of power, of superiority. He had done that. Somehow, he had made that happen.

"I knew you'd come to your senses." His grin raked through her.

"Did you...do that?" She could barely hear her own voice.

He shrugged. "Do what?"

My God. What sort of monster am I dealing with?

His hand disappeared in his trouser pocket. When it reappeared, his fist gripped a thick wad of bills. They looked like hundreds. "Here's two grand." He quickly peeled off several bills and held them out.

Numbly, she watched her own hand reaching out and closing around the bills. She wanted to toss them back in his face but instantly realized that would be impossible. The same horrible power that had created the fireball kept her fist wrapped around the money.

"Buy something sexy. Frederick's of Hollywood sells the stuff I prefer. It would help if you had bigger tits, but I understand you females have gimmicks for that. Do whatever it takes."

He went back to his desk, picked up his phone and asked Adele to connect him with someone named Lawrence Blunden. He pulled a cigar from his jacket pocket, sniffed it, and bit off the tiny end.

Ashley remained gaping at the bills. This was not right, and she was not going to go along with it. It didn't matter that this terrible man had somehow done something horrible to her mind. She would not become a prostitute.

Just put the money back on the desk blotter and leave.

She took one step toward his desk.

Waite's simmering black eyes focused on her as he lighted his cigar.

Do it. Dump the money and—

Waite's eyes grew brighter.

Her heart thumping, she spun on her heel and ran.

Chapter 30

Partners

As she and Chip crossed the parking lot, many people were getting in their cars and backing out of their spaces. It was well past six—possibly the end of the workday for many.

Tiffany hardly noticed the line of traffic inching down the aisle. She couldn't stop thinking of the dark-haired young girl they'd seen in Breath Mint's reception area.

The fact that the girl was there in the first place told Tiffany something was wrong. If you were forced to deal with a super demon, you faced serious trouble.

Tiffany could sympathize. Her own world had crumbled when she was just a few years younger than that girl. Just a handful of years after Daddy was accidentally killed by a drunken hunter, Mom, needing stability again, brought home the man who would be instrumental in turning Tiffany's world upside down.

Her new stepfather was a nasty man with cold, dead eyes, who wasted no time sneaking into her bedroom to say good-night by cradling her in his arms. But even at her tender young age, Tiffany felt it was wrong. Stepdad insisted it was okay. "Stepdaddies loved making their little girls feel special." But since "Mom would be jealous if she knew," Stepdad felt it best if they "kept it our little secret."

Just before Tiffany's thirteenth birthday, while Mom was visiting her sister in Chicago for the weekend, Stepdad came into her room one night. His breath reeking of whiskey and cigarettes, he cuddled up beside her on the bed and put his arm around her, telling her he loved her and wanted her to touch him, then fell into a drunken stupor.

Tiffany never told her mother. Thinking she had personally been guilty of causing the incident, she locked herself in her bathroom at night whenever she heard him coming up the stairs. But after five years of living in constant fear, Tiffany knew she had to leave.

One morning, while Stepdad was at work and Momma was out shopping, Tiffany crammed her favorite things into a suitcase. Carrying most of the money she had saved working weekends at the movie theater concession stand, she walked the eight blocks to the Greyhound bus terminal and bought a one-way ticket to Hollywood.

For three hours she sat on a hard wooden bench, agonizing over leaving her mother and the house where they had once been a happy family. A house that was no longer filled with warm memories. A house where a man she hated and feared now lived.

Seeing the dark-haired girl on Broad Waist's couch had brought everything back. Tiffany saw herself on that couch, lonely and miserable, desperately wanting relief from the pain. The image was even stronger than what she had experienced with Darcy McGill only days before, outside the novelty store in Raven, Ohio.

"What's wrong, cupcake?" Chip asked.

"What makes you think something's wrong?"

"How long have we known one another?"

"Two weeks? One week? No it's about ten days. Wait, now that I think of it, it's not quite—"

"Jeez Louise!" He crossed his eyes. "Sorry I asked, okay?"

"I accept your apology."

"Terrificoso. Now tell me something."

"Sure."

"What's bugging you?"

"It's really nothing."

"We've got enough worries of our own. Remember?"

"I remember."

"Good. For a second you had me frightened."

"Weren't you just frightened up there?" She pointed to the building.

"Why?"

"And you're frightened again?"

"What's wrong with that?"

"You can be frightened as much as you like. This is a free country, after all."

"Good. Then—wait a minute." He rubbed his eyes. "Tifferoo, are you trying to play with my head?"

"Not really."

"Good. I don't think I'm ready for something like that."

"Tell me when you're ready, okay?"

The dark-haired girl came out of the building, trudged down the walk, and approached a black

218

Honda about ten spaces down from the concrete steps.

"I've got an idea," Tiffany said, watching her.

Chip sighed. "I know I'll probably regret this as soon as it comes out of my mouth, but what the hell? Here goes. What's your idea?"

"We need to get around, don't we?"

"Get around?"

"To find Digger."

"Well, since he's not standing right here, it would be a safe assumption to say yeah, we need to get around if we want to find him."

"Wheels."

He frowned. "You mean like a car?"

"Or truck. Or van. Something with wheels."

"You're trying to tell me we'll find the Digger guy easier with you driving around?"

"I don't know my way around this place."

"Then what's your idea?"

"We need someone who lives here and has a car."

"You actually know someone who lives here?"

"Not exactly…"

"Don't tell me you're thinking of stealing a car…"

She couldn't believe he'd just said that. "You know me better than that."

"So how do you intend to get a car if you don't steal it? We can use fake money to buy one, but I don't see any dealers in the immediate area. Besides, it's getting dark."

"Follow me, okay?" She broke into a run, heading straight for the Honda.

***

Slumped over the wheel, Ashley struggled to fit the key in the ignition. It wouldn't work; her hands shook too much.

Easy. Take a deep breath.

She took a deep breath.

And continued to shake.

She sat back and closed her eyes. And tried hard to understand what just happened in that horrible man's office.

How could anyone do something like that? What powers could enable someone to inflict such pain? Such intense heat?

He was inhuman. A monster.

She had to get away from here.

But could she get away?

Someone possessing such powers would easily find her. To make matters worse, he was a businessman. And businessmen had contacts. And friends.

Even if he had no idea where she went, he could use his connections to find her.

There had to be a way out of this. She could never have sex with a stranger for money.

She loved a guy not very long ago. Just a couple of years, actually. She fell for him while she was living on the street.

She had been so silly back then. So naïve. She really thought he loved her and wanted to spend the rest of his life with her. She had no idea—at least, not then—that bad boys lived only for the moment. They had no conscience. No remorse. And they cared only about themselves.

It made her feel dirty, used. Discarded. Like trash.

It also opened her eyes, made her see more about life in those two years than she'd ever seen before.

But nothing could prepare her for what happened just a few minutes earlier. It terrified her, told her how easily her entire world could collapse.

Her worst fears had finally come true. She was going to become a prostitute. And nothing could stop it.

Drive, she told herself. Drive until you're far, far away. That horrible man just gave you enough money to get out of here.

Two thousand bucks. That was enough, wasn't it? It certainly was enough to pay for the gas it would take to get her to Pittsburgh.

But what then? Could she find Uncle Rob? Would he help her? Would he put her up while—

A tap on her window.

She cringed, twisting in her seat.

The beautiful blond lady and the slender redheaded guy she'd seem outside Mr. Waite's office stood just a few feet from her door.

They no doubt followed her to tell her something else about her new job. This lady was probably one of their escorts. She had to be. She certainly was beautiful enough.

She had no idea what the skinny guy did. He was probably some sort of errand boy.

But it didn't matter. If they were connected with the nasty man, they were either evil or in as much trouble as Ashley.

221

Ashley didn't want to know anything else. She didn't need more aggravation.

If she could just drive away...

But she couldn't. They had seen her. If she pulled away, they'd tell Waite. He would find her and do something even worse to her.

Another tap.

Her pulse fluttered as she rolled down her window. "Yes?"

"I'm Tiffany," the blond lady said. "And this is Chip."

Tiffany's bright smile quickly made Ashley forget her depression. Strange feelings of warmth filled her being.

"Just in case you're interested," Tiffany said. "We're doing an errand for that awful man. We wouldn't if we didn't have to. I can't stand him. He makes my skin crawl."

Ashley couldn't believe what she just heard. Was this lady lying?

Tiffany's large, glittering blue eyes said no.

"Really?" Ashley asked. "You're not just saying that?"

"He's disgusting. He's also arrogant and repulsive. Like I said, he makes my skin—"

"Tifferoo..." Her companion glanced nervously behind them. "I think you need to keep your voice down."

"Hush." Still looking at Ashley, Tiffany said, "Could we possibly ask you to give us a lift?"

"A lift?" Has she heard her right?

The redheaded guy said, "It's like this. I get in, Tifferoo gets in, and you cart us around like

222

groceries. Only we're not really groceries—not now, anyway. Under different circumstances, maybe. I do tend to wilt the ol' petals if I don't get enough sunshine and water."

"Will you please stop?" Tiffany elbowed him in the side.

"You know better than that, Tifferoosky." His ears wiggled and he farted.

Ashley couldn't help it—she laughed.

And unlocked her doors.

Chapter 31

Backyard Goodies

Cal parked the stolen Riviera in front of a single-story block building on Oak Ridge Road. The sign, Patti's Lounge, painted in sloppy black letters on a jagged piece of plywood, pierced the ground next to the front slab.

Cal got out and stretched. Slipping away from those damn Safari security guards had tired him out. No biggie. After some Wild Stuff, burgers, and fries, and a few hours with a hooker, he'd be good as new.

Digger wandered off to the other side of the lot and stared into the darkness.

"What the hell are you doing?"

Digger sniffed twice, then grinned. "I'll catch you later."

Damn. Dig was weirding out again.

In school, Cal had read about creative dudes like Michelangelo working on their masterpieces for weeks on end without bathing or eating. Edison did the same shit—

going weeks without taking a bath because he was too hung-up inventing stuff.

This might explain Digger's weirdness. Boy didn't care for whiskey, good food, women, or anything else a normal dude liked. Didn't even want to buy new clothes with the money he lifted.

Cal wanted desperately to learn to open locks and start up smooth rides without an ignition key.

He also wanted the skinny on how to con tourists out of wads of cash.

But if weirding out over elephant shit and eating dried-up leaves came with the package, he was going to have to rethink all this.

Before Digger could reach the hedges separating the back yard of the bar with another yard, Cal said, "You'd rather look for something funky-smelling in those bushes than go inside for a few stiff belts?"

Digger nodded eagerly.

Bummer. Dude was serious.

Cal needed to get on the stick and learn whatever he could as soon as possible. Then he could dump this weirdo.

He just hoped that learning a few of the basics wouldn't change him.

Last thing Cal needed was to start getting off on elephant shit instead of hot babes.

***

Cal took a table in a dark corner and ordered a double Wild Turkey on ice.

The place looked like somebody's basement. A pool table sat at the far end of the room. About a dozen small round tables filled the center of the main area. Half a dozen old farts sat drinking or nodding off. The air-conditioning was on full but couldn't dilute the heavy reek of whiskey, sweat, and cigarette smoke.

The juke was on soft, which suited Cal just fine. Sounded like one of those smiling Vegas dorks crooning about true love.

Two bone-thin chicks perched on stools tried making time with the bar guy, but anyone could tell he wasn't interested.

Chicks were too damn old. Probably had tatts everywhere to disguise the wrinkles.

Orlando had plenty of hookers to choose from. They were only a few miles from the Trail. He would rather pay a little more for something decent to look at, anyway.

When Digger came back from his hedge-sniffing excursion, he and Cal could pick up a hooker and find a room. Tomorrow morning, he'd force Dig to teach him the money scam thing. That was the world's greatest trick—even better than starting up rides. Imagine walking up to a dude and conning him into giving you twenty bucks...or forty...or a hundred. Cal had been trying that for the last two years but could only manage pocket change. Dig got money all the time and always made off with bills. Big ones, too.

He has to teach me. I'll leave his ass stranded in the middle of the porno district if he doesn't.

Cal was on his third round when Digger came back, smelling like he'd rolled around in something dead. Good thing no one was sitting at the next table. Otherwise, they'd probably be thrown out.

Dig plopped down clumsily in the chair and grinned stupidly. His eyes were glazed.

"What the fuck did you get into?" Cal asked.

"Found some cool plants in somebody's back yard."

Uh-oh. This sounded suspicious.

"Cool plants?"

"They smelled really neat. Super—I mean totally—cool. Wow. I mean wow!"

Cal had seen that expression before. The same glossiness, the same blood-shot eyes. Usually on guys smoking heavy shit.

Dig looked stoned.

"Tell me about those plants."

"Brought some with me." Digger reached into his pocket. He dropped a clump of dried brown leaves on the table, then picked up one and brought it up to his nose. His eyes grew. "Doesn't it smell good? I mean gooood..."

Luckily, no one cared about them, everyone napping or too busy getting drunk or buzzing along with Wayne Newton from the juke.

Cal picked it up for a closer look. Yep, just as he'd figured. He leaned toward Dig and lowered his voice. "You moron. This is grass!"

Dig squinted. "Really?"

"Yeah."

Dig looked confused. "But grass is green and skinny and smooth. This stuff is brown and crinkly—"

"I don't mean grass, asshole. I mean grass. Marijuana. Hemp. Weed. Smoke. You found somebody's home-grown stash!"

Digger giggled. "You sure are funny, Cal." He blinked. "What's Mary-wanna?"

"You're kidding me—right?"

Dig just grinned stupidly.

This boy had to be screwing around. Hell, everybody knew about grass. Knew about doughnuts, too.

It's just his weird-ass way of fucking with me.

"What'd you do with this shit?" Cal asked.

"Whaddya mean, Cal-Pal?"

"Listen carefully. Okay? Con...cen...trate. How'd this shit make you stupid? You smoke it?"

"Smoke it?"

Cal knew Dig didn't have matches but had to ask anyway. You didn't get this fucked up just by sniffing this shit. "Did you roll it up in paper? Hold a match to it? Light it? Then inhale and wait for the top of your head to pop off?"

Digger giggled. "You can be really, really, really funny sometimes."

"I'm serious, now. How'd this shit mess you up?"

"I wanted to mix it with rotten fruit but couldn't find any. I saw these little-bitty trees in a neat little row behind a house, but they didn't have anything on them but—"

"You got any more?"

"Trees?"

"Focus, now." He held up the clump in his fist. "This shit."

"I put a whole bunch in the car."

"A whole...bunch?" This sounded too good to be true. They could make some serious cash selling local weed and wouldn't have to worry about hitting tourists for a while. "How much is a whole bunch?"

"Those Walmart bags in the back seat of the car we took? I filled them up."

"Jesus, Dig... Five bags? Of home-grown grass?"

228

"I figured I could find some fruit in the morning and mix it all up and have it for breakfast."

All they needed now was for someone to walk past the Riviera and glance in the windows.

Cal jumped up. "We need to get outa here!"

Digger yawned. "I'd really like to munch on something. I heard a dog barking in the yard next door. If I could just make a stop there first—"

"C'mon." Cal found some bills in his pocket. "We need to split now!"

Chapter 32

Joining Forces

Colonial Drive had become a swollen mass of glaring headlights, growling engines, blaring horns, and biting exhaust fumes.

As the growing darkness gradually dimmed the tall, imposing buildings behind them, Ashley sensed her spirits lifting. Not all the way, but enough to help her start breathing again. The suffocating coil inside her had eased up considerably.

Perhaps it was because Tiffany and Chip, two strangers who seemed very nice, had distracted her, made her laugh.

But she had to remind herself that this was just temporary relief.

Flashes of her encounter with Mr. Waite came back. A sour taste filled her mouth. I am not a prostitute, she reminded herself. I will never have sex with a stranger for any amount of money.

"We know you're not a prostitute," Tiffany said from the seat beside her.

Ashley stiffened behind the wheel.

Was she hearing things? Imagining them? Maybe it was the darkness. Her night vision didn't seem to be working properly.

Tiffany's lips weren't moving.

But she'd somehow spoken anyway.

The explanation was clear: she was losing her mind. That nasty man did it. He did something awful to my head.

"You're not losing your mind," Tiffany said, once again without moving her lips.

My God. I am going crazy...

"No, you're not."

Why do I think I am?

"You're not used to someone with powers."

Powers. Like that fireball Waite had shoved into her skull?

No. Tiffany wasn't evil. She was beautiful. And nice. And sweet. She couldn't possibly be a monster.

But what sort of powers is she talking about?

"Tell you later."

"Where are we headed?" Chip asked from the back seat.

"Maybe Ashley can take us to her place, if that's all right. I don't think we'll be able to do much at this time of night anyway."

"My place?" Ashley's hands tightened around the wheel. Introducing Tiffany and Chip to Momma—especially if Momma was drunk—would not go well.

Tiffany smiled. "If you don't want us there, it's all right. We can find a motel."

"It's not that I don't want to..."

"Don't worry." Tiffany's lips had stopped moving again. "Your mother won't bother us."

Ashley sighed tiredly. "But you don't know her. She's been going downhill since Daddy—"

"Is he dead?"

"He left when I was little."

"And your mom's trying to cope."

"In her own self-destructive way."

231

"So did mine."

"Your father left you, too?"

"My dad was killed in a hunting accident."

"I'm so sorry."

Tiffany's beautiful face filled with sadness.

Strange, how much they had in common.

"What's the plan, then?" Chip asked. "I know I'm a little...messy-looking." Ashley snuck a peek in her mirror and caught him glaring at Tiffany. "I wouldn't want to embarrass anyone..."

"If you don't mind the living room couch," Ashley said.

"It sure beats a rock garden."

"A what?"

"Don't ask," Tiffany said.

Chip went back to looking out the side window.

"So what happened with your mom?" Ashley sent over to Tiffany.

"She brought home a stepdad to replace my father."

"And?"

Tiffany's eyes turned into glacier pools. "He liked me. A lot."

Ashley turned back to the road ahead. Which was worse? An abusive stepdad? Or a mother who stayed drunk? She wanted to say something to lighten the moment. To tell Tiffany she felt for her.

"I'm dealing with it," Tiffany sent over.

"It must have been terrible for you."

"Thanks for caring."

"I owe you and Chip my thanks as well."

"For what?"

232

She didn't know where to begin or how to say it. She somehow felt that Tiffany and Chip had saved her, although she had no idea why she felt this way. The fact that she no longer felt like driving away and never coming back was enough. At least, for now.

"Showing up when I was ready to…to…I don't know what I was going to do. I felt trapped and had no idea how to get away. You couldn't have shown up at a better—"

"Your place far from here?" Chip asked.

"Just a couple of miles."

"You live alone?"

"Just me and my mother."

Chip sighed. "I'll try to behave."

"You'd better," Tiffany said.

"You two are really nice," Ashley said. "It's hard to believe you both work for that…that Mr. Waite."

"Only because we have to," Chip said.

"How do you stand it?"

"I keep reminding myself that he won't hurt us as long as he needs us," Tiffany said. "Chip deals with it by hiding behind me while we're in his office."

"Hey, I've got issues."

"Even so, Waite is kind of overpowering."

"I know what you mean," Ashley sent over. "When he ordered me to be one of his prostitutes, I tried to leave."

"What happened?"

x

233

"A scorching fireball penetrated my head. I thought I was going to die. I don't know what he did or how he did it. I just know he did it."

"He did it, all right."

"How? What sort of power does he—"

"We're looking for two dorks," Chip said. "One of them also works for Waite."

"What about the other guy?"

"He's probably a local and doesn't even know Waite. We think they got together up here somewhere."

What did he mean by that? "Up here?"

"The first guy came up from Hell."

Had she heard him right? It sounded like he'd said Hell...

That just couldn't be, could it? Hell? The place the damned supposedly went after death?

Ashley cleared her throat. The words came out sluggishly. "Did you say...what I think...you said?"

"What did you think I said?"

"Sounded like...Hell..."

"Cool. Glad to see you're paying attention."

Chapter 33

Close Call

A skinny little Indian guy wearing a white turban rang them up at checkout. He glanced at Digger once or twice, wrinkling his nose and frowning.

Digger knew what that was all about. The weed he'd found. He smelled strongly of it. But that wasn't all. It felt almost like someone was crunched up inside him, pounding on his brain with a tiny hammer.

Weird stuff, though. Cal called it "grass." He had also called it a couple of other things Digger couldn't exactly remember. But it sure made the room move around funny. It was like being at sea, almost. It also made the inside of his mouth bitterer than anything else he had put in there. Even that dried-up fruit, leaves, and dog-smear concoction he found the day before hadn't left him with such a bad aftertaste.

Digger needed to stick with his favorite foods. This "grass" crap—as well as that funny doe-nut Cal had given him—was bound to mess up Digger's taste buds.

Cal bought two roast beef sandwiches, a small bag of chips, a cheap corncob pipe, and a bag of dried figs Digger found hanging from a metal tree near the cash register. Cal also found a small bag for his shaving supplies, some mouthwash, and a nifty leather kit with tweezers, nail clippers, and a penknife.

235

Digger picked up a box of Trojans from the display beside the candy bars and sniffed it. "What's this?"

Cal frowned. "Put it back."

"What is it?"

"Don't tell me you're that stoned."

Trojans. Troy? The Trojan horse? It didn't smell like horse poopers... Even if it was, the packet was much too small for a decent sample.

What else could it be?

"What's it for?"

"Forget it. You don't need it."

"Do you?"

Cal stared at it and shrugged. "Maybe I'll get a pack, now that I'm thinking about it." He pulled it off the shelf and dropped it on the counter with the other stuff.

The clerk pushed everything into a paper bag, rang it up, and gave Cal his change.

Flashing red and blue lights bouncing off the glass turned the parking lot into a fireworks display.

"What's going on out there?" Digger asked.

"A cop. What's it look like?"

"Think he'll see our ride?"

"It's the only car out there, doofus. I kinda figure he might notice it."

That certainly didn't sound good. "So what'll we do?"

"Sneak out through the back."

"What about all that neat stuff I found?"

Cal gave him one of his looks again. "I don't think trying to get it right now would be a real swift career move."

236

Cal had a point. They had taken someone's car. It would be stupid to think they could go back and grab the bags from the back seat. Digger could easily do it with a trick or two, but Cal would surely ask him a bunch of more questions about his gift.

But it might be worth a try anyway.

"Want me to see if I can sneak around while he's not looking?"

"You're an idiot."

Digger decided not to press the issue and followed his friend out through the back.

"Across the street." Cal pointed to the lights just beyond the busy intersection. "Lots of rides parked behind that steakhouse. But don't act suspicious and whatever you do, don't look at the cop."

Suspicious? He had no idea what Cal meant. "How do I not act suspicious?"

"Just keep looking stupid. Then we won't have anything to worry about."

Before Digger had time to think about what Cal had just said, a voice behind them yelled, "Hey, you!"

The cop stood behind the Riviera, his notepad out, his right hand resting on the gun in his holster.

"You talking to me?" Cal asked. "Or him?"

Frowning, the cop stared at Digger. "Turn around."

Digger didn't budge. Don't look at the cop. And don't act suspicious. Keep looking stupid. And don't do anything to the cop. Too many things to keep track of.

"You!" The cop sounded angry.

Cal elbowed him in the side. "Idiot. You want to get us arrested?"

"You told me not to look. Or act suspicious. Or—"

Cal elbowed him again. "I changed my mind, asshole!"

Dig turned to face the officer.

The cop jabbed a thumb at the Riviera. "Know anything about this car?"

"Looks like a Riviera," Cal said.

The cop sighed. "It belong to you?"

"I wish."

"See who was driving it?"

"We were inside, buying stuff." He held up the bag.

"Anyone else in there?"

"Just a hairy little guy with one thick black eyebrow, wearing a turban."

The cop stiffened and reached for his radio. "What's he doing in there?"

Digger shrugged. "He's behind the counter, operating the register. He doesn't say much, though. He seems like a quiet guy."

The cop groaned and dropped his arm. "Anyone else?"

Cal said, "I think I might've seen someone sneak into the john..."

What did Cal mean by that?

Digger turned. "I didn't see—"

Cal elbowed him again, this time really hard.

The cop snatched his radio from his shoulder and began talking into it.

Cal and Digger crossed the busy highway.

238

Chapter 34

Retiring for the Night

Teddy's Olds was parked in the drive behind Momma's Toyota.

Her heart sinking, Ashley pulled up to the curb and turned off the lights and ignition. Now what? Just go on in with her new friends and hope for the best?

It would be so nice if Momma and Teddy were in the bedroom, or maybe passed out on the living room sofa.

"Why not let me take care of this?" Tiffany's soft, soothing voice drifted into her thoughts.

In the darkness of the cab, Tiffany's face showed understanding and concern. Nonetheless, Ashley feared this wouldn't go well. "But how? Momma's impossible to deal with when--"

"Are we going inside or what?" Chip's chin rested between the bucket seats. "It's been a long day. I'm so tired, the ol' petals are starting to wilt."

Best get this over with. Ashley was exhausted as well. The ordeal with Waite had zapped what reserves she had.

With a heavy sigh, she pushed open the door. "Be forewarned. Momma has company. And she's probably drunk."

"So what?" Chip asked.

"We'll be barging in on her."

"And?"

"She's got company."

239

He shrugged. "I'm still waiting for the punch line."

"Why are you so dense?" Tiffany asked.

"That's the punch line? I'm disappointed. And still confused about why we should care about her mother being drunk."

"She's trying to seduce someone who's probably also drunk," Ashley said.

"In other words, she won't want to be disturbed," Tiffany said.

"Shuckers," Chip said, climbing out. "And I so wanted some quality entertainment before bedtime."

Teddy sprawled on the living room sofa, his jacket draped over the recliner, his tie pulled down. Tufts of curly red hair sprouted from his open collar. His glossy eyes instantly sized up Ashley, nearly popping out of their sockets the instant Tiffany walked in.

Momma came out of the kitchen, carrying drinks clinking with ice. She stopped cold and glared at Ashley.

"Momma...this is Tiffany and Chip."

Grinning, Chip pointed to Tiffany. "She's Tiffany. I'm Chip."

With a grunt, Teddy heaved himself up, buttoned his collar and straightened his tie. "I'm Teddy." He crossed the room, approaching Tiffany with quick, eager steps. "Where'd Lynn's baby daughter meet such a fine young lady?"

"Here's your drink." Momma stuck the glass in his face. Whiskey ran down the side, making tiny dark spots on the faded green carpet.

240

Teddy took the glass but didn't turn away from Tiffany. His grin remained. Momma's face broke out in blotches of red. Ashley recognized that look all too well. It wouldn't be long before Momma lost it.

"Tiffany," she thought, her pulse racing," if you're gonna do something, you'd better do it soon..."

***

Teddy's soft, clammy hand closed over Tiffany's like a damp washrag.

He was so much like Stepdad. The same glossy-eyed look. The same glint of slobber on his lower lip. The same way his eyes stayed so long on her breasts. The images in his head told her he was married but didn't take it too seriously.

Time for him to go home. His thoughts were clear, so she knew he wasn't very drunk. She wouldn't feel guilty for putting him behind the wheel and sending him on his way.

"So...where're you from, honey?"

"Peoria. And my name is Tiffany." It took her two tries to wrench her hand free.

"That's in Illinois, isn't it?"

"It was when I left."

He snickered. "Where'd Lynn's baby daughter meet such a delightful young lady?"

"Chip and I met Lynn's baby daughter in town today," she said flatly, and planted her next thought

(go home and drive carefully)

firmly into the man's overactive brain.

He yawned and suddenly noticed the cold drink in his left hand. "You know what? I need to call it

241

a night." He put the glass down on an end table and picked up his jacket.

Ashley's mom rushed over. "I thought you wanted to stay...longer."

He shrugged into his jacket. "All of a sudden I'm really tired. I overdid it at the board meeting this afternoon. I need to get home. Got that meeting at eleven and—"

"I just made fresh drinks. Just stay a while longer..."

Tiffany planted the same thought into the mother's brain. The woman went silent as Teddy shuffled over to the front door. As soon as he left, she set her drink down beside Teddy's glass and went down the hall.

"Not even a warm and affectionate good-night?" Chip scratched his head. "I'm hurt. And offended."

"Are you really?" Ashley asked.

"No, but I am confused."

"You're always confused," Tiffany said.

"What's your point?"

"The point is, you're always confused."

"So?"

"And befuddled."

"Doesn't that mean the same thing?"

"I'm so confused right now, I don't know."

The bedroom door slammed shut. He stared toward the hall, then turned back to Tiffany. "What did you do, lamb chop?"

"When?"

He sighed. "Never mind."

242

"Your petals really are beginning to wilt." She hoped he would just forget the whole thing. She didn't want him asking questions about her growing powers. Not now, anyway.

"They've obviously overdone it for the evening," Ashley said, looking relieved.

"My petals?" Chip asked.

"Don't be silly," Tiffany said.

"I'm only being myself."

"Same thing."

Ashley glanced at Tiffany. "Thank you so much..."

"No problem. Now can we do the sleeping arrangements? I'm kind of tired, too."

"Chip, there's the couch. It's more comfortable than it looks."

"Looks like the old Teddy Bear flattened one of the cushions with his oversized butt load. But how about my bud? Got a place for her?"

"Tiffany can sleep in my bed. I've got a loveseat—"

"I don't want to put you out of your own bed."

"I don't mind."

"But—"

"Jeez Louise." Chip dropped onto the couch and lay back. "If this is gonna turn into a catfight, I'd like to see the clothes flying off before I shut my eyes."

"You're boring," Tiffany said. "And really tacky."

"Best I can do when the petals are in the wilt mode."

***

243

Ashley shrugged out of her clothes. Tiffany sat on the edge of the bed, watching her. Ashley stepped into the closet and tossed them in the laundry basket, then sat down on the loveseat in her bra and panties.

Her mind reeled. She wanted to ask Tiffany the question that had been plaguing her but didn't know how to bring it up.

"Just ask," Tiffany urged.

Ashley smiled. "I keep forgetting you can get into my head. I imagine that comes in handy."

"Sometimes I hear more than I really want to."

"I can only imagine."

"You're wondering about that Hell thing, aren't you?"

"Was Chip kidding?"

"Not that time, I'm afraid."

It made no sense. There was no way a beautiful, sweet woman like Tiffany could come from Hell. Ashley refused to believe it. Bad people went to Hell. Good people went to Heaven. At least that was what she had been taught.

And what did that horrible Mr. Waite have to do with any of this?

"Waite's a demon," Tiffany said. "One of the really nasty ones."

Ashley tried to read Tiffany's expression. Her eyes said it all. It also explained many things. The man's arrogance. His dark aura. His intense hatred. The frightening episode in his office.

The car explosion outside the Café drifted into her head.

Why was she suddenly thinking about that? It couldn't possibly have anything to do with—

Tiffany's nod was slight.

"My God. He caused that?"

"Explosions get him off."

Her next question was even more important than her first. "If he's a demon...what's he doing here?"

"Every hundred years, one of them goes back down to the Pit and someone else comes up to take his place."

"For what?"

"To run things."

She continued staring at Tiffany, waiting for the woman to break out in laughter. Or say she was kidding. "Are you serious?"

"How else do you explain the Holocaust? The Taliban? Psychopaths? Serial killers? Child molesters? Kids who torture animals? School shootings? Oklahoma City? Nine-Eleven? You honestly think people with their small minds and knack for messing up simple things can actually do all this bad stuff on their own?"

A shiver ran up her spine. "We're actually being controlled? By demons?"

"Waite has brought up inferiors to work for him. One recently turned up missing. Chip and I have to find him."

"Tiffany, this doesn't make sense. You're...alive."

"We've been given substance while we're up here, but Chip and I are dead. Waite and his inferiors are also dead."

245

Trembling, Ashley reached for Tiffany's hand. Warm.

Tiffany closed her eyes. Her blouse instantly changed into a black tee shirt, her tan Capri's a pair of faded jeans. A pair of Nina Elisha clogs covered her feet.

Ashley immediately pulled away. "Wow..."

"I can wear anything now. It's just an illusion."

"I guess that's how you can slip into my head as well?"

"Among other things."

"Like what?"

"We'll talk more tomorrow. Right now, we need to get some sleep. Chip and I only have a couple of days to find Digger and his friend. Then we've got to go back down."

"Why were you even down there in the first place?"

"I was dragged from Limbo into Hell."

"Why?"

"A demon wanted me."

"For what?"

"Guess."

Ashley's jaw dropped. "You're not kidding, are you?"

"I wish I was."

Ashley's head grew hot. She wanted to close her eyes and wake up from this terrible nightmare.

"We both lost, didn't we?" she said, mostly to herself. "You were dragged into Hell and I'm about to become a prostitute. Doesn't seem like there's a God. Or justice. Or anything good out there to protect us."

"I don't want you to worry." Tiffany lay down on the mattress. "We'll figure something out."

"Do you honestly believe that?"

"I have to. So do you. So does everyone. Otherwise, what good is it, being here in the first place?"

Ashley turned off the light and lay down.

Tiffany was right. If you didn't believe things would turn out, you might as well just give up.

She just couldn't imagine how they'd get out of this. Not with a powerful demon calling the shots.

But as bad as things looked, she trusted Tiffany. No one could have handled Momma and Teddy so easily. And anyone who could read minds was someone you wanted on your side.

She decided to go along with Tiffany's wishes. Something in Tiffany's eyes made things seem better than they were even though the overall picture didn't look good at all.

Before she drifted off, Ashley promised herself that she'd find some way of helping Tiffany stay here with her.

DAY FOUR - Finding the Dung Beetle

Chapter 35

Morning Delivery

After breakfast, Tiffany helped Ashley wash the dishes while Chip sat at the table, munching on an eggshell.

Ashley couldn't believe Chip had eaten three of those as well as the coffee grounds right out of the coffee pot. Death sure did strange things to people.

"You actually like eggshells?" she asked.

He burped. "Doesn't everybody?"

"Don't forget his coffee-grounds obsession," Tiffany said.

"It's good for the petals."

"I just can't get over the fact that you and Chip are dead," Ashley said.

"You'll get used to it after a while."

For Ashley, getting used to all this had taken a back seat. She was trying to understand why things no longer seemed hopeless. Though she slept very little, sitting up frequently to make sure Tiffany still lay in her bed, that Tiffany hadn't been some illusion brought on by Waite's horrible trick, Ashley actually felt more at peace with herself.

Things had developed a dreamlike quality. Just twenty minutes ago, while Ashley fixed breakfast, Tiffany came in wearing a bright red tank top, light-blue hip huggers, and a pair of shiny black tennis shoes with a red streak spanning the outer rim.

This weirdness gave Ashley a strange sense of hope. If Tiffany could change her appearance, talk through her mind, and handle people like Momma and Teddy so easily, things might not be so bad. With Tiffany on her side, Ashley felt less helpless.

Ashley wiped her hands on a dish towel. Something suddenly occurred to her as she glanced at Chip. "Can you change your outfits as well?"

"Abso-damn-lutely."

"Then why are you wearing the same thing as yesterday?"

He grinned. "I'm what you'd call low-maintenance."

"Is that what you call it?" Tiffany asked.

"What would you call it, lamb chop?"

"A total lack of imagination."

"I could deck myself out in a clown's outfit, if you like."

"No need," Tiffany said. "The hair and the ears are more than enough."

"Oucherino."

The doorbell rang.

"I wonder who that could be." Ashley hoped it wasn't Teddy or someone else Momma had met at the bar.

"I don't know." Chip swallowed the last of his eggshell. "But since you have to answer the door anyway, why don't you find out?"

Ashley crossed the living room, approached the door, and peered into the peephole.

It was Daniel Grove.

249

A stab of heat sliced through her.

Tiffany came out of the kitchen. "Who is it?"

"The jerk responsible for my life going down the tubes."

"You'd better see what he wants."

The heat inside her grew. "I'm really not interested in anything he has to say."

"Do it anyway."

Ashley sighed. Tiffany was right. If Daniel kept ringing, Momma would hear it, get up, and ruin their pleasant morning. But she couldn't bring herself to open the door. She didn't want Daniel standing on her doorstep and surely didn't want to talk to him. He had built up her hopes. Her dreams. She trusted him, thought he really wanted to help her. She even wanted to go out with him again.

Tiffany's voice was soft and gentle. "We don't want to do anything to anger Waite. At least, not right now. The less we have to deal with him, the better."

She opened her mouth to protest, but Tiffany sent over a swell of soothing warmth, extinguishing the fire building up within her. Tiffany gently patted her shoulder and went back into the kitchen.

Her heart racing, Ashley eased open the door.

"Hi." Daniel smiled weakly.

Ashley said nothing. She could feel her left hand closing over the doorknob. Her right hand had become a fist.

"I wanted to stop by and see how you were doing."

How could he possibly show his face, let alone say something like that?

250

Be calm. Show him you're above all this. "Everything's peachy. Wonderful. Couldn't be better."

"You look really nice and—"

"Forget the compliments, Daniel. We're way past that, now."

He rubbed the back of his neck. She could tell he was uncomfortable. It made her feel a little better.

"This sudden change. It wasn't my idea."

"We've already been through this, remember?"

"I just want you to know that I had nothing to do—"

"You didn't stop it."

"If there was any way for me to do it—"

"I know. You'd do it in a heartbeat."

"I really would."

He sounded sincere, but she couldn't find it in her heart to let him off the hook. Because of him...

The rage fought its way back.

"I'll think of that when I'm with someone who's paid you and your nasty friend a lot of money to treat me like a piece of meat," she said.

"I wish you could understand how badly I feel about this."

"I wish you could understand how badly I feel about it."

"You honestly think I would've asked you to leave the O-Town if I thought this would happen?"

Bad enough she had to think about this at all. Or even try to determine Daniel's role in it. She wanted him gone. Off her street. Out of the neighborhood. She also wanted to hose down the stoop—as well as the driveway—as soon as he'd left.

"I don't know what I think right now," she said.

"I understand."

"Then you can also understand how angry and disgusted I am. How betrayed I feel. I liked you, Daniel. I thought…I even hoped…it might lead to other things."

He lowered his head.

She made a move to close the door. "If that's all—"

"I…brought something." He reached into his jacket pocket. His hand twitched as he handed over a plastic package. "A cell phone."

"But I already have—"

"This one's for your clients."

It took all her strength to open her fist. When he dropped it into her palm, she flinched at its coldness, its clamminess. It felt like something disgusting, something dead. It made her tremble. She wanted to toss it in his face. Or drop it and mash it with her shoe. She also wanted to scratch his face, then hurry back to the kitchen and wash her hands.

Her rage consumed her, and she slammed the door in his face.

Chapter 36

Cal's Brainstorm

Cal sat up and fought down the strong urge to puke.

Tasted like a slimy critter had crawled in his mouth while he was asleep, took a dump, then died before it could escape.

Damn weed tastes like shit, but it sure fucks up your head!

Whoever grew this batch really knew their shit. Probably made the family dog piss on it to spice it up. That was probably why Dig liked it so much.

Too bad Cal had only got to smoke one small bag he stuck in his pocket before their trip to the 7-Eleven. If that stupid cop who found the Riviera had any brains, he snatched the rest for himself. Fucker might be buzzed out of his fucking mind by now.

Of all the lousy luck.

He sat up and surveyed the dark motel room.

Alone again. They were too damn shitfaced last night to go back out and hunt down a hooker.

Where the hell was Dig? Probably crawling around in a dumpster, searching for his breakfast.

That boy was way beyond weird. Cal couldn't even get him to smoke the stuff last night. Sucker only wanted to eat it. Who in his right mind would pass up the chance to smoke some home-made, knock-your-head-off weed?

The door opened. A blast of blinding morning sunlight exploded in.

253

"Close that fucking door!" Cal buried his face in the pillows. The urge to puke grew even worse. "Wanna blind me?"

Dig closed the door, making everything dark again. "You'll never guess what I just saw."

Cal lowered the pillow. Fucker nearly blinds me, then expects me to play a stupid game. "Me giving you the finger?"

"The what?"

"This." Cal held it up.

Dig squinted. "What's that?"

"What's it look like?"

"Your middle finger."

"Good guess."

"What's it mean?"

Asshole's humor just ain't cutting it this morning. "Means I'm not in the mood for your stupid guessing games."

"There's a rodeo in Kissimmee this afternoon." His eyes got all bright and funny.

"So?"

"A rodeo, Cal. Know what a rodeo is?"

"A bunch of weekend cowboys trying to look cool flopping around on horses and bulls so they can get laid later on."

"I saw a bunch of pictures on the billboard." He giggled. "All kinds of neat critters!"

Cal sighed. Here we go again.

"You'll have fun, too. I promise."

"How can I have fun at a fucking rodeo? I don't like horses or bulls, and if I step in horse shit, I'll have a fucking bird."

Dig shrugged. "Might be ladies there..."

The dude had a point. "I guess I can put up with it for an hour or so if there are babes wandering around..."

"Let's get there early, okay?"

Cal lowered his legs over the edge of the bed. Fighting the dizziness and the sour taste in his mouth, he looked his friend right in the eye. "When are you gonna teach me some magic?"

Dig's grin dissolved. He sat down in the chair in front of the curtains. "I told you, I'll teach you one of these—"

"Listen up. I've been carting around your weird ass all over this crazy place for days. You'd be lost without me. Least you can do, give me a few pointers."

"After the rodeo, okay?"

Fucker's playing me again. "How long can it take to teach me that tourist money con?"

"It'll take a little while to cover the basics..."

It was time to up the ante. "I'll bet your boss can teach me."

Digger stiffened. "My boss?"

"The guy that makes you shit your drawers whenever I mention him."

Dig trembled.

Cal grinned. He'd obviously hit pay-dirt. "You never did say why you never talk about him."

Dig busily nibbled his lower lip.

"Well?"

"I messed up when I shouldn'ta...I just messed up..."

"Keep going. This is interesting."

Dig lowered his head and grabbed his sides. He had obviously done a bang-up job of messing up.

Cal found himself intrigued. "C'mon, dude... What'd you do?"

Silence. Still grabbing his sides, Dig gawked at the floor.

Cal's thoughts raced. Things were finally beginning to clear up. Dig had the Touch. He also had a boss. Could this mean Dig's boss also had the Touch?

Finding Mr. Big suddenly seemed a nifty idea. If Dig had really fucked up, the big man was probably looking for him. He might even be grateful if Cal brought Digger back.

Just how grateful?

There was one sure way of finding out.

"I'm still waiting," Cal said.

"I can't talk about this." Dig's voice became a raspy whisper. "You understand, don't you?"

"Sure." Best drop this—for now. "No problem. Let's just get out of here."

Dig looked hopeful. "Are we going to the rodeo?"

"It's where you want to go, isn't it?"

"Goody. Wow!" Dig jumped up in his chair. He clapped his hands together. "Let's go! C'mon. Hurry!"

"I need a shower first."

"Why?"

Cal shrugged. "I smell."

"I don't smell anything."

256

"You play with elephant turds and roll around in dogshit."

"So?"

"Your smeller ain't exactly something I'd want to trust in an emergency."

"But—"

"I ain't going anywhere without a shower, okay?"

While Dig pouted, Cal shuffled into the bathroom. He turned on the shower and got the water set at the right temperature. He rinsed out the dead taste in his mouth with a healthy gulp of mouthwash and brushed his teeth. Then stepped into the shower.

An hour at the rodeo wouldn't hurt anything. Maybe Dig was right; maybe he'd find a hot babe. Later on, he'd trick Dig into revealing where Mr. Big Shit was.

Fifteen minutes later, he toweled himself dry, packed his travel bag, and followed an excited Dig outside. They crossed the lot, where their stolen Caddie Supreme sat waiting.

A loudspeaker crackled behind them.

"Orlando Police Department! Freeze! You are both under arrest!"

Chapter 37

At the Mall

Her head enveloped in a warm bubble, Ashley parked the Honda in the front lot of the Mall.

Her palms were wet. She wiped them on the front of her jeans while staring numbly at the store entrance.

She had been here many times as a little girl with Momma and Daddy. They enjoyed coming here on Friday nights and Saturday afternoons. She fondly remembered the times she went with Daddy into the men's clothing store and laughed when he made faces at her in the mirror while trying on suit jackets. The times they had dinner at the Chinese restaurant before it closed and became an electronics store. The times Momma walked into a store, all dressed up, her head held high, little Ashley happy to be with her and anxious to grow up to be just like her.

A very long time ago. Maybe not in years, but in the many changes their lives had endured.

Once she realized the past was dead, Ashley experienced no further fond memories. The building itself had suddenly become a sort of edifice of doom before her very eyes. A large part of her new nightmare world. She was no longer a little girl and no longer with Daddy or Momma. She would no longer be going inside to watch Daddy make faces at her in the mirror. She would no longer be going into the Chinese restaurant for her usual shrimp plate and to watch Momma and Daddy giggle when it was time to crack open their fortune cookies.

This time, she would be going inside to buy the sexy outfits she needed for her new career. She was a hooker now. A prostitute. She would be giving her body to men for money. And all memories of her childhood were dead and buried.

If only she could close her eyes and transport herself miles from here...from Waite, from Orlando, from herself...

The nausea erupted low in her gut.

"I'll help you through this." Tiffany's warm voice drifted over.

Ashley forced the nausea back down. "I just don't think I can do it."

"Sure you can. Just open your door and--"

"That's not what I'm worried about."

"Just remind yourself that you're getting some beautiful outfits for free. Don't think past that."

"I can't help thinking what the outfits will be for."

"One step at a time, okay?"

"What about--"

"Are we going in?" Chip asked.

Tiffany told him to shush.

"Does that mean yes?" he asked.

"It means shush."

"Glad you explained things so well, precious."

With a deep sigh, Ashley used every ounce of will power she could find within herself to push open the door.

***

259

Two hours later, Tiffany and Ashley left the dressing rooms, paid for their purchases and left the store.

Chip, his red mop more disheveled than usual, caught up behind them. "Finished already? It's not even next week yet."

Tiffany knew he was going to whine about this. Men always did. Her dad constantly found some excuse to fix something at the house whenever her mom wanted to shop for clothes.

Boys will be boys, Tiffany thought. Even when they're dead.

"Not that I'm complaining or anything," Chip added. "Just that the ol' leaves always shrivel up when they're deprived of fresh sunshine for more than a week at a time—"

"Oh, stop. Finding the right outfits takes time. Here. Make yourself useful." She thrust two large bags at him.

He frowned. "Thanks, precious. Is it my birthday?"

"You really need to come up with better jokes."

"Best I can do when the ol' leaves—"

"You can be such a whiner."

"All right, all right. I'm through whining."

"Thank you."

"You want me to try these on now? Or the next time I want to look dazzling and mysterious?"

"They're not your color."

"How come guys can walk into a clothing store, buy whatever they want, drive home, eat supper, crack open a beer, and sack out in front of the tube in the same amount of time?"

260

"Guys don't care how they look," Tiffany said.

***

While Chip put the bags into the trunk, Ashley unlocked the doors and got behind the wheel.

She knew she should be depressed and angry. After all, she had just bought nearly two thousand dollars' worth of sheer sexy outfits to wear for strangers. But somehow she didn't feel that badly. Tiffany had made her feel much better. She even helped Ashley through her mental block of trying on outfits she wouldn't be caught dead wearing under normal circumstances. Tiffany made the experience a pleasant one, far from the traumatic horror she imagined for herself.

"I guess we need to look for Digger now," Tiffany said, sliding in beside her.

"Any idea where to start?"

"We thought that since you live here, you might—"

The ringing of the cell phone in Ashley's purse made her jump.

"Oh, no..." She mashed her back against the door, gawking at her purse as if a bomb ticked away inside it. She could tell by the strange ring that it was the phone Daniel had given her.

Her pulse hammered. Her skin buzzed as if she had just been scalded. "It's starting." Her voice sounded weak. "Already. Even before I've had a chance to—"

"Don't worry." Tiffany patted her trembling forearm. "This is where I come in." She closed her eyes.

"But what can you possibly—"

261

The ringing stopped.

Chip climbed in back. "We ready to start looking?"

Ashley couldn't stop smiling. Tiffany had done it. With her strange powers, she stopped the horror.

"Thank you so much," she sent over.

Tiffany winked. "We're ready," she told Chip.

262

Chapter 38

In Lockup

The small dark cell reeked of stale cigarette smoke, B.O., and stale vomit.

Digger paced the room. Cal sat on a bunk, his head in his hands. Digger could tell Cal still felt bad from that grass stuff Digger had found.

Digger also felt bad, but not because of the grass. Instead of heading off to the rodeo, they were tossed in the back of a squad car and hauled off to jail.

This was awful. This was just plain awful.

I have to get out of here. I want to see the rodeo.

It wouldn't be that much of a problem to get the cell door open. When you were a trickster, you always had something up your sleeve. He wanted to tell Cal what he planned to do, but Cal was in one of his moods. A headache from the grass, for one thing. And Cal was probably still angry with him for what he'd done in the squad car.

At the time, Digger wasn't thinking of Cal getting angry. He just wanted out of the squad car. And when Cal saw Digger's cuffs sitting on the seat as soon as the cop shoved him in, Digger thought his friend was going to freak out.

"What the fuck do ya think you're doing?" Cal whispered, his head jerking back around to the door slamming in his face.

"We're not going to the rodeo, are we?"

"No shit, Sherlock."

"I gotta get out of here!"

"I kinda feel the same way, but ya know what? We're kind of arrested at the moment. I don't think Blue Boy outside will go for us slipping away."

Digger shrugged. "Getting those off was no problem."

"Maybe not for you. Listen. And try to put this together." Cal shifted in his seat.

"Here." Digger reached for the cuffs. "I can get those."

"The hell you will." Cal pulled away. "Don't you realize that if we run, Blue Boy might shoot us?"

"For a stolen car?"

"For escaping. We'll have the entire police force looking for us. Even if you manage to get away from them, I'll still be here. You'll have to find your stupid rodeo all by yourself. That might pose a problem, too, since you don't even know how to drive. And don't count on hitching a ride. Not too many folks will pick up someone who smells as bad as you."

Dig sat back and sighed. Cal had just ruined everything.

I'll just have to do something later on.

He picked up the cuffs and slipped them back on.

Right now, Digger paced the cell, studying the distance between the bars and sniffing the lock. He didn't see much of a problem, slipping out of this cell. No one else was here, so it wouldn't be difficult.

"You're not thinking of doing something stupid, are ya?" Cal asked.

"That depends."

"On what?"

"How long we gonna be here?"

Cal sat back on the hard bunk and sighed. "We stole three rides, brainiac. Cops tend to take that kind of shit seriously. In other words, don't count on checking out your rodeo today."

"What'll they do to us?"

"First, somebody's gotta come in and book us."

"What's that?"

"You're not serious."

Digger just shrugged. All he could think of was a couple of cops coming in and swatting them with books.

But that didn't sound right. Why would they even do that?

"I don't know what that means."

Cal shook his head. "You're seriously strange if you don't know what being booked means. Here's what happens. A couple of cops come in, cuff us again, then take us to a room where they'll take our prints and our picture, then—"

"Take our prints?"

Cal held up his hands and wiggled his fingers. "These babies."

"What for?"

"They have to do that before they bring us back here."

"Why?"

Cal shrugged. "It's their thing."

Digger had a feeling Cal was being his usual sarcastic self. "You mean they do it because they like doing it?"

"That's right, Dig. It's their favorite thing. Keeps 'em busy. Entertained. Out of trouble."

Digger went over to the iron bars, studied them a few seconds, then eyed a small black box fitted into the ceiling. "What's that?"

"Sucker probably goes off if you mess around with the lock."

"What about that?" Digger pointed to another box mounted near the opposite corner.

"That's a camera. Like the one at the Ford place. Why? You don't want to wave and act silly again, do you? They'll shave our heads, clip our nails, stick us in a padded room, and force-feed us stewed prunes until our teeth fall out."

Digger pressed his chest against the bars, extended his arm, and pointed at the camera, then went to the other end of the cell and did the same thing to the black box. He covered the latch with both hands and closed his eyes.

About thirty seconds later, the door clicked open.

"Son of a bitch! How the hell do you do shit like that?"

"Shhh." Digger stuck his head out into the hall. "Stay close, okay?"

***

Outside, a guard sat behind a small metal desk directly across the hall, his nose buried in the Sentinel. Digger watched him through the small square window in the door.

266

"Now what?" Cal whispered. "I kinda think he'll notice if we just open the door and walk on out."

Digger knew this wouldn't be hard at all. Just a little of that telekinetic stuff he had learned from a couple of the subs down in Hell would be all it took.

Digger closed his eyes. You have an itch. Scratch it...

The guard immediately reached up and scratched his ear, then went back to his paper.

Cal shrugged. "That's it? We're supposed to sneak out of this fucking place while he's scratching his ear?"

"Let me try again." Digger closed his eyes. Scratch harder. Longer.

The guard lowered his hand, reached between his legs, and scratched, peering over his shoulder as he did.

Cal groaned. "Can't you do better than that? Make him whack off or something."

"Won't that get him fired?"

"Your point?"

Digger took a deep breath and focused.

Reach down there again. This time, slide your hand inside your drawers to get the job done right, then shift around so no one can see what you're doing, and—

The guard reached down and turned his chair toward the left. When he shifted in the chair, his elbow nudged the Styrofoam cup sitting on the desk blotter, tipping it over.

Cursing loudly, he jumped up and tossed the paper. He yanked open the bottom drawer of the desk, grabbed a handful of paper towels, and hastily wiped up the spill. He looked down at his wet trousers and cursed. Then tossed the empty cup and the towels in the trash. Shaking his head, he disappeared around the corner.

"That's the ticket." Cal slapped him on the back. "Let's clear out."

***

The big room bustled with male and female cops. Some carried papers and talked on phones. Others escorted handcuffed ladies in tight, revealing clothing to their desks. Three uniformed cops sporting brush cuts sat typing away on keyboards.

"Wanna just take our chances?" Cal asked. "Everyone's kinda busy. They might not even notice us."

Digger didn't reply. Even though he still wasn't used to this modern world, he knew they couldn't do that. The odds of them sneaking out without anyone glancing at them would be astronomical. Digger didn't want to do anything to jeopardize their trip to the rodeo.

No, they needed a distraction here. A big one.

"Something you might like to share?" Cal asked.

"I used to be able to throw my voice."

Cal gave him that look again, the one that made Digger feel genuinely stupid.

"I used to be able to belch, hiccup, and fart at the same time," Cal said, shrugging. "It's cool when you're ten. But when you're grown up, doing something like that'll kill you."

268

Digger wondered if Cal was joking again. Cal's solemn expression said no. But there must be some reason why he brought that up.

"What's that have to do with anything?" Digger asked.

"It makes just about as much sense as your voice-throwing thing."

Digger decided not to waste time arguing. He peered around the corner, took a breath, and opened his mouth wide.

A moment later, a high-pitched scream exploded down the hall marked RESTROOMS.

Three cops halted in mid-step, spun around, and bolted across the room. Half a dozen uniforms jumped up from their desks and followed.

Two young women in short skirts and low-cut blouses handcuffed to chairs watched the commotion, their heads darting in both directions.

The brunette with huge gold earrings and tatts covering her skinny tanned arms pulled at the cuffs. She twisted around as Cal and Digger rushed past. "Hey, honey! You wanna take me with ya?"

"Sure do, baby," Cal said, grinning. "You got the keys to those cuffs?"

She scowled. "What're you? Nuts? If I had those, I wouldn't need you."

"Dig? You wanna get those cuffs off this lady?"

Digger turned and stared at his friend. Cal looked sincere. "We have time for that?"

"Not really."

"C'mon, honey. I'll make it worth your while."

"Hear that, Dig? She'll make it worth our while."

Digger scratched the back of his neck. "Will she take us to the rodeo?"

"Well, honey? Will you?"

"Sure, baby. Just get me out of this."

"You got a car, baby?"

"No, but I know where we can get one."

Digger didn't think she was telling them the truth. She sounded like some of those harlots who used to dance at Caligula's banquets. And many of the ladies who performed for the super demons in the Castle. "C'mon, Cal. We really don't have time for this."

"Sorry, baby." Cal shrugged. "You heard the man. Another time, maybe? How 'bout Saturday?"

"Asshole!" She tugged violently at the handcuff.

"Sunday good for you? Maybe after church?"

She yelled a string of heated profanities as they scurried down the hall.

***

Outside, the parking lot across the street formed an endless sea of glittering shards of glass and metal. Finding another ride would pose no problem at all.

Digger and Cal rushed across the street.

Digger hoped Cal wasn't angry. "You're not mad, are you?"

"For what?"

"For not bringing that lady with us."

"Hell, no. Why the fuck should I be mad?"

"Maybe you wanted to bring her with us…"

"She wasn't my type. Anyway, that was really great what you did back there. You never did tell me where you came from, did you?"

"No. I never did."

Cal chuckled. "C'mon, Dig. We're buds. We've been through a lot, haven't we?"

Digger didn't like it when Cal got personal. He always had the feeling Cal wanted to know more than he needed to. There was no reason to let Cal or anyone else know about Braithwaite. It just wasn't safe.

"A long way from here," he told Cal.

"Miami?"

"Farther." Some nice-looking rides sat quietly in the shade of a palm tree at the corner of the big lot. Any one of them would serve as an excellent choice. "What kind of car do we want now?"

"I don't care, as long as it's comfortable and flies. When I met you on International Drive, had you been working there long?"

Cal was getting personal, all right.

"A few days."

"Before that?"

"Before that what?"

"What were you doing?"

"Same thing I was doing when we met."

"On International?"

"Church Street."

"When you came to town?"

Digger stopped walking and turned to Cal. "Why so many questions?"

He shrugged. "I'm thinking maybe we ought to stick around here."

271

"Why?"

"Church Street has just as many tourists as International and the theme parks. Maybe we should—"

"We need a ride." Digger resumed scanning the lot.

"We hit too many tourists in one place, they're bound to get the cops after us."

"I wanna see that rodeo."

"I'm kinda hungry. Haven't eaten in—"

"Don't they have food at a rodeo?"

"I could really go for a sit-down eating place."

"I wanna see the rodeo."

Cal sighed and went silent. Then he said, "You and your fucking rodeo."

They crossed the street and picked their way down the long aisle.

A dark-blue Lexus sat in the shade at the other end.

"How about that one?"

"Fine," Cal said.

"You sure?"

"I said fine, dammit."

"You're mad."

"Shut up and open up the damn car."

Digger sighed. Now he felt badly for upsetting Cal. But he had no choice. "Why are you mad?"

"I'm not mad."

"You look mad."

"I'm just hungry."

"Don't they have food at the rodeo?"

"We've been through this before. Yeah, they have food at the rodeo."

272

"Will you feel better after you have some food?"

"Yeah. I'll feel great. Fucking great."

"I'm glad."

"I'm glad you're glad. Now open up that damned car."

273

Chapter 39

Ashley's Brainstorm

Ashley kept up with the southbound flow.

She had no idea how to help her friends with their job. Orlando was a huge, sprawling place, with heavy traffic and chaos everywhere. The theme parks were miles from one another. Finding someone would be impossible.

"Is there something about this guy that would give me an idea where to look?" she asked. "I mean, is he the executive type? Should we be looking for software conventions, maybe?"

Chip laughed. "Not in this lifetime."

"Is he athletic?"

Chip chuckled. "I wouldn't exactly put him in that category."

This wasn't helping at all. "Does he like junk? Collectibles? Would he spend his time in flea markets? Antique stores?"

"Nope."

"Does he have any hobbies? Music? Art?"

"I wouldn't accuse him of having good taste, either, girl."

"Then what does he like? I mean, everyone likes something, right? Even though he's dead, he must have been fond on something when he was alive…"

"Our man is quite partial to fresh, tangy dung."

She glanced at him in the rearview. Grinning as usual. He might be in one of his impish moods. Or struggling with one of his issues.

"What did you say?"

"He likes dung. Shit. Feces. Poop. Scat. Muck. Droppings."

My God. She had heard him correctly. "And you say he actually likes it?"

"His spirit form is a dung beetle," Tiffany said.

"Ewww!" Ashley shivered. They were looking for someone who was actually a dung beetle.

Why should this shock her? She was hauling around two dead people from Hell. Just yesterday, she was in the office of a man who slipped a fireball into her brain.

Why should anything faze her?

"I hate to ask, but what does this…man…look like?"

"Messy," Chip said. "Average height. He's got a slight pot. His hair's a mess."

"I wouldn't talk," Tiffany said.

"I'll have you know my hair's what you'd call natural."

"I stand corrected. A natural mess."

"You can really be nasty when you want to be, Tifferoosky. And I hate to correct you, but you're sitting."

"We saw him at the Kilimanjaro Safari," Tiffany told Ashley. "But we lost him and his buddy when Security spotted them. If they were able to get away, they'll probably stay as far away from that place as possible."

"Which leaves us with the obvious question," Chip said. "Where should we look?"

"You honestly don't think they're still there?" Ashley asked.

"Why would they be?" Chip asked. "They'll be arrested if they're spotted."

"But he's . . . like you guys, right? Dead?"

"Hey, nobody's perfect..."

"What I mean is, if he's arrested, can't he do a trick or something and get free?"

"Judging by what Waite said, his buddy is probably mortal. If they're both arrested, Digger will get free, but his buddy won't be able to."

"And if he's depending on his friend for transportation," Tiffany said, "he won't want to leave him with the police."

The flash of an idea came to Ashley. "There are farms and ranches south of here," she said. "The St. Cloud area, particularly. East of Kissimmee."

"How much land are we talking about?" Chip asked.

"Miles."

"Terrificoso. Miles to go before we get bleeped. We've got to find that idiot or we're toast."

"There's usually a rodeo going on at the Kissimmee Arena during the middle of summer," Ashley said. "I believe there's one this weekend. It should be going on right now."

Chip sat up. "What's that?"

"Everyone knows about rodeos, don't they?" Ashley sent over to Tiffany.

"He's been down there hundreds of years."

"What does he do down there?"

"He's a plant."

"That explains his eggshell thing."

276

"But not the brain damage."

"Well? Is anyone gonna tell me what a ro-de-o is?"

"How about if we just drive there and let you figure it out all by yourself?" Tiffany said. "You might get lucky this time."

"You know something, Tifferoo? Being a butt-kicker has gone right to your head."

Chapter 40

A Kink in the Works

A strong sense of bad brushed Daniel's face when he opened the door to Mr. Waite's office.

The urgent phone call just minutes ago ("Get your ass up here now!") tore through Daniel like an electric prod.

Bummer. I should've stayed in bed.

Daniel suspected that he had messed up in some large way and was about to see his life flash before his eyes. He experienced the same feelings earlier, at Ashley's front door. The hurt and the anger in her beautiful brown eyes sliced coldly inside him like an ice pick to the gut.

Standing in front of the huge, tinted window and blocking most of it, Mr. Waite puffed busily on his cigar. He turned at the sound of the closing door. His small black eyes fixed on Daniel.

"What the hell happened with that cell phone?"

"Cell phone?" Daniel asked softly.

Mr. Waite shrugged. "Cell phone. You know, that expensive plastic thing mortals staple to their ears nowadays. What part of that don't you understand?"

"What cell phone, sir?"

Mr. Waite sighed. "How many of those things have you given out lately?"

It registered coldly. A finger of ice poked him at the base of his neck. He shuddered. "The one I gave Ashley?"

"There ya go. I knew that expensive college education of yours would help you figure it out."

No. She wouldn't. She was upset and angry— even furious...

But would she actually trash it?

He didn't know Ashley very well. He wanted to. In fact, he had planned to get to know her very well. He wanted to take her out as often as he could. And spend time with her. And maybe even get lucky.

But that was before Mr. Waite changed the game plan.

Yes, she was furious enough to trash the cell phone. But it would be wise not to tell Mr. Waite.

"That little bitch was slightly off her feed, wasn't she?" Mr. Waite said.

Damn... Daniel had forgotten. Reading minds wasn't much of a chore for someone who could cause explosions with the blinking of an eye.

"I honestly don't think she'd actually trash it..."

"Neither do I. She's kind of a weenie, actually. She came to see me yesterday about her new job description. Even tried to walk out that door. Couldn't handle it, though." He winked. "Think maybe she couldn't resist my charm?"

Daniel felt a jab of pity low in his gut. And intense anger at Mr. Waite for putting her through all this. But he knew better than press the issue.

"I don't know what happened, sir."

"You gave her a new phone?"

"Out of the box."

"Well, something ain't clicking. I just received a call from one of my coordinators. They tried

279

getting in touch with the girl and said the damned thing wasn't working."

"I wonder what happened..."

"They tried the number later on and didn't even get a dial tone."

"Those things happen all the time."

"That would be a definite oops, wouldn't it? But not when it comes to my new businesses. I'm building up a solid network. How many oopses do you think I'll tolerate, kid?"

"I understand, but cell phones aren't exactly reliable all the –"

"I know all about cell phones, kid. Balberith and I developed them personally. I'm sure you've heard the name before. Went by Balbor up here. He's a good organizer but kind of a klutz when delegating work. But his incompetence came in handy. Who do you think's responsible for so many American businesses leaving the country?"

"Really? Mr. Balbor is responsible for Chrysler and GM moving to Mexico and—"

"Among other things."

"And you and he developed the cell phone?"

"He was responsible for the computer as well. I didn't think it would catch on, but he assured me mortals would become addicted immediately. Sucker was right. How about that?"

"The computer was thought of...down there?" The idea sounded inconceivable.

Waite shrugged. "Mortals needed new toys. Mankind hasn't had a good old-fashioned major war in so long, we had to think of something just as effective. People aren't dying off quickly enough, kid. They need a helping hand. This planet's getting too crowded. The Big Man wants things simple when he comes back up. He's good, but sometimes he gets overwhelmed—know what I mean? We think he might be getting senile. That sucker's old..."

"But computers?"

"What better way of shifting things into high gear? It's caused identity theft, rip-offs, scams, and endless fuckups. It's so highly technical and complicated that no mortal is intelligent enough to actually control it. That was the point of the whole thing. To design something so complicated, so powerful, and so effective, mortals would instantly become addicted."

Mr. Waite chuckled softly. "Kid, it's doing exactly what we designed it to do. Serial killers can give helpful pointers to their adoring fan clubs and keep their legacies alive. Child molesters can get together, conduct all kinds of juicy little chats, and find out where all the schools and playgrounds are. Any idiot can find all the ingredients necessary to build any sort of bomb he desires. Or poison. Meth addicts can even find the best brand of drain cleaner on the market to inject into their veins. Privacy is dead. No one is safe. Everyone is fair game."

Daniel had heard several different accounts crediting technology to the Devil. But he had no idea the theories were true. And he was shocked to find out the cell phone was first thought of in Hell.

"See, kid, Balberith thought mortals needed help to get their asses moving faster. He was right. It's also an excellent method to monitor everyone while world governments are fighting about how to bypass the human rights issue so they can implant microchips into the general population." Mr. Waite pushed some cigar smoke toward the ceiling. "Injections would take entirely too long. Too many mortals would resist. But mortals can't resist the cell phone, can they?"

"I've been hearing about that for several years, now." Even so, Daniel didn't think it would happen. Not in America. Not in a free society.

"Kid, when you're talking about mortals, you're talking about stupidity. You've got the younger generations—or, as we like to call them, the walking dead—paving the way for the next generation. Each generation turns out to be around twenty percent stupider than its predecessor."

"In other words, the cell phone was actually invented to accelerate the process of killing people off?"

"Amazing, isn't it? You can now murder one another more easily on the highways. And with all this hilarious texting the walking dead—as well as all other mortals—are doing, highway slaughter couldn't be easier or more enjoyable."

Daniel always knew people were stupid, but never to this extent. He obviously had much to learn.

"Look how long it's taking the so-called leaders of the modern world to decide something dangerous has been going on. The cell phone had already killed thousands before anyone even suspected something was wrong." He shook his head. "I hate to say it, but sometimes Balberith shows remarkable ingenuity."

Daniel said nothing.

"Getting back to the real issue, kid... If I had developed the cell phone, it would work."

"But they usually do—that is, whenever—"

"They're still not perfected. Yet another sign that mortals are hopelessly stupid."

Daniel couldn't argue with any of that.

"Kid, find a phone that works and make sure that bitch gets it in her hot little hands today!"

Chapter 41

At the Rodeo

Fighting the crowd, Digger led Cal up the cracked concrete walkway leading to the open rear doorway of the Arena.

The huge area exploded with a plethora of scents—horse and cow shit, hay, feed, and fresh dirt as well as a pungent array of perfumes and colognes from the crowd.

Except for the sour stench of perfumes and colognes, this is like being in a dream...

Small piles of horse hockers peppered the walkway. Digger could easily tell the piles were from a horse. Cows left soft, foul patties. Digger preferred horse anyway due to its strong alfalfa-sweet feed scent. Despite the crowd moving amongst them, Digger couldn't resist stopping at each pile. He bent over, sniffing and licking his lips. Sweet. And fresh.

He reached down to grab a sample.

Cal shoved a knee into his butt. "You'd better not pick that up," he whispered harshly.

"I just wanted—"

"Keep moving."

"But—"

"You're a real sicko. Did you know that?"

"What's wrong with me taking—"

"You want someone to arrest us again?"

With a deep sigh, Digger gave the pile one last look, then joined the rest of the crowd on their way inside.

While the crowd flooded the admission gate, Digger veered off toward the pens. Cal tried steering them straight, but Digger kept moving off to the right, following the strong scents. The aromas grew much stronger as they went down a dark, dirt-covered corridor.

Straight ahead, workers and fancy-dressed contestants rushed up and down the aisles. One of them carried a first-aid kit while others barked at cell phones.

Digger bathed himself in the mixed fragrances. "Smell that, Cal? That's horse poopers. That stuff's almost as sweet as elephant or rhino. Know why?"

Cal sighed. "How can anyone care so much about shit?"

"It's my thing." Digger hoped Cal would understand without asking too many questions.

"That's something I wouldn't share with too many people if I were you."

"Horses eat grass and oats and hay. It makes their poop sweet."

"I'm so glad you told me. I always wondered about that."

Dig ran right over to the iron fence in the area marked Bulls. A huge black bull dozed inside a pen, his enormous horns resting between the bars.

Dig climbed the fence. "Hey, Cal! Look at this beauty!"

Cal rushed over and grabbed one of Dig's ankles. "You're gonna get us tossed out of here!"

"I just wanna have a closer look."

"Get down. Now!"

Digger tried lifting his leg, but Cal had a death grip on his ankle. He looked down at his friend, whose face was flushed, his eyes really big. He looked scared. Best do as he said. Cal knew modern mortals a lot better than Digger did. "Bye, Bully, see you later." He waved at the bull, then jumped down.

Down the next aisle, the Bulldogging sign advertised a row of pens half-filled with small groups of calves. Some dozed while others paced. Shit sat in fresh patties on the straw-covered floor. A large shovel leaned against the bars.

Digger could no longer stand the temptation. He had to grab a sample. What good was coming here if he couldn't bring a souvenir back with him?

"That smell's driving me up the wall!" He reached for the shovel.

"What the fuck do you think you're doing?"

"I'm gonna take a souvenir."

"You ain't bringing cow shit into my brand-new Lexus."

"I'll dump it in a feed bag." He stuck the blade of the shovel between the bars and dragged a pile toward him. "I saw empty bags scattered all over the—"

"Hey!" shouted a voice behind them. "What're you doin' with that shovel?"

***

A long line of traffic inched down the sandy path, toward the large horseshoe-shaped arena.

Ashley followed the procession to the rear of the building, where a huge grassy lot encompassed

286

an open field. Several vacant spaces showed a quarter of the way down the long row.

Ashley coasted behind a dusty blue SUV with a Texas license plate and some NRA bumper stickers covering the bumper, and parked beside a filthy black Super Cab also covered with NRA stickers, as well as one saying AMERICA, LOVE IT OR LEAVE IT and one saying MY EX GOT THE VETTE.

Tiffany had been to a rodeo once before, in southern California. She went with a man who owned one of the bulls selected for the bull-riding event. He was a pompous bore, constantly bragging about how much land and livestock he owned. After trying to impress her with his knowledge of thoroughbred horses, he took her into the back to show her how many rodeo people he knew.

The aisles and pens bustled with cowboys yanking on their horses and bullying the cattle. When her date met another well-dressed bore and the two men quickly engaged in a testosterone contest, Tiffany ducked out of the picture and took a cab back to her apartment.

Straight ahead, two short, slender Hispanic men in work clothes led a slicked-down black horse. The Hispanic closest to the horse kept snatching the lead rope. The animal yanked its head and pulled away.

Here we go again...

The Hispanic snatched the rope again.

Tiffany thought

(careful, you'll lose your balance)

and smiled when the young man tripped and stumbled to the ground.

His companion laughed and said something in Spanish which Tiffany interpreted as, "Why you sitting on your ass when we need to groom this mare?"

The first guy got up and dusted off his trousers. Gripping the lead rope with his left hand, he yelled some heated Spanish at the horse, then pulled his right arm back.

I wouldn't.

The Hispanic's fist missed the horse's mouth by a foot. The force of the blow spun him around. He lost his balance and landed flat on his back.

The horse raised its tail and dumped a sizeable wet load that missed the Hispanic by less than a foot.

"He drunk? Or just clumsy?" Chip asked.

"I wouldn't know," Tiffany said.

"Did you do that?" Ashley sent over.

"Yes, and if he tries it again, he's really gonna be sorry."

A third Hispanic joined the twosome. He was older, taller, and dressed in an open-neck brown shirt, black dress slacks, and shiny high-heeled white slip-ons. He wore several gold necklaces, gold earrings, a gold bracelet on each wrist, and at least three gold rings on each hand. He barked at the trainers in Spanish, then followed them closely as they led the horse past the sign that said PASO FINO AUCTION TONITE 7 PM.

***

Outside, Cal elbowed through the crowd gathering at one of the food concessions. He

288

reached the sandy road that circled the rear of the big building.

"That sure was close." He wanted to deck Digger for nearly getting them arrested again. But as long as they were able to get away...

He turned to see if Security had followed them outside.

No sign of them.

No sign of Digger, either.

Dammit. What the fuck is that moron doing now?

Squeezing through another small wandering crowd, Cal went back up the slope.

Digger, carrying an empty feed bag, rushed over to where that damned horse had just dumped a fresh pile of shiny brown. People kept their distance, swerving around him. Cal couldn't blame them. If he didn't have to keep Digger in sight, he would've left his sorry ass here long ago.

"What the hell do you think you're doing?"

Digger smiled stupidly and shrugged. "Horse poopers, Cal. I can't pass this up. It's fresh. Look at it. Still has steam coming up from it."

"Lovely. Steam. Horse shit. My dreams have come true. Now drop that fucking bag and let's get outa here. We're lucky Security gave us up."

"But—"

"No buts, dammit. You're not bringing horse shit into my Lexus!"

"I'll scoop it up and dump it in this bag."

"I don't care!"

"Cal, we can put it—"

289

"No horse shit in the damn car!" Cal snatched the empty bag from Dig, crumpled it up, tossed it onto the grass, and stomped on it.

Dig looked like he wanted to cry. "Why did you do that?"

"I needed the exercise. Why else?"

"That was a mean thing to do. A really mean thing to do."

***

Tiffany turned at the sound of the angry voice.

Just beyond the crowd, two young guys argued on the walk outside the building.

Tiffany let the crowd move around her.

The two guys looked familiar. The guy on the left wore a red shirt and black pants, the other guy a baggy brown shirt and jeans. His hair hung all over the place.

Just like Chip...

Was he the one carrying the elephant turd?

He was certainly interested in collecting that pile the horse had dumped.

Who else would be interested in horse poop?

"What's up, Tifferoo?"

"Isn't that the two we saw at the Safari?"

Chip watched silently. The crowds quickly moved away from the two young men as they came into the arena.

Chip's ears twitched. "Looks like the two we saw. Besides, I don't see anyone else in that crowd who wants to get that close to a horse patty."

Ashley shivered. "I know you told me all about that guy, but he's still grossing me out."

290

"As we told you," Tiffany said, "his spirit form is a dung beetle."

"I don't care," she said. "I see a guy who badly needs a bath standing over a horse patty."

Just then, the guy in the red shirt crumpled up the feed bag, tossed it on the grass, and stomped it. Then he grabbed the other guy by the shirt collar and they both disappeared around the corner.

***

Two cop cars sat parked behind the Lexus, their lights flashing. Three cops walked around the Lexus, talking to their radios, and looking around.

"Fine. Just fucking great." Cal frowned at the sight.

"Cops, Cal."

Groaning, Cal pointed to his eyes. "These work, ya know."

"They found the Lexus, didn't they?"

"Yours work too, I see."

"What can we do now?"

Digger was really beginning to bug him. Cal didn't even want to come here in the first place. The trip was a fiasco. He still couldn't believe he had let his idiot friend con him into dragging him here. Cal Krebs—a dyed-in-the-wool city boy spending a pleasant Saturday afternoon dodging animal shit. Afterward, Cal pulls his idiot friend down from a bull cage, then gets a little exercise when they're chased by Security for trying to steal calf shit. To top it all off, he and his moron friend entertain the crowd by engaging in a heated argument over a scattered pile of slimy horse crap.

291

Now, after all this, they try and steal another car in a crowded parking lot because the cops just found the stolen Lexus.

A sterling example of an entertaining afternoon in Tourist City, U.S.A.

He faced Digger and tried to keep his voice down. "How the fuck should I know? You see a turban on my forehead? You see anything on me that says The Great Karnak?"

"Who?"

"Johnny Carson? The Great Karnak? Don't tell me you

don't know—"

"Who?"

"The Tonight Show? Here's Johnny? The turban? The answer is?"

"I don't know what you're talking about, Cal."

"That's because you're an idiot."

"What does that have to do with—"

"Shut up. I've got to think."

"Think you can figure out something?"

"I have no fucking idea."

"What if you don't?"

"Then we stay right here until one of us finally figures out that we both need our heads examined."

"Let me guess. You're joking again."

"Fucking Einstein. I'm paling around with fucking Einstein."

"I think I've heard of him..."

"Doesn't matter. You're still an idiot."

"You guys need a ride?"

Cal spun around.

One of the hottest-looking babes he had ever seen in his entire life moved toward him. She wore a tight-fitting maroon tank top, a pair of tan Capri's that showed off her gorgeous calves, and open-toed pumps. She looked like a runway model, only with better tits. A tall, good-looking brunette flanked her on her left, a skinny small-breasted redhead on her right.

"Uh, hi." Cal had to clear his throat twice. His head grew cloudy. He couldn't take his eyes off those tits. Or that thick curtain of honey-blond hair.

"Hi."

Something was vaguely familiar about her. He had seen her before. And it wasn't too long ago, either.

"That's not your car, is it?" Blondie asked. "The one the cops are looking at?"

"Naw. That's not ours. We…hitched here."

"If you need a ride," the brunette said, "we're about to leave right now."

"No problemo," the skinny redheaded chick on the other side of Blondie said.

"Really? It's no trouble?"

"None," Blondie said.

I've died and gone to heaven. Here I'm thinking I'm stuck with Pig-Pen for the rest of my life, and I turn around and three hot babes are offering me a ride.

Cal grinned. "That would be just great!"

Chapter 42

Take No Prisoners

A filthy gray Toyota Supra sat in the drive.

Daniel cursed softly as he pulled over to the curb. The last thing he wanted was a confrontation with Ashley's mother. The woman was a mess. Talking to her would not be pleasant.

For nearly five minutes Daniel stared at the front door, gathering courage. The appearance of the house did not exactly make this any easier. The front yard needed mowed. The bushes lining the front stoop obviously had not been trimmed in months. The windows were covered with film and dirt.

Daniel had no choice. Going against Mr. Waite would be disastrous. Confronting a pathetic alcoholic paled in comparison to antagonizing a powerful, hot-tempered super demon.

Daniel didn't want to upset the status quo. He was incredibly lucky to be under Waite's tutelage. Mr. Waite knew how to make money. His new company had been pulling in thousands a day just from his two Orlando contacts. In just one business day, the new escort service had already earned Daniel more than a thousand dollars.

Even so, he hated getting Ashley involved in this. It was his fault that she quit her waitress job in the first place. If she had stayed where she was, she wouldn't be going through any of this. But as much as Daniel wanted her out of this, he couldn't see any way of doing it without making things worse.

The image of the seared BMW kept popping up in his head.

Despite his personal feelings, his fears, he forced himself to consider things from a different perspective.

He was about to become extremely rich. Personal feelings couldn't even enter into the equation. A thousand bucks a day from a single source translated into a sizeable fortune, one even his father would appreciate.

Sure, he liked Ashley. He liked her a lot. But wasn't the bigger picture more important than a relationship that probably would not go anywhere anyway? Even if Ashley forgave him and agreed to date him, they were not matched. She came from a broken home, had an alcoholic mother, and didn't even graduate from high school. To make matters worse, she was barely nineteen—nearly eleven years younger than Daniel. Even if they did hit it off, Mom and Dad would never approve. And if his parents didn't approve, it would cause major complications all around, both financially and emotionally.

Take no prisoners when pursuing great wealth, Mr. Waite had told him.

Although cruel, Mr. Waite's advice made sense. Daniel needed to do everything he was told if he wanted the success he had been obsessing over since college.

Recharged with this fresh burst of confidence, Daniel got out of the Vette and marched up the cracked driveway. He pressed the buzzer, took a

295

few deep breaths, and prepared himself to become his usual charming self.

The door opened. A heavy reek of stale booze and B.O. pushed outward, raking against his face.

Frowning and bleary-eyed, Ashley's mother wore a wrinkled flowered bathrobe opened at the neck, which showed off her wattle, protruding collarbone, and small freckled cleavage. Though tall, long-limbed, and reasonably slender, she carried the sort of gut one develops from years of heavy drinking. Her ruddy, whiskey-bloated face revealed signs that she had once been attractive, but too many rough years had tarnished her former image. Daniel guessed her to be not much more than forty, but she clearly looked fifty.

"Mrs. Parker?"

"Yeah?"

"I'm Daniel Grove. I'm a friend of Ashley's."

No reply.

"Ashley's not here, is she?"

"Her car ain't here. Do the math."

This was going just as well as he'd imagined.

Tossing her a quick smile, he said, "Do you know where she might be?"

"Nope." She grabbed the doorknob. "That all you wanted?"

His hand buried in the side pocket of his Versace, he gripped the package containing the cell phone. He suddenly lacked the power to pull it out.

Take no prisoners. The words hammered in his brain.

Yet his hand stayed right where it was.

Did he think that handing this repulsive woman the phone would make him feel like some sort of conspirator? A regular Judas?

It's not that. Not at all.

Handing her the phone meant moving closer. Entering her sphere. Inhaling the miasma of her breath.

And, worst of all, touching her.

The woman nauseated him. He needed to get away. Her foulness and unpleasant aura had made it difficult to breathe.

"That all?"

Daniel's empty hand slowly emerged from his pocket. "Sorry I—"

The door slammed in his face.

Chapter 43

A Carload of...babes?

As the big white building grew smaller in the rear window of the Honda, Cal settled back in the seat and sighed in relief.

Picked up by a carload of babes. Awesome. He had the strong feeling that he'd just stumbled into someone else's wet dream.

The brunette was sweet, but the blonde beside her? Wow! He hadn't been able to take his eyes off her. Her long, curly hair swept down over her shoulders like a thick golden veil. It made his temples pound.

The redhead sitting beside Digger wasn't even bad if you liked them skinny—

Jesus. The redhead was a guy!

How the hell?

"Something wrong?" Red asked.

"No. Nothing's wrong." Cal rubbed his eyes. When his vision cleared, he had a better look.

Yep. A guy, all right.

The excitement had obviously messed him up. Everything seemed to have happened all at once: the security dudes after them, the argument with Dig about the horse shit, then the cops finding the Lexus. It must have done something screwy to his head. The blonde's fault, no doubt. And the brunette's. Dig's, too—for getting him all riled up over a shovelful of horse hockers.

"What were those cops doing with that fancy car?" Red asked.

Cal figured innocence would work best. "Cops?"

Red nodded. "You saw them. Big and stupid-looking? They usually wear blue uniforms, carry guns and handcuffs, and toss you in the backseat of their squad car when you've been a naughty boy."

"I know what cops are." Cal glared. Red was not only a guy, he was also a smartass.

"They were acting nervous about something."

Cal shrugged. "Maybe someone locked themselves out of their car." No reason to let them know what happened. You could usually keep out of trouble by acting stupid.

This felt like the perfect time to act stupid.

"You said you were hitching. So why were you in the parking lot?" The brunette glanced at them in her rearview.

She reminded Cal of Jackie, the cheerleader babe he and every guy in high school wanted to jump. Jackie wore tight jeans all the time. She knew what it did to all the guys but wore them anyway. This chick was just as fine, only her boobs weren't as big—not that he could tell.

But you just didn't know nowadays, not until you got the top off and saw the goodies for yourself. Babes liked doing screwy things to their boobs. The ones who wanted to be stared at made them bigger and the ones who didn't want to be stared at knew how to make them practically invisible.

"We were looking for another ride," Cal said.

"Then you were leaving when we bumped into you?" Red asked.

299

Cal shrugged. "My buddy and me, we hate crowds."

"That's why you came to this shindig? Because you don't like crowds?" Red gave him the same accusing look as the cop at the 7-Eleven. Asshole.

"Wasn't crowded when we got here." Cal wanted the blonde to talk to him instead. Blondie looked just as good as any of those babes he had seen in those summer slasher flicks. The ones in wet tee shirts running around, screaming. Sure had the looks for it. And the tits.

"What's your name?" Blondie asked.

Cal grinned. About time she took over. Now he could stare at her without making her weird out. "Cal," he said. "Cal Krebs."

"How about your friend?"

"I call him Dig."

"Dig?" Red acted interested. It figured, two dorks bonding.

"His name's Digger."

"Digger?" The brunette glanced at them again in her rearview, this time longer.

Dig acted like he was trying to melt into the seat. Cal just couldn't understand it. The Touch thing sure was cool, but you had to wonder why it made you scared shitless around babes.

"My real name...is Cletis," Dig mumbled, almost to himself.

"Cle-tis?" Cal scratched the back of his neck. "You told me your name was Digger."

"That's my nickname."

"Why Digger?" Blondie asked.

"He likes digging for stuff." Cal didn't want to tell these babes what Dig liked digging for. Chicks grossed out easily. You had to behave yourself if you didn't want them to freak. And if you wanted to get laid.

At least Dig hadn't had the chance to grab a shovelful of cow shit before Security came after them. Or that pile of horseshit out on the walk. These chicks would have already dumped them to the curb. Dig smelled funky enough.

"What do you dig for?" Blondie asked.

Dig just shrugged like a shy little kid.

Blondie must have figured Digger was uncomfortable because she just nodded and smiled. Hell, anyone could see that he was just shy of throwing up. "I'm Tiffany," she said. "And this is Ashley. That's Chip in the back."

"Chip?" Cal wanted to chuckle.

Red frowned. "Something funny?"

"Nah. Everything's just cool." Cal forced himself to look serious.

"Where would you like us to drop you off?" the brunette said.

"We're just bumming around." Cal said. "No specific place in mind."

"Where'd you two come from?" Chip asked.

"Orlando." Cal wanted this asshole to stop asking questions. And also for not being a female. And for being a smartass. It was okay for a chick to be a smartass if she had nice tits and a tight little ass. But not okay for a guy.

"You want us to take you back to Orlando?" Blondie asked.

Dig stiffened. Cal thought his friend might be having an attack of serious cramps.

"Actually, we wanted to hook up with some ladies." He hoped they'd take the hint.

"You went to a ro-de-o to look for ladies?" Chip asked.

"Something wrong with that?" Cal hoped his quick glare would make this dork shut up. "Lots of chicks show up at rodeos."

"This is a coincidence," Blondie said. "We wanted to party tonight but didn't know exactly where to go. We're new in town and don't know anyone. Maybe you'd like to show us around. Sound okay with you?"

***

"Sounds awesome. Whatever you ladies want."

Cal Krebs grinned stupidly. For the tenth time in just a few minutes, his eyes wandered down the front of Tiffany's top.

Typical—a young guy with a small amount of brain cells and an excessive amount of raging hormones.

It was going to be so easy to handle him.

"What do you have in mind?" Ashley's thoughts drifted over. "I thought you had to take them both back to that monster in Orlando."

"I'd like to find out a few things first."

"Like what?"

"Like what they've been doing."

"Does that matter?"

Hunched forward in the back seat, staring at his lap, the Digger guy continued to be the poster child for sad and pitiful.

302

"I just don't feel right about taking them back. It would be like dropping off a stray puppy to be euthanized."

Ashley gave a slight nod. "I'm beginning to feel the same way. I don't know about Cal, though. He's a real jerk."

"But that doesn't mean he deserves to be taken back."

"Can't we just leave him somewhere?"

"That's why I have to find out a few things. They seem pretty close. It might ruin everything if we split them up."

"Dig says a party sounds just great, Blon—uh, Tiffany," Cal said.

"I guess we'd better get some refreshments first."

"Refreshments?" Ashley sent over.

"Cal seems the type who likes to get drunk. He might volunteer a few things if he's feeling relaxed."

"Good thinking."

"Maybe we can find a motel room somewhere," Tiffany added.

"Somewhere closer to town?" Ashley asked.

Digger stiffened in his seat. Tiffany was certain he had done that before, when she mentioned Orlando. She did a quick probe. A fleeting glimpse of Breath Mint flashed prominently in his head. She understood immediately. To Digger, the word "town" meant facing the super demon. She couldn't blame him for being terrified.

It made her wonder just how evil Digger actually was. He was living in Hell, but that didn't

303

mean anything to her. Chip had also been living in Hell. He was anything but evil. He was definitely mischievous. He was also silly and ignorant. And genuinely irritating. But not nearly as bad as her stepfather or most of the movie people she had known. And certainly not from the same wicked mold as Gutril, Breath Mint, or those scary creatures chasing her in Hell.

Digger was shy, quiet, and obviously uncomfortable in the presence of women. Tiffany didn't know much about demons, but from what she'd already seen, that sort of behavior wasn't consistent among them.

She definitely had to find out more about all this.

Chapter 44

A Little Tweaking

Dad and Mr. Waite sat in a corner booth of the crowded restaurant.

Daniel hurried through the glass doors at a few minutes before six. Mr. Waite sat stiffly, his massive arms crossed over his huge chest. Dad looked uncomfortable sipping his drink.

Before taking his seat, Daniel ordered a vodka martini from the short, white-haired waitress standing beside him.

"About damned time you got here," Mr. Waite said. "Just to relieve the boredom, I almost caused one of the waitresses to have a heart attack."

Daniel had only gotten the man's phone call half an hour ago. He was leaving the Parker home and quickly found himself trapped in downtown rush hour traffic. Only a helicopter ride could have made better time. "Traffic was bad," he said, trying to sound pleasant.

"Really? Traffic was actually bad? In Central Florida?"

Daniel knew better than argue. Something was obviously bothering Mr. Waite. Daniel didn't like the way Dad stared off into space. He didn't seem all there.

"How are you, Dad?"

"I'm a stupid asshole, son."

Daniel stiffened in his seat. Had he heard him correctly? Dad's eyes weren't focused. Daniel couldn't help wondering what had gone on before he'd gotten here.

"Pardon me?"

"I said I'm a stupid asshole."

Mr. Waite drank some red wine. "It's disheartening, isn't it, kid? Finding out about your old man at this stage in your life?"

"Dad? Are you feeling—"

"He feels fine, kid. Right, Grove?"

"I feel just fine, Daniel. For a stupid asshole."

Daniel didn't know what to say. Something weird had obviously happened.

"Your old man and his buddies have made a few colossal blunders during the last twenty-four hours, kid. I told you about it. My Arab land deal? Well, your father is just expressing an accurate assessment of his behavior. He's suddenly showing remarkable insight, if you ask me."

Daniel remained silent. He could only guess the discomfort Dad had endured over this.

"What do you think, Grove?" Mr. Waite had more wine. "Learned your lesson?"

"Yes I have, Mr. Waite, even though I'm a stupid asshole."

"How many times do you think you've uttered that phrase during the last twenty-four hours?"

Dad sighed deeply. "Too many—even for a stupid asshole."

"How'd the little woman enjoy your epiphany of self-analysis?"

"She told me to knock it off."

"Would you like to?"

"I really would—even though I'm a stupid asshole."

"I guess you've learned your lesson. You may stop doing it."

"Thank you." Dad had a big gulp of his drink.

Still staring at Dad, Mr. Waite said, "I've arranged this pleasant little get-together for two reasons. One, to show your kid how I react when people piss me off." Mr. Waite rested his huge forearms on the table and interlaced his fingers. "The other reason, of course, is to find out how you did with your little errand."

Daniel's drink came. He was grateful it was strong. He downed nearly half of it. How could he possibly tell Mr. Waite what happened? How could he squirm out of this without arousing the man's wrath?

But when he felt the heat from Mr. Waite's small black eyes settling on him, he realized it was too late.

"Oh, fine. You wimped out, didn't you?"

"Well—"

Mr. Waite blinked. "You gave her the cell phone?"

"Not exactly..."

"You did or you didn't. There's no third option here. Unless, of course, you added something. You didn't, by any chance, violate the girl, did you, kid? Not that there's anything wrong with that. She is our property now."

"I...didn't do that, sir."

"Okay, then. Tell us what did happen on your recent adventure."

"She...wasn't home."

"So then, you just dropped it off."

"Her mother was home."

"Okay. We seem to be on a roll. You gave the phone to the mother?"

"I didn't think it would be the right thing to do..."

Mr. Waite turned to Dad. "I take it your boy, here, favors his mother's side of the family?"

Dad turned pale.

Waite's insult made the hair stand up on the back of Daniel's neck. Demon or not, Waite just went too far. "Sir, it isn't fair to—"

"Think I'm being a tad judgmental?"

"Well, sir..."

"Somewhat critical? I could be stretching things a little, but let me try a slightly stronger phrase. Unduly cruel, perhaps?"

The image of the smoldering husk of the BMW flashed before his eyes. What's wrong with you? You want to die because of a stupid insult?

"No, sir..." Daniel drank more of his drink.

"Let's try this with baby steps. Why didn't you give the mother the cell phone?"

"I...didn't like her..."

"Pardon me? For a moment I thought I heard you say you didn't like her. You know, something a little boy might say about one of his teachers? Possibly the one who wouldn't let him eat his crayons?"

"She's very unpleasant and negative."

Mr. Waite lowered his voice. "Unpleasant?"

Daniel nodded. He couldn't back out now.

"Negative?"

"Yes, sir..."

Mr. Waite shifted in his chair. "Boy, since I've obviously overestimated the level of your brain activity, I'm going to have to make my orders a bit clearer. Let's try this again. A little slower, of course, so you can absorb them better. Ready?"

Daniel forced himself to ignore the insults and nodded dutifully.

"You give Mumsy the phone. Mumsy gives it to Princess. That's it in a nutshell. If Mumsy forgets or loses it, you tell me and I give her one or two legitimate reasons to be unpleasant and negative. Understand now?"

"Yes, sir..."

"Grove, tell Junior what an imbecile he is."

"Son, you're an imbecile." Dad stared blankly at his half-empty glass.

"Tell him what he needs to be doing."

"Son, you need to do exactly what Mr. Waite says."

Mr. Waite poured more wine from the bottle at his elbow. "I told you I'd make you rich and powerful, did I not?"

"Yes, sir."

"I can't do it if you fight me, can I?"

"No, sir."

"I won't do it if you piss me off."

"No, sir."

"The rich get richer and more powerful when they listen to us. Isn't that right, Grove?"

"Absolutely."

"They understand what needs to be done, and they do it, no questions asked. You need a more analytical mind, kid. You have to understand once and for all that there is no room for sentimentality or emotional involvement here. Get it?"

"Yes, sir." Daniel felt small, insignificant, and powerless. A stranger in his own body. I need to stand up to him. Right here and now.

Mr. Waite needed to know Daniel was his own man. Daniel had backbone. And ideals. And plans. Daniel realized his mistakes and possessed the intestinal fortitude to correct them. It was his fault he had stuck Ashley in the middle of this. She was too nice, too innocent. She had no business being involved.

Tell him, right here and now. Sure, he can turn you into a blot of ketchup staining the tablecloth. But if you don't stand up to him, you'll never have any self-respect again.

Daniel looked Mr. Waite in the eye. "Sir, I need to—"

A bright flash erupted in his head. The room swayed. He gripped the edge of the table for balance. His temples throbbed. His head grew warm. Then hot. Then sizzling. He forced his eyes shut. The blood thundered violently through his limbs. The room grew warmer. The clattering of dishes and silverware gradually diminished.

A sudden silence filled his head.

All former thoughts had vanished. Something about Ashley, about her being nice. And ideals. And plans. And ketchup—or was it mustard?

The swaying stopped. The throbbing in his temples also stopped. The heat swelling within him ebbed, then vanished.

He opened his eyes. His vision grew cloudy with patches of black. He rubbed his eyes. He suddenly realized he'd been sweating.

"What was it you wanted to say, kid?"

Daniel's mind remained blank.

A plan. What was it about a plan?

"You all right, son?" Dad asked softly.

"I think so..."

"You sure?"

"Grove, your son feels differently about things. Look at him. Everything just clicked. He's all grown up and mature and filled with all kinds of business savvy. Ready to kick ass." Mr. Waite grinned.

What the hell happened? What was I thinking of when--

"Your boy just realized the error of his ways. Isn't that so, kid?"

"Son?" Dad looked worried.

Ashley...

I was thinking about Ashley...

Or was it her mother?

An image of a door slamming in his face brought a clot of heat billowing right back, enveloping his neck.

The bitch slammed the door in my face. I didn't want to get too close to her, so she slammed the door in my face. I sacrificed my business because of a stupid drunk.

"Feel differently about things, kid?"

"Yes, sir." Daniel looked around the dark, crowded room. Funny, he'd forgotten where they were. Steakhouse. Heavy traffic outside. He couldn't even remember coming here.

How long have I been here?

Did I black out?

What happened?

He felt as if he had just woken up. As if he had been asleep. But instead of feeling refreshed, he felt foolish. And angry. Just as he did when he was caught for doing something really stupid as a kid.

Foolish and angry. Mostly angry. Angry with himself for not giving Ashley's mother the cell phone. That's what he was thinking about. That damned cell phone.

Why the hell didn't I give that drunken bitch the cell phone?

Why should he care about a stupid drunk? That phone represented another five hundred bucks a week padding his pockets. An additional twenty-five K a year.

No more sentimentality or emotional involvement. Business was business.

After dinner, he was going right back to Ashley's home.

312

Chapter 45

Party!

Cal, his back propped up with pillows, sat on the motel bed. A bottle of Jack Daniel's rested in his lap.

Digger sat on the other bed but was not drinking. He was looking down at his lap.

Staring at Digger from her seat in front of the motel window, Tiffany did a brief probe. Digger felt confined. Trapped. And embarrassed.

Cal had a slug of Jack's and belched. "Wanted some of this stuff at the rodeo, but they didn't have any. Just soft drinks, hot dogs, and French fries. And funny hats." He had another swallow and shook his head. "Florida's the fucking funny hat capital of the world. Every time they have a shindig, they sell a boatload of stupid hats. Every kind of hat you'd ever want. How come they sell so many funny hats?"

"Because tourists have so many funny heads?" Chip said from the padded seat next to the television.

Cal ignored the comment. "No booze, though. Too many fucking kids running around. Can't have any booze where there are fucking kids."

"How come so many babes want kids anyway?" He downed more Jack's. "They're just little assholes that get on your nerves."

"Maybe they like little assholes," Chip said.

"Why is that?"

313

"How should I know?" Chip shrugged. "I'm only a babe when the situation calls for it. It's not like I can actually think like one."

"You're an asshole," Cal said, and had another slug of whiskey.

"Thanks." Chip grinned. "Didn't think you liked me."

"I don't."

"Then stop with the compliments. You'll get my petals all aflutter."

"I hope he nods off soon," Ashley sent over from across the table. "He's really nauseating."

"Who?" Tiffany sent back. "Cal? Or Chip?"

Ashley just smiled.

"At least Chip can be manageable if you threaten him just the right way."

"What's Cal doing with Digger?"

"That's what I intend to find out."

"Last time I partied?" Cal grinned. "Me and this hooker I picked up, we had our own little get-together. Yesterday, maybe? Night before?" He sighed. "Don't remember. Remember that damn Tweety bird on her ass, though." He turned to Tiffany. "How come so many females get tatts on their asses?"

"I wouldn't know."

"Your ass doesn't have a tatt?"

"Nope."

"You sure?"

"I think I'd remember something like that."

"You might be lying."

"Why would I lie?"

"Babes lie all the time."

314

"I don't like tattoos."

"Your ass doesn't need one." Cal hiccupped loudly. "It's fine just the way it is."

"Thank you."

"Tweety bird, eh?" Chip asked.

"Damn straight. Right smack-dab in the center of her ass cheek."

"Which one?"

"Huh?"

"Which cheek? Everyone's got two. A left one and a right one." Chip scratched his head. "Now that I think about it, though, I do recall seeing something with just one. It was down in the rocks, crawling around--"

"What the fuck's it matter?"

"I guess it really doesn't. It's not like we're down there, for one thing. And it's probably long gone by now. I think I saw it years ago, so it's probably been scooped up, digested and shat back out by Sibrius."

Cal squinted, staring at Tiffany as if seeing her for the first time. "You remind me of somebody I saw a little while ago."

"Really?" Tiffany glanced at Chip.

"You're one babe a guy doesn't forget. Unless he's gay. Even if he's gay, he'd remember. Sort of a jealousy thing, maybe."

"Where did we meet?"

"Can't remember." Cal lowered his gaze. "Change your shoes?"

"Of course."

"When?"

"Just a little while ago."

315

"Was I here when you did it?"

"In a manner of speaking."

"What was I doing?"

"Sitting there with your bottle. Like now."

"They sure are great-looking shoes. Look good on your feet, too. Expensive?"

"Thank you. Very."

"You didn't have to do it, though."

"What do you mean?"

"You coulda just kicked them off with the rest of your things."

She should have seen that one coming...

"Damn straight." Cal chuckled. "Why don't you and your buddy just take your clothes off and we'll have a real party?"

"Maybe later," she said.

Cal turned solemn again, staring at the whiskey bottle. "Sure don't remember you changing those shoes... You'd think I would've noticed, tight?"

"A lot of guys don't notice things like that."

"I wish I could do that," Ashley sent over.

"You can only do it when you're dead."

"That's right. I guess I forgot that tiny detail."

"Tangy stuff." Cal had another swig. "Yeah, me and Dig, we been hitting all the hot spots in Orlando ever since...since I caught him on International Drive, moving in on my turf."

"Your turf?" Chip asked.

"The tourists come down here, hit the souvenir shops and the fast-food places and end up broke before they can make it to the theme parks." He chuckled. "Dumbasses. That's why you gotta hit

316

'em at the right time. Otherwise, they're all tapped out and can't give you money."

Tiffany figured Cal was just a few minutes away from nodding off.

"And you met Digger there?" she asked.

"I'm standing at the corner, sizing up a mark. There he is, lifting cash from this Asian family. From Asians, no less. Know how tight they are?"

"How tight are they?" Chip asked.

"So tight, they squeak. And they don't even speak English. Makes it even tougher to bum money from them. Know how hard it is, getting cash from someone who only speaks gibberish?"

"How hard is it?" Chip asked.

"Fucking impossible. But Dig, here? Walks right up to them and they hand him a wad. I mean a fucking wad. Tens, twenties... Big money, baby."

"From Asians," Chip said.

"Slanty-eyed, tight-fisted pricks."

"How'd you do it?" Chip asked.

Digger didn't reply.

"Fucker's got the Touch."

Tiffany blinked. Now they were getting somewhere...

"What's that?" she asked.

"Knows some neat tricks. He can unlock things. Start up cars. Get money. Me and Dig, we're tight. He even knows how to fix old cars and get them running again. Dig's one classy dude for a dickhead."

"Is he for real?" Ashley sent over.

"He thinks he is," Tiffany sent back.

"How can you be classy if you're a dickhead?" Chip asked.

Cal glared at Chip. "You sure are an asshole. How'd you get hooked up with two such sweet babes?"

"It was their lucky day."

"I'll bet." Cal turned to Tiffany. "Know it was your lucky day?"

"Ashley and I will always consider ourselves very fortunate for the experience," she said.

Cal stared at Tiffany, possibly to see if she was being serious. Then he sighed and lifted the bottle again. "Dig here? He likes shit, even plays in it."

"Really?"

"I mean shit. Crap. Weird, huh?"

Digger lowered his head even more.

"Different strokes, as they say," Tiffany said, watching Digger.

Digger raised his head slightly. His eyes moved in her direction.

"Boy's beyond different," Cal said. "But he can do really neat stuff. See, he's wired all wrong. If he was wired right, he'd be like us—all normal and shit, ya know? That'd be okay, I guess, but he wouldn't know anything really cool. But he's wired different and does cool things, and if you can do cool things, you can act weird, right? Dig doesn't care much for stuff everyone else likes, like drinking and women. Right, Dig?"

Dig made no reply.

"He's all weirded-out and messed up right now. He always gets like that with women around. And

318

you two?" He giggled. "You're too much for ol' Dig. Know what I mean?"

"I think so." Tiffany was just about ready to make Cal call it a night. They heard as much as they needed to. Digger had been humiliated more than enough.

"She sure was a weird chick." Cal had another slug of whiskey.

"Who's that?" Chip asked.

"Hooker we picked up. Looked good in jeans. Real good." Cal frowned. "You really are an asshole, you know."

"I've been told that before," Chip said.

"Nighty-night," Tiffany sent over gently.

Cal blinked and stared at his bottle. "Weird." He yawned. His head fell back onto the pillows. "This is a neat party...ought to...take...your clothes off..."

Tiffany waited a few moments. Then: "Cal?"

He was already snoring softly, a sloppy grin covering his features.

"Digger?"

He slowly met her eyes.

"How would you like to take a walk with me right now?"

He blinked. "Right now?"

"Right now."

His eyes grew. "Outside?"

"I think we both need some fresh air."

319

Chapter 46

A New Mindset

Daniel flicked off the ignition, sat back in the comfortable leather seat, and stared at the Parker house.

Why do I feel like I just woke up?

Why does this feel like a brand-new day?

I don't even remember driving here.

How else could he have gotten here?

The restaurant. The talk with Mr. Waite. It had rejuvenated him, made him feel like a new man.

And he did feel very differently indeed. As if a heavy fog had been lifted from his shoulders. He could see much clearer.

Mr. Waite's image flashed before his eyes.

Just a few minutes with Mr. Waite was all it took to fully understand the game plan. Things had to be seen from the viewpoint of the true professional. The success Daniel had lusted after all these years would now happen.

Mr. Waite was right about Ashley. The truth was harsh but had to be acknowledged before Daniel could proceed. Ashley was no different from any of the other dozens of females he had seen waiting tables or working the registers at drugstores. She was the essence of mediocrity. She came from a broken home and had quit school. She had no ideas or plans for improving her situation.

Her home was an eyesore even for this low-income neighborhood. Her mother was a pathetic mess. As pretty and as savvy as Ashley was, she was destined to become a carbon copy of her mother.

Five hundred bucks a week.

The phrase popped into his head almost magically. That same phrase had been popping up ever since his last meeting with Mr. Waite. Five hundred bucks a week translated into twenty-six K a year. And all that was required for the process to start was a simple two-minute visit with an unpleasant woman.

Daniel climbed out of the Vette, marched up the drive, and pressed the buzzer.

Just hand it over, get back in your car, and leave. Two minutes of your time. No fuss, no muss.

The door pulled open.

Dressed in a bulky, loose-fitting pullover and faded jeans, Ashley's mom appeared in the doorway. Her hair was matted. Her eyes were glazed. The frown crinkling her features from his last visit hadn't faded.

"You again?"

Best keep this short and businesslike. No smile or little-boy persona this time. Showing his good side would be a waste of time. Besides, he didn't want this repulsive mess to think this was pleasant for him.

He pulled the small package from his pocket and held it out. "This is for Ashley."

She just stared at it. "What is it?"

"Please make sure she gets this as soon as possible." He wanted to tell her that her future depended on making sure Ashley got it. He decided not to. If this woman screwed up, it was her own dumb fault.

She just shrugged, took the package, and slammed the door.

Feeling triumphant, Daniel strutted back to the Vette.

A wide grin took over his features.

Five hundred bucks more a week, he thought as he flicked on the ignition.

Chapter 47

A Chat with Digger

The night was warm and muggy. Heavy traffic sounds roared down South Orange Blossom, past the motel. The smells of charbroiled burgers and burnt onions mixed with the exhaust fumes shooting from the highway.

Tiffany followed Digger past the dumpsters and the long row of parked cars in the rear lot. Digger walked quickly, his head up, sniffing the air. He exuded the same excitement as a dog when freed from the confines of a tiny cage.

Digger seemed like a nice guy. Quiet and shy, and totally harmless. Much like the stray dogs Tiffany had brought home as a child.

Tiffany couldn't believe someone like Digger was sent to Hell in the first place. It made her wonder how many others were there who shouldn't have been.

But that didn't matter right now.

What mattered was how she could ask her questions without scaring him. Digger had to know what was going on. Who Tiffany and Chip were. Why they were at the rodeo. He had to know what they had to do and why they had to do it. And since they were quickly running out of time, he had to know now.

"We know where you're from, Digger," she said softly.

Digger spun around. Even in the haze of the streetlights she could see the white horror taking over his features. "Where I'm...from?"

She approached him slowly. "Chip and I are also from Hell."

Digger gaped at her. "You, t-too?"

"Yes."

"H-How did you—"

"That's not important. What's important is that we have to figure out what to do."

"Do?"

"Breath Mint sent us."

"Who?"

"Your boss—whatever his name is. He sent us to find you and take you back to him."

Digger cringed. He stepped back. "That was you? At the Safari?"

She nodded.

"You've been following us? To take me back?"

"Don't worry, I'll figure out something."

He wrapped his arms around himself. "You can't. Nothing you can do. I'm doomed. Doomed!"

"Don't give up yet, okay? I'll do my best to think of something, but I'll need your cooperation."

"Cooperation?"

"First of all, why'd you run away when you came up here?"

He blinked. "Run away?"

"From Breath Mint."

He lowered his head. "It doesn't matter. Not now."

324

"Everything matters."

He didn't speak.

"Is any of this because of Cal?"

He sighed. "It wasn't all his fault." He shook his head. "I...I just can't...I can't do what I'm supposed to do."

"What are you supposed to do?"

"I'm supposed to do bad stuff to the tourists. Make them, you know, wreck their cars and get hurt and lose all their money."

"Why can't you do it?"

"I've tried. I really have. But every time I do something, I feel bad about it. Cal thinks I've been taking money from these people. I haven't. I make it look like I'm doing it just so he thinks I am. I just walk up to them, say hi, then imagine a bunch of money in my hand. Then I show Cal the money. He thinks I took it from the tourists. And when he needs money to buy something, I give him some." He sighed. "Cal wants me to teach him some of these tricks, but I can't do that."

"Is it because you're an inferior? Because you're unable to pass your powers off to a mortal?"

Digger shook his head. "Cal...he's bad. He'll hurt people. He doesn't like anyone very much. I can tell. He—" Digger turned away.

"Why do you stay with him, then?"

"When I came up here, I did what I was supposed to do. I didn't like it, but I did it. Then I met Cal and he told me all about these neat fun things. I didn't get to do much when I was alive. I was only eighteen when I died."

"I didn't know."

325

"I was a court jester for Caligula. I...tripped...on a step...during one of my juggling routines...and made him spill his wine goblet in his lap. He had me beheaded."

"Just for that?"

"He wasn't very nice."

"I've heard. You were sent to Hell for that?"

"My family, we performed black masses for the court. My folks, they did all sorts of nasty things. My dad was a shaman, and my mom was a witch. I didn't know any better, so I did stuff with them. Family, you know..." He shrugged.

She remembered the many times she wished bad things would happen to Stepdad. "I understand."

"I'm not bad, though. At least, not like the supers down there, or even the subs. They really enjoy doing bad things. I only do bad things when they order me to."

"And this all changed when you met Cal?"

"Everything sounded like so much fun. Driving around to all these neat places. Picking up ladies. That's Cal's idea, but I went along with it because he likes it so much."

"He conned you into doing what you've been doing?"

"It wasn't like that. You see, two thousand years ago, we didn't have half the stuff I see here now. You've got these neat cars that take you places much faster than horses, and really fun things I'd never seen before. Like that Safari place. And the rodeo. I just wanted to have fun. When I was alive, I had to entertain Caligula and all his people. If I

326

didn't do it or if I didn't do it good enough, they'd torture me right there, and everyone would laugh." He sighed. "But no one ever made me laugh."

"Except Cal."

"I never had a friend...before."

"You didn't want to be alone."

"Down below, you spend your time hiding from supers and subs because they always want you to do something you don't want to do. But up here, being alone is totally different. I heard about how big this place is, how crowded. I knew I would be scared and confused. At first, I was terrified. I didn't know where anything was, so I got on a tour bus and took it to International Drive, where I saw all these strange people with funny hats wandering around. I bummed around for a few days, wondering what I was going to do. Then Cal walked over to me one day, really upset, telling me I needed to find another place to work. I had no idea what he was talking about. I just nodded and said sure, I could do that. But when he saw the money in my hand, he wasn't mad anymore. In fact, he acted really friendly after that. Even cracked a few jokes. That made me laugh, and I wasn't scared or confused anymore."

"And instead of reporting to your boss—"

"When I first came up, His Excellency gave me one of those funny little phone things so he could talk to me whenever he wanted."

"What happened to it?"

He looked down at his feet. "I didn't want any trouble. Cal asked me about it. I didn't want him to find out what was going on. And I didn't want His Excellency to…to find out about Cal."

Tiffany had been right about Digger. He really was a nice, sweet guy. Just another unfortunate soul doomed to spend eternity in the same dark, foul place as she and Chip.

"Do you really think you can help me?" Digger asked hopefully.

"I don't know. But I'll certainly do my best."

Chapter 48

Some Final Arrangements

Satisfied with how things went with the Grove kid, Braithwaite finished his bottle of port wine before leaving the restaurant.

The kid's father wore his usual worried look as he slipped a twenty beneath his plate for the tip.

"Something wrong?" Braithwaite asked.

"Just a little worried about my son."

"The kid's doing fine."

"I honestly hope so." Grove avoided looking him in the eye.

Braithwaite could read the man's thoughts. He wanted to know what his son was involved in but didn't want to ask.

Best not tell him anything for the moment. Grove, as well as the rest of the Diocese, had much to do to remove themselves from Braithwaite's shit list. Any discussion of the kid right now would surely delay the process—especially if Grove said something stupid again. Braithwaite had enjoyed his meal. He didn't want to cap the evening by turning a Diocese member into an escaped mental patient wandering South Orange Blossom Trail in an orange suit with no recollection of the last twenty years of his life.

Braithwaite went out into the warm, muggy night. He wanted to walk back to his penthouse suite but had to make an important call first. He sat down on a park bench, pulled his cell phone out of his jacket pocket, then punched in the appropriate numbers for the long-distance call.

The soft, familiar voice quickly came on the line.

"Mr. Waite," the man said in perfect Arabic.

"Mohammed," Waite replied in equally perfect Arabic. "And how are things in Cairo?"

"They are as well as can be expected. The arrangements in Florida—have they been made?"

"All that is required is your presence."

"The land we wish to purchase. It is sufficient for our needs?"

"There are several parcels that might interest you. It will probably take two days for you and your associates to view them all. Two of these are presently resting on golf courses."

"Excellent, excellent. The Americans, they love their golf."

"They seem to be very happy and content, paying large amounts of money to chase a little white ball around in a mowed field."

"How much area shall we be able to purchase?"

"I have estimated nearly two hundred acres you should have no difficulty acquiring."

"The owners... They are motivated?"

Braithwaite sat back and grinned. Motivated wasn't quite the right word. Pressured was more appropriate. But now was not the time for such a discussion.

"I have talked to them," he said. "They understand the situation."

A slight pause. "And the price has not changed?"

330

"It comes out to between two and five million per acre."

"Perfect. It is well within our budget."

"How long do you think it will take to develop these properties?"

"A recent talk with my Iraqi associates suggests that we will cause much less attention if we proceed very slowly. They have given me an estimate of between five and ten years for full development."

"That is very wise. Americans usually do not make much of a fuss if they do not suspect anything or see anything out of the ordinary. This is how the land for the theme parks was purchased nearly five decades ago."

"No one in America will know our plans until everything is fully operational."

"Excellent. Then we shall see one another sometime this Saturday afternoon?"

"I shall look forward to it."

"Give my regards to my colleague, Agaliarept."

"He goes by the name Aghali Areptuli to our people. We have not seen him for some time now. He is heavily involved in his recruitment campaign for future training camps."

"How's the bad boy doing?"

"He has, I believe, recruited four hundred so far. His personal goal is two thousand. He intends to reach that number by the time we begin sending our associates to Florida to begin our developmental plans."

"I have no doubt that he will achieve his goal."

"You are correct, my friend. Aghali is a very driven individual."

331

Chapter 49

Tiffany's Plan

Lost in thought, Tiffany followed Digger back to the motel room.

Neither Ashley nor Chip had budged from their seats. Cal snored loudly, his mouth wide-open, his chin covered with drool. The half-empty whiskey bottle remained wedged between his legs. Digger didn't seem to notice anyone as he assumed his former position on the other bed.

Time to take Chip aside and tell him what she had in mind. She knew he wouldn't like it, but he had to know anyway. She couldn't do this without his help. "Chip? Join me outside, okay?"

"Why?"

"We need to talk."

"About what?"

She was in no mood for this. "Guess."

He shrugged and jabbed a thumb at Digger.

She frowned. "Why don't you just say his name? You don't want anyone guessing, do you?"

"There are only three other "anyone's" in the room, angel. I'm sure one of them already knows what this is all about. Unless the second one's a total imbecile, she probably also has a pretty good idea. The third one wouldn't notice anything if you covered him in gasoline and lit a match."

"Just shut up and come outside with me, okay?"

"Well, since you're asking so nicely..."

He joined her on the walk leading to the machines between the buildings.

Tiffany had no idea how to present her idea. No matter what she said, Chip wouldn't be happy. He wouldn't approve of anything that might go anger Breath Mint. But she was determined to handle this her way. She couldn't take Digger back. She liked him too much to make him face Breath Mint.

"I take it you've got something in mind." Chip pulled a plug of grass from the small patch near the edge of the walk and sucked on it.

She nodded. She could tell he was already suspicious.

"And going by your silence, as well as the blank look on your face, I'd say you're planning to do something I'm really not gonna hate."

"I don't want to take Digger back," she blurted out.

"I just knew you'd pull something like this. He gave you a sob story." He tossed the grass over his shoulder. "Fell for it, didn't you?"

"Of course I did."

"He's a dung beetle, Tifferino. That's bottom-of-the-barrel, even in Hell. I'm only a flower and I'm way above him on the food chain."

"What does that have to do with anything?"

"He's a dung beetle."

"He can't help what he is."

"But he's a dung beetle. One of those gross-smelling wormy-looking things that comes crawling around the rock garden, sniffing around all the time."

"Did he bother you?"

"Actually, we liked him coming around."

333

"See there?"

"Don't get all silly and starry-eyed and romantic, now. We liked him coming around because he always picked up the stray shit the supers dumped on our petals."

"He's not a bad guy at all. He shouldn't even be down there."

He didn't reply.

"You agree, don't you?"

"About what?"

"You're not listening to me, are you?"

"You're silly and glossy-eyed and romantic. When you're like that, you use your girlie parts instead of your brain."

"He's not a bad guy."

"He's a dung beetle, precious. Who cares if he's bad or not?"

"I do."

"That's only because you're a sap."

"Maybe I am. But I just think—"

"Baby Cakes, if Braithwaite even suspects we're trying to pull something, we'll both be sent back down there quicker than you can blink those long, curly lashes. They'll skin us with a dull deer antler, then stick us both in the Sea of Entrails without a paddle for the next five hundred years."

"The Sea of what?"

"Ever heard of Shit Creek?"

"I thought that was just a figment of—"

"Think again, muffin."

She brushed that image aside. She couldn't let herself be distracted. "Listen. If we work this right, Breath Mint won't suspect a thing."

"Don't tell me you've already got something in mind."

"I've already got something in mind."

"I told you not to tell me that."

"It's true. And it's very simple. Just hear me out, okay?"

Chip rubbed his eyes. "Why don't I have a warm fuzzy about this?"

"Broad Water intimidates you."

"So?"

"You freak when you get within one mile of him. You melt into a messy gob of mush when you're around him. You turn totally brainless and slobber. If you weren't a flower, you'd leave a trail of slime."

"I get it, all right? Stop the character references and just tell me what you've got in mind."

"I intend to tell Breath Mint we didn't find Digger."

"That's it? Your big plan?"

"Simple, huh?"

"Simple isn't exactly the word I'd use."

"What word would you use?"

"Totally asinine, ridiculous, dangerous, and tacky."

"What's wrong with it? And that's six words."

"For one thing, it won't work."

"Why not?"

"He's a super demon, honey bunny. He can read minds."

"I'll make sure he won't read mine."

"And how, pray tell, will you do that?"

"He already thinks I'm a dumb blonde. The rest will be easy."

"And just how do you intend to keep him from tapping into that luscious melon?"

"I intend to act like a dumb blonde."

"And that'll accomplish what, exactly?"

"He won't be able to get in there to read anything."

"Lamb chop, this won't work for one very important reason."

"What's that?"

"You're not a dumb blonde."

"Boiled Wafer doesn't know that."

"He will."

"I'm really good at acting dumb."

"Precious, there's a lot at stake here. Are you totally sure you can pull this off?"

"How can you even ask me that? I used to live in Hollywood."

DAY FIVE - Reporting to Braithwaite

Chapter 50

Raising the Stakes

After the beautiful Tiffany lady and her friends left, Digger sat at the table in front of the motel room window, watching the main highway through the parted drapes.

He still couldn't believe he was free. The blond lady hadn't lied to him when she told him she'd think of a way. She had even discussed it with her friend, the trickster named Chip. Chip hadn't wanted to do it, not at first. Digger could tell by the way Chip kept shaking his head as they left. Digger suspected Chip might be afraid of the blond lady. Digger couldn't understand how anyone could be afraid of such a sweet, beautiful lady. It baffled him that someone like her was sent to Hell in the first place.

But the more he thought about it, the more he realized how many others he'd seen down there who didn't seem to belong. Chip also didn't seem to belong. He was a trickster, but he wasn't evil or bad. At least, not like the inferiors or subs.

But that didn't matter. Digger was free.

Before they'd left, Digger asked them what they were going to tell Braithwaite. The blond lady just said, "Don't worry about it, just stay away and

337

blend in. If you can, try to leave the state and get as far away as you can."

It sounded like a terrific idea. If he could just convince Cal...

Cal suddenly opened his eyes. After a loud groan, he struggled to sit up. His whiskey bottle rolled off his lap, onto the bed sheets.

He rubbed his eyes, yawned, and glanced around the room.

"Where'd everyone go?"

"They're gone."

"I can see that, brainiac. Where'd they go?"

Digger shrugged. "They're just...gone."

Cal rubbed his temples. "They didn't say where?"

"Nope."

Cal didn't say anything. He just continued rubbing his temples. When he stopped, he turned back to Digger and glared.

"Cal? Why do you look so mad?"

"You can't figure it out on your own?"

"I never know what's going on in your head."

"It's like this, Einstein. When I blacked out, there were two sweet babes sitting at that table. Now they're gone, and you're there instead."

"I just told you. They left."

"I got that." Cal jabbed a thumb at his head. "This works, ya know."

"We can find other women. We did before."

"Sure. No problem. This is Florida. Babes are everywhere. Just open the door and they'll stampede right in."

"We'll find one, Cal. All we need is a ride. And we both know that's no problem."

"Right. No problem."

"You still don't look happy."

"I have a head the size of a fucking basketball, all right?"

"So…you're happy, then?"

"I'm happy, all right? I'd do a fucking cartwheel, but I really don't want to want to throw up before I've had my breakfast. Now…where the hell did they go?"

"They just decided to leave."

Cal continued staring. Digger could tell his friend was trying to figure this all out.

Suddenly Cal's eyes grew, as if something had just popped into his head. Digger didn't think this was a good thing.

"Dig, how'd those babes happen to be right there to pick us up?"

Digger shrugged. Maybe if he acted stupid, Cal wouldn't be able to put any of this together.

"That rodeo was jam-packed. How'd those babes get where we were?"

"They…walked?"

"You know what I mean, dammit. Don't play dumb."

"I…don't know what you—"

"Babes like that don't pick up strange guys. Even you can figure that one out. Those two were fine, especially Blondie." He shook his head. "She was some serious wet dream. And chicks like that don't pick up just any asshole—especially two assholes like us."

"Maybe they just—"

"They were following us, weren't they?"

Dig swallowed. His pulse quickened. "Following us?"

"I saw Blondie at the Safari place. She even called out for me. Why'd she do that, Dig? Why was she out there in the brush, hiding from those security dudes just like we were?"

Digger stared at the floor. If he could leave right now, he might be able to hitch a ride in the back of one of those small trucks if he could find one hauling a bunch of stuff. Maybe if he checked out the parking lots at these breakfast places—

"They have something to do with your boss, don't they?"

Dig flinched. Oh no. He was putting it all together.

"They work for him."

A sheet of ice slid down his back, making him shudder.

"Your boss is looking for you, isn't he?"

Digger's gulp was audible.

"It's all about that damned cell phone, isn't it? He kept tabs on you, and you trashed the phone and now he's looking for you. He sent those three to find you, didn't he?"

Digger glanced at the door again. He didn't want to leave Cal but didn't see any other way out.

"Why'd they leave? Why didn't they take you with them?"

Dig stared at the floor. He couldn't look Cal in the eye. Digger was a trickster just like Chip. He could do a bunch of neat tricks, but right now, Cal was the one with all the powers.

"Dig?"

"It was the blond lady. She...felt sorry for me."

"So?"

"She decided to tell...my boss...she couldn't find me."

"You mean they were looking all over the damn place for you but decided to just call it off?"

A nod.

Cal sat there, scratching his jaw. Digger hoped his friend would just drop it and suggest going out for breakfast. Or looking for another car to lift. Cal should be hungry about now. If Digger suggested breakfast, he wouldn't have to worry about Cal figuring out any more of this. "Maybe we should look for a place to—"

"Won't Blondie and the others be in a whole bunch of trouble?"

Digger blinked. Trouble. The realization slammed through him.

He should have thought of this before, but he hadn't been thinking clearly. He was too busy being happy about getting his freedom back. They were going to leave without him. He wouldn't have to worry about being taken back to Braithwaite.

But now that Digger's thoughts cleared, he realized what he'd actually done. Cal was right. All three of them were in trouble. Big trouble. And it was all because of him.

"If your boss sent those three looking for you, won't they be seriously screwed when they go back and tell him they couldn't find you?"

Digger looked down at his lap. And felt bad. Real bad.

The beautiful blond lady was so good to him, too...

"Well?"

"I...don't know."

"If your boss ordered them to find you, I'll bet he'll be majorly pissed when they go back empty-handed."

Majorly pissed? Cal had no idea. When a super demon was pissed, a whole bunch of innocent people would be hurt or killed.

"That was awfully mean of you, Dig. An awfully mean thing to do."

"It was her idea." He didn't know why he said that. The statement hurt as soon as it had left his lips.

"You're really cruel, Dig."

Yes. He was cruel. He just said it was her idea. That took balls—as well as a large amount of cruelty.

I really deserve to be in Hell...

"A babe feels sorry for you and takes the fall. So what do you do? You let her do it."

"She...she insisted."

"I'll bet she held a gun to your head, didn't she?"

She insisted. That was almost as bad, as lame, as saying it was her idea. You are bad, he heard himself saying. You do belong in Hell.

But what could he do? How could he make this right without endangering his freedom? Without returning to Braithwaite?

"What can I do?" He felt helpless. And hopeless. All he had wanted was to have a little fun for the first time in his life. Now he faced the cold realization that he had destroyed three people who had gone out on a limb to help him. "I can't do anything to fix this."

"I think we should look up your boss."

"No!" They couldn't. That was the point of being with Cal in the first place, wasn't it? Tossing the cell phone? Doing fun things without hurting anyone? He couldn't go back. Couldn't!

"You gonna be able to handle it if he fires all three of them?"

Dig turned away. If only Cal knew. If only he knew what Braithwaite was. How he operated. If only he knew Braithwaite didn't fire people, he destroyed them.

But why should he? Cal would only know if Digger told him. And Digger wouldn't tell him. Telling Cal would be the worst possible thing Digger could do. Not knowing. That was their only prayer.

Not knowing.

That might also be Digger's only prayer as well. . .

Cal wouldn't know about Braithwaite. And Digger wouldn't know about the three people who'd let him go.

You won't know, his mind told him. You're here. You won't have any idea what will happen to the blond lady and her friends. For all you know, they won't even go back to see Braithwaite. Maybe they'll drive away. They all know about the super demon. They all know they shouldn't go back to him—especially after having failed their mission.

"I won't know about it." Saying it aloud made him feel a little better. "I won't hear about it because we'll be—"

"You don't think he'll send anyone else after you?"

Digger's heart raced. If only Cal hadn't said that...

"If you pissed off your boss as bad you said, he'll send someone else after you. Count on it. And what if he sends guys next time? And I don't mean guys like that skinny redheaded dork. A regular guy ain't gonna feel sorry for you. He'll just haul your ass back, no questions asked."

Digger wanted to come out of his skin. There had to be a way out of this. If he didn't have to face Braithwaite...

He jumped up and paced. "I can't go back. I just can't!"

"Maybe he won't be so pissed if you tell him you're sorry. Ask him to give you another chance. I'll even put in a good word for you. Maybe he'll hire me on as your assistant."

Digger stopped pacing. Cal had just started up that spiel of his again. Trying to find out about Digger's powers. Digger's "Touch," as Cal liked calling it. Wanting to learn about it.

"He won't do that."

"How do you know?"

"He just won't. He's not…he's not like that."

"He needs you, doesn't he?"

Braithwaite didn't need anyone. He used inferiors and subs. He used mortals, too. But he didn't need anyone.

"If he needs you, he won't fire you."

"You don't know him. He wouldn't—"

"A smart guy wouldn't fire someone he needs, would he?"

"You don't know him, Cal. You…you just don't know him."

"I'll be right there beside you. I'll convince him it wasn't your fault. I'll tell him it was me. I got you sidetracked."

Digger began staring at the door again.

"You want whatever happens to Blondie, the brunette babe and Red, on your conscience?"

Digger's head throbbed. The suffocating feeling of guilt had come back. She was such a sweet, beautiful lady. He felt almost like he was standing in a flower garden when she was with him. She made him feel good about himself. For the first time in two thousand years, Digger didn't feel dirty or filthy.

She was like an angel. She may have been in Hell, but it was a mistake. She wasn't a demon; she was an angel.

Cal put his hands on Digger's shoulders. "Your boss won't do anything before he finds out what's been happening. A smart man finds out all the facts before he does anything."

345

Digger pulled away and turned to face the door. "He doesn't do anything a normal person would do."

"Then we need to convince him how important we are, don't we?"

Digger sighed. If only Cal knew...

But Digger couldn't possibly tell him.

"How bad do you feel about Blondie?"

He felt horrible. He wanted to strangle himself right now. If he wasn't already dead, he'd kill himself.

If anyone was an angel, she was. And she didn't deserve what faced her if they went back to tell Braithwaite they'd failed.

"Don't you think we ought to try and get her out of this mess?"

"How?"

"She got you out of trouble, right?"

You're bad, Digger. You sent an angel back to the super demon. You belong in Hell.

"I belong there," he said softly to himself.

"Good. Then we'll just go back and tell your boss how it was our fault she and her friends screwed up."

Back to Braithwaite. To be sent back to Hell.

Digger put his head in his hands. You're bad. You deserve to stay in Hell. You're a demon. Demons do bad things. "I can't!"

"You want her to take the fall for this?"

"No!"

"Maybe we can get to them before they go talk to your boss."

346

I'm not bad. Not really. But there's only one way I know to prove that.

I need to rescue her. I can't let her suffer for something I've done. I need to do something. Anything.

"Dig? I don't mind. I really don't. We're buds, ain't we?"

She's the only one who ever helped me. The only one who ever looked at me without laughing. Or frowning. Or judging me.

She's an angel, and I need to rescue her.

"You can't do this, Cal. I have to do it—all by myself."

Chapter 51

Meeting with Mr. Waite

Braithwaite did not expect to see them this soon.

He also didn't expect them to come back with the brunette instead of the dung beetle.

It made him wonder if he was dealing with two morons. The brunette looked nothing like the shit bug. Whatever would possess them to bring her here?

Maybe they forgot what their mission actually was.

That would just figure. He obviously underestimated them, considered them incompetent, not total imbeciles.

He sat forward, rested his elbows on his desk blotter, and carefully lighted his cigar. Staring at them, one at a time.

The blonde seemed nervous, which made him feel a little better. Behind her, the stinkweed stayed close, nearly touching her, trying his best to keep out of the line of fire. Behind the stinkweed and about a foot or so to the right, the brunette stood stiffly, her bone-white hands clasped together in front of her.

Braithwaite pushed a thick plume of dark smoke toward them. "How'd you three hook up?"

"Outside in the parking lot," the blonde said. "After our last meeting here."

Blondie wasn't exactly giving him a warm fuzzy. "That makes a good when. Now...how

348

about trying for a good, old-fashioned why? It won't get you off the hook, but it'll go a long way toward making me think you're not really as stupid as you appear."

"We needed transportation to find Digger. This city's much too big to cover without a car. We just bumped into one another."

As ridiculous as it sounded, it made sense. But they still needed to tell him why the dung beetle wasn't with them. "All righty. That sounds reasonable...but it doesn't explain why you didn't bring back the shit bug."

"He...got away."

"Ya don't say?" He sat back and considered his next tactic. He could turn the three of them into puddles of cat piss staining the carpet. That would make things interesting, but it wouldn't help him find the dung beetle.

It would also stink up the office.

He had asked the Legion to send up a dozen or so inferiors, two of them specifically to look for the stink bug. However, judging by how the Legion operated nowadays, this would probably take several days. Maybe even weeks.

Braithwaite wanted the stink bug here now.

Too bad the blonde hadn't come through for him. He hadn't expected her to show up empty-handed. He had her pegged as the take-charge type. The kind who could entice any mortal male to do her bidding. Not the sort who didn't accomplish what she set out to do.

She was obviously no different from the tens of thousands of other females he had known throughout the centuries. Eye-candy and a variety of sweet smells seemed to be the summation of their existence.

The brunette tried her best to keep her head up but the fear oozing from her kept her from maintaining any degree of confidence. "You," he said. "Whatever your name is."

She straightened. The scent of her fear evaporated. Apparently she didn't enjoy being addressed as "You." Her large almond eyes glistened. "My name is—"

"Fine, fine. Just make believe I addressed you by your given name and we'll continue from there. We need to talk about a certain cell phone you should now have in your possession."

She shrugged. "It…didn't work."

"The Grove kid didn't give you another one?"

Her eyes glazed over. She had obviously been spending too much time with the blonde. A damned shame stupidity was contagious. But since the Dark Prince actually preferred this behavior in mortals, Braithwaite should work around it.

"I wasn't home," she managed.

The three of them were probably out looking for the shit bug at the time.

"So…the shit bug got away." He pushed another plume of cigar smoke at them. "That's the bottom line. Now explain."

"He and his friend just slipped away in the crowd," Blondie said. "That's easy to do with so many people wandering around."

That didn't sound quite right. The blank look on Stinkweed's face told him something weird was

350

going on. "That the way it happened?" he asked Stinkweed.

"Y-Yes, sir..."

Braithwaite sighed and rubbed his chin.

It was time for a little probing.

Chapter 52

Cal's Big Chance

Cal parked the stolen Mercedes in the crowded lot behind the skyscraper. At the other end, the glass doors of the building sparkled in the late morning sun.

Digger could not move. The last four blocks had been unbearable. His breathing became painful and he began sweating more than ever. He hunched down in the comfortable suede seat, his fists in his lap. He knew his smell was getting stronger when Cal turned off the air-conditioning and rolled down the windows.

"This the right building?"

Digger didn't reply. He couldn't find his voice. He was thinking of Hell.

He'd soon be returning. He knew it, felt it. There would be no more riding around, looking for neat things. No more finding fresh animal piles. He'd be a dung beetle again, crawling around in the hot darkness, looking for things Sibrius or one of the demons had dropped. Staying half-buried among the piles so the demons wouldn't find him and carry him inside the Castle to torment him.

"Come on," Cal said, swatting him on the shoulder. "This won't be bad."

The sudden contact snapped him out of it. His eyes grew. Poor Cal. He had no idea what he was getting into.

But this is unavoidable. It has to be done. I have to save the angel and her friends.

"You don't know him. You don't know wh-what he'll do..."

"I told you before. I'll do this. You can stay right here."

Bad enough the beautiful blond lady and her friends had sacrificed themselves for him. There was no way Digger would let Cal do the same thing.

"I can't let you do it alone, Cal. No. I have to go in there. And I have to do it alone."

"I thought this was all settled. You're too chickenshit, so I'll go in. I'll even act like I don't know where you are. I'll just say I met Blondie and the others at the rodeo and—"

"That won't work."

"Why not?"

"He'll know."

"How will he know?"

"He always does."

"What is he? Some sort of fucking mind-reader?"

If only that was all Braithwaite could do...

Digger gripped his sides. He couldn't let his only friend face the demon. "I've been thinking it over, Cal. You can't go in there."

"It'll be okay, I promise. From what you said, he wants you to mess with the tourists, take their money—which you've been doing, right?"

A nod.

"Look around." Cal pointed toward the street. Throngs of sloppy-dressed folks shuffled up and down the sidewalk. "Stupid fucks are everywhere. This is Orlando. Dig, if your boss wants to make money off the tourists, he's gonna need you to stick around. And if I can swing this right—"

"You just don't understand."

"Understand what?"

No reply.

"Talk to me, dammit!"

"He doesn't need anyone. If someone doesn't work out, he just gets rid of them and finds someone else."

"Look. I know you're scared of him, but—"

"He's a demon, Cal. A demon!"

Cal stared dumbly at him.

Digger wanted to strangle himself. He hadn't wanted to tell him, but it just slipped out. As his mind reeled, he realized that it had to come out. There was no other way he could convince Cal not to go inside.

"What the fuck are you talking about?"

Now that it was out, Digger had to tell him everything. Cal might not understand or believe him, but at least it was the truth. "He's from Hell." Digger shivered. "I'm...from Hell."

Cal continued to stare. Then he laughed. "C'mon..." He swatted him again. "You can do better than that. I've heard some lame ones in my time, but this—"

"It's true."

Cal shook his head and chuckled.

He thinks I'm crazy. Good. Maybe now he won't want to go in the building.

"You don't have to do this, you know," Cal finally said.

"Do what?"

354

"Give me this bullshit."

"It's true. I swear."

Cal rubbed his eyes. "Listen. It's like this. Your boss is gonna teach me a few things. I don't care if he is a demon. I don't even care if he's an angel or one of those gremlins in a bad horror flick. Or even something Sigourney Weaver had to shoot with that fancy interstellar zapper gun she totes around."

"Who?"

"It doesn't matter, okay? Whoever this asshole is, he's gonna teach me a few of those damned tricks." Cal shoved open the driver's door.

"B-But…you can't!" Digger scrambled to open his door and jumped out. "You can't do that!"

"Why the hell not?"

"You just don't understand!"

"Sure I do. You just told me. Your boss is a fucking demon. One of those ugly dudes with horns, a pointed tail, and slobber coming out of his mouth. Right?"

"I d-don't know what you mean…"

"You think I'm some dumb shit? You don't want me meeting him. Admit it."

"I don't want you meeting him."

"Dig, you're really an asshole." Cal slammed his door. "You think I'm gonna believe a cockamamie bullshit story like that?"

"I'm telling you it's the truth!"

"Yeah. You work for the Devil. Sure."

"He's not the Devil. He's a demon."

"Same thing, right?"

"No. Demons aren't nearly as bad as the...as him—"

"Doesn't matter worth a shit. I want this, and you're not gonna ruin it for me. I know I can be good at it too, dammit. Look at you. You couldn't come up with a good idea if it bit you in the ass. I can come up with good ideas all day long. You're pitiful."

"No. It's nothing like that!"

"Bullshit. You're the one with the Touch, but if I can do the same things you can do, you won't be special anymore—"

"That's not it at all!"

"I'm gonna make your boss give me what you've got. I deserve it, too. Don't you think I deserve it?"

"It isn't that I don't—"

"Well, I think I deserve it. That's all that matters. I've been at the short end of the stick all my fucking life. It gets old after a while, ya know? I saw shit at school every fucking day. Rich kids getting all the babes while they laughed at schmucks like me. See it on the roads, too. The rich jerks in the expensive cars cutting folks off 'cause they're in a big fucking hurry to start ordering around shitheads like me all day. See shit everywhere. There's the lucky ones and the unlucky ones. Why the fuck do I always have to be unlucky, for Chrissakes?"

Digger couldn't speak. Cal didn't understand. He just didn't understand.

"Devil, my fucking ass!" Chuckling, Cal hurried toward the building.

356

Chapter 53

Tying up Loose Ends

Slipping inside Stinkweed's feeble brain proved ridiculously easy.

Images of the dung beetle and his friend running away from three men in tan uniforms. Elephants pulling leaves from trees. Crocodiles basking in the sun. A bus filled with tourists moving along a bumpy dirt path. A glimpse of the dung beetle and his mortal friend in a crowded parking lot, arguing over a feed bag and some horse shit scattered on the pavement.

Then...

The Limboite from the back, bending over. And from the front, with a close-up on her titties.

For an idiot, Stinkweed showed a remarkable level of good taste. But nothing bouncing around in that unruly red mess told Braithwaite anything that would make this fiasco any clearer.

"Where'd they get away from you two?" Braithwaite asked.

"Kissimmee Rodeo," the blonde said.

"What were you doing at a rodeo?"

"We figured he'd go there."

"Why?"

Blondie shrugged. "Livestock."

"Silly me." Braithwaite found himself thinking about the Castle again. Demons definitely made more sense than mortals. Even the feeble-minded ones like Alachua, who ran around in the Valley of

357

Decay, doing bad bird calls. "You haven't seen them since?"

The blonde shook her head. Stinkweed, looking confused, stared at her.

Something was definitely going on...

Time to penetrate that luscious golden skull.

A labyrinth of images. Colors. Streaming faces. At first he thought he was riding a carousel gone berserk. The Kilimanjaro Safari once again flashed prominently. Elephants. Crocodiles. Birds. Tourists wandering through the village. The tour bus driver. A tree.

A fucking tree?

He probed deeper, past the Safari images. Another shot of the tour bus. A flea market. A grinning old man with a cigarette stuck between his lips holding out a cheap necklace.

The Valley of Decay.

Gutrillus Canus pulling her out of the Meddaworld. A dump. A grassy field covered in trash. A coffee shop. A dark-haired mortal wrestling with a well-dressed mortal in a crowded dining room. The dark-haired mortal kissing her, pushing her down on a bed. A pickup truck, its bed piled with feed sacks. A good-looking, half-naked moron with crinkly blue eyes and a silly grin, offering her a drink at poolside—

Enough!

Braithwaite rubbed his throbbing temples. This female was a mess, her head even more cluttered than Stinkweed's.

His intercom buzzed.

This was not the time for interruptions. "Adele, I told you—"

"Two, um, gentlemen to see you, Mr. Waite. They say you've been looking for them the last few days."

What the hell was this? "The last few days?"

"Yes, sir. Shall I tell them to leave? Or shall I insist on—"

"Describe them."

A pause. "Well, one of them is about twenty, maybe six feet tall, slender—"

"What about the other one?"

A much longer pause. She lowered her voice. "Um, this gentleman has dirty brown hair. It's very, well, tousled." She lowered her voice even more. "He could use a little, er, cleaning up, sir. He appears to have fallen in dirt or mud. His trousers, they're very..." Adele sighed. "He's wearing a baggy brown shirt and is very upset..."

"Have them come in immediately." Braithwaite sat back and grinned. He had no idea what was going on, but this was bound to be entertaining. That was the one thing about mortals that never failed to impress him: the fact that you never knew what they were up to.

"Those two idiots you just said got away?" he said, watching Blondie closely.

She swallowed. "What...about them?"

"They've decided to look me up on their own. Convenient and all sorts of interesting, wouldn't you say?"

***

Cal reached for the door marked MR. WAITE.

Digger grabbed his wrist.

Cal pulled free. "Lemme go!"

"Cal, you can't do this!" Digger, the jerk, had gone loony. His face was pale, he was shaking, and he smelled really ripe. Stronger than Cal could ever remember.

"Asshole." Cal didn't care how messed up the dork was. No one would fuck this up. "Go wait in the damned car."

"You'd better go in," the dark-haired lady at the desk said. "He doesn't like to be kept waiting."

Cal shot Digger a glare. "Moron." He pushed the door open.

Blondie, the Ashley babe, and the skinny redhead huddled close together in the center of the room, gawking at him. Blondie's eyes were huge. He could almost hear her voice in his head saying

("get out of here right now!")

but figured it had to be his imagination. It was Dig's fault. The asshole had him all messed up.

A dude sitting behind the desk watched him behind a thick pillar of cigar smoke. Looked like one of those specially blended numbers the big shots bought for ten bucks apiece.

Mr. Big, no doubt. Sucker was huge, for one thing. Yard-wide shoulders, a big round head, and enormous hands. He was dressed in an expensive-looking dark suit.

Dude had scary eyes, too. They went clean into your head. Cal could almost feel him in there, sizing him up.

"And who the hell might you be?" Mr. Big's booming voice filled the room.

Cal cringed. Wow. With those lungs, this dude could scare the hell out of anyone. No wonder Dig was scared shitless of him.

"I'm Cal," he said. "Cal Krebs."

Mr. Big slowly stood.

Cal's jaw dropped.

Fucker must have been six-and-a-half-feet tall and probably went well over three hundred, maybe even three-fifty. Made that actor dude that played Perry Mason in the old TV show look like a little shit. Wow...

"Didn't think I'd see you again, dung beetle. Was it something I said? Something I did? Or did all this have something to do with that cell phone you were too stupid to hold onto?"

Dung beetle?

Cal turned. Dig had followed him in and stayed close to the doorway, trembling.

Why did this ginormous dude just call Dig a dung beetle?

"Close the door."

Gulping audibly, Dig closed the door softly, then tiptoed over to stand behind Cal.

"Who are you? And what are you doing here?" Mr. Big slowly circled his desk. His eyes stayed on Cal.

"I'm Dig's bud. We've been working together since we hooked up on International Drive a few days ago."

Mr. Big puffed on his cigar. Didn't say anything.

Cal figured he was making headway. Just two guys shooting the breeze. No problem. Dig was making this out to be way worse than it really was.

"International Drive," Mr. Big said. "And you met him there?"

"Sure did. He was taking money and—"

"Taking money?"

"Lots of it." Might as well try and impress the dude.

"And where is all this money?"

Dude had to be kidding.

Cal shrugged. "We spent it."

"On what?"

"Booze and women, mostly. Motel rooms. Food." Cal grinned. "The rest we just pissed away."

Judging by the scowl, Mr. Big didn't like that.

Guess I should've phrased it better.

"Lots of hot babes in this town—know what I mean?" Cal winked at Blondie. She didn't wink back. She just stood there, her eyes really big. Funny, how this dude scared everyone.

Well, he wouldn't scare Cal.

"All sorts of honeys," he told the dude. "You're a guy—you know what I mean, don'tcha?" No harm in a little bonding. All guys thought alike where babes were concerned. Even a rich, important dude like this big boy.

"Where did you find this mess?" Mr. Big asked, glaring at Digger.

Mess? What the fuck is he talking about?

"Uh, listen here, Mister—"

"Shut up."

362

Who the hell did he think he was? Sure, he was big and loud, and had tons of money, going by the suit, the cigar, and the office…but calling Cal a mess? Just because they spent their money on fun?

"I asked you a question, Dung Beetle."

Digger trembled even worse. "On In-International—"

"I really need to express myself better. I guess I got a tad careless and assumed you two have been carrying around an actual working brain cell. Which, of course, seems to be highly improbable. What I meant was, whatever possessed you to waste your time with this—this—"

"Uh, sir?" Time to speak up. People had been dissing Cal all his young life. This was his one big chance to defend himself. "I ain't a mess."

"Really?"

"You got it." Now was a really good time to let the man know who he was dealing with. Maybe Cal had wasted money. You had to grab your fun when you got the chance. But that didn't mean he wasn't motivated. All he needed was a chance to prove himself. "I'm cut out for bigger and better things."

"I'll just bet you are." The big man grinned.

Cal grinned back. If anything bonded two motivated guys, it was talk of success. This dude wasn't so bad. Now that he understood what Cal had in mind, he realized Cal wasn't a mess at all. Cal wasn't any different from anyone else—he just hadn't gotten any breaks. If he had lucked out once or twice in the last couple of years, he might have his own office as well.

363

No, this boy wasn't bad at all. Put his pants on one leg at a time, just like everyone else. Probably even left the toilet seat up, too.

"You think so?" the big dude asked.

"How's that?"

"You think I'm like everyone else? I leave the toilet seat up?"

Whoa. Dude's good. Reading my mind like it's no big deal. It made Dig's tricks kind of lame. What good was taking money from stupid tourists if you could read minds?

Maybe he could teach Cal tricks like that one.

"You want to learn tricks." The big man blew a huge plume of gray smoke toward Cal's face.

Cal brushed it away and grinned. Dude did it again. And didn't even make it look hard. Wow. I've gotta learn this shit!

"I'd love to learn some nifty stuff. Just like Dig, here." He reached back to swat the dork on the shoulder. Dig pulled away. "Dig's cool. The way he gets money from people and all? I'd give anything to be able to do that."

"Anything?" Mr. Big said. "Really? You'd do anything?"

"Sure would. Think you can teach me? Dig's been promising to teach me some tricks, but I don't think—"

"You're right." Mr. Big's eyes had actually grown brighter.

"Right?" Cal asked. "About what?"

"Idiots like you don't think."

Dammit. He's dissing me again!

364

"You're wrong about that." Cal decided to keep his cool, no matter what. Keeping your cool while you were being dissed took balls. Mr. Big might even be impressed. "I ain't no idiot."

Mr. Big boomed laughter. Everyone in the room cringed. "Would you like to prove that?"

"Huh?"

"Can you actually prove you're no idiot?"

Cal grinned. That was no problem. "See, I really wanna learn the Touch. I can learn real fast, too. Just teach me and I'll show you. I'm really motivated. Idiots don't wanna learn anything. They aren't motivated, either. That should prove I'm no idiot."

Mr. Big nodded. "Sounds good to me."

Cal sighed in relief. It was working. It was actually working.

"You want to learn a trick?"

Great. It was finally happening. Dig could pout and whine and lie all he wanted, but Cal's determination would win out.

"Anything you wanna show me will be just awesome," he said.

"I'll show you a trick to end all tricks. Okay with you?"

Wow. Cool.

"Okay. I mean, yeah. Just let me know what you're gonna do and—"

"You said you and Digger are friends?"

"Yeah. I guess." Cal glanced behind him. Dig had backed away some more. A strange white color had taken over Blondie's face. Red shook more than ever right now. Even the Ashley babe was

365

shaking, although Cal couldn't understand why. Just two dudes shooting the breeze, right?

"Are you or aren't you?" the big man asked.

"Yeah. Sure. We're buds."

"Then you must know what he likes."

Now what was he getting at?

"Huh?"

"What does your friend like? What turns him on? What really turns his crank?"

Cal shrugged. "Shit. Turds. Especially animal shit. All sorts of—"

Mr. Big's eyes flared, forming jagged white shards. "Here's a trick of all tricks. An idiot like you will really appreciate this one."

Mr. Big's eyes turned into lightning bolts and shot right out at Cal.

A giant hot fist slammed into his gut. The smell of burning flesh rose from the floor, disappearing seconds later. Cal's sudden scream was immediately cut off.

Everything instantly turned black and cold.

Cal had the sudden sensation of falling…

***

A steamy brown turd lay on the gray carpet where the idiot had been standing.

Blondie, Stinkweed, the dung beetle, and the brunette all gaped at the disgusting object. Good thing the dung beetle was already dead. Otherwise, he would probably have had a coronary.

Now it was time to wrap this up. Braithwaite had things to do.

"You. Shit bug."

The inferior froze.

366

"I brought you up here for one purpose. How could you fuck it up?"

"I-I…I couldn't…I—"

Blondie started to say something.

"If I were you," Braithwaite said, "I'd keep those lips pressed tightly together. Unless, of course, you'd like me to tweak them a tad? Make them bigger? Smaller? Shape them into something more avant-garde? A foghorn, perhaps?"

She immediately closed her mouth. Good. She was paying attention.

"This place is crawling with tourists, shit bug. They come here specifically to act stupid and spend all their money. They're all idiots. They don't need much of a push. How the hell could you fuck up such a simple task?"

"I-I…we j-just, I mean, I didn't want to—"

"I have this nagging feeling I'm not going to get much of an explanation from you, am I?"

The inferior shook violently.

"Is that a yes or a no?"

The shit bug continued shaking. The odor around him grew rancid.

"I'll take that as a definite no. Unless, of course, you've actually got something to add."

The shit bug muttered something incomprehensible.

"I guess what you've got to add won't matter much if no one can understand what it is. Let's make this brief. Pick up what's left of your friend."

The inferior cringed.

Braithwaite sighed. "Having trouble with that order as well? I'll make it simple. Listen carefully.

I'll even say it slowly, so you'd better listen. You're. A. Shit. Bug. Your. Friend. Is. Now. A. Piece. Of. Shit. You. Like. Shit." Braithwaite shrugged. "Get it now?"

Still trembling, the inferior carefully picked up the turd and held it carefully in his palm. He tried looking at it but didn't seem to be able to.

Braithwaite wanted to laugh. A gutless shit bug?

But at least the idiot was able to pick it up. Braithwaite rubbed his hands together. "Now put it in your shirt pocket. It's beginning to smell up my office."

With shaky hands, the inferior did as ordered.

"Excellent." Braithwaite nodded. "Once you're back down there? Let Balberith, Asmodeus, Olivier, and the others know what a colossal idiot you are. I'm sure they'll have some interesting jobs simple enough for you to handle without screwing up."

With a flick of his wrist, Braithwaite sent a jolt of sparkling flame toward the pitiful oaf.

Squealing in agony, the inferior instantly melted into a pool of brown wetness seeping into the carpet.

Cringing, the threesome backed up toward the door.

"I didn't say anyone could leave."

Everyone froze.

"Excellent." Braithwaite rubbed his palms together and grinned. "I'm pleased that everyone has decided to come together and rally for a change.

How'd you all like my little demonstration? Impressive, wouldn't you say?"

"They didn't deserve that," Blondie said, her eyes glacial pools.

Braithwaite regarded her curiously. She apparently decided to turn defiant again. Good. "Think I overdid it a little?"

"You shouldn't have done it at all."

"Maybe, but since I've already done it, what you or anyone else thinks doesn't matter." Braithwaite winked. "Personally, I enjoyed the turd-in-the-pocket thing, thought it was a particularly nice touch. This way, when the shit bug goes back down, he'll have his friend right there with him. I'm pleased."

"You're the only one here who is," Blondie said softly, her eyes still burning.

She was beginning to piss him off again. "Just be glad I don't do the same thing to you, your idiot flower friend, and your incompetent waitress buddy."

"Why don't you, then?" Blondie gazed steadily at him.

Stinkweed and the brunette cringed behind her.

Braithwaite grinned. For a scatterbrain, she sure carried around a giant set of 'nads. Maybe she actually would make a good demon when he sent her back down…

"I would, but something very important came up. I need all three of you. At least, for right now. Actually, you and the brunette are all I really need, but since my associates have been known to explore

369

bizarre avenues from time to time, Stinkweed might prove useful as well."

"Useful?" Blondie asked.

"Several international colleagues of mine are arriving in Orlando this evening. They are extremely wealthy and demand to be properly entertained during their brief stay. See that you don't disappoint them. Or me, especially."

"What is it you'd like us to do?" Blondie asked.

Braithwaite roared laughter. "You actually want it spelled out?"

"I'm not a prostitute," she said flatly.

"Guess what? Tonight, you are. So is your friend. And Stinkweed, if my associates desire it. You'll all be required to perform. Make sure you perform well."

"I don't perform," Blondie said, glaring.

"You have one of two choices. You either perform or follow the same adrenaline rush that idiot and the shit bug just had. Since I'm still all giddy and happy-go-lucky from my last miracle, I'll let you pick." He glanced at his watch. "You've got five seconds."

Blondie said nothing.

"Excellent." Braithwaite snorted out another thick knot of cigar smoke. "Time to notify your chauffeur." He picked up his phone.

Chapter 54

An Unpleasant Errand

Daniel reached for the doorknob and discovered that he didn't want to turn it.

He had done this same sort of thing dozens of times before, but somehow, this was different. Negative vibes? Some strange invisible force had taken hold of his hand, forcing him to open the door even though he really didn't want to.

He should not dread this visit at all. He was becoming his own man, and he'd soon be very rich. And even if he did have to face certain unpleasant tasks, he was confident he could follow through on all of them.

The call from Mr. Waite just three minutes ago (Get up here right now!")

sounded anything but pleasant. It probably had something to do with the escort service. Mr. Waite might want him to take hold of the reins. So be it. Daniel was ready for just about anything.

But when he opened the door and saw Ashley standing there with two others, he realized in that one instant that he was still clinging to remnants of his former self.

I can do this.

I might not be able to look Ashley in the eye, but that's an entirely different matter, one I'll have to work on if I want to succeed.

"Kid, you're a chauffeur tonight." Mr. Waite stared at him from behind his desk. The cigar in his mouth spat out tiny tendrils of gray smoke.

"A…chauffeur, sir?"

"Good memory." Mr. Waite winked. "A successful businessman always boasts an excellent memory. Now take these three to the best women's fashion store you can find. They need to look like escorts. High-class. Yes, even the redhead."

Daniel tried looking at Ashley and her friends but found it difficult. "Escorts, sir?"

"Kid, you're beginning to sound like a bad echo. You won't have time to find a limo, so use the brunette's car." Mr. Waite stood and dug into his pocket. "You'll need some cash." He pulled out a large wad and ripped several bills from it.

Daniel had no idea he would have to cart the escorts around. This was supposed to be high class—so why not use their regular chauffeur service?

"No time for regular service." Mr. Waite had obviously read his thoughts once again. "This is a rush job."

That explained it. It also told him that Mr. Waite was counting on him.

You can handle this. You can handle anything.

A hint of doubt drifted softly into his head but quickly disappeared. He watched himself grabbing the bills from Mr. Waite's massive fist. "No problem, sir."

"Good deal. The Village Resort Hotel, Disney Village. Presidential Suite. Get there as quick as you can. Make sure my friends go to bed happy tonight."

***

372

Tiffany slid in the back seat with Chip. Ashley got behind the wheel and Daniel Grove climbed in right beside her.

"You're our chauffeur?" Chip asked.

"Shut up," Daniel snapped.

"Does that mean yes?"

"It means shut up."

Chip shrugged. "I thought chauffeurs were polite."

"You sure have a big mouth," Daniel said.

"I also thought they wore funny suits and weird hats and drove a limousine."

"I just told you to shut up."

"I'd just like to know why you're not wearing a hat. And why you're not driving. Don't chauffeurs usually drive, too? You're not driving. I can tell."

Daniel groaned. "Will you just—"

"You know how I can tell?" Chip grinned. "One, you're not sitting behind the wheel. Two, the Ashley babe is sitting behind the wheel. And three—"

"You can be really irritating, you know."

"I've been told that before. But to finish what I was saying, this isn't even a limousine."

Sighing, Daniel turned to Ashley. "Get on Colonial and head east. Then make a right on Semoran. We'll be going south."

Tiffany could tell something was bothering him even before they got into the car. He had shown up in Breath Mint's office only ten minutes earlier and stood stiffly in the doorway, avoiding their eyes. He cringed when Breath Mint ordered him to take the three of them to meet his associates at Disney

373

Village. He made no comment, but his eyes shifted in Ashley's direction, stopping short before dropping to the carpet.

He sounded really angry. And he barely met Ashley's eyes.

"Find out what's wrong," Tiffany sent over.

Ashley glanced at her in the rearview. "I think Chip just set him off."

"He was angry even before Chip ruffled his feathers."

"Can't you just do one of your mind things instead?"

"I can sense that he's angry with you about something."

"Can't you find out?"

"I think it would be more effective if you tried talking to him. Isn't he the guy who came to your house yesterday morning?"

"He's also the guy who got me to quit my waitress job. And he's different. I mean totally. He used to be funny and charming and witty. He was also polite and caring. I wanted to jump his bones."

"Well, I have this strong feeling Waite did something to his head. Just feel him out, okay? If we can't find out anything that way, I'll slip inside and have a look around."

Ashley fiddled with her seat belt. "What's wrong?"

"Just drive."

"You sound upset."

374

"This sure is exciting and mysterious." Chip grinned. "I'm having oodles of fun. How about everyone else?"

"I told you to drive," Daniel said curtly to Ashley. He shot a glare at Chip. "And you to shut up. Do it. Both of you."

Chip turned to Tiffany and scratched his head. "I forget what I'm supposed to do—drive or shut up."

"Don't be funny," Daniel snapped. "I'm serious."

"How can I be funny if you're serious?"

"Just can the comedy, all right?"

"I can't help it," Chip said. "I get confused when I'm scared. When I'm confused, I do my funny routine. I don't like being scared. It wilts the ol' petals—"

"Shut the hell up!"

Chip wrinkled his nose and twitched his ears. Then he sat back and shook his head. "Pooper," he muttered.

"Drive." Daniel turned his eyes to the front.

"Something really odd has happened," Ashley sent over to Tiffany. "You may be absolutely right about that nasty Mr. Waite doing something to him."

"Let me see what I can find." Tiffany tapped into the man's skull. An image of Ashley and Daniel having dinner at a crowded restaurant, both laughing—

The image quickly dimmed, replaced by Breath Mint's enormous shadow looming over him.

She should have known. Breath Mint had manipulated this guy's head. Daniel Grove would never be the same.

"What's up, Tifferoo?" Chip whispered, watching her closely.

Uh-oh. . . He's suspecting something.

She shifted her probe, aiming directly at the unruly red mop.

Distrust and hurt. And fear.

She suddenly realized she should have brought him into this earlier. They had been through a lot together. She was doing him a grave injustice.

But it wasn't too late. Besides, they needed his help.

She sent her thoughts hurtling toward him:

"We need to figure out some sort of plan, and fast!"

***

Tifferoo's voice thundered into his head.

Flustered, Chip stared at the big blue eyes. Still the same old butt-kicker with the same clueless expression she developed and perfected from living in Hokeywood. Still sexy, sassy and delicious...

But somehow different now.

Yepperino. Her powers had grown. Big-time.

He tried an experiment: "Tifferoo? You up there somewhere?"

Her faint smile made him more at ease. "I'm here."

"How long have you been able to—"

"Just a little while."

"You've been doing that with the Ashley babe?"

376

She blinked the way she also did whenever she felt guilty about something. Then, a slight nod.

"Since when?"

"Not long."

"I'm hurt. And disappointed. And depressed. And taken aback."

"Taken aback?"

He shrugged. "I was on a roll. But the fact remains. I'm devastated by this sudden epiphany of betrayal and rejection."

She squinted. "But you don't look devastated..."

"I hide my feelers pretty well."

"How can you hide anything when I'm in your head?"

"Good point. But why didn't you tell me? I thought we were buds."

A sigh. "It's kind of hard to explain."

"Try."

"Would you believe it was mostly girl talk?"

Now he knew she was lying. Ol' Tifferoo was helluva butt-kicker, but her irritating habit of being the poster child for Good and Honest wore thin most of the time. She was obviously lying, probably to spare his feelings. Tifferoo had great potential but would never become a successful demon. Too soft, for one thing. Too sweet. And honest to a fault. Her flaws were a definite no-no for any sort of complicated demon work.

"No," he told her.

Before she could reply, Rich Boy abruptly twisted around in his seat.

***

377

Daniel didn't like the sudden silence.

The three of them might be planning something.

Time to let them know what was really at stake. It would be a grave mistake for them to try anything. They all saw what Mr. Waite was capable of. One quick call and the three of them would have plenty to worry about.

He didn't want to get Ashley in trouble, but sometimes a man had to do things he just didn't want to do. Especially if he wanted the money train to run on schedule.

"We need to get something straight before we do anything else," he said.

"Like what?" the blonde asked.

"The three of you had better act appropriately or an extremely important business transaction will be seriously compromised and will cost us billions of dollars."

Ashley had stiffened at the word "transaction." "We certainly wouldn't want that," she muttered, staring straight ahead.

He ignored her. Feelings didn't enter into this. Thanks to Mr. Waite, everything had become clear and simple. Daniel now fully understood how wealthy and powerful a man could become under the right supervision. And if he didn't let sentimentality come into play.

"Before we get to the hotel, you ladies will need new outfits."

"I already have new clothes," Ashley said, still avoiding his eyes. "We bought them yesterday morning. They're still in the trunk."

378

"Has Mr. Waite approved of them?"

"Any normal man would approve," she snapped.

"Well, your friend needs an outfit," he said. "We'll get her something sexy, flashy, and expensive. Once we arrive at the hotel, that's where you both need to shine. These men have come all the way from—"

"What about me?" the redhead asked in a soft voice. "What am I? Chopped liver?"

Daniel turned in his seat and found himself gazing into the blinking green eyes of an irritated woman.

***

"Very nice." Tifferoo's voice floated softly into Chip's head. "Now's the perfect time to play with this jerk."

"As long as he doesn't call the boss and ask what the hell's happening."

"Don't worry, I'll take care of that."

"My hero."

"Heroine."

"Whatever." To Rich Boy, Chip said, "There are three of us, you know. I realize I'm not blonde or beautiful, but I can still turn a few heads when I want to. You ought to see the damage I can do passing a construction site in a halter top and tight jeans."

Rich Boy gawked at Chip. "Uh, sorry. I guess I...I mean, I thought...aren't you a—"

"A what?" Chip glared.

"I guess I wasn't paying much attention in...in Mr. Waite's office."

"What are you trying to say, honey?"

He shook his head. "I'm really confused."

"You look confused, baby."

Daniel rubbed his eyes. "I could've sworn you were a—"

"This is my true hair color, dammit. Maybe it looks slightly different inside a car than it did in that fancy-shmancy building back there. I mean, just because I don't get my color from a bottle like some girls..." He glanced in Tifferoo's direction and scowled. "That doesn't mean I should be left out of the picture. How can anyone not be impressed with this package?" He stuck out his skinny chest, twisted in the seat, and pushed his hair over one shoulder. Tifferoo turned her head so she wouldn't crack up. "How many ladies do you know who can scarf down six dozen fish sticks in one sitting and still be able to squeeze into a three?"

Rich Boy's color had paled. He couldn't take his eyes off Chip. "Listen... this is really confusing!"

"What's confusing about it, honey? I've got this super-fast metabolism. I'll bet Blondie, here, hasn't seen a three in years. And take a gander at our raven beauty at the wheel. Ask her if she can squeeze into a three. I'll bet she's at least a five. Go ahead, honey. Ask her."

Rich Boy swallowed loudly. "I need...to find...find out something..."

The cell phone appeared magically in his hand. He nervously attacked the buttons.

380

"While you're talking to your boss," Chip said, "be sure to mention how you've been ogling my titties."

Rich Boy said nothing. He continued frantically pressing buttons.

"He's about to have a problem," Tifferoo sent over.

"Damned cell phones," Chip sent back. "Told you they'd never catch on."

Rich Boy frowned at the phone, then stuffed it back into his pocket.

"Something wrong?" Ashley asked.

"Not a damned thing." He sounded angry.

"Yepperino," Chip went on. "A size three. No matter what I eat. Ever since I was growing up in Athens, Greece. That's downtown Athens, by the way. I can eat whatever I see and forever stay a three. I remember one time—"

"Can't you just shut up?" Rich Boy said irritably.

"When can I talk?" Chip asked. "I'll bet these important clients of yours would love to hear how I can stay a three--"

"Listen to me. All of you." Rich Boy twisted around sharply in his seat. His eyes were huge. "You don't tell them anything unless they ask."

"Wow. That important, eh?"

"Exactly."

"Is that why we're buying clothes?" Chip asked. "A good idea, if you think about it. I mean, I look as cute as a button in these old things, but I clean up real—"

"Don't talk unless you're asked."

381

"He's really scared," Tifferoo sent over.

"You can thank me later, Tifferoosky."

"Our first stop is the Florida Mall," Rich Boy told Ashley. "We'll hit Victoria's Secret. Pick out a couple of outfits and then we'll be on our way."

"Victoria's Secret?" Chip asked.

"That's what I said."

"Sounds like oodles of fun!"

Rich Boy said nothing. He was too busy trying to work his cell phone again.

"How will I look in one of their sheer numbers?" Chip sent over to Tifferoo.

"Ridiculous."

"Even to morons who make their women hide their faces and bodies in burlap tents and never let them shave or use deodorant?"

"When you put it that way, you just might have a teensy chance."

Chapter 55

Careful Preparations

The luxurious Village Resort Hotel, situated just a quarter of a mile from one of Disney Village's most prestigious golf courses, boasted several floors of luxury suites overlooking the meticulously trimmed, sloped countryside.

A silver double stretch limo parked in front of the hotel gleamed even in the shade of the wide concrete Porte-cochere. The uniformed chauffeur standing beside it resembled a young Omar Sharif.

Thick polished pillars, comfortable furniture, and huge potted plants dominated the open area. Enormous crystal chandeliers hanging from the mirrored ceiling made the area appear even larger and more ornate.

The constant dinging of elevator doors sounded like slot machines in a gambling casino. Guests wandered from the elevators to the hall, where a black sign stenciled in white letters advertising Seafood Buffet 12 – 3 P.M. pointed their way. Mixed aromas of sautéed shrimp and grilled fish drifted out into the main area.

"That smell is making me hungry." Ashley boarded the elevator and put down her Victoria's Secret bag on the carpeted floor in front of her.

Daniel followed them in. "I'm sure they'll have something for you upstairs." He pressed the button that would take them to the third floor.

"The smell reminds me of the last time I had oysters," Ashley said, staring at the back of his head.

Standing beside Ashley, Tiffany could see Daniel's reflection in the shiny metal doors. He was staring at the floor. She could tell Ashley's comment hit home. A brief probe flashed that same picture of Ashley and Daniel in the restaurant one moment before Breath Mint's huge, foreboding image once again took over.

"I could go for some fresh dirt," Chip said. "My petals—"

"If I were you," Daniel said, turning to glare at him, "I'd start seriously thinking about using the off switch for your mouth."

"I'd use it if I could figure out where it is," he replied. "Lately I've been having trouble thinking things through. You see, I was a blonde once—"

"Shut up."

"You sure say that a lot."

"I agree." Tiffany frowned.

Chip reddened. "Somehow, I had the feeling that remark wouldn't do too well with this crowd."

***

Daniel led them to Room 303.

The small, comfortable suite provided an open living room-kitchen area, three bedrooms, and a large dressing area.

"You'll have about half an hour to change into your outfits and make yourselves ravishing," he explained.

"Half an hour?" Red said. "For ravishing?"

384

He was growing tired of this smart-assed bitch and her uncontrollable mouth. He had to remind himself that he only had to deal with her minimally. It was up to Mr. Waite's Arab associates to shut her up. Judging from what he'd heard about Arabs, they knew exactly how to keep their women silent.

"Yes," he said. "Ravishing."

"Sexy is about all I can manage, but—"

"Shut—"

"I know," Red said, nodding. "Shut up."

"I was wondering how long it would take."

"I might need a little more time for that, too," Ashley said.

Daniel forced himself not to look at her. Looking at her instantly brought back the guilt. But when he turned away, everything went back to being all right again, and he could think clearly and concentrate on business. With this one trip, he was going to earn around five thousand dollars. A lot of money for a single phone call, a brief meeting, and maybe an hour of his time.

More than enough money to justify putting up with a big-mouthed bitch and a few random guilt feelings.

***

A black-haired, clean-shaven guy around thirty opened the door. He wore a dark suit and smelled faintly of rosewater. His blinding smile showed perfect teeth. "Daniel Grove?" he said in perfect English, with just a hint of a British accent.

Daniel nodded.

"Please come in."

A man about the same age stood behind him. He was also clean-shaven, well-dressed, and smelled of rosewater.

"I am Kahlil Ayalliah," the first young man said. "And how is our mutual friend Mr. Waite?"

"He welcomes you and has instructed me to see that you are given every comfort."

The other man bowed and shook Daniel's hand. It was warm and dry. "I am Samir Shalhoub."

"Your English is perfect." Daniel was suddenly embarrassed for his slight southern drawl from too many years of Florida living.

"You are most kind," Kahlil said. "My cousin Samir and I are interpreters for these gentlemen. We are both graduates from the University of Alexandria and hold degrees in Business Administration as well as Foreign Languages and Diplomatic Relations."

Through the ornate archway, four dark-skinned, heavily bearded men in their mid- to late-fifties sat grouped together in the large, elaborately furnished living room. They were dressed in dark silk suits and wore white turbans. Two men sat on the sofa in front of the large, tinted picture window overlooking the swimming pool and tennis courts. Their companions faced them in armchairs. All four puffed away on cigars while engaged in rapid conversation.

"They are very important men," Kahlil said softly. "We insist that you do not ask their names or attempt any personal inquiries or information."

"I understand completely."

"We appreciate your cooperation." Samir smiled briefly. "These gentlemen shall be in this country only a few days and have instructed us to make all arrangements with the understanding that their identities be closely safeguarded."

One of the men suddenly barked something in Arabic.

Samir and Kahlil turned in unison and bowed.

Samir replied softly in the same language, then whispered to Daniel, "They wish to meet the ladies, if it is convenient."

Daniel consulted his watch. "I will give them ten more minutes, then collect them. They should be ready by then."

***

Chip came out of the bathroom wearing the sheer sleeveless gown Rich Boy had selected for him at the Mall. It was a navy-blue and too tight in all the wrong places. It felt like a rope had been looped around him and tightened, digging into his pits.

Tifferoo stood in front of the vanity mirror in the next bedroom, fluffing her hair. Her red sleeveless outfit fit like a second skin.

"You okay?" she asked.

"Why?"

"You look, well, silly."

"I need a little more information than that, Blossom Flower."

"You're trying to touch your ears with your shoulders." She went back to fluffing her hair.

"Best I can do in this straitjacket."

387

"You took the wrong size. I told you that back at the store."

"Rich Boy wants it tight."

"Rich Boy's an idiot."

Hmmm... Something very strange here. Tifferoo's outfit had also been too tight. But right now, she looked comfortable, and was moving around effortlessly. The seams hadn't even come apart.

"That outfit actually fits?" he asked.

"Now it does."

"What did you do?"

"Left it on the bed. This is one of my creations." She gestured to the floor. "Like the shoes?"

The high-heeled black pumps glittered with clusters of small diamonds stuck in each center, right below her instep.

"Those diamonds real?"

"Of course." She turned back to the mirror.

He shook his head. "You and your shoes."

"I love shoes."

"I never would've guessed." He went back to admiring her outfit. "Looks terrificoso, Tifferoosky."

"Not bad for something I just whipped up, huh?"

"Why didn't I think of doing that?"

"Maybe you're just nervous."

"Not hardly."

"Caught up in the excitement?"

"Excitement?"

388

She shrugged. "You're about to meet some fabulously wealthy men."

"Are you excited?"

She sighed. "You know how I feel about rich men."

"Me, too. I was more excited when you were kicking Gutril's ass in Ohio."

"Maybe you're just not cut out to be a female prostitute."

"Right on both counts."

Ashley appeared in the doorway in her glittery off-the-shoulder gold gown thingy. Her shins and most of her thighs showed clearly. The wide front slit running from the bottom of her skirt came to within two inches of Forbidden City. Her six-inch, open-toed platforms made her grip the door frame for balance.

"I feel like I'm on stilts," she whispered.

"You'll be okay," Tiff said. "Just don't move too fast, bend over, or turn around."

"I've got to get out of this stupid thing." Chip went down the hall to the other bedroom, peeled everything off, and stood in front of the mirror. He didn't really care much for fashion, but this was an exception. He closed his eyes. The same outfit appeared magically, like a form-fitting body stocking. He left out the collar completely, which felt like a bug doing irritating things to the back of his neck.

He went back down the hall.

Ashley and Tiffany hadn't budged from the vanity mirror.

He couldn't understand the fuss females made over their appearance. They were about to meet a group of rich jerks interested only in stripping them naked and pounding them senseless. But instead of being nervous and jumpy, Tifferoo and the Ashley babe acted as if they were going to some fancy coronation.

Even after several hundred years, he'd never understand women.

"Look," he said. "They're only super rich camel jockeys paying for a romp in the hay."

Tifferoo shrugged. "We know."

"I honestly don't think this'll turn into a romance type of thingy."

"We certainly hope not." Ashley wrinkled her nose.

"They probably just want to get their rocks off with American women."

"We know," Tifferoo said.

"Then why all the primping?"

Tiffany gently patted her cheekbones. "A girl always wants to look her best."

"Even for horny assholes?"

"Especially them."

"I'm intrigued, befuddled, and in awe. Please explain this nebulous nonsense."

"They're so much more fun to frustrate," Tifferoo said, shrugging.

"A girl doesn't want to frustrate a nice guy," Ashley said. "It's almost like kicking a puppy."

The explanation sounded so simple, he felt like an idiot for not figuring it out for himself. "Now I get it."

"What did you do?" Ashley squinted at him. "Your outfit fits much better."

He thrust out his skinny chest and fluttered his lashes. "A little of this, a little of that..."

"I like what you did with the collar. Where is it?"

"Left it on the bed with the rest of the trash."

"Good. It looked ridiculous."

"Speaking of looking ridiculous," Chip said to Ashley. "If you drop something, don't try to pick it up. Those stitches might blind someone when they start flying around the room."

"I know." She tried pushing it down farther over her thighs. "I can feel the air conditioning on my...navel."

"Listen," Tifferoo said. "We don't have much time. We have to figure out our strategy before Daniel Grove comes back."

"Go right ahead," Chip said. "Let those ratifying realities rip."

"First of all, we need to face facts. Breath Mint is only one phone call away, so I don't think it'll be wise to—"

A knock at the door.

They all froze.

"You'd better be finished in there." It was Daniel's muffled voice. "You're being summoned."

"So much for figuring out our strategy," Chip said.

"What'll we do?" Ashley's face paled.

"Don't worry," Tifferoo said. "I'll think of something."

"But we haven't been able to—"

"C'mon, dammit." Daniel pounded. "You've had enough time."

"I'm really nervous," Ashley whispered uneasily.

Tiffers reached for the knob. "We'll be okay. Just follow my lead."

Chapter 56

Meeting the Arabs

The door opened.

A well-dressed young man with large black eyes and long dark eyelashes smiled brightly at Tiffany. "Good afternoon, ladies," he said softly, maintaining his smile for Ashley and Chip.

"I'll be back to collect them in a couple of hours," Daniel Grove said behind them.

The young man's dazzling smile did not waver. "We shall send for you when my employers instruct me to do so," he said amiably.

"Mr. Waite would like me to check in, nonetheless."

"If that is his wish..." The young man bowed.

Daniel stepped out into the hall. "I'll call in about two hours, then."

"Thank you for your cooperation." The young man eased the door shut and extended an arm. "If you will please follow me..."

Tiffany, Chip, and Ashley followed him down the dimly-lit carpeted hall, into the first room on the left.

It was a small bedroom, with two single beds and the appropriate furnishings. Three long black silken garments were spread out neatly on the beds.

"Please," the young man said, gesturing. "You are to put these on."

"What are those?" Chip asked.

"They are the Abayah. My employers require each of you to be covered from the shoulders down to your feet."

"What about the stuff we already have on?" Ashley asked.

"Yeah," Chip said. "It wasn't exactly the highlight of my day, squeezing into all this crap."

The young man smiled politely. "You are to slip the Abayah over everything before you meet the gentlemen."

"It took us an hour to put this on," Chip said. "My pits are still tingly and chafed."

"I am so sorry," the man said.

Tiffany picked up a small black scrap of silken material. "What's this?"

"That is a Hejab," he replied. "It covers the hair."

"They want us covered so they can do the unveiling." Tiffany frowned at Ashley and Chip.

The young man bowed and reached for the doorknob. "Please do not take too long." He bowed before leaving.

**

Four stout, heavily bearded men wearing dark suits and white turbans lounged on the sofa in the large, elaborately furnished living room. All four smoked cigars and sipped champagne. They all froze when Tiffany and the others followed the young man into the room.

Four pairs of large, black gaping eyes shifted from Tiffany to Ashley, then to Chip before returning to Tiffany and Ashley.

394

Tiffany suffered a flash of déjà vu. She imagined herself back in Hollywood during one of their auditions. The same leering eyes, the same slobbering lips. It would not be long before they were forced to disrobe. But unlike the Hollywood dogs, these men would not make requests. Their glazed, unflinching eyes clearly said they were totally in charge.

One of the turbans said something to the young man, who quickly bowed and whispered, "I am to give you whatever you wish to drink."

"I'm not thirsty," Tiffany said.

"Neither am I," Ashley said.

The young man remained bowing. "I suggest you have something anyway. Otherwise, you'll offend them."

"Then what happens?" Ashley asked. "Higher oil prices?"

The young man kept his bright smile. "They are accustomed to having their demands satisfied."

"Well, since you're asking so nicely, I'll have a strawberry daiquiri," Tiffany said.

"I'd like a glass of white wine," Ashley said.

"A large pitcher of ice water for me," Chip said.

The young man's smile relaxed a fraction of an inch.

"She's on this weird diet," Tiffany said. "Without her water, she gets really silly."

The young man nodded politely, then straightened.

"And a small orange juice for a chaser," Chip added.

395

The young man produced a cell phone and spoke softly.

One of the turbans chuckled loudly and said something in rapid Arabic. The others nodded eagerly.

A young guy resembling the other young guy entered the room. "You ladies have just been given a great compliment. Our employers are quite taken by the beauty in your eyes and the way you carry yourselves."

Turban Number Two whispered something to Turban Number One. They both laughed. Tiffany suspected it was a dirty joke. It was a shame that even huge amounts of money could not improve a man's character.

Turban Number Three barked something to the two young men, who both bowed, then started down the hall.

"Where are you guys going?" Tiffany asked.

"We have been instructed to retire to our rooms."

"Who's gonna interpret what they say?" Chip asked.

The second young man grinned. "Not necessary, I assure you."

Turbans One and Two patted the cushioned seats beside them. Turban Three, slouched in an armchair, finished his champagne. Turban Four grunted something and stroked the arm of his chair suggestively.

"I suddenly feel very popular and dirty," Chip said.

"Welcome to our world," Tiffany said.

"Now you know what it really means to be a woman," Ashley whispered.

Turbans One and Two patted the seat again. So did Three and Four. Two muttered something. One loosened his tie, Three his belt. Four flicked ash from his cigar.

"This isn't going very well, is it?" Ashley asked.

"How can you say that?" Chip said. "They seem to be enjoying themselves already."

"I meant for us."

Turban One produced a pair of handcuffs from his jacket pocket. A fierce expression took over his dark, bearded face. Slobber glinted his lower lip as he gestured to Tiffany.

"Looks like the program has just dropped a notch or two," Chip said.

***

Turbans One, Two, and Three dragged Ashley and Tiffany into the second bedroom and slammed the door.

This room was just like the one containing the Abayah and Hejab. That is, except for the ping pong paddle, spiked leather dog collar, handcuffs, and rawhide cat o' nine tails lying neatly on the big double bed.

"I'm really scared," Ashley sent over.

"Don't worry," Tiffany sent back. "I won't let them hurt you."

Dangling the handcuffs from one hand, Turban One gestured for her to approach. Turban Two had pulled his pants down and pointed to the floor at his feet.

Turban One barked something in a loud voice that Tiffany interpreted as, "On your knees before your master!"

Turban Three grabbed Ashley by the wrist, pushed her down on the bed, and flipped her over. He had already begun pulling up her Abayah.

Her voice was raspy and weak, partially muffled by the pillows. "Please, Tiffany...please do something before—"

The rest of her plea was muffled as Turban Three buried her face in the pillows. Turban Two reached for the dog collar, sat down beside her, and fiddled with it.

A slow burn crept heavily down Tiffany's back. This was worse than anything she had gone through in Hollywood. Not because of what these men were doing but because she, Ashley and Chip were expected to endure it.

Tiffany hated being here in the first place. She was furious with Breath Mint for what he had done to Cal and Digger. Digger hadn't deserved the fate he'd been dealt. Neither had Cal. And Ashley certainly didn't deserve any of this.

I may not have enough powers to battle Breath Mint, but I can certainly make sure he knows who he's been trying to push around!

Her slow burn grew, scorching her flesh. It was time to get back to her butt-kicking ways. She wanted to send these men somewhere but knew she couldn't. Even if she had the powers, she wouldn't use them. She wasn't evil; being nasty just wasn't her forte.

However, she could get Ashley, Chip, and herself out of this without too much damage.

Turban Two dropped the dog collar on the bed. He straightened, grabbed her, and began wrestling with her. One and Three hastily grabbed the ends of the Abayah and pulled.

Tiffany instantly created a huge wart covering her chin.

While Turban Three reached for the collar, Turban Two grabbed her by the neck and pulled her close. Spotting the wart, both men gasped.

And froze.

Tiffany thought

(translate this)

and said, "You guys should really be ashamed of yourselves."

The men gawked at one another.

One said in Arabic, "The golden-haired whore speaks our language!"

Two said, "If only Allah had not cursed this wench with the sign of the beast upon her chin."

Three said, "Allah would not approve of such a disfigured young beauty defiling our bodies."

Tiffany said, "If you don't like the sign of the beast, I'll make him go away. And by the way, I'm not a whore."

Her wart disappeared.

The three men gasped.

Tiffany sent over a message to Turban Two

(turn around and put your hands behind your back)

and the man, protesting loudly, instantly did as she suggested.

To Turban One, she suggested

(cuff your friend)

and the man frantically muttered, "I cannot! I cannot!" But even as he fought hard to pull away, his hands fastened the cuffs to his associate's wrists.

To Turban Three, Tiffany sent over

(pull your friend's pants down)

and the man instantly protested: "I cannot do this! Allah, please help me! This will disgrace me and—"

Tiffany sent over

(good night, sleep tight)

and the three men collapsed quietly onto the mattress.

Ashley sat up and surveyed the scene. Her hair was a mess as she stared at the three on the bed...then at Tiffany...then at the three again...then at the bondage toys, before going back to Tiffany. "What...how did you...what happened?"

Tiffany shrugged. "I guess they were more exhausted than they thought."

Ashley continued staring at her. "But how...when...what did you do?"

"Jet lag can be a scary thing," she said, smiling.

***

His small black eyes glazed, Turban Four sat in the armchair, motioning for Chip to remove the Abayah and Hejab.

Chip did so.

He then gestured for Chip to remove the rest.

"You really don't want that," Chip said. "You're liable to see something pop up you're not expecting right now."

The man chuckled and nodded, gesturing again.

"Hmmm..." Chip scratched his chin. "Maybe that's exactly what you'd like to see."

The man chattered away softly in Arabic. He pointed to Chip, then to the floor, then to his crotch.

"A man of simple tastes, eh? Pardon the pun."

Grinning, Turban Four nodded.

Chip instantly made his outfit disappear, revealing his svelte, adorable male form.

The Arab gasped.

Grinning, Chip did a quick pirouette and nearly tripped. "You like my Baryshnikov?"

The man slowly got to his feet. Stared at Chip's face. Then Chip's member. Then his face again, his hair. He swallowed loudly and whispered something in very rapid Arabic.

"I take it you're more interested in the extra accessories than the Baryshnikov?"

More frantic chattering.

"Let me take a wild guess here. I'll bet you'd like to know what I just did, huh?"

The man's eyes swelled in their sockets.

"You'd like to know where Mr. Happy came from?"

The man continued chattering softly, as if in a chant.

"Have you ever been told that you guys look really silly with all that crap-wrap wound around your head?"

The man whispered something that sounded almost like a prayer.

"But I'll bet it cuts down on most of the aggravation when you sit down at a pay toilet and there's no paper on the roll, huh?"

More whispering.

"Listen. If all you're gonna do is stand there and pray, I guess it's time for my show-stopper. Watch this and be prepared to be dazzled." He spun his head around like a top, made a noise like a crazy loon, crossed his eyes, and farted loudly.

The Arab backed up, bumping against the armchair.

With a soft groan, he closed his eyes and collapsed.

Chapter 57

A Swift and Graceful Exit

Down the hall, four doors extended beyond the one with the sleeping Arabs. The two rooms across the hall served as the master bathrooms. The next room was empty.

The end room contained two single beds, an entertainment center, and a reading area cluttered with textbooks.

The young men sat in the room. Both still wore their suits. One sat in a chair, reading a textbook. His partner worked a laptop in the far corner. They both looked up sharply when Tiffany opened the door.

The one reading the textbook gasped and rose from his chair. "Yes, please? Is there something you request?"

The young man working the laptop looked up and blinked. "Can you please explain why you—"

Tiffany shot the word

(sleep)

into both their heads. The first young man fell back into his chair and sprawled forward, his textbook dropping to the floor. His friend also slumped forward, his head thumping the desk blotter.

Tiffany stared at them, suddenly remembering the boys in the van she had dealt with. Her powers were beginning to frighten her. If she wasn't careful, she was liable to really hurt someone...

403

But at least they had worked well enough to get them out of this.

She quietly eased the door shut on her way out.

***

"What did you do, angel?" Chip asked when Tiffany came back.

"The boys are sound asleep."

"You're really good at that," Ashley said. "I'm so glad. This could've been horrible."

"It's far from over," Tiffany said.

"I have this funny feeling they're gonna come to very shortly," Chip said. "At the same time, too. And when they do, they're gonna wonder why they still have their clothes on and why they're not having sex. Even an idiot can figure that one out, pumpkin."

"I'll need to do something else, then. Something to seal the deal."

"I'll bet this has nothing to do with anything evil, does it?" Chip looked disappointed.

"You actually have to ask?"

"One can always hope."

"I'm not a demon, you know."

"I really wish you'd quit bringing that up, lamb chop. It's so depressing."

"They're sleeping," Ashley said. "Isn't that enough?"

"The two boys shouldn't be a problem, since they don't know what happened. But these four need some sort of hex. When they come to, they're going to wonder what went on. Then, of course, there's Daniel. He's due to call in."

404

"Can you do hexes, muffin? That borders just a tad close to evil, you know..."

"Not good hexes."

He sighed. "Since I've always been standing around in the rock garden, and never had the chance to see what was really happening, I may be out of touch...but I've never actually heard of a good hex."

"Neither have I, but what have we got to lose?"

"What are you guys talking about?" Ashley looked confused. "I've heard of hexes, but I always thought they were bad."

"They are," Chip said. "They're really fashionable with witches, gypsies, vampires, and demons. It actually means "witch" in several languages. But take the totally tantalizingly tangy Tifferoosky, here, and she'll no doubt turn it into something so sweet, it'll curdle your insides—"

"Oh, stop. This won't be a normal hex. More along the lines of a strong suggestion."

"But good," Chip told Ashley. "We do only good stuff now."

"That would be really cool if good stuff came from Hell," Ashley said, smiling.

"Yeah." Chip rubbed his temples. "Good stuff coming from Hell. Now I've heard everything."

Sometimes he was so dense...

"Just keep thinking that if I can pull this off, they won't want us back down there," Tiffany said.

"Uh-huh." Chip was still rubbing his temples. "Get sent to Hell and start doing all sorts of good stuff. The demons won't go for that at all. They'll kick your butt out. Yep, works for me..."

405

"We're wasting time," Tiffany told him. "Now let me think. I have to figure out a good suggestion for these four."

"What sort of suggestion?"

The Arabs had come here to do business with Breath Mint. Whatever this was, it was evil and would affect a lot of innocent people. "Something that'll scare them into hurrying back home and staying there."

"And you think you can actually do this?"

"I have to try."

Tiffany stared at the three sleeping on the bed, then visualized the fourth sacked out in the main room. She closed her eyes. "Go back home and forget about what you were going to do here. This country is not for you. You have humiliated yourselves and your culture and will suffer the consequences if you protest in any way."

Satisfied, she opened her eyes.

"What was the hex, dearest? Make it so they'll pee their pants and forget who they are whenever they walk past the microwave?"

"Even better," she said. "I'm sending them back home."

"Now can we please leave?" Ashley asked uneasily.

Tiffany stared at the snoring Arabs. They sure didn't look evil or nasty. Just middle-aged men with hairy paunches and adenoids.

But they were also friends of Breath Mint, and this made her extra wary about leaving them right now. Something else was definitely needed. Tiffany couldn't leave this room with a clear

406

conscience until she'd done all she could to make sure these evil men didn't harm anyone.

To Chip, she said, "What's his name again? That demon guy you're so afraid of?"

Chip sighed patiently. "Braithwaite, my beautiful, alluring, golden-haired but sometimes scatter-brained goddess."

"Thank you. And don't call me scatter-brained." She closed her eyes again and sent them one last message:

"Tell Braithwaite that you had a lovely time and that you have to hurry back home due to urgent business."

She opened her eyes and smiled at her friends. "Now we can leave."

Chapter 58

Trouble Brewing

At around seven that evening, after an excellent dinner of sautéed shrimp and scallops, Daniel sat back while his waitress carefully placed his third martini on the napkin at his elbow.

Her nametag said Lucy. She was tall and slender and had the thickest brown hair. She looked about twenty, maybe twenty-two. As she sauntered back to the bar, he wondered how happy she was working here. Perhaps she might consider working as an escort. A grand or two a night would definitely beat what she was making here.

He sipped his martini. Strong. Good deal. When she came back, he would have a little chat with her, find out what her goals were.

Speaking of escorts...

It was time to phone Samir. It was almost two hours and, according to Mr. Waite's instructions, time for their status report. Daniel had wanted to drive back home but decided to stay here for the night instead. This third martini had already made him tired. He didn't want to risk his life on the roads.

Especially when he was well on his way of becoming a wealthy man.

Maybe he could con Lucy into joining him for the night. She certainly had been giving off enough vibes.

He decided to feel her out when she came back to his table. He could present his business proposition, then ask if she wanted to hear more about it when her shift was over. If he was right about the vibes, he'd be spending a pleasant evening in a luxurious hotel suite with a hot-looking young babe.

First things first. He pulled out his cell. Better make sure things were going all right. If everything was running the way it should, the Arabs would want no interruptions for the rest of the evening.

Samir answered on the third ring. "Yes?"

"Samir? Daniel Grove."

A pause. "Yes. Hello."

The hairs on the back of Daniel's neck stirred. Samir sounded as if he had just woken up.

"Samir? Everything all right?"

Silence. It sounded like Samir was stifling a yawn.

"Samir?"

"I am here."

"What's happening there?"

"I...don't know," he said in a soft voice.

Daniel stiffened in his seat. "Pardon me?"

"I seem to have fallen into a very deep asleep."

Daniel fought to keep the panic in check. "Samir, what's going on?"

"I have somehow...been derelict...in my duties. I am so sorry. The ladies...they have gone. My employers...they shall wish to speak to me. I really must go now."

What the hell happened?

"The girls just left?"

"So it seems."

Something had gone seriously wrong. Samir seemed alert, sharp, and bright. Not the type to fall asleep on the job. "You didn't hear them?"

"As I have stated, I was asleep. Kahlil, as well. It must have been the jet lag. I vaguely remember talking to the blond lady before, I believe, Kahlil and I retired to our room. But everything is fuzzy. The two of us seem to be suffering identical symptoms."

This made no sense. "You just left your employers and the women?"

"We were instructed to do so. Please. Forgive me. I must see if my presence is required." Samir hung up.

Daniel stared numbly at the cell phone. The dark, air-conditioned restaurant had grown quite warm. The people passing his booth gradually grew hazier, then disappeared. The darkness of the room encircled him, becoming a hot, suffocating blanket.

Was this really happening?

Or was he hallucinating?

He rubbed his eyes.

The guests became visible again. Voices and laughter grew louder. The tinkling of silverware and the distant banging of pots and pans caused a flood of warm relief shimmering up his limbs.

His mind kicked into overload.

Those girls did something.

But what?

He scrambled for his cell phone.

Mr. Waite needed to know what was going on.

Immediately.

***

The sharp-featured, dark-haired man in the tailored black suit sat in the window booth, watching the Grove boy and waiting for his important call. The clock above the bar said it was a little past seven—just two minutes since Grove had made his call.

Grove sat at his table, staring at his cell phone, then trying it again.

The dark-haired man grinned. He had already gotten a dead signal.

This one would have to wait.

Good deal. The inevitable would be delayed—at least, for now.

The dark-haired man had a sip of white wine as the wash of headlights shot past the tinted windows.

Strange. This was remarkably similar to a meteor shower. In some ways, the hectic activities of mortals mirrored certain phenomena of the universe. Except, of course, for the fact that mortal activity inevitably ended in destruction.

His cell chimed its familiar soft C major chord.

"Yes?"

"George, we've jammed the boy's phone."

"For how long?"

"I'd say fifteen minutes should be sufficient."

"You don't think he'll be suspicious?"

"What if he is? He is presently powerless. It is how we prefer him to be."

"You're not worried about him finding a pay phone?"

"From what we have already observed, the boy's waitress will distract him considerably when she returns to his table."

411

"Well, I'm right here," George said. "If he does decide to use a public phone, I'll have to make other arrangements to delay his call."

"Good. We're agreed, then? We'll wait fifteen minutes, then unjam the line."

"What about the other line? Have you taken precautions?"

"It was trickier, of course, but we managed. He'll experience difficulty too."

"Good. That man needs difficulty. It'll give him character."

"Always the optimist. Later, George."

"Later." He pocketed the cell, raised his glass, and had another sip of wine.

Fifteen minutes should give the Limboite and her friends more than enough time to slip safely away.

***

"Kid, I've been trying to call you!" Mr. Waite sounded more upset than usual. "Something wrong with your goddamned cell phone?"

"Possibly, sir. I tried calling you as well."

"One of these days I'm gonna have to find someone who can actually fix these pieces of junk."

"Is something wrong, sir?" Daniel could tell something was bothering the big man.

"I'm not sure. I've got this gut feeling something went wrong at the hotel."

A trickle of ice tapped Daniel between the shoulder blades. He shivered. Hopefully, this was just a normal gut feeling. There was no way the man could actually know what went wrong—was there?

412

"I kind of feel something, too," he said, trying to sound vague.

A pause. He heard Mr. Waite sigh. "Just tell me what you know, not what you feel."

Daniel didn't immediately reply. If he said as little as possible, he wouldn't incriminate himself. He decided to tell the big man what he knew for certain, and nothing else. "They didn't want me to stick around, so I'm not sure what went on."

"Those Arabs value their privacy. You haven't talked to anyone, then?"

"Just Samir. He sounded upset but didn't tell me very much."

"I'll call you right back."

***

Braithwaite could tell something had gone wrong. The kid was holding back. This was not the time to take chances. He had put in considerable hours to arrange this land deal. Agaliarept would not hesitate to contact the Dark Prince about such a monumental blunder.

Mohammed answered on the second ring.

"How has the evening been for my friends?" Braithwaite asked in Arabic.

"It has been…enjoyable, my friend," Mohammed replied after a slight pause.

Enjoyable. The uneasiness in the man's voice was obvious. Something happened that was not on the agenda.

He needed to get to the bottom of this immediately. "It pleases me that my friends and associates are enjoying themselves."

413

"Yes. Indeed. We must thank you once again for your hospitality and the generosity of your staff. But something very important has come up. We must return to Cairo immediately."

Braithwaite stood up. "What did you just say?"

"We must return home. Some urgency has arisen which demands our immediate attention."

"Urgency?"

"We will be leaving within the hour. We must thank you for your generosity and—"

"What about our land deal?"

"Yes. How awkward. We must talk about that some other time."

"Mohammed, what in hell's going on?"

"Like I have just said, an urgent business matter. We must tend to it immediately—"

"What happened with the girls?"

A pause. "Yes. The ladies. They were…very nice, very obliging. We must thank you for their lovely presence."

"Nothing else happened that I should know about?"

Another pause. "It has truly been a most enjoyable visit. We must get in touch again very soon."

Braithwaite put the cell phone down on his desk blotter. His thoughts raced. The "ladies were very nice." They were "very obliging."

Could the man have been more subtle than that?

And a mere two hours later, after a long plane trip and in spite of a multi-billion-dollar land deal, they were packing their bags to fly back home?

414

It didn't take Braithwaite long to put two and two together.

Those bimbos pulled something.

The Limboite, no doubt. She was obviously the ringleader. She was arrogant and defiant. Probably still steamed over being dragged into Hell by Gutrillus the idiot.

But what could she do? She wasn't even an inferior and had limited powers. Other than the appearance-altering trick all the neophytes experienced when they first came back up, she had nothing.

So…what happened?

And where were they? They were given strict orders to stay there.

When Braithwaite got hold of them, he would send their sorry asses down to the Valley and let Sibrius and the rest of the pack chase them through the woods for the next hundred years.

Braithwaite buzzed the kid again.

"Sir?"

"Find those bimbos. And when you do, bring them back to my office."

"But I have no idea where they might have—"

"Kid, guess what kind of mood I'm in right now."

A pause. "I'd say you're really pissed."

"And what happens when I'm really pissed?"

"Things get blown up?"

"Go on."

"People die?"

"Kid, you've got possibilities. Now…guess where this leaves us."

"You want me to find them."

"Exactly."

"I do have a question about one of them, sir…"

"What is it?"

"The redhead. Is he a he? Or is she a she?"

"The redhead is an it. And sometimes even that's pushing it."

"I think I understand, sir."

"Okay, then. Now listen… We're wasting time. Find them before I get more pissed than I already am. Understand?"

"Yes, sir."

"If you find them soon enough, there just might be portions of this tacky town still standing when you get back. But mind you, I'm not making any promises."

***

George left the bar and went out into the muggy evening air.

People wandered around the hotel in droves. Traffic roared from the highway running straight ahead at the end of the trail. Florida sure was one hectic place.

He pulled out his cell and pressed the appropriate button.

"Everything all right?"

"They got away."

"Any idea where they're going?"

"North, I think."

"You think?"

"The only thing I'm sure of is that they've escaped the clutches of the super demon."

"We can't blame them, can we?"

416

"Of course not."

"Just make sure you don't lose them again."

George stopped walking. "What do you mean, again?"

"It is bad enough the three of them are involved in this. And even worse that the twosome stumbled onto forbidden soil."

"They didn't stumble, they were—"

"I know, I know. We all know. It is a black mark for us all."

"I intend to make it right."

"You can only do so much, George. They are dead. They have come back, but we cannot possibly undo the fact that they have already passed. That has been altered only a few times in the past, but we're all painfully aware how our superiors feel about undoing final decisions."

"Oh, yes. I'm fully aware of that."

"For a moment, you sounded like you had forgotten."

"I just don't feel they should spend their time dodging demons."

"If we do our jobs correctly, they shouldn't have to worry about that ever again."

"I intend to see that this works."

"Well, make sure you're not far. Braithwaite is not a very forgiving soul."

"He's a demon. Forgiving is not in his makeup."

"Just don't lose them."

"Get busy with your usual triangulation quadrant work and we might all get lucky."

George pocketed the cell.

417

And disappeared into the approaching night.

EPILOGUE - Leaving Florida

The Long, Long Drive

By nine o'clock, the sky had become an endless mass of dark blue.

As Ashley drove north, the sunset cast a shimmering blanket of gold upon the still surface of the ocean.

Tiffany couldn't stop agonizing about Digger and Cal.

She felt sorry for Digger and had let them go. It was the nicest thing she could have done. She had no idea Cal planned to trick Digger into meeting Breath Mint. If she had suspected something like that would happen, she certainly would have done things differently.

Cal had sealed their fate. Cal and his big dreams. A loser who sacrificed his own life and the life of his only friend for something totally unattainable. Cal wanted to be special. To have something no one else had. Digger wanted only to have fun. To be free.

They both wanted to live. To be happy.

It was the same dream everyone had. It was her own dream when she got off the bus in Hollywood, a naïve, starry-eyed kid away from home for the first time in her life. Facing a different world. A world where fantasies and dreams came true. A world much brighter and happier than the place she had come from. The darkness and the tears would remain back home where she had left them. She hoped she would never see them again.

A new darkness and fresh tears came when she tried to build her new life. Heartbreak followed. And frustration. And depression. But the most frightening revelation of all was the knowledge that people were cruel and nasty everywhere.

It took her own death to make her realize that the world could only be this way when run by demons. But as long as someone existed with the power to do good, things wouldn't be quite so bad.

"Why so quiet, honey bunny?" Chip sprawled in the back seat, his hair fluttering in erratic clumps as the warm evening wind slapped through the open window.

"Just thinking," she said, sighing.

"That never works for me."

"That's because you don't do it right."

"How am I supposed to do it?"

"Some other way."

"Thanks a lump. I'm so glad you explained it so clearly."

"Any idea where we're going?" Ashley asked.

"Just drive," Chip said. "We'll let you know when to stop."

"Breath Mint must know what we did by now," Tiffany said. "He'll have people looking for us. Is there anyone in Orlando you won't mind never seeing again?"

Ashley went silent. A quick probe told Tiffany that Ashley was thinking of her mother and feeling badly for how things turned out.

"There's no one," Ashley said softly.

Tiffany understood her friend's sadness and guilt. She herself had experienced that same thing

420

on the bus ride to California. Tiffany hadn't wanted to leave her own home but had no choice. Her only regret was that she hadn't had the chance to tell her mother good-bye. She hadn't even left a note because she was afraid her mother would rush to the bus terminal and bring her back home.

And because of that hopelessly sad situation, Tiffany had died without her mother even knowing about it.

"You need to tell her good-bye." Tiffany felt as if she was talking to herself.

Ashley gently wiped away the tear drifting down her cheek.

"It'll stay with you if you don't," Tiffany said.

Still no reply.

"It happened to me," Tiffany said. "I'm dead and it still haunts me."

Ashley stared straight ahead. Tiffany couldn't tell if her friend was sad from seeing her mother as she was now or remembering how she'd been before their world had shattered.

"I'll give her a call when we stop for gas," she whispered.

***

They pulled into a QwikStop a few miles north of Jacksonville, parking beside one of the two gas pumps in front of the brightly lit block building.

Ashley got out her cell and with a large sigh, crossed the cracked concrete lot to make her call.

Chip approached a nozzle and stared at it. Then he gazed at the building. Then Tiffany. Then the building again.

Tiffany could always tell when he had an issue. Right now, he looked like he was waiting for someone to come outside. "Are you…waiting for someone?"

"Steve or Bill."

"Who?"

"Last time I was up here, these guys were running around."

"What guys?"

"They all wore dirty overalls, were covered with grease and oil, and had a cigarette sticking out of a corner of their mouth. Their names were Steve or Bill."

"Just Steve or Bill?"

"They threw in a Bob or Mike once in a while, but mostly it was Steve or Bill."

He was making even less sense than usual. "And they did what, exactly?"

"Those were the names stitched on their pockets. You probably had to be named Steve, Bill, Bob or Mike to do the job because those seemed to be the names that came with the uniform."

Tiffany sighed. He was taking even longer than usual to explain himself. "And just what did Steve, Bill, Bob, or Mike do, pray tell?"

Chip sighed. "They'd put gas in your car, silly girl. They even cleaned your windshield and checked your oil."

What was he talking about? She didn't remember such a thing. Dad always pumped his own gas ever since she could remember. But then she reminded herself how long it had been since Chip had been up here. It sounded weird, but maybe that's how things were back in the fifties and sixties. "I don't think they're around anymore."

"Where'd they go?"

"Exactly when you were up here last?"

"In the late fifties."

"I hate to tell you this, but Steve and Bill are probably dead."

"All of them?"

"Even Bob and Mike."

"Wow... That's a giant bummer."

"If any of them are still around, they're probably sitting in a rocker, soaking their dentures."

Chip suddenly went all pouty and bummed out. "I don't think I like this modern world. Bad enough you have to pay for television that used to be free and walk around with a cell phone sticking out of your ear that doesn't even work half the time. Now you're telling me you have to pump your own gas."

"When you put it like that, living back then does sound a lot simpler."

He went back to studying the nozzle. "You just stick this metal thingy in the gas tank hickeymajig on the side, right?"

"Didn't you ever pump gas before?"

"Steve, Bill, Bob, or Mike would never let me do it."

"I guess it's time for you to learn. Just do it."

"You have money? Or should we wait for the Ashley babe to finish her phone call?"

"I think we might need a credit card."

"One of those plastic money thingys?"

"That's what a credit card is."

"Cash might work better."

"You're right. Credit cards leave trails."

He replaced the nozzle. "I'll do it. I don't think I can handle this gas-pumping thingy anyhow."

"It's not that complicated."

"It's not that."

"What is it?"

"I feel a whole bunch of remorse and other crappy stuff coming on."

"You're not serious."

"You wouldn't understand. It's a guy thing." He wiped his left eye, then hopped over the concrete island and jogged toward the building.

Ashley came back, pocketing her cell. Her eyes glistened.

"Your mom home?"

"Sort of."

"Drinking again?"

"Always. She was so busy yelling at me about that stupid cell phone Daniel dropped off at the house that she didn't even care why I called."

"Well, at least you tried."

"Too bad she won't remember."

"But you will."

"Will it matter?"

"One day."

***

After they got back in the Honda, Ashley sat behind the wheel, staring out into the night. "I have no idea where to go."

Tiffany felt a pang of guilt. Because of them, Ashley was uprooting her former life and taking them hundreds of miles from her home. And her mother.

424

But what choice did they have?

Because of Breath Mint, they all had to get as far away as possible.

"Where we end up is strictly up to you," Tiffany said. "It doesn't matter where Chip and I go."

"Just so it's not back down to that old rock garden," he said.

"If I have any say in it," Tiffany said, "you'll never see that horrible place again."

"My hero."

"Heroine."

"Whatever."

"My father has a cousin who lives in Pittsburgh," Ashley said. "We were buddies when I was little but we kind of lost touch. Uncle Rob's in fashion design and has contacts in that area. I've always wanted to try that."

"Pittsburgh's pretty close to Ohio," Chip said.

"That's right," Ashley said. "You and Tiffany did something in Ohio before you came to Florida, didn't you?"

Tiffany grew silent. They sent a subordinate demon back down to Hell.

But she also met the only man she had ever loved.

She hoped Lou was okay. If he was going on with his life since she walked away from him.

Of course he's okay, Princess. Your spell made him forget about you. And if you're lucky, he will find someone else.

Her decision had been necessary. The relationship she and Lou once had, the love they

425

had once shared, could never be rekindled. What she and Chip had done in that quiet little town no longer mattered in the great scheme of things.

They had to get away and hide. Breath Mint wasn't going to accept what she and Chip had done. He would have dozens of inferiors up here before long, searching for the three of them.

There had to be some way of identifying inferiors, but it would not be easy. However, it was the only way she knew to avoid going back down to that horribly dark, disgusting place called Hell.

"Tifferoo? You still with us? Or did you take a quick stroll back down Memory Lane to visit your favorite restaurant owner guy again?"

"All I care about right now is getting away," she said, forcing herself back to the present.

"Does that mean we're going to Pittsburgh?" Ashley asked.

"That's what it means."

Ashley fired up the ignition. They pulled back out onto the Interstate, which would take them farther away from Orlando.

And from the nasty demon Breath Mint.

ALSO BY DAVID BERARDELLI

www.ingramcontent.com/pod-product-compliance
Lightning Source LLC
Chambersburg PA
CBHW011652010726
47499CB00010B/3224